A BRUSH WITH FIRE

ART OF THE DEAD *series*

A Brush with Fire: Art of the Dead Book 2

Copyright © 2010 by Jody Summers

This is a work fiction. All of the characters, names, incidents, organizations, and dialogue in this novel are either the products of the author's imagination or are used fictitiously.

More books may be ordered through booksellers or by contacting:
JS Books Publishing
7301 Ranch Road 620N Suite 155
Unit 300
Austin, TX 78726

info@jodysummersbooks.com

ISBN: 978-1-7331775-2-8 (sc)
ISBN: 978-1-7331775-3-5 (ebook)

Printed in the United States of America JS Books Publishing rev. 4 date: 10/19/17

A BRUSH WITH FIRE

ART OF THE DEAD *series*

JODY SUMMERS

This book is dedicated to my two beautiful daughters who are both doing a magnificent job of proving the viability of my "grow-a-buddy" program. Thank you both for all your support. Who could have ever hoped to have one daughter who is not only an aspiring actress but also a great editor and another adept at filming and film editing. What a blessing!

CHAPTER

tabula rasa—(tăb'yə-lə rä'sə) From the Latin tabula, tablet and rasa, erased. Defined as: The mind before it receives the impressions gained from experience or a need or an opportunity to start from the beginning.

The smoke smelled delicious. It sent cascades of goose bumps all over her body making her nipples stand erect in the tight black jumpsuit.

Flesh burning. The thick, cloying smell with which she was so familiar. She had set the sun loose in the house, and it was beginning to shine. With calm, metered steps she began to descend the staircase of the huge Victorian home. The blue sculptured carpet beneath her feet would be gone soon, she thought happily, as she slipped the permanent match back into the little backpack she always carried with her.

It was called a permanent match. It was an odd little tool she had found at a craft show in Texas many years ago, and it had fascinated her. Little had she known all the wonderful uses she would find for it in the years to come. A four inch section of deer horn, pointed on one end, was drilled lengthwise at the other to hold a finger-thick bar of magnesium, which in turn held a slender cylinder of flint embedded along its side. A nine inch length of leather was inserted through a small hole drilled through the side of the deer horn near the point. The leather had a knot on one end. The other end went through a two-inch length of hacksaw blade. It was an ingeniously simple device.

Merely use the blade to scrape a few shavings from the magnesium bar, then hold the flint close to the shavings while, again using the hacksaw blade, to strike sparks from the flint into the magnesium. It made a lovely white flash and almost never failed to start a fire at once.

The crackling sound from upstairs was growing, and she knew time was getting short. Although very little additional smoke had made it downstairs, the smells of the growing conflagration seemed to be following her like a specter in the night. Time was definitely getting short. She'd have to be gone soon, before the alarms began.

Passing through the kitchen, she paused to turn on all the burners on the stove. The thought crossed her mind to use the match again, but it would be too dangerous. Other deliberations disappeared as an explosion rocked the house. She turned her head sharply, wildly gyrating the feathers on her mask. The sun would reach here soon. She had to go. Smiling beneath the layers on her face, she made her way out the back door, locking it, needlessly, behind her.

There was a stand of trees at the back of the property, just inside the privacy fence; perfect cover, she thought for the hundredth time. Moving quietly in her dark cat suit, invisible among the flickering shadows of the evening, she reached the center of the huge back yard and paused. Kneeling, she slowly and gingerly slid the colorful mask from her face, and set it down reverently in the grass facing the now violently burning upper stories. Feathers danced in the breeze, and the distorted rictus of a rainbow smile flickered in the glow of the flames, giving the wooden edifice an apparent animation it didn't possess.

Her look of satisfaction was still hidden beneath another fabric mask, as she backed away to stare briefly at her handiwork, then ran for the fence at the back of the yard. The six-foot privacy fence presented her with no more than a few seconds challenge as she jumped, grabbed the top and quickly pulled herself over with grace a cat would envy.

She was two houses away, still moving deftly in and out of the shadows, when she heard the sirens begin in the distance. She laughed.

CHAPTER

Sean felt like he was floating on air as he lead Ebony back to the barn. She'd said, "yes"! All that remained was to plan when they wanted to have the ceremony. The buoyant sensation left him feeling as giddy as a drunken sailor. The moments it took to get the spirited stallion back into the barn and cared for passed in an unnoticed haze, and the idyllic grin plastered on his face was in danger of becoming a permanent fixture. He'd never thought he could feel so wonderful.

After what, to Sean, seemed like no more than five minutes, but in reality was more like forty-five, he walked in the back door to the kitchen. Immediately he was assailed by a myriad of sensations from Kira. Sean's empathic abilities were extraordinary to begin with, but in the last few weeks they seemed to have grown tremendously and most especially as they related to the woman he loved. Now they told him something was wrong. She was puzzled. Scared? Uncertain maybe? It was a jumble of all three, and Sean couldn't quite separate them.

The fact that Kira hesitated to look at him the minute he walked into the kitchen only served to accentuate his misgivings. She looked up, and smiled, but the smile lacked substance. It moved her face but never touched her eyes and certainly had no sincerity behind it. Sean's reaction was almost immediate.

"What's wrong," he said bluntly. It wasn't a question as much as a statement, and Sean knew that she was familiar with his abilities.

"I just got a call," she stammered out slowly.

"Yeeeeaaah," Sean replied, encouraging her to continue with the exaggerated syllable.

"Well, someone else wants me to do a painting." She began, leaving the finished sentence somehow unfinished.

Kira had started a new business dubbed, 'the Canvas of Life', just a few months prior; it consisted of mixing the ashes of the deceased, or cremains, with her paints to produce tribute paintings.

"That's great," Sean responded, still waiting for the catch that her tone and his senses both told him was coming.

"Well," she began again, her voice pregnant with hesitation. "The call was from the FBI."

"What?" Sean exclaimed eyebrows rising up to his scalp.

"Yeah, it was a guy by the name of Joshua something, and he said he'd read John Thornton's report."

John Thornton was the Louisburg detective that had helped Sean and Kira deal with the resolution of the thirty-plus year old string of murders that involved Sean's supposedly adopted father.

"What was this FBI guy doing reading John Thornton's report?" Sean pressed, his mind racing ahead with the possibilities.

"Apparently, any submission of a report that resolves a previous serial killing case is routinely read by someone at the FBI, and because of a case he was working on, it ended up on this guy's desk," Kira answered, reciting back nearly verbatim the explanation Joshua had given her.

"Okay, so why did he call you?" Sean couldn't decide how to react to all this, but he had plenty of suspicions in the meantime.

"That's just it," Kira answered, puzzlement implicit in her voice, "Besides mentioning my paintings, he didn't exactly say."

"Well, what did he ask?" Sean's emotions were escalating from curiosity, to concern, to protectiveness.

"He asked if he could come out here and meet with me." Kira looked as perplexed as Sean felt.

"When?" Sean asked, ignoring this last bit of information.

"Tomorrow."

"Tomorrow! Wow, it must be something important."

"That's what I was thinking," Kira responded evenly.

~

Kira wasn't sure how she felt about the whole situation and certainly wasn't sure if she was interested in doing a painting for the FBI. What the heck would the FBI be wanting with one of my paintings anyway? The really scary part though, was that she was thinking she might have an idea of what they could want, and she didn't have any desire to be part of that either.

~

So, what did you tell him?" Sean asked, after a protracted pause.

"Well, I told him okay."

"Hmmm, so that means he's going to be here tomorrow, then."

"Yep."

"Okay. Then I guess we'll know tomorrow," Sean responded, mentally putting the subject to bed. That conversation at least satisfied Sean's questions about what he'd been sensing from Kira. The puzzlement and the twinge of fear now made sense, which left his mind free to return to a previous line of thought.

"Kira, I want to contact my Dad."

Kira stopped and stood stock still. One eyebrow climbed quizzically, and a smile bloomed on her face. It was hard to look at Kira's face and not smile back. She was a former model, and the beautiful sculptured curves of her face could animate a stone.

"I think that's wonderful Sean," was all she said. But then as an afterthought she added, "When do you want to call him?"

"Oh, I was thinking that calling him in the morning should be fine. Maybe we can catch him before he goes to work. If he works, that is."

"That's a good idea," Kira added, following his train of thought. "Especially since he's in Colorado and we're an hour ahead of him."

Sean's thoughts were already moving on. He couldn't deny that the thought scared him. His roots had been a mystery to him all his life.

It had been just recently that he'd discovered all the strange circumstances surrounding his real parents or, for that matter, that he was adopted at all. As a result he now had a birth father who wanted to meet him.

"What time did the FBI guy say he would show up?" Sean asked, thinking about his own plans for the day.

"Probably around two or three tomorrow afternoon," she said.

"Did he say where he was coming in from?"

"He offices out of Austin, Texas,"

"Austin, huh?" Sean replied vacantly, his thoughts dancing on. "Well, I guess tomorrow's going to be an interesting day."

"Tonight could be interesting, too," Kira said, obviously changing the subject.

The comment brought Sean's head up sharply, and he paused briefly to take in the smile and the gleam in her eye. His senses confirmed what he saw there. "Well aren't you the insatiable vixen," he commented wryly.

"With you I am. Why don't I grab us some wine and meet you in the shower?"

"I'll go start the water," he said, promptly turning and heading for the stairs.

The sounds of passion and play were a stark counterpoint to the crickets chirruping outside under the stars on that warm summer night. It was a treasured respite from all they had just been through, but their momentary peace on that quiet Kansas farm was about to change again. The evening meandered away.

Sean's eyes popped open. Light was filtering in through the window. He must have slept through the rooster crowing. Kira's smell filled his nostrils, and her body filled his arms. The night before had been extraordinary and even now, with her body backed up to his and the feel and smell of her filling his mind, he couldn't get enough. Still, his thoughts were elsewhere. His mind was rehearsing the phone call he was destined to make this morning, and his subconscious was telling him that he was harboring considerably more fear than he was willing to admit.

All his life, he'd believed that Jason Easton was his father, and just as he was preparing to accept the horrible truth about his father, he'd discovered that, in fact, Jason Easton wasn't his father at all. In the course of the investigation, Sean found out his real father was alive and desiring to meet him. For days he'd put off even making the call, using Kira as an excuse. He wanted to ask Kira to marry him before he called his father, but that had been the last excuse he could make himself accept. Now, the day was here. Shortly he was going to call his dad and say . . . say what? Hello? He guessed that was where he was going to start but what to say after that? Too many unknowns to venture a guess, he finally decided. The whole line of thought had his heart racing enough that, despite how wonderful Kira felt, he was going to have to get up.

Gently, Sean disentangled himself from Kira, trying his best not to disturb her sleep. Pulling away from her was almost physically painful; he felt as though he could die happy if he could just spend the rest of his waking moments holding this beautiful woman. But his mind was cutting no slack for his emotions, and he wanted a clear head when he made this phone call. It was 6:45.

~

Kira felt Sean carefully disengaging himself from her and, though she was still mostly asleep, a sensation of sadness swept through her. Maybe sadness wasn't the word. Incompleteness would be more accurate.

One eye opened slightly to the movement of him silently slipping into the bathroom. Closing her eye again, she tried to go back to sleep. The sight of him, however, brought back memories of the night before, and her mind climbed its way to consciousness of its own volition. Her next thoughts were on the day's events and brought with them a certain amount of trepidation.

Why did the FBI want her to do a painting for them? As that thought sunk in with all its implications, she awoke completely and sat up in bed. She decided to go downstairs and start some coffee. Monday morning, she thought, what a week this was going to be . . . and she didn't know the half of it.

Joshua Harrison was just getting to the office. It actually *was* his office, not just one of the many he'd been using in towns around the country for months. Regardless, he was only going to be there for an hour or so this morning before he had to head out for his flight.

His flight. What was he doing, he asked himself for the fiftieth time. Grasping at straws was the answer that came to mind, but then again, grasping at straws had been defining this case for weeks now.

Joshua was a tall thin man with an unattractive hawkish face, dark, rather oily hair, and old-style horn-rimmed glasses. Owing to his appearance, he had never had much of a social life, and after college had been recruited for the FBI, quite by accident, when someone from the local office had struck up a conversation with him at a career day on the UT campus. His ungainly appearance overshadowed the presence of an extremely keen analytical mind, and, after a few minutes conversation, the recruiter had the sense to realize he had discovered an asset he couldn't pass up.

Josh had been flattered by the offer, and over the last ten years had become one of the premier serial crime investigators for the FBI. His intelligence was certainly an advantage, but he had also proven to have an uncanny knack for ferreting out criminal motivations which had proven time and again to be an invaluable tool for hunting them down.

But now, after three months and eight arsons, he was finding himself at his wit's end. Not only did there seem to be no discernable motivation for the string of fires, but they hadn't been able to find any bodies either.

People had turned up missing with each arson, but the bodies, traces that are always so easy to find in a fire, were missing. Bodies are such important clues in determining motivations and methods that their lack in this case had greatly added to the overall puzzle. Surely some of the missing victims must have been in their homes when they burned? But, if so, where were the bodies? Bodies just didn't burn that quickly.

Not to mention this string of arsons was making an untrackable trail across the country. No one would have even connected them if it wasn't for those stupid masks the arsonist was leaving. That was the reason Josh had nicknamed the perpetrator the Mask Maker because of the stupid masks, and what did they have to do with anything anyway? It gave him headaches just to think about it.

CHAPTER

Sean walked into the kitchen in his jeans and an undershirt. His hair was still wet from the shower, and his other senses were being accosted with morning delights. The fragrance from the coffee Kira had made filled his nostrils, and the sight of her in her bare feet, wearing only a long, thin T-shirt that danced delicately around her subtle curves, was nearly enough to arouse him where he stood. She turned to look at him, a twinkle dancing in her eyes as she brought him a cup of coffee. His smile grew in response, as they sat down at the table together.

"Good morning, sunshine," she finally said as she leaned over for a kiss.

"Good morning, yourself," he responded, giving her only a gentle peck on the lips in a thoughtful attempt to guard her from his anticipated morning breath.

"How are you feeling this morning?" she asked, carefully lifting the hot coffee to her lips for a sip.

The thought crossed his mind that she was referring to the wine the night before, but he dismissed it and got to his real feelings. "Scared, actually."

"About calling your Dad I presume."

There was a short pause as Sean sipped his coffee and gathered his thoughts. "Yep, you got it. The funny thing is I can't imagine why I'm so nervous about it. It's not like there is any fault here, or I don't know that he wants to talk to me." Sean's words trailed off in unspoken frustration.

"Sean this is your DAD. You're a grown man, and it's the first time you've ever gotten to speak to anyone biologically related to you.

Nervous is normal. Quit fretting. Besides, it'll all be over in just a little while anyway."

At that, Sean's eyes came up sharply from his coffee cup. He had never thought of it that way before but it made perfect sense. "I guess you're right."

With those words she reached over and rubbed him on the shoulder, drawing a smile.

"Right," he said, pursing his lips and thinking again how wonderful it was to have her in his life.

"Do you want me with you when you call him, or would you rather be by yourself?"

The question caught him off guard because his thoughts hadn't ventured quite that far ahead yet. He thought for a moment before answering. Kira's presence would be a great support on the one hand, but on the other there was something about the moment that seemed intensely private and personal.

"I think I'd like to do it alone." He considered adding the words 'if you don't mind', but his senses were already telling him she didn't so he left it unsaid.

Kira smiled and nodded, her next words confirming his supposition.

"I think that's the way I'd want to do it too." Then she abruptly changed the subject. "Do you want to eat something real quick before you call?"

Sean glanced at the clock. It was 7:30, 6:30 in Colorado. Surely he wouldn't leave for work that early. "Yes, I think I would," he answered, "and I think I'll make it."

After a quick breakfast of French toast and bacon, Sean headed upstairs. Passing the den, he glanced at the painting of his adopted dad, Jason Easton, sitting peacefully in the rocking chair on the front porch of this very farmhouse. *Peaceful*, he thought, as he recalled what a protracted nightmare it had been to bring that whole episode to this point. A part of him wondered at their decision to leave the painting in the house, after all they'd gone through. Somehow though, seeing him sitting peacefully in that chair had reminded them both of the good they had finally accomplished by solving that mystery. With that thought, he made a sudden decision to make the call from Jason's old bedroom. Turning from the painting, he bounded upstairs. It was 8:05.

He went into his bedroom. His and Kira's bedroom; he corrected himself with a smile, grabbed his cell phone, and went back into Jason's old room. As he entered, he remembered distinctly the horrible odor that had pervaded this room for so many years, and all the events that surrounded getting rid of it. It made him wonder again what might have happened to him if he'd never met Kira.

He sat there just a moment, letting his feelings range out. Now, all that lingered was a serene sense of peace and an emptiness in the room. That was good. Sitting down on the bed, he looked at the phone in his hand. Well this was it. Curiosity and fear blended together into a smooth rope through his nervous system. He tried to imagine what the call would be like, grinned at himself at the attempted stall, and dialed the number.

He answered on the second ring. "This is Aubrey," a low metered voice said.

Sean hesitated briefly, considering how to address this man, then spoke.

"Aubrey, this is Sean Easton." That was all he got out before his voice seemed to stop on its own. He was simply at a loss as to what to say next.

The momentary pause on the other end of the line seemed interminable. A fraction of a second before he spoke, Sean sensed recognition from within that pause.

"Sean! You finally called. I was hoping you would. Where are you calling from?"

"Uh ... my home in Kansas," Sean felt like he was stumbling on the words. After the initial sense of recognition, he felt overwhelmed by the sensation of joy pouring into him from this stranger on the phone. But Aubrey's next words stopped him cold.

"You're feeling bewildered," he began simply. "I understand. I've been so looking forward to this call since I found out you were alive, but I've been struggling over what to say, how to begin. It's all too amazing." His words abruptly halted, but all Sean could think about was the first sentence.

"How do you know I'm feeling bewildered?" he asked, but as he heard the question leave his mouth he recognized a sharp needle of fear on the other end of the line. That, in turn, puzzled him even more. The conversation ground to an uncomfortable stop, and silence reigned across the ether for long, long seconds.

~

Aubrey's thoughts were racing. He wasn't prepared to reveal this part of his personality so abruptly to his new-found son, and he was afraid that Sean would think him strange at best, loony more likely. But the question was direct, and, as the seconds continued to stretch, Aubrey was aware of a kind of sympathy coming from Sean. It encouraged him, and he finally broke the silence. "Well son, I seem to have this tendency to sense people's feelings whether I want to or not. Part of my life it just seemed like a nuisance, but as the years passed I have simply come to accept it. And I apologize in advance if it disturbs you," but he instantly knew Sean wasn't disturbed.

~

Sean felt the swell of relief and camaraderie rise like a full moon tide. He had the same trait as his dad! It was the bridge he had needed in order to cross the gulf of the unknown with this stranger who was his father.

The words began to pour out of him. "I understand perfectly, Dad, I've struggled with the same thing all my life!"

~

At hearing the word, "Dad", Aubrey's eyes continued to flood at the realization of having truly found his son. He was sixty years old, and his life had just begun again.

From that point on the conversation was a free-flow banter. Time slipped away.

Kira had been sitting downstairs fidgeting and had started some more work on her current painting. There were very few of his ashes left, and the work was nearly finished. It turned out to be more of a portrait, something she hadn't done yet with her new business, but she was too keyed up about Sean's call to concentrate.

She was just getting ready to mix the last ashes with paint when she heard the door open upstairs. The door to Jason's room, she thought fleetingly. What an interesting location he'd chosen for his first call to his dad. The quick thunks on the stairs told her Sean was coming down, and she swiveled on her stool to face him. Even without Sean's senses, she felt the excitement precede him.

Before a word came out of Sean's mouth, Kira caught the sparkle in his eyes. She knew that look; she saw it frequently when he looked at her. For one fleeting instant, Kira felt a stab of jealously followed immediately by embarrassment and then a rueful smile. Fortunately, Sean was so excited he missed everything but the smile as he crossed the space from the stairs to the den.

"That may have been the second most wonderful moment in my life," he began, eyebrows raised in wonder.

Kira could hardly fathom what it must be like to be meeting your real father for the first time in your life at 32, and with no associated emotional baggage to intervene.

"What was he like," she asked, giving him the lead to go.

Sean paused for a second before looking back up into Kira's eyes. "He was like me," he said simply. Another moment passed in silence before he continued. "Kira, he sounds like me and ... and ... well ... he's an empath like me too! Or maybe it's more accurate to say I'm an empath like him."

"He offered that up right away?" Kira asked, surprise metering her words.

"Well, it sort of came out. He sensed my feelings, and I noticed it and asked. I don't think he really wanted to tell me that yet."

"Welcome to my world," Kira giggled. "I should have guessed that it wouldn't be something he could keep from you. So, I guess you admitted to your shared trait."

"Oh yeah! Kira, I can't wait to meet him. It's so weird thinking about meeting someone biologically connected to me after all these years. It almost feels like . . . I don't know, finishing the puzzle about yourself, I guess. I think it's going to end up making me sad I never got to meet my mom though."

A little specter of gloom settled over them, but Kira wouldn't let it stand. "Oh for heaven sake, don't borrow problems, be happy for what you do get to do. You've not only found your dad, but now you have someone you can share a conversation with without speaking."

Lifting his eyes, Sean chuckled. "Spoken like a true friend," he answered simply, letting the shared moment linger.

"Well, when are you going to see him, or is he coming out here?" A vague look of consternation crossed Sean's face before he finally took her gently by the shoulders.

"Kira, do you mind if I go out to meet him alone? I don't want to leave you for a minute, but somehow meeting him alone for the first time just feels right."

"I completely agree. It'll be emotionally charged enough without having to worry about any interaction between him and me. Besides, I'm not going anywhere. There'll be plenty of time for him to meet me."

CHAPTER

The plane ride was only thirty-five minutes to Dallas and then an hour and twenty, after changing planes, to get to KC.

The plane was crowded out of Love Field but, fortunately, Joshua had managed an aisle seat. He pulled out the report to read. There had been another arson. This time it was just outside of Washington DC in Reston, Virginia.

Josh looked down at the report. The constant roar of the airplane screaming through the air at 450 miles an hour and the muted sounds of the flight attendants and passengers made a good setting for him to concentrate. Yet, even though the seat beside him was vacant, he was still reluctant to begin reading.

He'd been chasing this arsonist across the country for months, and still it seemed he had more puzzles than answers. The fires were definitely arsons, as they had found a variety of accelerants at the different fires, and a single unidentified one that burned exceptionally hot. The odd thing was the continual lack of any human remains. Contrary to what the lay person might believe, bodies don't burn easily. Bones, especially, don't burn easily and certainly not to ash in the typical house fire. The one exception might be the occasional grounder, a building that burned completely to the ground before the fire department arrived, and those were typically only in rural areas where the fire department was quite a drive away and the fire was well underway before it was even reported. That simply wasn't the case with these fires. They were all in urban areas.

There were always bones at the scene if a victim had been there and, usually, tissue regardless of how charred it might be. At each fire, though, someone from the residence had turned up missing, and the police had to assume the connection but none of their bodies had yet been found. As a result, the arson teams had gone back a second time to search for human remains only to come up empty handed. The entire MO had been nebulous to non-existent. Even different accelerants had been used at the first four fires and more than one at some locations, which had so far been in different cities along the eastern seaboard.

The only things that connected the arsons for the investigators were the one unidentified accelerant and the arsonist's signature of leaving bewildering, Picasso-esque, hand carved and heavily painted masks at each site, facing the fire from the backyard.

It was when the third of these appeared that the FBI had decided to call in Josh who promptly began scanning reports and tied in the first fire, which had no mask, to the others by the lack of a body of a reportedly missing property owner and the mention of the unidentified high temp accelerant.

Joshua was good at what he did; he had been chasing arsonists and killers for fifteen years for the FBI. He was, typically, only called in on the most difficult cases, and this case, being unusual with its lack of remains, its lack of consistent accelerants and even its lack of apparent motive, had certainly qualified. They had called him after the third fire and now after eight, he knew precious little more than he did before.

With all these thoughts whirling through his mind Joshua hesitated to look down at the report. Finally though, his eyes settled on the first line. Reston, VA right out of Washington DC, $750K home burned on a Saturday night. The fire department got the alarm at 9:30 in the evening and made it to the fire by 9:45. Even arriving within fifteen minutes after the report, the fire department was greeted with a wildly prodigious conflagration.

The two-story, white, colonial house was rapidly being consumed. Fire was raging out of all the upstairs and downstairs windows like tongues of the devil as the fire trucks pulled into position. The fire was so hot, the lead fire truck had to be hosed down by a second one to keep it cool.

It took them over three hours to finally extinguish the raging flames, and it was the next day before investigators got around to finding the mask in the back yard. Any possible signs of forced entry were eradicated in the blaze and, again, no remains were found.

The house had been owned by Susan and James Grace. James had reported Susan missing while he was travelling on business, due to his inability to contact her for 24 hours even though she carried a cell phone.

Josh put the report down. Same as the other ones, he thought. It got him thinking again about where he was headed, and again he felt a little stupid.

His good friend David in the serial homicide division had read that damn report by some backwater detective in nowhere Kansas about this woman who had solved a thirty year old serial killing mystery by doing a painting from the ashes of the murderer, and David had passed it on to him because they'd been talking over beers about how this current investigation was going nowhere.

It'd seemed worth a try that night, but when David called him in the morning with the lady's and the detective's phone numbers, he'd been hesitant to follow through without the alcohol haze to influence him.

"Come on!" David had urged, "What have you got to lose but a little of the department's time, and who cares about that?" They had both laughed, and he had made the call. Now, sitting here on the plane, he realized that there was something else to lose here: other people's lives. People were dying, almost daily. Still, he had no better leads at the moment, and the stop-off wasn't going to take that much time away from his trip out to Reston.

Sighing deeply, Josh looked out the window. The plane was descending. Farmland, he thought ruefully. Oh well, he'd be on the ground shortly, and he could get this little joy ride over with.

CHAPTER

When Kira came upstairs, she found Sean sitting at the computer. She walked up behind him, glancing over his wavy black locks, and put her hands on his shoulders.

"Whatcha doin'?" she asked, beginning to knead his shoulder muscles.

"Well, I came up here to look at flight schedules, but I think I'm mainly just procrastinating."

"Still nervous about meeting your dad?" She leaned her head around as she asked, trying to catch his eye.

"Maybe some, but I think I'm more distracted about this FBI guy coming here to talk to you." As he finished his sentence, Sean quit looking at the screen and swiveled his head to meet Kira's gaze.

"It is a little odd, isn't it?" She began. "But I can't decide whether I'm more nervous or more curious about the whole thing. I mean really, why would the FBI want me to do a painting for them?"

Sean held her gaze for a moment before responding. "To catch a killer, I'm guessing."

Kira's eyes widened a bit as the idea settled in. "That thought crossed your mind too, huh?"

"Oh yeah," he answered. "But that doesn't tell us *why* they need you to do one. I don't imagine that the killer is already dead this time, though. This guy's time frame seems to speak to more urgency than you'd expect if they just wanted to resolve an old unsolved case."

Sean had swiveled his chair around while he was talking. Now, Kira stepped up and straddled it leaving her sitting in his lap and facing him with her arms on his shoulders.

Her tone changed as his expression softened. "Well, I guess we'll find out shortly won't we?"

"Yeah, I guess we will." Sean's tone was somewhat resigned, but he reached his arms around Kira and hugged her with his head on her chest.

"Whatever it is, Sean, it'll be okay," she answered wrapping her arms gently around his head.

"I hope so," was all he said. They held each other like that for a moment or two until the doorbell rang. Sean sat up, and Kira leaned back and looked at her watch.

"I guess it's that time. I'll go get the door."

"I'll go with you," he said. Smiling, she stood and crossed the room.

Kira was a little taken aback at the slender hawkish features and general oily appearance of Joshua as she opened the door. She decided his smile was genuine enough, though, as Sean slid up beside her.

"Joshua Harrison," he said, simply.

He also had a well modulated voice, she noticed. "Kira McGovern," Kira answered, taking his hand in a firm handshake. She was a little surprised at the comfortable strength of his grip. His appearance didn't lend itself to the expectation of strength. Josh quickly shifted his gaze to Sean, who was already reaching out his hand.

"Sean Easton," he said sensing his impatience as their hands clasped. It puzzled Sean for a second, and he almost missed Josh's gaze flicker to Kira and then back to him.

"She's my fiancée," he added, answering the unasked question in Josh's eyes. Josh looked a little embarrassed and hurried on.

"I'm sorry to barge in on you folks on such short notice, but I'm kind of under the gun on this current case."

"Come on in and tell us about it," Kira offered, stepping back from the entrance. As he walked in Kira continued. "Let's go have a seat in the kitchen while I make some coffee, Josh, and you can tell us what you have in mind."

They all walked through the house with Kira leading and Sean bringing up the rear. Sean noticed Josh pause as they passed the easel in the den where Kira had her current painting. Even from the back Sean could see Josh's gaze shift to the face of his supposedly adopted father in the painting Kira had done.

Pausing, Josh asked, "Are these some of your paintings, Kira?"

Kira turned, hesitated, then smiled.

"That's them," she answered.

"And these are the ones that have dead people's ashes mixed in with the paint?"

Kira's brow furrowed at his phrase as she answered haltingly, "We call the ashes cremains and yes, those are two of them. Why?"

~

Josh turned his gaze from the paintings back to Kira before answering. Her beauty caused him to hesitate. Her chestnut hair, dark eyes and dimpled angular face were positively breathtaking even without makeup. Josh was unaccustomed to being around such beauty, and it distracted him. Gathering his thoughts he forced himself to continue.

"Well," he began, now starting to sense the delicate ground he was about to tread, "I heard the story about you and these paintings." He finished as tentatively as he'd started not certain of the reaction he might get, but suddenly becoming very sure that this was all very real for these people. His own predilections and lack of belief in anything he couldn't see, were about to get him in trouble.

Unfortunately, there was another part of the story he hadn't heard, and that was about Sean's empathic abilities. Right now, Sean should have been his greatest concern.

~

Sean was clearly sensing both Josh's incredulousness and his disdain. What he couldn't discern was whether that disdain was for the work or for the people.

Either way, it was making his hackles rise, and he was on the verge of saying something about it when Kira chimed in.

~

"What exactly have you heard about my work, Mr. Harrison?" Kira crossed her arms under her breasts and leaned back slightly, her entire tone and demeanor virtually screaming 'I dare you' to anyone with sensitivities beyond that of a stone.

Josh was certainly not the most sensitive of people when it came to human interaction, but it would have taken a moron not to have some inkling of the potential hostility blossoming here. So, trying to tread carefully, and failing miserably, he began, "Well, I read the report about you doing paintings with the ashes of dead people."

"Cremains," Kira interrupted.

"Eh, yes, cremains . . . and then I guess you achieve some kind of psychic perceptions about them, and that was how you solved the Easton murders."

~

All Sean heard was 'Easton murders'. He had never heard them referred to in that way, and it stopped him cold. He was an Easton. His thoughts were abruptly drawn to Kira who was in a quandary of her own. All *she* had heard was 'psychic perception". Even though early on she had heard that word from a client, she and Sean had seldom used it to refer to what they had experienced, and coming from Josh, it seemed to give the whole occurrence another dimension.

~

'Psychic perception'; as it sunk in, Kira decided that the term was probably accurate enough. As a matter of fact, it seemed to pigeonhole the whole episode into a manageable little lump of thought. It was just that she didn't, in any way, shape, form or fashion, think of herself as some kind of psychic.

She was a painter for heaven's sake, not a Medium to the dead. Or was she? The thought was still rolling around her mind when she realized Josh was speaking again.

~

". . . and the funny thing is we haven't been able to find any bodies. Maybe you don't know, but it is extraordinarily difficult to burn bodies up completely, and though people living in the houses have been reported missing, there've been no remains found in the houses."

Kira's mind was still trying to shift gears as she asked, "So what is it you think I can do, Mr. Harrison?"

"Josh, please," he began. But he was thinking how these people were already making him uncomfortable, as if they could see inside his head or something. "And we were hoping that you might come to one of the sites, take some ashes and do a painting and tell us something that might give us a lead."

Kira's mouth hung open slightly. She had had an idea that they might ask her something like this, but now, hearing it, it just sounded too strange to accept. The silence got heavy before she finally answered.

"You've got to be kidding me?" She began. "You actually want me to go with you somewhere to a burned down house, pick up some ashes and do a painting?"

~

Hearing it stated like that, Josh felt sheepish, like hearing his own doubts recited back to him. He'd kind of expected her to jump at the chance to do her thing. Part of him already thought it was a stupid idea, and hearing her restate it seemed to magnify the stupidity of the notion. His voice faltered a bit as he answered. "Uh . . . well . . . Yeah. That's what we were kinda hoping."

~

Sean had been quiet since the beginning of this little interchange, just weighing words against the sensations he was getting. Kira's bewilderment was both palpable and understandable, but what had begun as a feeling of antagonism for Josh's disdain was slowly melting into sympathy for the sensations of frustration and desperation he was now getting from the guy. He took the opportunity to weigh in with a bit of logic.

~

"Josh, we have no idea how or why Kira's abilities work. Certainly, we have no reason to believe that she could use ashes from inanimate objects to glean some kind of impression. Maybe I should recount to you what Kira has done. She's mixed ashes of the deceased with paint and done tribute paintings for relatives. In the process she has received images from the deceased, either in the work itself or in dreams while doing the work about their lives. In the case of my adopted Dad it happened to be the murders he'd committed that no one knew about. We don't know how or why it happened, and we were initially as skeptical

23

as you must be. But we surely accept it now."

~

Josh was amazed, and he didn't get amazed often. He was realizing that he hadn't thought this through. He'd really given so little credence to the possible veracity of the story that he hadn't let his mind gravitate to the specifics of what it entailed. Now, in their presence, and hearing Sean's words, Josh found he *did* believe them; he suddenly realized that he *did* care whether Kira helped him or not. He allowed himself a glimmer of hope to actually believe that Kira might be able to help. His mind raced to make the adjustment, and he altered his tack accordingly. They needed to know his problem, and he'd better show some sincerity too.

"Folks, I know you don't know me from Adam. And, frankly, on the way over here I was thinking that this was a huge waste of my precious time. But, contrary to my initial judgment, I find myself believing you, in which case, I need your help. I have an arsonist out there who is lighting fires and, I believe, killing people. There have been eight fires so far and twelve missing people, and we don't have a clue. We haven't been able to find any bodies. The only clue we have that even ties the fires together is these stupid masks the perp is leaving in the yards." It all came out in a rush. Josh stopped, took a deep breath and looked directly at Kira. "And ma'am if your abilities can in some way help us solve this, you'd be saving lives rather than just offering tributes to the dead."

~

Sean had felt the sudden shift in Josh's attitude and was certain that his words were sincere. But the whole idea of Kira getting involved scared him on some deep primal level. There was a bad guy out there.

A real bad guy and Sean didn't want Kira anywhere near that. He knew it wasn't his decision though, so he kept his mouth closed and turned to Kira himself. Consternation and confusion were what she was feeling, that much he knew.

~

The words, 'saving lives' had really hit home with Kira. Could she truly help save lives? Would her abilities work in the fashion he was suggesting? Her mind ranged back to recent events with Sean and his adopted dad. Well, she thought, they had in that instance. Maybe it would be worth a shot. As she let herself consider the possibility a shard of fear slid into her, but she couldn't justify it rationally. She was just going to be at the site after the fact and then doing paintings. How could she possibly come in contact with this arsonist? And if that wasn't a possibility what was there to fear, really? She glanced over at Sean who was watching her intently then shifted her gaze to Josh.

~

"So, if I was willing to do this, when would you want me to go and where?"

Josh stared back at her for a moment, impressed with her courage, then replied. "Washington DC was where the last arson occurred, just night before last, so that's the place. As to when, well as soon as possible, today, or tomorrow if you can."

"That quick?" Kira answered nervously. The immediacy he was suggesting seemed to make it more real for her.

Nervously, she looked over at Sean who smiled and offered, "Well, I can't say I'm thrilled about you doing this, but if you are set on it, you could go while I go out to meet my dad."

~

This statement brought a questioning look from Josh briefly, until he reminded himself of what else had been in that report, that Jason was only his adopted father and not legally adopted at that.

~

Kira felt a bit confused. Being in Kansas now, she was beginning to know what Dorothy felt like getting caught up in that Tornado.

"Ok I'll do it," she heard herself say. She saw Josh nod as a tiny thrill of excitement coursed through her. It was, after all, a new adventure, but another pang chased the excitement. She didn't like being away from Sean.

Well, she was going to be away from him for a bit regardless, but the thought pulled her gaze to his face. His features were smooth, almost too smooth, with a bare hint of mirthless smile clinging to his mouth. "What's wrong?" She asked him instinctively.

His brows knitted at the question, and his hand came up to rub his chin while he thought. "I guess I have a bit of a bad feeling about this," he replied finally. "I don't know why, really. I just do."

Kira moved to him and put her arms around his waist, hugging him. "It'll be ok, Sean, you'll see, and I'll be back pretty quick anyway." As she heard herself say the words, an idea occurred to her. She slid back from Sean turning towards Josh. "I'll have to do the paintings *there* won't I?"

"Well, yeah," Josh answered with a hint of sarcasm. The emotion did nothing for his hawkish features, Kira reflected distantly.

"Then I'll only do this on one condition. I want you to fly Sean out whenever he's ready to come."

"Not a problem, Kira. And by the way, we will be paying you, too."

Funny, Kira hadn't even thought of that aspect. "How much?" She asked, her curiosity roused.

"Twenty-five hundred a week if that's ok, plus expenses."

Kira smiled, "Yeah, that'll be fine." It was about what she charged for a painting anyway.

~

Sean couldn't shake his sense of foreboding, but he liked the idea of at least being able to join her right after he visited his dad.

His mind had been full of the portents of that meeting until Josh had arrived and shoved them onto the back burner. Now they re-emerged, and Sean saw how the timing was going to play out.

"Okay, Kira, you may as well go with Josh, and I'll book a flight in the morning to go see my dad. When I get back I'll see where you are and fly out to meet you. Sound like a plan?"

~

Kira, smiled again. She was impressed at his shifting gears to accommodate her even though she was well aware of his misgivings. "Sounds like a plan, sweetie. But I'm going to miss you." She turned to Josh and her tone turned to business, "So, when do we leave?"

~

Josh had been paying close attention to the interplay. These two were definitely sharp and definitely in love. He roughly shoved down the wisp of regret at his self-imposed solitude and answered Kira a bit too roughly.

"My flight was for 6:30. I'll see if they have another seat on that one." And with that, he pulled his cell phone from his pocket, stepped away from them, and began to make the call.

CHAPTER

Poena was finished with the body. She closed her pack and turned to the little box she'd brought. It was time to let the sun loose, but first she had a few windows to open. Her chest heaved inside her black, fire-proof, Nomex suit, and her breath was hot inside her multiple masks, yet she smiled. Her grandpa would be happy.

Moving quickly on sneakered feet, she opened windows at either end of the upstairs of the large house.

She needed plenty of air to feed the sun. Going back to the bedroom, she stood over the body, pulled out the permanent match and struck the flint with the blade. The flash on the tiny trail she'd made was bright enough to leave afterimages in her eyes, even before it hit the main mass of powder. She quickly backed away and made for the staircase. It wouldn't be good to be too close to the sun when it lit.

The familiar anger welled up inside her. They're paying now, she thought, as she smelled the first wisps of the acrid smoke. Anger quickly turned to satisfaction. The smoke thickened. Burning flesh. She inhaled deeply, taking in the rich, thick fragrance. Already, she was pulling the top mask from her face as she opened the back door. It slid easily over the fabric beneath it. Experience told her she had several minutes, at least, before there would be any alarms. She'd disabled the fire alarms in the house, so no warning would be sent until one of the neighbors reported the blaze, and they were surely all asleep.

It was 3:30 am. Gaining the center of the backyard she paused to look at the mask she had just taken from her face. Even with just the dim neighborhood lights she could see the colorful twisted smile painted on the mask. No feathers this time. Beautiful, she thought. "Now, you watch this," she said to the mask as she set it down carefully in the grass facing the brightly lit upstairs windows. The look on her face was a cross between triumph and loathing.

If anyone could have seen that smile beneath her black, nomex mask, it would have chilled their bones. That grin would have looked more natural on a starving feral dog that had cornered a rabbit.

Just then an explosion shuddered the house. Ducking instinctively, surprise registered on her face, which then turned to anger "DAMN!", she said. "Too soon." But then she began to run, and as she ran she laughed. Yes, Grandpa would definitely be happy . . .

The Flight out to Washington was uneventful. Josh wasn't talking very much, and Kira's thoughts were vacillating between a nebulous fear of what she was getting herself into and a surprising sense of loneliness at leaving Sean behind. The last time she'd been separated from him had been just before she moved from New Orleans and had begun the painting of Sean's dad. That was when the worst of the dreams had begun, and she could barely stand to even recall those. She used to travel like this all the time when she'd been modeling, jetting all over the world to stand in front of a camera with some beautiful backdrop. Even with all the glamour, it had been a lonely existence and didn't even compare to the fulfillment she was now experiencing with Sean.

She glanced out the window and watched the terrain slip by for a moment. What *was* she doing, she asked herself. She had been persuaded by the idea of being able to save lives, but who was she kidding?

Sure, she had experiences with knowing things about the subjects of her tribute paintings, but that was no reason to believe she was going to be able to give the FBI any useful information by doing a painting of . . . of what? Which ashes could she even use to do her paintings? Had Josh thought of that? Did he figure she could just scoop up some ashes from the burned down house and she would get images from that? Probably. The entire situation was so absurd! Well, whatever he had in mind, she'd find out soon enough. She looked out the window again and stared at the world six miles below. I hope Sean gets out here soon, she thought, and not for the last time.

~

Sean was staring out the kitchen window at the thick green woods. He loved this ranch. It represented peace to him and now, with Kira in his life, it felt more like home than he had ever imagined.

Having her gone left him feeling ill at ease; he was even finding it difficult to focus on the few things he wanted to do in the morning before he left to see his Dad. His Dad. Just referring to him like that felt odd. Here was a man he'd never known and the only biological connection he will have ever experienced. Images of his adopted dad flashed through his mind. Well, his *pseudo* adopted dad, anyway. All those years working on this farm with the man he thought was his father seemed like a story from a mystery novel. The fact that, in some way, it hadn't been real continued to jar him. But it had been real! Just not the reality he believed at the time. He had a real father to look forward to now, though.

Thinking about it made him nervous on one level, but totally excited on another. What would he look like? Would his dad look like him, or more accurately, would he resemble his father? Whatever else happened, Sean had a certainty that meeting his father was going to be momentous on a personal level and, somehow, very very important in his life. But in what way?

With those images in mind and, yet another brief flicker of missing Kira, he pushed back from the table with a half finished sandwich and headed out to the barn. There were some horses that needed his attention.

~

Reading his reports and pointedly trying to ignore Kira, Josh chided himself unmercifully. What kind of *fool* was he? Taking some psychic painter half way across the country to help him solve an arson? This was just plain stupid! When he saw David again he was going to kick his ass for talking him into to this foolishness. On the other hand, what harm could it do? The FBI had okayed the expenditure, and he certainly wasn't getting anywhere with this crazy firestarter, so, what the heck.

He finally found some mental refuge by letting his mind wander back to the case itself. Where was he hiding the bodies and why? And why was there always this severe hot spot at the arsons? What was the accelerant the guy was using and why? *Damn!* He thought. What's the use? If he had to use some kind of psychic to catch this whacko then, so be it. But I'll be damned if I'm going to waste a lot of time with it.

He almost huffed out loud as he turned his attention back to the reports.

It only lasted a few seconds, though, before he cast another furtive glance at Kira who was still staring out the window. Damn, that woman was beautiful, he thought. She bore a strong resemblance to Jennifer Anniston. Almost visibly shaking his head to clear it of those thoughts, he looked back down at the reports. There had been another fire while he was gone, complete with mask in the back yard. Soon he was engrossed in the details.

Josh didn't like to fail. As a small kid with awkward features, the only thing he ever seemed to be able to do right was solve puzzles. All kinds of puzzles. He could put together a 1000 piece jigsaw puzzle in a couple of hours, and he was always the first one to solve the little interlocking metal puzzles, usually so fast that everyone accused him of having seen them before. He even kept a little solved Rubik's Cube on his desk at the office. It was the one thing he could always count on and, ultimately, the impetus that had led him into the FBI, to solve the puzzle and, in this case, to catch the killer.

CHAPTER

It was Tuesday morning and Aubrey was just getting in his car to go the airport to pick up Sean. The skies were that rich, deep blue that only seems to come at higher elevations, and a warm stiff breeze was blowing out of the mountains.

He was feeling nervous, and excited, and found himself trying to remember how many times he'd cried over the years, lamenting the son he'd never gotten to raise. To have his son, Sean, come back into his life at age sixty was nothing short of a miracle. He almost teared up again at the thought.

It reminded him of the day he had reported them missing. The emptiness. The torment of not knowing. The police had tried for months to find any trace of either of them, all to no avail. In some ways, the situation had been worse than finding out they'd been killed. Just not knowing. It had left him in a quandry of indecision; when to quit hoping and when to begin to grieve. He had hoped for a long, long time. Pain had fuzzed his memories. He couldn't even recall how long it had been before his heart finally gave up, but he did remember that it was like a ripping sensation inside of him. It was the reason that he'd never remarried, and why he'd decided to spend his years in solitude in the mountains outside of Denver. Well, one of the reasons anyway.

It was a solitude that he'd found peace in over the years, and even come to enjoy. The other reason for his self imposed seclusion was his empathic ability. It was unnerving enough to have the capacity to be consistently aware of the emotions of the people around you, but his was way more than simple empathy. It was like empathy elevated one order of magnitude. Just short of psychic, he liked to think. It had haunted him as a youth making what should have been normal companionship with others a misery, until he'd discovered ways to control it. He'd even created ways to use it, but for all his established control, he still found it easier to simply live in solitude. Except for his lovely Laura. Being aware of her emotions had always been sheer delight, and she'd harbored no fear of his abilities, but rather relished in them. He forcibly tore his mind away from thoughts of her. He wasn't going to ruin his first day with his son.

~

Aubrey was a tall, lean man with a weatherworn face, flashing deep-set brown eyes, and an easy, engaging smile.

In his youth, his hair had been coal black, but now he kept his remaining stately silver locks cut short. He would typically smile at the thought that his hairline had never receded. He'd been a computer analyst until he retired, and these days spent his time writing and analyzing stock investments.

He started the engine of his little BMW and put the top down. The motions were mechanical, things he'd done so often that they required no thought. It left his mind free to think again about his conversation with Sean . . . Sean—a good name, Sean, it could have even been something he might have picked himself. But he didn't pick it. His son had been named Eric. Aubrey shook his head, those thoughts were too frustrating. The idea of having his son raised by the very murderer who had killed his wife was just mind boggling. It would be interesting to hear that story from Sean, to hear what it was like. His thoughts continued to flicker back to Laura, and back to his life in general. It had been a good life, though lonely.

It seemed he and Sean had one thing in common already, and he was thrilled by that connection, even if it was one that had caused him problems. He suspected that Sean didn't anticipate the depth of that connection, or that with that connection as a starting point, Aubrey might just have something valuable to teach his prodigal son. Their mutual ability should also allow them to become closer, faster than either of them could imagine. The notion made him smile, as the wind in the convertible whipped his hair. It was going to be an interesting day.

When he finally made the last turn to enter the airport terminal area, he glanced up at the airport in the distance and studied its white canopied points intended to mimic the snow capped peaks behind him. He'd lived here for almost 30 years. It was a peaceful place to be.

Approaching the parking lot, he slowed and, as the wind noise subsided, he noticed he was getting more anxious by the second. Would his son look like him? Would he be comfortable talking to him? Eventually, all he could think about was that, after all these years, he was finally going to get to see his son again.

His smile felt plastered permanently on his face while he parked the car, then raised and secured the top.

~

Sean boarded the plane at 10:30AM. With the time change he'd arrive in Denver at 10:50. He couldn't decide what feelings were weighing on him the most, his concerns for Kira or anxiousness about meeting his father. What would it be like? What had it been like for his dad? What do you say to your father when you meet him for the first time at age 32? He'd been wrestling with what to even call his father when he first saw him. Father, Aubrey, Dad? Nothing seemed or felt right. Well, he would just have to cross that bridge when he got there.

His thoughts were interrupted by the flight attendants announcing the safety features on the Airbus 300. Moments later, the plane roared down the runway and into the sky. It always amazed Sean that his ears would start popping so quickly after they left the ground. They must change the cabin pressure right away, he thought absently.

There was no one beside him in the row, so he spent the time staring out the window and watching the terrain glide by. He hadn't flown enough to be complacent about the scenery, and it produced a calming effect on his mind. He loved heights.

Kira was in Washington by now with Josh. He couldn't help but wonder how that was going. He continued to have a bad feeling about the whole thing and wasn't even sure why. No matter how many times he tried to convince himself that there was no possibility of Kira coming in contact with the arsonist/killer, the grave forebodings wouldn't subside. His anxiety about not being there with her was almost as powerful as his anxiousness about meeting his father.

That thought led him back to his father and their conversation on the phone.

He knew that his father shared his empathic abilities, but there was more there, some indefinable sensation when he touched on his father's feelings; it was almost as if, when he reached with his mind to feel his father, his father ... pushed back? Was that it? Did it feel like he pushed back somehow? Sean wasn't even sure what he was talking about. These sensations seemed to defy words. And the more he tried to pin the feelings in his mind, the more they seemed to slip away from him. It was maddening. Oh well, he sighed to himself, he'd know soon enough.

He turned his attention back to the window and the crisscrossed patterns of the farms of western Kansas.

CHAPTER

Stepping into the hotel room shower, Kira found herself thinking once more about how much she was missing Sean, and the whole thing just shocked her. She'd been so independent all her life. Nevertheless, it caused her to smile but not even those thoughts would remain still. She was supposed to meet Josh this morning and go out to the last arson site.

With the hot water soothing away her tension, she picked up the rose scented soap and let her concerns glide away like the sudsy foam on her body. She had plenty of time, so she planned to languish here for awhile and make the most of it. Mental images of standing in the middle of a burned out house with her easel set up and her paints out trying to do a painting kept haunting her. That was silly, of course, but every time she thought about trying to do a painting with the ashes from one of the arson sites, that was the image she kept getting. What if it didn't work?

Frankly, Kira was quite skeptical, and if it didn't, would they want her to try several times? She sighed over the hiss of the warm water. It didn't matter.

All she could do was try and see where the attempt took her. From there Josh and his FBI buddies would have to decide where to go with it.

Her mind flitted back to Sean. He'd be making his way to the airport by now. She was so excited for him to get to meet his dad. What a special blessing to have happen later in life even if the circumstances surrounding it had been extremely odd.

She paused, realizing she was humming a tune to herself. What was it? And as the answer came, she started laughing out loud in the shower. The tune going through her head was John Denver's song "Rocky Mountain High". Well Sean, she thought, smiling to herself as it occurred to her that the name Sean was the Irish equivalent of John, I hope you enjoy your Rocky Mountain time.

~

Aubrey had parked the car and walked into the terminal. He couldn't go all the way to the gate without a boarding pass; he couldn't pass through security. Things had certainly changed over the years. He checked the video monitors and saw which gate Sean's flight was coming into, and knew just where he could wait to watch. He'd even made one of those little white signs to hold up that said "Sean" on it, though he had a feeling he wasn't going to need it. There were still fifteen minutes before Sean's flight arrived, so he took the time to find a little Starbuck's kiosk and grab a Grande Latte and biscotti. He hadn't had breakfast and that would just hit the spot.

That idea set him to wondering if Sean drank coffee, or if he drank alcohol for that matter, or what kind of food he liked . . . so many many things he wanted to know about his lost son. Sitting down, he waited anxiously and sipped his hot, aromatic brew.

~

The flight touched down gently, and Sean watched the plane taxi, feeling nervous.

Part of him almost wished he did have someone beside him to talk to for a distraction, but no, that would have encompassed its own problems. This was definitely better. The tone dinged as the plane stopped at the gate, and Sean's anxiety quotient soared off the scale. As he stood waiting for the other passengers to deplane, he realized his heart rate had slipped into overdrive. "Good grief," he whispered to himself, "calm down Sean or you'll come off as a frightened child when you first see your dad."

Walking down the corridor out into the gateway area, Sean scanned the crowd for anyone that might look like his dad, until he realized that he wouldn't have been able to pass through security. He'd have to wait till he got past that point to begin looking for him. Quickly, he moved on down the hallway, dragging his little wheeled bag that belonged to Kira. The slight exertion calmed him noticeably. It was a long corridor back to the security check point, and, for Sean, the moments seemed to drag interminably. He finally arrived though, and, as he passed, he slowed almost to a halt, and, again, began to scan the crowd in earnest.

~

He has his mother's eyes. It was Aubrey's first thought when he saw Sean pass by the security checkpoint. It made his heart race immediately. Even with all the comings and goings of the myriad of people in this busy airport, he couldn't have missed those eyes if he'd tried. To his surprise, it brought tears of happiness and sorrow at the same time, seeing his son, and remembering his wife. He was up and moving before he was aware he had stood, leaving the coffee cup forgotten at the little table.

~

Sean was still scanning the crowd, unsure as to exactly what to look for since he'd never seen his dad, but somehow certain that he'd know him on sight. When he caught the abrupt movement in his direction from the Starbucks across the corridor, he knew it was him. He was absolutely certain.

Angling his stride toward the man moving to him, he saw features that he knew as his own: deep-set eyes, familiar smile, and the easy grace with which he carried himself. Yes, here before him was his genetic father. Unbidden tears appeared in his eyes as he traversed the last few steps to the father he'd been robbed of . . .

~

Even at a distance, Aubrey was already aware of the flush of warmth suffusing his son, and it drew even more tears from his eyes. "Damn!" He said to himself, as he quickly wiped his face, "I didn't expect to get teary." Without any idea as to how the greeting was supposed to go, Aubrey flowed wordlessly into Sean's arms in a rich, warm embrace . . . and then something strange happened.

~

Sean found himself hugging his dad with a surprising abandon, no words seemed necessary, until he felt the tingle. It reminded him of touching his tongue to a nine-volt battery, but it wasn't coming from his body. It was inside his mind. He was, at once, aware of the sheer joy coming from his dad, and then suddenly he heard, "Thank you Lord! After all these years, thank you!" It surprised him so much he recoiled from Aubrey to look into his eyes. "Did you just say, 'Thank you, Lord?'"

Aubrey smiled. "Not out loud I didn't, but that's what I was thinking."

"What do you mean, not out loud. I just heard you." Sean felt confused and even a little scared. What was his dad suggesting?

"You heard what I was thinking, Sean. I didn't voice a thing."

"But I can't do that? I can read people's emotions, but not their thoughts," he countered, trying more to convince himself than anyone else. "And, frankly, that's bad enough sometimes." Then he realized what he'd just voiced and suddenly felt embarrassed. He'd not been sure he wanted to admit the extent of his abilities to his father at all, much less in the first sentence. Aubrey slid his arm around Sean's shoulder, leading him. "Do you drink beer, Sean?

I'd like to share a beer with you, and we can talk about this. We have a *lot* to talk about; I was hoping to bring up this topic later, but it seems you're too strong for that. Let's at least have a beer or two before we get into the tough stuff."

Sean's mind was racing. Tough stuff? He felt confused and warmed at the same time. It did feel good to be here with his dad, but what was this new thing??? It was a mark of his excitement that, for at least a few minutes, Kira vanished from his thoughts.

CHAPTER

Kira was dressed and putting on the last dab of makeup she was going to bother with. She was feeling comfortable in blue jeans and a sky blue cotton shirt and old, low-heeled Roper boots. It seemed like the perfect apparel for stomping around in a burned out house, she thought to herself. At that moment the phone rang and she looked at her watch. Eight o'clock. Well, he was prompt, that was for sure. She turned from the mirror to grab the phone off her bed.

"Glancing at the number to be sure, she answered, "Good morning, Josh."

"Hi, Kira, I'm in the parking lot. Are you ready?"

Direct as usual, she thought a little ruefully. Well, he never professed to be a diplomat. "Yeah, I'll be right down," she replied briskly, hanging up the phone as she reached to turn off the light. From her room on the fourth floor, she took the elevator down and breezed through the lobby with her purse in one hand and her box of paint supplies in the other. He was in a white four-door pickup, waiting under the awning.

"Good morning," he said with his angular, hawk-nosed smile, as she hopped into the truck. Then added superfluously, "All set?"

Kira smiled at him, wondering how those glasses managed to sit on that sharp nose of his, before replying, "We have to stop by an art supply. I have to get a canvas and an easel."

"That's what you said yesterday, but they don't open till ten; so, I figured we could stop by the site first, have a look around and maybe pick up some ashes."

"Where did you have in mind for me to do the work?" she asked, deciding to address first the image that had haunted her dreams last night. Most of the conversation with Josh so far boiled down to business, so Kira had already developed the knack of dispensing with the pleasantries. Besides, she was beginning to dislike the way he looked at her. Not that it was something unusual for her, especially during her modeling years; it was just that now, with Sean in her life, she found that type of attention more distasteful than she used to.

"I just figured we'd find a spot back at the office. We have a small conference room that should work, if that's okay with you?"

"Oh yeah, that's fine," she answered simply, turning her head to the unfamiliar scenery passing by them. Moments passed in silence and, again, Kira felt anxious about the entire situation.

~

Josh steered the truck through town with an easy familiarity. Kira seemed nervous. Josh, for his part, was typically quiet to begin with, and this woman unnerved him on several levels. As a result, his silence came more easily than usual especially since it was interlaced with a few uncomfortable glances at Kira. Damn, that woman was beautiful, he thought. He'd never had occasion to be around someone this gorgeous, and was finding, to his chagrin, that he didn't handle it very well. It didn't matter though, he told himself, the fire scene was close by, and he'd have plenty to occupy his mind shortly.

~

Kira watched as Josh pulled off the main drag into a beautiful, hilly residential neighborhood. The houses were spacious, varied and obviously expensive. If there was a house in here under $750 thousand, Kira would have been shocked.

"Is this the neighborhood of the fire?" she asked, surprise showing in her voice.

Josh took the opportunity to steal another glance at her as he answered. "Yep, this is the place. It's just down the next street."

Kira just shook her head in response, thinking what a waste to burn down a beautiful house in this gorgeous area. She was still reflecting on it when Josh slowed. Kira caught her breath as her eyes connected with the charred ruin. Josh stopped the truck at the curb.

Most of the exterior walls were still standing but very little of the roof remained intact. What little of it was left Kira noticed was made of slate. Very heavy. It must have collapsed quickly when the underlying support burned. A few of the interior walls remained standing and blackened beams leaned at a slant towards the center.

After stopping, Josh didn't hesitate to step out of the truck and walk briskly up to the miserable structure. Kira just followed numbly, still trying to assimilate the idea of this intentional damage. After her experiences with Jason's picture and all those murders, she found it surprising that a burned out structure would have this much of an impact on her. But it did somehow. It seemed bigger than life, and, as such, its destruction felt substantially more devastating.

Josh pushed open the front door. Kira grinned at herself briefly, realizing that images of knocking on the still functioning door had just crossed her mind. It's funny how your mind works, she thought. Stepping through, Josh slowed, his eyes roving intently around him.

His focus piqued Kira's interest. "What're you looking for?" she asked. "I mean, clues, I know, but what specifically? This time Josh didn't turn to look at her. He was already absorbed in his study of the surroundings displaying a singular intensity. He spoke absently over his shoulder as he studied.

"Burn patterns for one. Most people don't realize that fires burn in predictable patterns. Those patterns can give significant clues to the origin of the fire and even the fuels or means used to start it."

Josh tiptoed forward through the rubble, continuing to look down.

"Watch your step," he offered casually over his shoulder. Suddenly, he stopped, looked left and right, then peered up for a moment at a gigantic hole in the ceiling where the second story had apparently fallen through.

"For instance," he began again, his voice taking on the tone of an instructor, "See this? This fell through from upstairs and whatever caused it was extremely hot! What bugs me is I'm not sure what kind of accelerant this could be. Once upon a time I saw a fire that was started with rocket fuel, and it burned this hot, but that was extremely unusual. Ammonium nitrate could do this too, and it's a lot easier to get, but using it involves an explosion and there's no evidence of that here. So that brings us back to rocket fuel. I mean it's not like just anyone can get their hands on rocket fuel and whatever he's using, he's used it in all the fires, so he seems to be able to get plenty of it."

Kira was listening intently. Her interest was riveted, and Josh's expertise was obviously above question.

"And you see that "V" pattern over there on the wall? Something there was a source, or at least a secondary source for fire, but it didn't burn as hot as the stuff from upstairs. That's why you see the "V" pattern, sources that burn really hot burn in a cylindrical shape."

"Why do you say secondary source and not primary?" Kira asked.

"Because this section that fell from upstairs was where the fire started, and if you look up through this hole, you can see parallel scorch patterns on the wall. That was done from the intense heat source. So any other "V" patterns we see have to be secondary sources."

"So, lower temperature fires make the V or cone patterns, and higher ones make the cylindrical ones."

"Right," Josh answered, pausing a moment to look at her. He seem about to speak, but turned back to his work instead.

Josh's litany had gone on for several minutes. He seemed to like to think out loud as he worked, and Kira had the sensation that he'd probably be saying the same things whether she was there or not. She wasn't bored though. She'd had no idea of the complexity of the science of fire investigation. Following his gaze as he spoke, she took in the details of what he was pointing out. Presently, he stopped and started shaking his head.

"Damn! I know someone was here when this fire was started. I can feel it! But where the hell are the remains????"

"Why didn't they just burn up?" Kira asked, surprising herself.

Josh turned to her looking slightly irritated. "Don't you remember me telling you at the house? Bodies don't burn easily. Oh yeah, the flesh burns quick enough but there's usually even some of that left. The bones, on the other hand, take extreme heat and quite a while to actually burn to ash. Fire departments almost always get to a scene too quick for the bones to burn much, but there are no damn bones at any of these sites, only missing people. It makes me wonder if the perp isn't dragging them off somewhere. If he is, he's not leaving any clues to that either."

Something occurred to Kira at this point. "Why do you keep refer-ring to the fire starter as a 'he'? Did you get a clue to that at one of the fires?"

Josh smirked slightly, "You are smart aren't you? No, actually we don't know it was a 'he'. It's just that, statistically, the vast amount of arsons are started by men, something like 80/20 men over women. I don't know the psycho babble on it, maybe a power thing or some-thing. Anyway, I'm just assuming a 'he'." At this point, Josh stopped abruptly and looked up at Kira. "Do you have some preference as to where you get your ashes?"

Kira tightened her lips slightly, annoyed. She was still chaffing at his left handed compliment about being smart. It presupposed that he'd assumed her to be stupid up until that point. Also, his question had caught her off guard, and his tone was absolutely condescending.

"Josh, I don't *get* my ashes, as you put it. They are given to me by the survivors of the deceased. I've never done this before remember? I haven't a clue where to *get* my ashes!"

"Oh . . . that's right, sorry." Josh said, looking a little sheepish, which seemed to inspire him to be a bit more helpful. "Well then, I suppose we'll just have to guess." With that, he pulled a heavy duty zip-lock bag out of his front pocket and began poking around. "Do you want to pick some out, or do you want me to do it?"

Kira felt a little disgusted. This was nothing like what she'd done before, and she still wasn't sure how she felt about it. It just seemed wrong and a little scary. Nevertheless, she didn't want Josh to do it. He just didn't care. Somehow, she knew that it had to be her.

"I'll do it," she said finally, and began to look around as Josh word-lessly held out the plastic bag for her to take. She was feeling a little bit silly as she took the bag from his hand, until her eyes locked on a particular spot about three feet to Josh's right. She had no idea why she had focused on that place, but she nevertheless stepped gingerly through the rubble, and made her way there.

"How do I scoop them up?" She asked and to her surprise Josh reached into his other front pocket and handed her a medium size scoop. "Do you always carry that with you?" she asked, a bit surprised.

"Yep. It's part of the tools of the trade. I carry a few more things with me too."

"Oh," she said, nodding as she returned her attention to the rubble below her. She felt pretty certain that she didn't want to know what else those things were.

The ashes in this particular area seemed a little lighter in color, and, though she still had no idea what had drawn her attention to this particular spot, it felt right somehow. Felt right, she thought, I'm an idiot. Still, she carefully bent down and, using the scoop, filled the zip lock to the top. Standing back up and sealing the bag, she turned to Josh, who was staring at her.

"That what you need?" he asked.

Shrugging her shoulders and nodding she answered, "I think so."

"Well, I need a few more minutes, and I need to get a few samples myself, then we can go."

"Okay." Kira answered simply, feeling silly standing there, holding the bag. She was suddenly aware of a tickling in her nose, and her attention turned to the ash all around her. Well, I guess that's not surprising, she thought as she began to make her way out of the house. Josh was engrossed and, for the moment, ignored her completely. He continued to poke around and pick up the occasional bit, then his gaze would fix intently first in one direction then in another, and Kira could almost see the cold calculation in his eyes. Then he moved toward the back of the house and disappeared through the back door.

Kira moved over to the door and waited. Something felt odd here. Being in the presence of this act of violence and holding a small piece of its result. She looked at the bag and her nose involuntarily wrinkled as if she smelled something bad, which she didn't, well not anything new at least. What am I going to get from these, she thought? A chill spider-walked down her spine, followed by a tiny needle of fear in the pit of her stomach.

Glancing around the ruined house, she had a sudden, unexpected determination well up within her. "I'm gonna get you," she whispered to herself. "You can't do this to people and be allowed to get away with it."

Josh appeared in the back door at that moment, as if he had heard her voice, and stared for a second. Kira was on the verge of becoming uncomfortable when he said, "You okay? You look a little upset."

"Just angry at the idea of someone doing this to someone else." She answered truthfully.

"Tell me about it. I've felt that way so many times I guess I've forgotten about it. Anyway, I'm done here. Let's go back to the office."

"Fine with me. What's that in your hand?"

Josh glanced down at the wildly painted mask he was holding. "It's a calling card from the perp. I can't believe forensics didn't tag this and bring it in. It was sitting in the back yard like the others. I guess since the other fires weren't in this area, it didn't occur to them to look for anything in the back yard."

"He leaves masks?" Kira asked surprised.

"Every time but the first."

"But why?" Kira was staring at the thing as Josh approached. It was painted in reds and blacks and looked like something from a Chinese art show.

"That's the fifty dollar question! They're different every time, too." He slipped it into a plastic bag as he spoke, and took off his gloves while Kira followed him back to the truck.

After that warm greeting, Sean followed Aubrey out to the parking lot. When they got there Aubrey pulled keys from his pocket, and pushed a button. Lights flashed and a quick chirp sounded from a black BMW convertible.

"Nice car," Sean said, smiling.

Aubrey looked over his shoulder, smiling back, "Well, it's an indulgence, that's for sure. Why don't you put your bag in the trunk while I take the top down?"

"This thing has a trunk?" Sean quipped with a smile.

"Not much," he answered, pushing the trunk button and reaching in for the latches to the top, "but enough for that bag."

They both hopped in the car, but Sean was focusing on what he was feeling *from* his father, rather than about him. There was something warm coming from him. It included happiness, joy, curiosity and something else... anticipation? What was that about? What was his father anticipating?

Whatever it was, being around him felt right. It offered Sean a unique sense of completeness.

~

Aubrey turned and looked sharply at Sean as they both plopped down in the seats. Sean was thinking about him, Aubrey thought, and exploring the meaning of the feelings he was receiving. Happiness. That was where Sean was now, feeling happy about what he was sensing. That's a good place to start, Aubrey concluded. It was time to move on.

"So Sean, how bout a little Bar-B-Que with that beer? Are you hungry?"

"Sounds great to me," Sean said, as Aubrey pulled out of the parking lot. "Just lead on."

After a moment or two of surprisingly comfortable silence, Aubrey leaned his head towards Sean to make himself more easily heard over the roar of the wind in the convertible. "So, I imagine this all came as quite a shock, huh?" He began.

"At least," Sean answered frankly.

"Did you ever have an inkling about your differences from Jason?"

"Well," Sean began hesitantly, exploring his feelings on the question. "I guess it never occurred to me to question it. I mean, what did I have to compare it to anyway? Not to mention, Jason wasn't the most open man in the world. Asking him too many questions never seemed to get anywhere except his bad side."

"Ah," Aubrey replied, gently nodding his head with understanding. "And how old were you when you first realized you were so sensitive to people's feelings?"

Now, Sean turned sharply to Aubrey, who was still leaning close. There was a silence between them that would only have been quiet to an outside observer as they measured each other's feelings. "Being aware of the feelings happened pretty young. Realizing that it was something everyone else couldn't do, took a little longer."

"Yeah, I remember," Aubrey replied thoughtfully, causing Sean to stare at him again.

Well, at least it confirmed what he already knew.

Words seemed to fail at that point, and the roar of the highway wind was the only sound in the car. Finally, Aubrey spoke up again.

"Sean, have you ever tried to focus on those sensations you were getting? Tried to command them or direct them or have any effect on them at all?"

It was an interesting question, Sean thought, exploring his memories for an answer to the penetrating query.

"Not until very recently," he finally answered. "Not until I met Kira have I had the occasion to try to do that."

"Really?" Aubrey replied.

"Yeah, I actually got so tired of outside feelings intruding on me, I got to be somewhat of a recluse. Just finding whatever excuse I could to stay away from people, and living on a farm gave me plenty of excuses to do just that."

"Yeah, me too," Aubrey said, "Even when I got to the point where I could dim or mute what I was sensing, it was still easier to just be alone." More moments passed until Aubrey suddenly changed the subject. "You know, I never could truly accept that you were dead either."

"What?" Sean said, surprised. His mind was still whirling around the concept of sharing this extraordinary trait with his real father.

"Well, the fact that you both turned up missing but were never found was really hard on me, because I kept sensing that you weren't both dead but there was no proof. Still, after months and months of hoping and waiting for a call from the police I finally had to accept the fact that you both were gone. Rationally, anyway. I don't think my heart ever did accept it. I guess now I know why."

A wave of sadness broke over Sean. At first he thought that it was his own, then realized it was coming from his dad. His dad, he thought. I guess that's what I really want to call him

It dawned on him then that his situation wasn't the only odd one, and having never had any children, he could only imagine what it must have been like to suffer for a wife and child that you could only presume to be dead.

"I'm sorry you had to go through that," he finally said out loud.

"Thanks, son," Aubrey replied automatically.

At those words a vast feeling of warmth overcame Sean. He wasn't sure he ever remembered Jason calling him son. It left him with a feeling of belonging he'd never known before, and a gratification that approached the sensation he felt from Kira. Wow, was all he could think as the little sports car tore through the afternoon amid the roar of the freeway winds.

CHAPTER

Poena stepped out of the shower, wringing her long dark hair into the towel. The smell of smoke and the delicious smell of burning flesh were gone. Her svelte curves rippled as she reached for the second towel to wrap around her. The lean, whip-strong figure had been honed from years of gymnastics and that, coupled with her dark creamy complexion and the lovely contours of her face, made her a sight to stop traffic. She cared nothing for that, though, unless it gave her an advantage over her targets.

Joy suffused her entire being. The thought of last night's deeds gave her a feeling of accomplishment and satisfaction that she couldn't match anywhere else. Her grandpa would be so proud. She was using the wonderful lessons he'd taught her and wreaking the vengeance of which he'd only dreamed. It brought warming memories of his gentle smile to mind, and her smile bloomed in response.

Today she had another mask to make, and then she'd have to go to work. Both labors of love. By late afternoon she'd have the mask set up to season, and it'd be ready for paint by tomorrow. Then she could go into work and, again, enjoy the delicately sweet smell of burning flesh.

Having been off for the last two days she was certain that there'd be a back log of cremations for her to do. The funeral home got many of them done quite promptly at the relative's request, but there were always some that were less hurried and they tended to back up on the days when she was off. Not today. Today she'd get caught up. The smile that spread across her face would have stopped the hearts of most men, and if they were the right men she would have happily stopped those hearts more forcefully.

But no, she knew who her targets were. She always knew, and she must remain selective. She'd researched tirelessly to find the right ones, and there were several more waiting on her list already. But the mask had to be ready first, and a few more preparations had to be made. She'd need to replenish the sun, do some scouting, and then establish the proper timing. Soon, though, soon she could continue with her grandpa's work. Smiling even brighter, she moved downstairs to get some breakfast. It was going to be a wonderful day.

In the kitchen, she started the coffee, then opened the refrigerator to get some eggs. She glanced at the zip lock bag on the second shelf. Pausing, she picked it up to inspect the flesh it contained. Turning it slowly around, she grinned at her work. *Perfect*, she thought. I can get to work on this right after breakfast. Replacing the gruesome remains on the shelf, she reached for the eggs. She needed to hurry and eat. There was so much to do.

After leaving the art supply store, which took a few moments to find, Josh drove quickly back to the office. He had several things on his mind, and Kira seemed ill at ease. He was anxious to be out of her presence anyway; between her abilities and her looks, being around her simply unnerved him. He had too much to do to be distracted like that.

There were several samples he'd picked up that he wanted to get back to the lab; maybe this time he'd learn something useful. If he could just figure out this damn high temperature accelerant, maybe that would help. Or maybe Kira would come up with something useful. Ha, he thought. Oh well, she can't do any worse than I'm doing on this case, that's for sure.

~

Kira felt edgy. A part of her really didn't want to start on this painting. The whole idea was giving her the willies. The more she considered what she was about to do, the more she wished she'd never agreed to it. She felt certain it would be better when Sean got here. She wondered when that would be, and felt reassured and thankful that she had included that condition. She'd call him as soon as she got to Josh's office.

With that thought to calm her, she began to consider the other aspect of what she was attempting. If she could get any clues from the victims that actually helped stop these fires, then it would be worth it. Something about being at the fire scene offended her to the marrow of her bones, and she found she truly *did* want to stop this arsonist from setting any more homes ablaze.

Ten minutes later, they arrived at the building, and Kira had to hurry to keep up with Josh as he crossed the walkway towards the office. It made her feel like he wanted to get away from her, not that she objected.

Josh was continually making her feel uncomfortable. It was tickling the old reflexes she had honed as a model. The way he looked at her made her edgy, which was probably one reason why she was dragging her feet to begin with. This whole project was requiring her to be around him, and the more she was in his presence the more she wished she wasn't.

Once she was in there, she was going to have to actually *start* on the painting, and she was still more than just a little ambivalent about doing that. She'd never tried anything like what she was about to do, and, she realized, that was the other reason she was dragging her feet.

Aubrey and Sean had stopped at a quaint Irish pub, and they'd enjoyed corned beef sandwiches and beer. Conversation flowed easily as they shared the stories of their lives. Like Sean, Aubrey had been a football player. Having never seen anyone genetically related to him, Sean found it incredible to notice the things that were, in fact, genetic. Small things like an odd smirk when he thought something funny, that Sean had seen in photos of himself. The unusual angle Aubrey held his fork, that Sean had noticed about himself and never seen anyone else doing. There was also a sensation of completeness he kept experiencing, that he'd never known before. Amidst all this, was the pervasive feeling of joy wafting off his father in gentle waves.

"I can't begin to tell you what a delight this is for me," Aubrey was saying. Sean had to forcefully pull his thoughts from his revelry to refocus on his dad's words.

"You know I know that already," Sean replied with a conspiratorial smile.

That was the biggest joy for Sean, someone who could understand and share his gift, what it meant and how it worked. He felt understood as never before.

"Yes, I do," Aubrey answered with a nod. A few seconds later the smile slipped off his face, and he turned serious.

"There is something important I want to talk to you about though, Sean."

~

The sudden change of demeanor was emphasized by the feelings Sean was sensing. It jerked Sean's attention like a cold touch in the dark.

Whatever this was, Aubrey certainly felt serious about it. In response, he simply leaned forward on his elbows and waited.

~

Seeing and sensing the increase in Sean's attentiveness he continued. "Have you been able to sense people's thoughts yet?"

"What?" Sean answered, eyebrows lifting in surprise. "You mean their actual thoughts, not just feelings?"

"Yes, their actual thoughts. I didn't begin to be able to do it until I was in my late twenties, and, still, it seems to come and go, or maybe I'm just more in tune with some people than others. I don't know, really. I'm around so few people these days it's a little hard to tell."

Sean stared at his father. This was not something he wanted to hear. As a matter of fact it was terrifying. He'd struggled enough trying to deal with his awareness of people's emotions. If he suddenly began to be able to hear their thoughts too . . . well . . . he didn't even want to consider it.

"I know it's scary," Aubrey continued sensing his thoughts, "but I wanted to at least prepare you. It came as quite a shock to me, and I have thought many times that it would've been nice if I'd only had a little forewarning. On the other hand, you may never have that ability or you may find your gift takes another tack, but Sean," he began locking his eyes onto his son's, "it *is* a gift. Good can come of it if you let it. I truly believe that it's a gift from God that we're supposed to use."

Wordlessly, Sean continued to stare, absorbing what his dad was saying. Aubrey simply sat quietly, patience etched on his features and filling his mind.

"But, Dad," there he'd said it, he'd called him Dad. Good, he thought. "I don't know that I want that kind of . . ."

Sean wrenched back and gasped followed an instant later by Aubrey virtually imitating him.

"KIRA!" They shouted in unison.

"We have to go," Sean said, reaching for his cell phone, barely registering any surprise at Aubrey's simultaneous reaction. After dialing the number, he glanced back up at Aubrey who was already putting money on the table.

56

"Back to the airport," Aubrey said, no question in his voice. Sean just nodded. He was punching buttons on his phone as he followed Aubrey out of the restaurant.

Kira had everything set up and began mixing paint. She was trying to decide how much ash to measure into the titanium white she was going to start with, when it occurred to her that this was different than her other paintings. She didn't have to use *all* the ashes this time. This wasn't even a human's remains or, at the very best, not all of them. More than likely, none at all. Which brought her mind to another topic, what's going to be the subject of the painting? When she was doing works from deceased loved ones the subject matter was vital, but in this case the act of doing the painting was the point, not the resultant work. How strange, she thought. Still, if I'm going to paint it, it has to be something that interests me. She paused a moment to just settle on the stool and look out the window. An image of the ruined home she'd just seen floated into her mind. It offended her all over again, such a beautiful home, a place of refuge for its occupants. She could see in her mind's eye what the beautiful old colonial must've looked like before the fire. That's what she'd paint, the home itself!

With new resolve she finished mixing and looked at the canvas. Another Tabula Rasa, a blank canvas for her to bring to life. But what would come with this attempt; anything? Memories of the horrors that had accompanied her last painting forced themselves to the surface. Nightmares. Wicked visions. Physical manifestations. She shuddered. No. This wouldn't be like that one. Nothing could be like that one.

Her mind shifted. Columns, white columns. That's where I'll begin. Adjusting her position on the stool that Josh had fortunately been able to scrounge up for her, she planted her right foot on the floor to its usual position, adjusted her palette, and raised her brush.

As the tip of the bristles touched the surface a flash appeared before

Kira's eyes. It was an image of a face. Clear, but so fast that she couldn't make it out, and along with the image was a jolt to her hand and wrist. It felt like an electric shock. Involuntarily, Kira yelped as she pulled back from the canvas.

"Oh my God," she whispered out loud. "Not again!" Momentarily stunned, the memories of the terrible ordeal she'd experienced with Sean sped through her mind. The ashes of the man that had raised Sean; a serial killer that had never been caught; a man possessed by an evil he couldn't control. Making her way through that experience had nearly been the death of her and Sean. She couldn't do that again!

She lowered her brush as the tremor of fear grew in her mind, then raised it again. If this could save lives, she could do it. Determined beyond any reasonable explanation, she touched the brush to the canvas, absorbed the slight jolt and let her thoughts float away.

Her unique method of painting was an unconscious, or maybe a subconscious talent. Touching brush to canvas let her mind wander and her hand dance in an undirected fugue of artistic expression. It was a spiritual, soul touching experience with possibilities far beyond anything she could imagine.

The flames seized her.

Heat! The feel of flames on her face. Memories of a bonfire she'd experienced with Sean came to her, but NO . . . This was hotter, wilder and more . . . more . . . she struggled with the feelings she was having . . . pleasurable. That's what it was! She loved the flames. Their merry crackling, their raging heat, the varied smells they produced. It was wonderful. Then the smell hit her, thick almost sweet . . . Oh my God! It was flesh burning, human flesh! But before the revulsion could grab her, Kira was suffused with other feelings; pleasure again, joy, a positive delight in the heady aroma before her . . .

BEFORE HER? Where was she?

At the thought, she lifted her eyes beyond the immediate flames. A room. A bedroom. A house. She was in a house, and it was burning. Abruptly, she felt herself running, smoothly and easily, a familiarity with the movement that far exceeded her own.

Exceeded her own? What was happening?

Down the stairs, through the house, her breathing was obstructed.

But by what? There was something covering her face.

When she glanced down at her hands they were gloved and she was holding a plastic bag containing something bloody in one hand and a colorful decorated sort of mask in the other. Through the kitchen. Stop, check the burners. Gas? Yes. Turn them on. Must move quickly. Stay focused, move smoothly. An explosion rocked the upstairs. She smiled. Happiness. She felt so happy. Out the back door. Kneel, set the mask down, then run.

~

Moving with her characteristic grace, Poena glided in the rear entrance of the funeral home. She was smiling as she went to punch the clock. She loved her work.

"Hello Roger," she said to the pasty faced proprietor as he rounded the corner from the chapel.

"Well, hello, Poena. It's good to have you here today. We have plenty of work for you to do." His smile looked painted on. An affectation he was used to donning, with no emotion behind it.

"Any cremations?" she asked cheerily, already knowing the answer. There were always cremations to do in this busy mortuary. Her demeanor was something that puzzled and occasionally bothered Roger, but she was so efficient at what she did that he never bothered to pursue his concerns.

"Why yes, actually we do. Four, I think."

"Great, I'll get to them first, then," she answered and turned toward the crematorium. "Never fear the flames," she repeated in her mind, words from her grandpa's mouth. "Never fear the flames, my dear. The flames will set you free."

She loved remembering her grandpa's words. She remembered them all. He'd been so wonderful to her when her mom had left. Over and over again through the years, he'd told her his amazing stories. Even when his mind got cloudy later, he had told his brave, sad stories. She had loved him so much. But in another way those wonderful stories had hurt her and scared her. They were frightening and sickening and it was so sad that Grandpa had been forced to . . . No. That wasn't important now. What was important was that she was finally making him proud.

The bodies were stored in roll out drawers much like the morgues at the hospitals. Cold, dead remains, awaiting the fire of purification, unlike Grandpa's stories where the bodies were still warm and breathing when the fire took them.

A chart hung on the wall by each one; name, date of death, promise date for the remains. She reached for the chart feeling useful and cheery . . . A face flashed in her mind and was gone. She stopped dead in her tracks, unsure what had just happened but awaiting more.

"Embrace the fear," Grandpa had said. "Let it pass through you."

No more came. Still she waited, frozen in place, with the certainty of expectation.

There! Flames in her mind. It was a memory of hers. Someone was there! There? Who? It was a woman. She thought for a moment. It must be one of *them*.

Her grandpa warned her many times that one day they would come for her, and she must be prepared. Well, she had seen that face now, and she *would* be prepared.

Grinning broadly, Poena turned back to the clipboard. She was now just as certain that no more visions were coming as she had been earlier that there would be more. Besides, there was work to do and then preparations to make.

CHAPTER

Once back at the airport, Aubrey drove Sean right up to the departure doors.

It didn't even occur to Sean to question his father's instant and accurate recognition of his feelings *and* his thoughts, until he was already on the plane. It was a foregone conclusion that they'd be in touch again. Soon.

"I'm so sorry to have to rush off like this Dad," Sean was saying as he pulled his stuff from the little car. "I wanted more of a visit. Especially for the first one."

"Don't think about it. You have to go. She needs you," Aubrey answered in warm reassuring tones. He meant them too; Sean could feel it.

As he spoke, Aubrey reached into the glove box and handed him something.

"Here, I want you to have this," he said, as Sean paused.

Not having a clue as to what was in the little box, Sean took it, thanked him and expressed regret again at his sudden departure.

~

Sean's gift was so powerful, Aubrey reflected. His awareness of it seemed to have been growing ever since he laid eyes on the boy. And interestingly, Sean seemed to have no idea. Something was about to change with him, though, something with his gift. Aubrey couldn't have described how he knew this or what shape it would take exactly, but his certainty of it was unshakeable. And, amazingly enough, Sean seemed to have found a woman with some abilities too. That should prove interesting, he mused.

Looking back in the car window Sean said, "It was really wonderful to meet you, dad. We'll get together again soon."

Aubrey smiled, "I know we will, son." The warmth of saying and hearing those words 'son' and 'dad' connected them both more than anything else either could have imagined. He'd have another little surprise when he got a moment to open the little box. It warmed Aubrey inside to have at least that little token to give to Sean. He only wished he could be there when he opened it.

"Now hurry up. Kira needs you!"

Smiling, Sean turned and nearly ran into the terminal. The feelings of warmth for his dad were already being drowned in his concern for Kira. He put on more speed. It was going to be close to catch his flight.

Josh left the lab in a huff. Nothing, dammit! Not one new hint on that damn accelerant, and the only new thing on the mask was that the paint on it was a *very* typical acrylic.

On a hunch, he'd been on the phone calling anywhere that might have rocket fuel to see if any had turned up missing. So far all he'd gotten were three no's and several questions about his sanity. It was maddening. But he felt pretty sure he could rule that one out.

The lab seemed to think that the samples he'd brought represented a higher heat than could be generated from ammonium nitrate, but it had to be something readily available, he was sure of it.

Still mulling over these thoughts, he passed the office Kira was using on his way to the restroom. He decided to peek in and see how she was doing. He opened the door without knocking. He really didn't want to disturb her, he told himself, and did a double take. Kira was collapsed on the floor by her stool! Paint was splattered on the carpet near her palette and brush, which appeared to have fallen from limp hands when she fell.

For one brief moment Josh just stood there, too shocked at the sight to react.

"Oh my God!" he finally said as he bolted into the room. Racing to her side, his eyes were drawn up to the canvas she'd been working on. She'd made amazing progress, he thought. It was a house. His thoughts shifted back to Kira, who was beginning to stir slightly.

"Kira," Josh said, gently shaking her shoulders. Merely touching her affected him. Damn, why did she have to be so beautiful! Kira's eyes fluttered, then she gasped slightly and looked up at Josh. Her eyes were still unfocused, and Josh was certain she wasn't seeing him for a few seconds until she finally spoke.

"Josh? . . . Shit! . . . where is . . . damn it, just like Jason!" Her eyes suddenly focused and Josh had to lean back quickly as she abruptly sat up, glaring at the canvas. Not having any of Kira's previous experiences to draw on, Josh was at a complete loss. The whole episode just added to the general apprehension he had from being around this woman

"What's wrong Kira? What happened?"

"I saw someone," she answered, then looked at him.

The question must have been all over his face because she hesitated then continued.

"Josh, I have visions while I'm painting. That's how it works. That's how we found all those bodies in Kansas."

The clipped, pointed statements got through to him. Still struggling to grasp the unreality of what he was being faced with, Josh asked lamely, "You saw one of the victims?" a twinge of hope creeping into his voice.

"No. I think I saw the killer. I have to call Sean." Rising from the floor with a gentle pull from Josh, she picked up her paintbrush and palette and turned to set them on the table by her things. Reaching in her purse, she pulled out her cell phone. "Sean already called me," she said smiling. "I should have guessed."

"Guessed what?" Josh asked, impatience swelling in his tone. "Saw the killer?! What the . . ." But she wasn't listening. Josh felt like he was playing catch up in a marathon where everyone else had a two hour head start. His life had been interesting enough, but he'd never encountered anything that was beyond what his senses could take in. Sure he'd seen a few TV shows, but that was just TV. Only now he wasn't so sure.

"I should have guessed that Sean would have already called," Kira finally answered, ignoring his other question and putting down the phone after listening to Sean's message. She turned to look back at the still perplexed Josh. "He's already on his way. No doubt he sensed it when I had my episode."

"Sensed it? What episode?" Josh echoed lamely, feeling a bit like Alice in Wonderland. Silence reigned for a moment before Josh thought to ask something coherent. "Well, what can you tell me about what you saw in your uh . . . your vision." Josh could barely bring himself to say the word.

"Let me think about it a bit, Josh. I'd prefer to wait until Sean gets here anyway. From his message it should just be another few hours."

CHAPTER

Sean was seething with anxiety. He'd attempted to call Kira before he'd boarded the plane, but she hadn't answered. His thoughts were a gathering storm, gaining strength, but not yet resolved into a cohesive unit.

He knew something was wrong with Kira, but he didn't know how he knew, what had happened, or how bad. Or did he?

Closing his eyes on instinct, Sean took a deep breath and then another. The drone of the plane engines seemed to help him relax as he forced his thoughts into focus and slowly, deliberately, brought a clear picture of Kira into his mind. Her thick chestnut hair and large almond eyes, bold jaw line, slender graceful body, curvy legs, dainty fingers . . . there! He could feel her, he was sure of it. She was scared, then surprised, then confused, then curious and back to scared . . . No, what was that? A face. Another face? Then it was gone.

Sean inhaled sharply as things seemed to go black. He opened his eyes suddenly still drawing in breath. She was unconscious. Kira was unconscious. Somehow he was certain of it. But . . . He focused again, she was still okay. Okay. He wanted to do more, but there was nothing to be done from the plane, and he wasn't really even sure how he'd just done what he did. She was okay, he repeated to himself as he visibly relaxed into his seat, but his thoughts wouldn't hold still. Damn! She could only have barely begun. Why was she already having problems? Surely it couldn't be as bad as doing Jason's paintings? Or could it? He had no idea, but he'd be there soon and whatever it was, he'd be with her.

While he sat there, stewing in his own concerns, he found himself thinking of the little box his dad had given him. The thought was a welcome distraction. He'd stuck it in his carry-on and forgotten about it. Now, he reached under the seat and pulled out the small bag, rummaging through it until he located the little box.

Slowly, feeling as though he was handling something precious, Sean opened it and was surprised to find a slender, old-style cigarette lighter nestled inside. It was gold, and as he picked it up, his thoughts raced, trying to imagine why his Dad might have given him a gold lighter. Maybe Aubrey thought he smoked. Did his dad smoke? No, Sean didn't think so. As a non-smoker himself he felt pretty certain that if his dad was a smoker he'd have smelled it on him. Why then? Prying the lighter from its fitted little slot, Sean turned it slowly in his fingers. It was simple and elegant. As he turned it over his eyes locked on the delicate inscription etched into the smooth surface. It was in a gentle script and as such was a bit difficult to decipher. He switched on the reading light above him and turned it long ways. The inscription suddenly stood out plainly.

To Laura with Love, a reminder of the little light you brought into our lives. Aubrey

The small lighter he was holding in his hand belonged to his mother. A sensation sizzled through him that took him a moment to label. It felt something like the warmth he was so familiar with when he was close to Kira, but different. His Mom. Suddenly tears were in his eyes as he tried to imagine the mother he'd never known. Everything about her was a void, even the bits of information Kira had picked up about his mother from visions she'd been reticent to share because they were so entwined with Laura's death. After meeting his dad, the lack seemed greatly magnified. That one little moment of connection to a biological parent gave added depth to the loss that still remained. His thoughts lingered there for a moment until he felt the weight of someone else's gaze upon him. Self-consciousness quickly replaced his other feelings and then resentment at the intrusion, rapidly on the heels of that. A surreptitious glance to his right confirmed his feelings and caused the inquisitive lady to quickly turn away. With an effort he repacked the emotions, shoving them down for later. Right now he had Kira to think about. Later, he could grieve.

Sean called Kira when he got off the plane, got the address of Josh's office and asked about what was going on. She said she would tell him when he got there.

So with his imagination in overdrive and the navigation system on the rental car set, he hurried his way through the unfamiliar streets of Virginia, glancing absently at the lush vegetation that was so unlike his native Kansas.

All he could figure was that it must have been some type of strong vision. He'd been with her when she'd had those; first when she did the painting for Wes, whose wife had committed suicide, and then, much worse, when she did his dad's painting. Well not his dad, Sean corrected himself, Jason. The man who had raised him. The more he thought about it, the harder it was for him to imagine them finding any ashes that Kira could actually use, or at least ashes that they knew to be from one of the victims. Josh said they hadn't found any remains, and if they couldn't find any bodies what was Kira working with? The thoughts rolled around in his head but no answers were forthcoming.

His restless mind shifted to another puzzle, his dad's reactions. His dad had the same reaction at the same time as he did, Sean thought. But how could his dad do that, he wasn't connected to Kira ... but he *was* connected to me. He read my thoughts! I guess that's what he was talking about, Sean concluded. The sensation of warmth that Sean had experienced when he was with his dad suffused him again, and so did the foreboding statement that his abilities could change. Reading thoughts ... shit ... that's all I need.

Almost missing a turn, Sean redirected his attention to the route he was trying to follow. The computer said he was still about twenty minutes from Josh's office. Once he was there he'd get some answers.

CHAPTER

That woman's face was haunting her thoughts. Somehow, Poena knew it was important, but she wasn't sure why.

She'd had nightmares before and sometimes the faces of victims swam through her mind either before or after the fires, but never had she had a vision as clear as this, much less while she was awake. Maybe it was a sign from God. Maybe he was showing her the way she had to go. She'd be wary. She'd see the face again. God would show it to her, and Grandpa's voice would tell her what to do.

She shook herself mentally and returned to the work at hand. There was much to do before she could leave, and then she had a few hours at her other job, where she could replenish the sun. She also had some more research to do and plans to make. Her life was not only fulfilling but delightfully busy, too.

Whistling happily, she slid the first body on her list of cremations onto the ceramic tray that she would then slide into the crematorium. She anxiously anticipated the smell that accompanied her work. It wasn't as intense as what she experienced at her own fires, but it was still satisfying. It reminded her of her mission, and that reminded her again of her grandpa's inspiring stories.

Josh had taken Kira to grab a bite to eat and kill some time. For him, it was not only to let her calm down while they waited for Sean, but a chance to be around her some more. He was beginning to recognize that Kira was weighing too much on his thoughts, and though he tried to fight it, he was afraid he was losing the battle. It would be good for Sean to be there. Two hours and two Jack and cokes later, Josh returned her to the office.

~

Kira was thankful that Josh had left her alone in his office. He had done so reluctantly and not before gushing over her effusively for what seemed like years. She was so anxious for Sean to arrive.

Standing there by herself, she turned to stare at the painting again, and it occurred to her that she had picked an odd perspective. The house was turned at a sharp angle to the front rather than straight on. It allowed the viewer to see not only the front of the house, but the side also and a good portion of the back yard. The columns on the front were going to end up being seen at an oblique angle. "Why did I do that?" she wondered.

~

Poena knew she must don the mask her grandpa had described to her in such detail as a little girl. Of all the masks that littered her life, this was the true one; but this one was not a physical mask. It was a mask to hide emotions so that tormentors would never see her fear or pain. It resided in her mind just like Grandpa had described; just like he had used to protect himself from his tormentors for so many years.

For Poena, it was usually represented by the masks she created. Not this time. This time the mask must be put on so that she could protect herself. Now, when that woman tried to see her, all she would see was her mask. She would never see the real Poena again!

~

Kira was still pondering the perspective of the painting and trying to decide whether to try to paint some more, when Sean virtually burst into the room.

"Kira," he said breathlessly as he ran to her.

She turned and flung herself into his arms. "Sean, I'm so glad you're here."

"Me too. Kira, I . . . I *felt* something, and I knew I had to get here."

Kira smiled over Sean's shoulder as she hugged him. "I know."

"Perspective?" Sean said out of the blue as they continued to embrace. "What about perspective?"

Kira levered herself away from Sean with both hands on his shoulders and looked straight into his eyes. "What? That's exactly what I was just thinking about," she commented, surprise and a touch of concern evident in her voice. "Perspective of the painting," she continued. They both turned, at that, to look at the painting.

"See how I've turned the image of the house? You can see the side and some of the backyard? I can't understand why I did that."

Sean let that puzzle slide and got back to what was dragging on his curiosity. "Kira, you have to tell me what happened," he began, staring into her eyes.

"Sure, but let's get Josh. That way I won't have to explain this stuff twice."

Fifteen minutes later, Kira finished recounting the story to Josh and Sean. For several long minutes the silence hung heavy in the air.

"So you think you got a glimpse of the killer?" Sean finally said, "Not one of the victims."

"Yes, I'm sure it was the killer. I just didn't get a very clear look at her face."

"*Her* face?" Josh asked surprised.

"Yeah it was a she, long dark hair . . ." Kira's gaze slid away, remembering.

"And how do you know it was the killer?" Sean asked

"Well for one thing, she *loves* the fire. She likes the smells of things burning especially . . . flesh," Kira shivered involuntarily and grimaced at the memory, "and the heat and the power of the flames . . . and . . . and . . ." Kira suddenly focused and turned to Sean. "Oh, Sean I . . ." the fear made her features blanche.

"Felt her!" Sean finished for her. Kira simply nodded, completely missing the fact that Sean had finished her unlikely sentence, as he swept her into his arms. "Oh my God," He murmured absently. "Not again."

"Not again? You *felt* her? What the hell are you saying, Kira? You're saying you really saw this woman . . . like in your mind?"

~

Josh was lost and confused and frustrated. No matter how upsetting being around one of these two seemed to be, it didn't hold a candle to the discomfort of being around them both.

~

But Sean and Kira were too engrossed in their own memories so Josh's questions hung unanswered.

CHAPTER

Poena walked back into her little rental house. She was tired. It had been a good day. After finishing at the funeral home, she'd gone to her four hour shift at her other job. She only kept that job because of the one important side benefit. Gently, she set down the box she'd brought back with her. The Sun, she thought to herself. She had plenty to last awhile. Now, she could focus on her next victim and *that face* she'd seen.

Moving to the laundry area she began to unbutton her dusty overalls as images of her grandfather floated up into her mind. The only father she'd ever had.

"Wear the mask," he'd said. "You always have to wear a mask. If they see your fear they'll take you first. Never let them see your emotions."

She could almost remember his crackling dusty laugh as he had recounted how he'd managed to survive. It made Poena feel proud to hear his stories of how he'd succeeded where so many had failed. Remembering his rickety, gaunt skeleton, she could easily visualize how he must have looked back then.

But with her pride in her grandfather there always walked the specter of fear; the deep blackness of terror that those same memories had engendered. It had been the nexus of her nightmares since her childhood.

She'd never focused on that, though. She couldn't really. Consciously, she barely recalled it at all, but it was there, with her, always.

Who was this face? She asked herself. She'd had something like this happen before . . . in the beginning. Walking by someone in the grocery store she'd received this mental flash in her mind, and she *knew* that person was one of them. She'd let a couple go by before it occurred to her that God and her grandfather wanted her to be the instrument of retribution for the suffering they had caused.

So the next time she was confronted with the same flash, she followed. It was in a grocery store, and it was a woman. She'd signed a credit card slip and Poena had managed to see the name. Later, she'd taught herself to do the research on the internet and, after weeks of painstaking study, she finally learned that the woman was indeed the spawn of one of them.

If Poena couldn't punish them, she could at least punish their progeny. That first time, she'd been so filled with excitement. To finally find her purpose, something she could dedicate herself to that would mean something. She could almost see her grandfather smiling down at her from Heaven and nodding his approval. Now, she could exact the justice that her grandfather's stories demanded.

Her initial research on the internet had taught her much, and soon she was quite adept at finding anything she needed or wanted with very few keystrokes. In part, it was her permanent match that gave her the best idea. She'd known from the beginning that fire had to be the route she'd use, but the match had given her the stroke of genius to do her work without getting caught.

Stepping carefully out of the dusty overalls, Poena moved towards the bedroom and her shower. She paused to admire her nakedness as she passed the full length mirror. Her svelte figure and dainty curves were augmented by her long black hair. She knew she was beautiful and, occasionally, used that to her advantage; but it seemed a distant thing to her, like mountains in the background of a painting, beautiful, but not a focus.

She didn't linger long. It was time to get cleaned up. There was still a lot more work to do tonight.

After her shower, she dressed in a pair of shorts and a T-shirt, giving no more thought to the advantage the short shorts put to her shapely legs. It was comfort and convenience that drove her choices of attire.

Walking back into the kitchen, she opened the refrigerator and picked up the zip-lock bag with the flesh in it. She'd salted it with the un-iodized salt. She wasn't really tanning the skin, just stopping the decomposition and keeping it flexible until she could finish the next mask.

Deciding it was doing fine, she placed it back in the refrigerator and moved back to her den. Masks had always been central to her grandfather's stories, and she was surprised when it came to it, that she had a talent for carving the base structure out of wood. She'd actually done pretty well, with even her first try, but since then she'd become much better.

Sitting down on the couch, she pulled the raw, wooden mask out of the drawer in the end table. Her carving knives were there beside it. Contentedly, she began to work. A little more off the cheek bones, reshape the nose slightly, finish cutting the nose and eye holes. By tomorrow it would be ready for the skin and the skin would be ready for her. Yes, the filth would face up to their sins . . .

As she worked, her thoughts turned again to that woman's face. She was certain that this face was one of them. But she'd never had a vision this strong. This one must be important, very important somehow. She'd see that face again. She knew she would, and when she did, she'd find out who it was and why it was so important.

CHAPTER

Images of the nightmares of Kira working on his adopted dad's painting danced through Sean's mind. It took him a moment to separate the fact that his own memories were being augmented by those from Kira.

The act of doing that painting had been such a horrible ordeal that Sean preferred to steer clear of those memories, yet here they were again. How could this new experience be as bad as that one, Sean wondered. That situation had been a very unique brush with evil. Surely this couldn't be like that. But the sensations he was receiving from Kira were so strong! And the remnant of Kira's memories of the Jason experience was making the hair on the back of his neck stand, all by themselves. And now, coupled with these new ones! It was almost too much to handle.

Burning flesh. Kira was remembering the smell of burning flesh again. Sean was convinced he could even smell it himself, and so strongly that it nearly nauseated him. The next thought, 'I hate this!' came to him.

Sean froze.

Am I reading her thoughts?

Surely not. He decided to test it.

"Burning flesh?" He asked tentatively looking in Kira's upturned face. Her beautiful eyes widened, and her mouth sagged slightly. He sensed Josh watching them intently as Kira merely nodded to Sean's question and hugged him again.

~

As she held him close, a little flicker of uncertainty coursed its way through her mind. My thoughts. He *is* reading my thoughts now. The realization seemed to coalesce in her mind. It scared her slightly. Or did it? This man that she loved could read her thoughts? Was that good or bad? She had long since become used to the idea of him being finely tuned to her emotions, but this was a long step beyond that.

Holding him there in that office, with Josh watching, she examined her feelings. I don't know, she finally decided. I don't know how I feel about that.

~

For his part, Sean was more certain how he felt about it. He didn't like it. An old adage floated up in his mind, 'ignorance is bliss'. That phrase had a new meaning for him now. Vainly he tried to push away the whole train of thought.

Unbuttoning Kira's blouse . . .

WHAT? Turning abruptly, Sean faced Josh, shock and anger warring for dominance on his face. "Did you?" But the question died as the color rose sharply into Josh's cheeks. He *had* been thinking of Kira, imagining himself unbuttoning her blouse. No! This was too much. Sean choked down the urge to say anything else. What could he say? Challenge Josh's inappropriate thoughts? To what purpose?

Bewildered at the amazing turn of events and not knowing what else to do, Sean simply slipped his hand around Kira's waist and said, "Come on let's go back to the hotel. I want to check in, and we can talk some more about what we do next."

They barely said good bye to the stunned Josh as they left the office. Numbly Josh trailed behind.

~

Watching Sean and Kira walk out to the car, Josh stopped and stood like a statue. What had just happened? He had the incredible sensation that Sean knew the thought that had flitted across his mind. The thought had even surprised him but . . . Sean KNEW! How could he possibly have known what I was thinking? And what was this connection between Kira and the painting, or rather the killer? And it appeared that Sean might be able to read her thoughts, too! Who was this guy? Who was this couple? A chill trickled through him. These things just didn't happen in his life. First some crazy arsonist that wasn't leaving a trace and now these two. Good God, he thought, I must be losing my mind.

Still staring, he watched Sean and Kira drive away. Josh's embarrassment was battling with his intense disbelief, for precedence in his thoughts. He acknowledged neither. I have to do something, he finally told himself, and with that, he turned back toward his office. I'm going to bug the lab techs again. Someone better figure out that damn accelerant!

~

Sean's mind was reeling. Kira was sitting quietly beside him in the car as he drove towards the hotel. She was feeling tense and uncertain towards him.

Damn! Two thoughts in a row. He'd sensed two thoughts in a row; first Kira, then Josh, and not just feelings—thoughts! DAMMIT! I don't want to be able to DO this! His spinning thoughts were near panic at the ramifications. And not just any thoughts either, he railed at himself. That son-of-a-bitch is having fantasies about my fiancée.

He stole a glance at Kira who was still sitting quietly in her seat. But she felt a teeny bit distant. Damn! Sean forced his mind into some semblance of calm.

Finally breaking the silence, Kira spoke. "Sean this *is* scary, but it's different than with Jason." Sean looked at her again and focused for a moment, thinking. With the first part of her sentence he'd been certain she was going to be referring to him, but it was the new painting she was commenting on. A tiny part of him felt relief. He wasn't ready to face the other topic.

"A different kind of connection?" he asked, tentatively phrasing what he was getting from her. It caused Kira to stop and stare at him. Shit, he thought, he'd done it again.

"Okay, Sean, what's going on? That's the third time you've spoken my thoughts now. Is this something new or something you've been keeping from me?"

79

He sensed fear coming from her, before shock and dismay overtook his features. "Kira, I'd never keep anything from you! This is something new, something that seemed to happen while I was visiting my dad. And, frankly, something that's scaring the hell out of me!"

"You mean just that quick? The change happened during your short visit with your Dad? That's a bit hard to believe."

"Yes, just that quick, and, to make it worse my dad warned me that this might happen."

"Warned you?" Kira stared at him as he spoke. "Warned you that *what* might happen?" This whole development was frightening her a bit more than she wanted to admit. Still, she was glad to be getting it out in the open. Keeping anything from Sean felt absolutely foreign.

"Reading thoughts, not just feelings. And apparently it is something he's had to deal with himself."

"Your Dad's like you? He told you this when you were with him?"

Sean, was smiling. "Yeah, he looks a bit like me too, Kira, and some of his mannerisms made me feel like I was looking in a mirror. It's such a strange feeling to be around someone you're genetically related to . . ." Sean's voice trailed off as his thoughts chased each other.

~

Kira had always had family around her, and she was suddenly struck by the sensation of how empty it would be to have gone through your whole life and never experienced the simple closeness of someone that was related to you by blood. The thought made her smile with happiness for him. So much so that she momentarily forgot the sensations of trepidation continuing to slither their way into her thoughts. She realized Sean was still talking.

~

". . . him and no matter what he did or said I found myself catching snippets of familiarity with a word or a phrase or a mannerism. It was really amazing. Well, more like fulfilling really." As he finished the sentence he looked at Kira, who was staring out of the window, and it occurred to him that he hadn't gotten his previous question answered. "Wait a minute Kira, you never told me what was different about this connection from the one with Jason."

~

Kira had to refocus her attention. Her thoughts had been wandering so far afield that she'd barely heard Sean's last sentence. For a brief moment her eyes followed the verdant landscape rolling by the rental car. "What?" She asked, suddenly jerking her gaze back to Sean. "I'm sorry. What did you ask?"

"The connection in the painting Kira, what's different than before?" he repeated.

This was where her thoughts had been while he'd been talking so there was no pause in her response. "Two things really; one, this is more personal than the other times. I mean, there were times with Jason's painting where I felt like one of the victims, but even then it didn't feel as personal, as close, as it did this time. I mean, Sean, this person is alive! And second," here she paused and locked eyes briefly with Sean, "I think she saw *me*."

"What?" He responded reflexively. "You're kidding right?" Now it was his turn to experience fear. The idea that this killer had glimpsed her, scared him to death.

"Kidding! Are you nuts? I'm scared out of my mind! It felt like she was looking at me in that vision just as surely as you're looking at me now. It gives me the chills just to remember it."

"Yeah, I can feel that from you," Sean replied simply.

Sean parked the car and hand in hand with Kira walked into the hotel lobby. It was a Hilton and an older structure with a lot of character, nestled in among the tall trees and copious landscaping. The big dark wood counter and lush burgundy carpet didn't register with Sean at all. His thoughts were too occupied. Right now, it was just another place to stay.

~

Kira was also nearly unaware of the transition. Her fears assailed her like a hail storm in the wind. They were hitting her from all directions. First this damn painting and now Sean's new-found ability. How can you live with someone who can literally read your thoughts? Even Josh

81

was freaking her out with the way he was looking at her. Suddenly, Kira felt enormously alone.

For the first time since her mother had died, she was struck by the profound separateness that marked her life. Sean was her lifeline and any barrier between him and her feelings for him was like carrying a stone in the ocean. She had to get past it. She *had* to!

~

But Sean's abilities were no where near as complete as Kira feared. While he watched her face and felt the fear well within her, he desperately wanted to know what she was thinking. It was just a jumble. He caught something about 'him' and then something else about 'alone', but that was it. Did she want him to leave her alone? Suddenly, his own rising fear prompted him to simply ask.

The lady handed Sean the key to their room.

"That's room number 506," she said brightly, "have a nice stay."

"Thanks," Sean said. Then he murmured, "Shit!" causing Kira to turn her head sharply. He merely smiled at her as he recalled that 506 was the same number as the haunted room at the Eldridge hotel in Lawrence they'd stayed at while doing Jason's painting. They hadn't actually stayed in the haunted room that night, but even the room next door had proven too close for comfort

"I wish I believed in coincidences," he said out loud as he walked down the big hallway, trying to ignore the increasing sense of foreboding.

~

Sean followed Kira into their room and closed the door behind him.

"Kira, what's wrong?" The question riveted her eyes on his. The weight of the question was far in excess of the simple syllables that composed it. It was the perfect phrase at the perfect instant. He couldn't read her every thought, and she could see the fear and pleading in his eyes, overlaid by his extreme concern. Her heart melted. How could she doubt this man who loved her, and so what if he could read her thoughts? In answer she grabbed him and began to cry, feeling stupid, vulnerable, and relieved all at the same time.

~

Holding her, Sean felt the warmth of her feelings wash through him, and he could breathe again. Moments passed in intimate silence.

Her tears slowly subsiding, Kira's thoughts returned to the problems at hand and crystal clarity seemed to overtake her. Gently she pushed back from Sean who still held her in silence.

"Sean, just like we had to finish the painting of your d . . . I mean Jason, we have to finish this. We have to catch this woman before she kills again."

Sean nodded his head at the earnestness in her voice, but his thoughts were still racing, and he answered with a non-sequitur that caught her off guard. "Do you know Josh has the hots for you?"

They locked eyes for a brief second, and then both broke out laughing. Once Kira could catch her breath she answered, "Actually, I did." Then she made a face like biting a lemon, and they laughed some more.

Poena was ecstatic. Her research had finally paid off. She'd found her next mission. The family was seventy-five miles away, but that wasn't a problem. She'd travel across the country if necessary. The wife was the right blood, another descendant, and in a few days she'd die for her grandfather's crimes.

Lovingly, she stretched the face of her last victim over her newly carved mask. To make it look smooth, she had to hold each area in place for a few moments while the special glue took hold. She started with the chin and then slowly smoothed the skin up over the carved lips and lower cheeks. Hold. Wait. Perfect. The simple stretching of the skin over the wood of the mask often took more than forty-five minutes and required relentless patience.

Sometimes she was even required to do a bit more carving on the underlying wood structure to properly accommodate the skin. But she enjoyed exercising her patience. "*Arbeit macht frei*" It was a phrase her grandpa had taught her; it meant 'Work can set you free'. Her dedication to that idea was one more quality that set her above other people. Her grandfather had always told her she was special, and moments like this confirmed his words.

"Patience can save your life," he used to say. Once the skin was in place, she'd go wash her hands and give the mask an hour or so to dry then she'd begin to paint.

The mysterious face floated up to her mind's eye as she stood over the sink with the water running. An attractive woman, but she definitely had the high cheek bones and the angular features of one of *their* progeny. She had to find out more about this woman so she could begin her research and prove what she already knew. This one must be important, maybe even the most important, she thought. Maybe even the last one she needed to find. But time was on her side, and right now she needed to begin planning her next fire.

As she ran over the details in her mind, the problems seemed to delineate themselves. This was a two story house in a high-dollar neighborhood, and it backed up to the river on one side, causing two problems. First, her ingress and egress were limited secondly; these high-dollar neighborhoods were much more suspicious in general, therefore, much more difficult to traverse without drawing attention too quickly. It was critically important that she not be detected too soon, and have authorities called before she was ready. Even with the sun at her disposal she needed time for the evidence to be consumed; not nearly as much as she would without the *sun* but some still ... Finally, there was no back yard for a quick escape into another neighborhood, and no adjacent neighborhood to hide her car and minimize suspicion. Just that damn water. Wait! That was it! She'd *use* the water! She could make the *sun's* enemy, her friend.

That was what her grandpa had taught her, 'make the enemy your friend'. The water could provide stealth. It could provide ingress and egress. It could provide a quick means out of the neighborhood. Still, the fire station was too close. It was the first time she'd picked a target where the fire station happened to be in such proximity. She'd have to do something about that too. It was going to require a bit more thought. She decided to go sit down and think, and make a few calls to a sporting goods store while she waited for the mask to dry. The mere challenge of the endeavor made her pulse race. She could do this, and it would make her grandpa proud.

Sean was wrestling with Kira's decision to continue working on this painting, or on this job in general. He could understand her feelings easily enough, but his bad feeling about the safety of this venture was growing exponentially with every new tidbit of information. The killer saw her? What if that was true? "SHIT." Sean whispered. And he had no reason to doubt it based on his previous experience with Kira's abilities. Would the killer act on her perception? Would she believe what she saw, or understand it if she did? What if the quarry decided to hunt the hunter? A real-live murderer stalking them was certainly a fresh wrinkle in their repertoire of new experiences, and it was one Sean didn't want to contemplate.

~

"What are you muttering about?" Kira asked, though she was pretty sure it had something to do with this new job, and she wasn't real sure she even wanted an answer.

Sean had already expressed his misgivings about it, and hearing it all again wouldn't make her feel any better about her decision.

"Oh, nothing new," he said. Seconds passed, and he was thankful that she let it drop at that.

The afternoon was sliding by as they settled into their room. Sean reflected on how often a hotel room was just a hotel room, regardless of the price. It seemed like, more often than not, what you found yourself paying for was everything else but the room. From the green floral pattern on the bedspread, to the short pile, brown carpet and the heavy, forest green blackout drapes, this was every hotel room in the country that cost more than fifty dollars a night.

Sean decided to take a shower just for the relaxation of it. Also, Kira was lost in thought, and he sensed that giving her a little time to sort out her day would be a much appreciated idea. Nevertheless, he decided to ask her to join him.

"Hey, Kira. This is an oversize shower. Wanna share it with me?" Sean intentionally called from the bathroom to make it easier for Kira to say no, which he was certain she would. "No thanks, Hon. I think I'll just relax out here and think a bit if you don't mind."

"No, that's fine," Sean replied, smiling at the anticipated response. "I'll be out in a few."

"Okay."

~

Kira stacked up several pillows on the bed, took a few deep breaths, crossed her arms on her chest and closed her eyes. She wasn't inclined to sleep though; her thoughts were churning *way* too fast for that. The question that was bothering her the most was the nature of the connection with the girl in the painting. Even describing it to Sean and Josh as 'much more personal' and that the woman saw her, still didn't seem to scratch the surface. It was almost as though she shared some history with this woman she'd never met, some intimate event that had involved them both a long time ago. But what could that mean? It couldn't be a real memory because Kira was certain she'd never seen this woman before.

Winnowing through her memories proved to be as frustrating and fruitless as she'd anticipated. Eventually, the only conclusion she could draw from the situation was that she was going to have to go back and work some more on that painting. It was the only idea she could come up with that might glean any more information.

No matter what, she was certain that this woman *had* to be stopped. She just had to be. And even that certainty seemed too powerful for the amount of information Kira currently possessed. Against all her intentions, her mind sought some relaxation of its own, and amidst the thrum of the shower in the other room, Kira drifted off to sleep.

~

With his eyes closed, languishing in the shower, letting the hot water relax him, Sean felt Kira's turmoil. Something about the painting, still. Then, something about a connection. His eyes popped open. "What was he doing?" he asked himself. "Damn! Am I trying to practice or something? I don't want to be able to do this!" But even as the words crossed his mind for the tenth time in the past few hours, he knew it was going to be useless. He was what he was. If he had to have this ability, at least he may as well try to make the most of it.

Closing his eyes again, he let his mind reach for Kira and just as his thoughts touched hers, he felt her relax. She'd fallen asleep. He smiled. Good, he thought, she needed it. Gently, he let his own thoughts slide away, back to the farm and the horses and things that were simple and fulfilling.

~

Josh's afternoon hadn't been so relaxing. After coming up with bupkis from another visit to the lab and getting virtually run out by the lab people he was harassing, Josh went back to his makeshift office and sat down in front of his computer in a funk. He doodled around on the internet for a bit, more as a means of letting his thoughts wander than anything else, until he glanced up and saw the mask sitting on his desk. The mask, he thought to himself. Maybe I better chase that angle for a bit. And with no further adieu he directed his Internet rambling to the history and making of Masks.

Two and a half hours later, his eyes weary from staring at the computer screen, Josh leaned back in his chair and took a deep breath. He'd learned about masks from Africa, the Incas, the Romans, the Chinese, Russia, masks for Theatre, and masks for religious rituals. He'd even learned the difference between anthropomorphic (human) and theriomorphic (animal) masks.

But the only tidbits of information that stayed with him were the references that masks could represent supernatural beings or ancestors, and that anthropomorphic masks were frequently used in ceremonies involving dead or departing spirits. Well, he was certain these masks involved a few of those. Still, something in those little tidbits tugged at the back of his mind. There was a bit of an answer in there if he could just pull the parts together. But what??? Maybe he was still missing some little piece of the puzzle to make sense of what he'd read.

Josh sighed again and closed his eyes. He had the feeling it was going to be a long night. That thought led him to wonder what Kira and Sean were doing. Maybe he should call them. No, he decided. They'd had enough today, better to wait and let them call him. Surely they'd call him in the morning anyway.

Vague feelings of embarrassment drifted through the back of his mind, which led him to think of the abilities of his two new associates. "DAMN!" He said out loud to the emptiness of his office. The sooner this case is over the happier I'll be.

Frustrated, he pushed his chair back and marched out of the office. "It's time for a drink," he voiced to the empty hallway as he made for the front door and his favorite local watering hole.

Kira woke up with a start. Fire! She'd been dreaming of fire. The stench of burning flesh lingered in her memory, a smell she'd never experienced before in her life, but now it was an odor that she was intimately familiar with and one she'd never be able to forget.

The hotel room was still dark and the air conditioning still droning when she turned her head slowly over to Sean. In the dim light, Kira could see his eyes wide open and him smiling at her.

"Good morning gorgeous. Did you have a bad dream?"

Kira smiled back at him delightedly and snuggled in close before answering. "Well, not like the ones I used to have, but not real pleasant either."

"You want to tell me about it?"

"Not really. It was mostly just flames anyway . . . And burning flesh."

"Icchhhh! I'm sorry I asked. So, what's on tap for today?" He asked changing topics abruptly and reaching his hands around her.

Kira responded pliantly, if somewhat distracted. "I think we should get some breakfast and go back to Josh's office. I want another crack at that painting."

The previous day's fear returned with a vengeance and Sean hesitated before replying, but in that brief pause he sensed the intensity of her determination and it short circuited his planned dissuasions. Instead, he glanced over his shoulder at the clock on the nightstand. It was 7:00 already, and he really *was* hungry.

"Okay, Hon, I'm with you. Do you want to shower first or do you want me to?"

Feeling playful and wanting in some ways to test his new abilities, she said, "Do you really have to ask?"

Smiling and grabbing her hands as he sat up, he realized he didn't. "Together it is then." And Kira virtually chased him into the bathroom, giving not a thought to the fact that he'd guessed right.

~

Breakfast at the Hilton was a more formal setting than either cared for but the buffet they offered left nothing to be desired. They were just sipping on their second coffee when Kira's cellphone rang. Kira fished it from her purse and looked at the display. It was Josh.

"Hello," she said simply, attempting to stifle the unwarranted irritation she found herself feeling.

"Uh, Good morning," He began tentatively, a bit put off by the tone of her one word greeting. "I didn't wake you did I?" It was 8:20.

"No," she responded more brightly, "We're just finishing up breakfast and then heading your way."

"Great. That was what I was going to ask. I'm at the office already." She sensed he wanted to say more, but he didn't. She thought he was probably fishing for their time of arrival at his office anyway.

"Yeah, we should be there in about forty-five minutes or so. I want to get back to work on the painting."

"Do you think you'll learn anymore from continuing with this painting?"

Kira thought for a moment. It was a question she'd already considered yesterday. "Well, I can't be sure, Josh, but I have a feeling I will, and if you don't have another recent fire site for us to visit then I may as well try."

"Okay. Well, I'll see you when you get here then." It felt like he wanted to get off the phone, and she had a memory of him staring at her that prompted those same feelings.

"Okay, Josh, see ya in a bit. Bye."

~

Josh stared at his phone as he slipped it back into his pocket. He took a deep breath. Fear. It seemed everyone was seething with it. Kira was afraid to do the painting, Sean was afraid for Kira, and now he was afraid of having thoughts that Sean could sense, about Kira. That *was* what Sean had done! Even though Sean hadn't said a word, Josh was convinced of it. Shit! How do you *not* think about something? Well, he knew the answer to that. You couldn't. The only thing you could do was think about something else. Still, having those weirdoes in his office made his stomach queasy. If he'd known what he was getting himself into before he contacted them, he'd have left them both in Kansas and just kept trying to chase this puzzle himself, which got him thinking about the case again.

A female? Kira said it was a she . . . hmmm less than 20% of arsonists were female and for serial arsonists it was even less common. Could she be right? The profile for a female arsonist was different, and it did include more residential than commercial fires. Hmmm . . . He'd have to think about that. Female arsonists were also much more prone to set fires for emotional reasons. The residential thing fit and the emotional thing could as well. Regardless, he told himself, he had calls to make. He could worry about the psychic duo when they got here.

~

"Listen, Sean, I want you to ignore anything you sense from Josh about me." Kira began out of the blue as Sean parked the car at Josh's office. They had been silent most of the drive since Josh's phone call and this comment took Sean a bit by surprise.

"Why would you want me to do that?" he asked.

"Well, I'm betting Josh has a clue what you sensed from him, and I'll bet it's scaring the hell out of him. It won't help things if Josh decides he's afraid to be around us. I think I scare him enough as it is without you adding to it."

"But he's thinking about . . . well . . . lascivious things about you! And how could he know anyway?"

"You don't always have to have a gift to pick up feelings, and anyway, they're just *thoughts*. If he doesn't act on them they're still just thoughts. If you're going to be able to read people's thoughts at all, you better start thinking about the difference between thoughts and actions. Don't *you* ever have thoughts that you're not proud of, thoughts that flash into your mind, and then you're ashamed? You may even consciously force those thoughts away from you, but they were still there right?"

Sean was provoked into silence by her words.

Walking slowly up to the office, he thought carefully about what she'd said. It was definitely something to consider. He'd certainly experienced fleeting images or even sometimes lingering ones that he wasn't proud of, and even some that had down right shamed him. What if someone else had read his thoughts at those particular moments? It wasn't something he liked to consider, and it resulted in a significantly more tolerant perspective. His mind unfocused briefly as he noticed the cool, moist, morning breeze brush across his face.

She was right, he thought. But how do you filter that? What's the difference between ideas that you intend to act on, and ones that just come into your mind unbidden, especially shameful ones? Every man woman or child who was brave enough to be honest with themselves could recall such momentary aberrations. It wasn't a topic he could deal with quickly. He was going to have to give this a lot of thought, and maybe get some advice from his dad, but in the meantime he realized Kira's advice was sound enough.

"I think you're right, Kira, thanks. I'll try." She just smiled back at him as she opened the door to the office, and he was rewarded with a surge of warm fuzzy feelings flowing from her. It was a measure of his distraction that Sean even let her open the door, as he was typically meticulous about his manners.

~

Josh felt his stomach jump as he saw the couple walk in the door. He squelched the feeling though. He was going to have to deal with these people a while longer, and he couldn't be twitching every time they were around.

Kira had on a tight black sweater and jeans. She looked positively . . . NO! Think about Sean. Think about the case, anything else.

"Good morning," he offered, smiling. When Josh smiled, his narrow lips pulled the skin between his nose and mouth down slightly, accentuating the hawk effect of his long, slender nose, and causing his glasses to slide a little.

"Good morning Josh. Did you have any luck finding anything out on your end?" Kira was still one step ahead of Sean, who remained silent, but at least he didn't glare.

"Not really. I did a little research on masks, but all I came up with was stuff about ancestors, spirits and rituals. I can't figure out the connection yet."

"Hmmm," Kira began, "Well maybe I'll come up with something else today."

"I hope so," Josh answered simply.

~

The comment had sparked Sean's curiosity, though. "Is there any chance I could look at one of the masks?" He had no idea what he hoped to learn. It was more of a hunch than anything else. At that moment a fleeting thought of his dad crossed his mind. It didn't seem to go with the flow of his thoughts, but he was so preoccupied with other events, he let it drop.

It was the oddest thing. Even now, with Sean gone, Aubrey continued to receive sensations from him. It was like they had forged some kind of link by finally meeting. Like Sean, Aubrey had never met anyone else with his same abilities, and the possibility that those abilities might interact in some fashion had never crossed his mind.

But it seemed that he was having these images of Sean every time he closed his eyes and impressions of feelings from him even when he was awake. It was heartwarming and unnerving at the same time, to find this connection with his son.

There was some part of him that had the notion that this connection was important somehow, but he couldn't for the life of him imagine what that might be.

Yet, large as that may seem, that bond still paled next to the sheer joy he was experiencing from finally getting to meet his son. The warmth that brought to his heart was only rivaled by the moment he had heard on the phone that his son was actually alive. It was a tremendous justification for all the intervening years he had dared to hope. That hope had been the last gift he could give his beautiful Laura, and now it had borne fruit. A tear trickled from his eye at the memory of their love. He'd never had anything like it before or since and, from what he sensed, Sean might have the same thing. The idea made him smile

He let the thoughts drift away and again devoted his attention to the stock research in front of him. The snow continued to fall outside the office window of his big log home. He was so accustomed to the beautiful sight of the snow in the mountains; he seldom stopped to enjoy it these days, like living in the middle of a rose garden and not stopping to smell them.

CHAPTER

Poena was typically careful not to do or say anything that would draw attention to her. Instinctively, she was aware that anonymity was her friend. So she was acutely aware of any regard she might draw as she pulled back into her driveway with the lightweight black canoe strapped to the roof of her car.

Still, it was daytime on a weekday so with a little luck there wouldn't be any curious eyes watching. Unfortunately, her tendency to be a recluse was curious enough in itself that doing anything that might seem like a social outing would probably garner undue consideration from her nosey neighbors. This time though, no one was there to see. Listening nervously to the low screeching sound as she opened the garage door with the remote, Poena pulled the nose of her old Subaru wagon partially in.

With as much economy of movement as she could muster, she quickly and efficiently untied the canoe and slid it off onto the garage floor. It was one of the new Kevlar canoes and, therefore, much lighter than it would appear. Smiling to herself as she looked briefly around the empty neighborhood, she backed the Subaru up and closed the garage door. Now it was time to paint, she thought, as she gracefully breezed into the house via the front door.

Humming to herself, she walked through the house to the kitchen. Opening the oven door, she carefully slid the mask out and set it on the table. Though she didn't need any heat from the oven, it seemed to her a good place to let the skin cure until she could paint it, nothing to startle anyone that might peer in through a window. Caution was the key to survival and anyone spying one of her masks before it was painted would certainly be startled.

Poena admired the realism of the mask. With the human skin stretched over her wooden carving, the mask had an amazingly life-like quality. Many times she'd considered leaving it like that, unpainted, untainted, but again her cautious nature took over. No one would guess the nature of the mask in its finished form, and the less evidence the investigators had, the better. Not that any of those idiots were ever going to catch her; but still, her grandpa had preached to her about caution in all things, and she knew his advice was good, even if she didn't always agree.

Black paint this time. The paint was already sitting there on her kitchen table. She would add some contrasting colors later, little marks of beauty, and some feathers too, but first she wanted to paint the entire thing black. Black was especially fitting for this granddaughter of a jackal.

The grin Poena exhibited at that thought would have frightened children to tears. She sat herself at the kitchen table and began to work contentedly.

CHAPTER

Kira walked into the little office with her eyes riveted on the painting. She could feel her pulse elevate slightly. That awareness seemed to feed on itself and her anxiety went up proportionally. Taking a deep breath and forcefully pushing away her fears, she began unpacking her supplies. Moments later, palette in hand, Kira sat down on her stool, garnered her courage, and raised her paintbrush.

Sean was already weary of sensing Josh's nervousness. The unrelenting quality of it had gotten old fast. Josh wanted to make some coffee before they went into his office. Kira had declined, restless to get to work, but Sean had heartily agreed.

The coffee can was empty when Josh opened it, and cursing quietly he left the little break room saying he'd be right back. Thankfully, his nervousness went with him. With nothing else to do, Sean sat at the break table and looked around. The room was devoid of any décor. White walls, white refrigerator, water cooler, round white table, and vending machines were all that was in there. Sean figured you couldn't expect much personality in a small FBI office, which got him thinking about where everyone else in the office was, until the tension from Josh preceded him into the room, coffee can in hand. At least the coffee proved palatable.

~

Later, as Josh lead Sean into his office, the strain of being afraid of his own thoughts was weighing on him. It was like a wet, vibrating slug in the pit of his stomach, and he was concerned that Sean would notice that too.

~

He could, and the feel of it was contagious. Sean had to question his own nervousness, as though his body was responding in sympathy to what he was sensing. He shook it off and tried to focus on the mask sitting on Josh's desk. He didn't want to glean any of Josh's thoughts because he was uncertain of his ability to mask his own feelings if he did. Hmmm, he thought, as those words slid through his mind. 'mask my own feelings ... '

That phrased seemed to resonate with him. His eyes drifted back to Josh's desk. Something there ... something about ... the sensation slipped away as Josh seated himself at his desk and reached for the mask on the far side.

"Well, here it is," he began, holding the thing out to Sean. "The lab has checked it over repeatedly. It's carved wood and ordinary paint. The other adornments, feathers and such can be bought at any hobby store."

Kira's presence was nestled in the back of Sean's mind. She was about to begin painting, he realized, as he looked at the gold paint and gaudy red lips of the thing Josh was passing to him. It reminded him of Mardi Gras. Feathers swayed capriciously with the movement and Sean's fingers closed on the edge ... Thunderous emotions exploded in Sean's mind. Horror, terror, pain, sadness! His heart lurched at the shock and power of it. A cacophony of feelings roared through his mind like a mountain river after a storm.

He'd never felt anything like it! It felt as though he was standing at the base of an avalanche watching it descend towards him. Then more feelings, different this time, came in another momentous wave. Shock, surprise, confusion, fear ... Then abruptly ... KIRA ... she bolted to the forefront of his mind! She was in trouble! He had to reach her. Involuntarily, Sean loosened the grip on the mask in his hand and then ...

~

Poena felt an ice cold hand reach into her heart and squeeze. The paintbrush in her hand stopped in mid stroke, and suddenly a kaleido-scope of images cascaded through her mind. Chestnut haired woman, black haired man with eyes like the sea, the last house she had razed, masks . . . they almost seemed to meld in her mind. Eyes staring at her from the dark. The woman! That face. That one she'd seen before, but the man, he was something new. The woman was reaching out to touch her. The man beside her was also reaching but not to touch her, to touch . . . her victims! What was he doing? Her mask! She had to put on the mask like her grandpa had taught her. Then no one could see her . . .

~

Stroke after stroke, Kira's hand was moving mindlessly. Her thoughts glided serenely over memories of the past few days, when a flash of light exploded in her mind and raced through her, sending heat coursing up her arm.

Long, dark-haired woman, cold, empty, flames, heat, hatred, dark water in the night. The images chased each other through Kira's mind like an accelerated film. Her mind swam trying to keep up with the speeding flow. A hammer swinging, the low dull thud of a body hitting the floor. Hands reaching for *her* face . . .

~

In an unearthly nexus of unimaginable clairvoyance Sean, Kira, and Poena collided at a single point. All three, with abilities, tapped and untapped, in three different locations, mentally raced at each other like three columns of water thundering from three fire hydrants, all meeting at some other worldly point in an instant in time. A Super Collider of psychic force. They met, meshed and exploded in a supernatural detonation of mental might, each feeling the tremendous recoil.

~

Sean stood up, abruptly stepping back as if struck, eyes glazed, he knocked over his chair and his senseless fingers lost their grip on the mask . . .

~

Poena dropped her mask and paintbrush, as what felt like a huge blunt force knocked her back against the kitchen wall.

~

Kira gasped as her paintbrush dropped. Trying to stand she tangled her feet in the overturning stool and went down.

~

Two thousand miles away in his mountain home, Aubrey experienced a burst of white light in his mind. Reeling, he gasped for breath and dropped the papers he was holding, back onto his desk. Seconds later his vision cleared. "What the hell was that?" He said out loud. But his only clue was a sharp lingering image of his new-found son with vague images of other people and places superimposed on it.

~

"Kira!" Sean suddenly heard himself shout. Ignoring Josh's growing shock and barely hearing his outraged curses as the mask hit the floor, Sean raced from the room.

Seconds later, Sean burst into the little office to see Kira sitting on the floor staring at the painting. Her left hand was on her heart, and as she heard the door burst open, she jumped and raised a hand to point at the painting above her on the easel.

Sean first noticed the flames that were beginning to issue from the two upstairs windows, then he saw the figure sitting in the back yard, dressed in black, legs crossed, hands placed meditatively on knees. The face was another mask. Tearing his eyes from the painting, Sean rushed over to Kira.

"Kira are you okay?"

~

Josh was apoplectic. What the HELL had ever come over him to deal with these two whackos! Walking around his desk, he reached for the mask on the floor. The bottom corner had broken off. Chips of paint and a couple of small shards of wood littered the low pile carpet. DAMN! Mishandling evidence was not something he was accustomed to have happen in the cases he worked.

As he reached to pick up the mask he noticed . . . something . . . there under the paint. Was it . . . leather? It was definitely another layer under the paint and over the wood. What the hell?

101

Josh drew the mask closer to his eyes. They suddenly widened in recognition, and he abruptly turned to leave the room, other concerns forgotten. How the hell did the lab techs miss this he fumed as he stomped off in the direction of the lab?

~

Poena's eyes opened, and she took a sharp, deep breath. She bent to pick up her mask as a slow smile bloomed on her face. It was a cold wicked smile, devoid of mirth, full of self-satisfaction, and underscored with evil. "Kira," she murmured quietly, testing the syllable on her tongue and ears. "Now I've seen you both," she said out loud to no one. "And we'll meet again soon." She looked again at the mask she had just picked up. No damage was done, and she felt certain her mental mask had done its job. No one had seen her face.

No thought of the 'how' or 'why' of the extraordinary circumstance that had left her with this new information even flickered across her senses. As a matter of fact, there wasn't a single facet of Poena's life that she ever considered strange.

Therefore, one new psychic incident wasn't about to garner too much attention. She happily repositioned herself on the couch and resumed her painting. She had work to do.

~

Sean lifted Kira gently off the floor.

Her eyes never left the painting as she began to speak. "Poena. Sean, her name is Poena. I saw her, or at least I kind of did. I must have tried to paint her too but . . . well . . . the mask . . ." Kira's words faltered as her thoughts chased each other too swiftly, but Sean understood.

"I think I sensed one of her victims," Sean added quietly. Kira whirled to him.

"You what???"

"I reached over to take that mask Josh was handing me and I felt . . . emotions . . . horrible emotions." A shiver chased the words down his spine. "I'm certain it was one of the victims, but I don't know how or why."

Now looking at Sean, Kira realized that he was looking as shocked as she was feeling. Instinctively, she reached to hold him. "Good Lord, Sean, what are we getting ourselves into?"

"We could stop. We could quit this right now and go back home. Lord knows Josh would be glad to see us go . . . well, see *me* go anyway." Kira didn't even grin at his feeble attempt at humor.

Instead, she looked Sean straight in the eyes. "I don't think we can, Sean. Not now. Not only do I want to stop this woman, but I think she's seen *us* too."

There was no answer to that, and Sean just stared at Kira. He knew she was right. He could feel it too, and if this woman had anything to do with the feelings he had just experienced, he wanted to stop her as much as Kira did.

"On the other hand," Kira began again. "I don't want to paint anymore today. Let's get out of here."

"I'll second that emotion," Sean added heartily.

They both turned and walked back towards Josh's office to let him know they were leaving, but when they got there, he was gone. Sean noticed the small mess on the floor.

"I must have dropped the mask, Sean said bending down. "And apparently it chipped a little. Oooo I bet that pissed him off. I wonder where he went?"

"Maybe he went back to the lab?"

"Let's go see," Sean replied, moving back towards the door. Kira followed closely as Sean glided out of the room.

"Have you been to the lab?" Sean asked.

"No, have you?"

Rounding the first corner, Sean stopped suddenly, seeing Josh. Kira, lost in her own thoughts, nearly collided with him before she realized the change.

"Kira, are you okay?" Josh flustered out. "The way Sean rushed out I thought . . ." Josh stopped, cocked his head and changed subjects. "Where are you two headed?"

Sean immediately sensed something from Josh. It didn't quite resolve into words though. Disgust. Shock. Anger. Curiosity. Anger was currently the strongest of the four.

"We were looking for you," Sean responded pointedly.

"I was in the lab," Josh's gazed flickered to Kira and then nervously back to Sean's face. "I found out something as a result of your clumsiness."

Feeling embarrassed, Sean answered, "I'm sorry about that Josh but I..."

"Forget it." Josh interrupted impatiently. "It turned out to be a good thing. We discovered something important about the masks."

Sean sensed the disgust rise to the surface as Kira came up beside him, facing Josh.

"What did you find out?" She asked.

"Underneath the paint on that mask is human skin." Sean sensed the words a fraction of a second before they came out of Josh's mouth and therefore his expression soured a second before Kira's hand shot up to cover her mouth in disgust.

"Oh my God! She cut off someone's face?!" Kira's eyebrows furrowed and her head tilted slightly toward Sean in the throes of her revulsion.

"That's what it looks like," Josh answered simply.

"You think it was one of the victims then?" Sean asked

"We think it was a victim from a previous fire."

"Let me get this straight," Sean continued, appalled by his own revelation. "You think this whacko cut the face off one of her victims and put it on a mask she left at her next victim's house?"

"That about sums it up, yeah. It had to be a previous fire because it takes a while to tan skin to use like this. Anyway, we're checking the other masks now but we feel certain it'll be the same for them too.

I guess the good news is that now we'll have some DNA samples and with a little luck we'll be able to match them up with one of the missing people from one of the fires."

Kira was almost too repulsed to speak as she listened to Josh's explanation, but finally words came to her. "What kind of sicko would cut the face off a victim and make a mask of it?"

"You said it," Josh replied. "A sicko. A real sicko. I just hope they were dead before she did it. "

"But why?" Kira asked as she grimaced at his suggestion.

~

"That's a good question, and if we can figure that one out we'll be a lot further on our way to catching this crazy bit . . . woman." Josh surprised himself at catching and softening his language. His gaze flickered from Kira back to Sean, who'd been listening quietly.

~

For his part, Sean was just wading through the intensity of Josh's and Kira's reactions. The emotions from each were thick in the room. Kira's revulsion and Josh's determination were the two most prevalent. Sean was noticing again how difficult it was for him to glean his own emotions about a situation when he was being bombarded by strong emotions from others.

A question came to him, though. "Will this help you find her at all?"

"Finding the skin? No, not really, but what it will do will be to turn this into an official homicide case, not just an arson, so we'll be able to get more manpower on it. What we need to figure out is some kind of motive for what Ms. Sicko is doing." The tension seemed to flow out of Josh as he focused on the particulars of the case.

"I have a feeling that whatever it is, it's going to be something as demented as her actions," Kira theorized.

"Boy, I'd have to agree with that one," Josh added. Sean stood there, listening vacantly, but his thoughts were elsewhere.

He was considering something else about that mask, and suddenly he decided he wanted to be out of there where he could talk openly with Kira.

"Kira got another impression from the painting that shocked her, and we were coming to tell you we're leaving for the day."

The slight change of tack didn't faze Josh at all but motivated his curiosity. "What did you see, Kira?"

Kira paused, glanced over briefly at Sean, then back to Josh as she folded her arms under her breasts. "I saw her Josh. And her name is Poena."

Josh blanched but recovered quickly. His hawk nose seemed to almost quiver like a dog testing a tantalizing scent. "You saw her face?"

was all he got out.

Kira thought for a moment as if puzzled, then answered, "Yes, I guess I did see her face come to think of it. At least for a second, and then it was gone."

"Can you draw it? And a name, you got her name?" Josh's thoughts were chasing each other out of his mouth he was so excited.

"Well, certainly I can, I . . ." Kira faltered as a thought struck her. ". . . you know, I think I already tried once, in the painting I was doing, but it came out with a mask on."

Sean's head turned sharply at the realization of what she was saying. "I think we need to get out of here and think for a while Josh. This has all been too taxing."

"Yeah, okay," Josh answered, but Sean knew he was lying. It was anything but okay to him. "But listen, it would be really helpful if you could sketch that face, Kira."

"I know," Kira answered, exhaustion and resignation evident in her voice. "But . . ."

"We can maybe come back tomorrow and give it a try, Josh," Sean interrupted. "Right now we're getting out of here."

"Okay, I understand. Well, as soon as possible would be great. Just let me know."

Sean sensed something from Josh about having all he could handle for one day. Well, that went for all of them. He turned, leading Kira by the arm. "Alright then, we're outta here. If you need anything urgent feel free to give us a call. We'll be back at the hotel."

"Will do," Josh answered, following them back towards the front.

Kira was noticeably silent as Sean pushed open the glass front door.

They remained quiet, riding in the car through the tree lined hills and streets of Reston, each deep in their own thoughts about the recent events.

Moments passed before Sean turned to Kira and finally broke the silence. "Kira, that was the strangest thing I ever felt," Sean began, seemingly out of the blue.

Kira tracked him though, going unerringly to the thought he was referring to. "Touching the mask?"

"Yeah. I don't know what's happening to me. Ever since I went to meet my dad I have begun to be able to do new things. Half the time I can actually read thoughts now, and when I touched that mask I got . . . a . . . jolt, I guess, of the feelings of that dead person whose skin was on it. Or at least, I'm pretty sure that's what I got. I don't have any proof, so I guess I'm just guessing there, too. But if I'm right, I've certainly never gotten any feelings from the dead before."

~

Kira turned to Sean briefly, and the forlorn look in his lovely blue eyes melted her heart all over again. That little boy look. Over and over during their relationship, Kira had been struck by how many times Sean made her think of a little boy. It was one of the endearing foibles she loved about him.

"All I can tell you is that I understand. I'm having similar feelings about slightly different experiences myself. I feel like my whole world is changing, and I don't know what might happen next. It seems like the only anchor to reality I have is you."

Sean smiled, "Yeah, I know what you mean." He experienced a burst of warmth toward her in response to the feelings he was sensing and her words. His smile faded quickly though as his thoughts wandered back to the mask, and then, strangely, to his dad. The vague notion flickered into his mind that he *had* received feelings from the dead before. Or at least he thought he had, once in New Orleans when he'd first met Kira. That line of thought was chased from his mind however, by the next one that he voiced. "Kira, if the feelings I was getting really are from a victim. This woman doing these things must be vile."

Already nodding her head, Kira answered, "Vile or crazy or both, but what scares me more is I'm beginning to think she's smart too. How could I have been trying to paint her face and have it show up with that mask on? What's up with that?"

"I think you had just begun painting when I touched that mask. I wonder what she was doing at that moment."

Sean turned his eyes from the road briefly and just looked at her. She was feeling puzzled, scared and . . . intrigued. Smiling, he returned his eyes to the road. He had to admit, this *was* getting very interesting. He just couldn't imagine where it all would lead.

~

They hadn't even bothered to call Josh the previous evening and, surprisingly, he didn't try to call them.

Neither of them had been to the Capitol before, so after having lunch back at the hotel, they trekked the forty-five minute drive into DC and made like tourists. By evening they were wearier, more patriotic, and in substantially better moods than when they'd left.

Rather than making any more decisions, they decided to eat dinner back at the hotel. With glasses of wine in hand the conversation finally turned back to what they had both been avoiding all day.

"Sean, I think I want to get some paint supplies for here at the hotel."

Sean didn't even act surprised. "You want to just pick up the stuff from Josh's office tomorrow?" Sean was pretty sure he sensed the answer to this already, but he asked anyway.

"No. I don't think I want to see Josh. I'd rather just get some new stuff."

"Sure, we can do that first thing in the morning. Whatcha' got in mind?"

"I don't know. I just want to have some stuff here in case I want to paint some more."

Sean knew there was more to it than what she was willing to say, but decided to let her have her privacy. Something about drawing the killer was floating in her mind, but he was quickly coming to understand how unnerving his ability could be, and he didn't want to upset his fiancée any more than was absolutely necessary.

"No problem," he answered before changing the subject. "Whaddya say we do that in the morning then go back to DC. I still want to see the Smithsonian and that could take most of the day."

Kira's answering smile warmed him to his marrow. "Sounds perfect."

J osh woke them the next morning with an 8:00 am phone call. Sean answered it.

"Are you two going to help anymore or just keep spending the government's money on your personal vacation?

~

Sean sensed the attempt at humor but was also aware of the seriousness behind it. And worse, Josh's tone didn't convey his intentions worth a damn. He decided to react to what he heard this time rather than what he knew.

~

"Hell, Josh, I thought this might be our only chance to recoup some of our tax money, so we were making the best of it. Have there been any more fires?"

"No not so far. But we did identify the person whose face was on that mask."

"Really, who was it?"

"It was who we expected; a Julia Anderson, formerly Julia Wagner. She was the wife of the owner of the last house. The woman he reported missing."

"Does that help any?"

"Not really. Homicide already called me twice yesterday, and I'm afraid they're going to end up being more of a pain in the ass than a help. Seriously though, are you and Kira coming in today?"

"I don't think she wants to work anymore on the painting she started. We're going to get some supplies for her to have at the hotel today and go take in the sights one more day. But let us know if there are any more fires."

~

Josh was a little disgusted with them, but he figured there wasn't much else to be done at the moment, so he let it pass. "Okay, just keep your phone with you, and I'll keep you posted."

"No problem," Sean answered, "We'll talk to you later then."

"Okay, bye."

"Bye, Josh."

Kira, still under the covers, looked up at Sean as he turned back from the phone. "Well," she said, "anything important?"

"Yep. It's another vacation day on the government nickel." Sean said brightly, sliding back under the covers, "And we're supposed to do some undercover work!"

Kira just laughed as he grabbed her.

~

An hour later, they had fallen into a brief nap. About thirty minutes into that nap Kira's eyes popped open, remembering the agenda for the day, then noticed Sean staring at her.

"Well, good morning again," she said sleepily, beginning to stretch.

"I love you," he answered, leaning in to kiss her on the neck.

The kiss sent chills down her body, and she shivered as she pulled Sean close. "I love you too." Feeling the warmth and strength of Sean's body against hers, she added, "So when are you going to marry me, Mr. Easton?"

~

Sean's body was already responding to her naked caress, and it was all he could do to fashion a reply. "Anytime you say, Ms. McGovern."

Those were the last words either of them spoke for a while. Not the last sounds, just the last words.

Later, Sean pulled out his laptop while Kira got dressed. He was looking for art supply places that were more convenient to their direction back to DC than the one she'd used previously. He found one, and after a quick breakfast at the hotel, they were off.

The day passed quickly. With all worries temporarily forgotten, they got Kira's supplies and enjoyed both the drive to DC, and their protracted tour of the Smithsonian. Looking at all the aircraft, Sean was dazzled just like a little kid.

~

Kira could only grin at this newest example of her favorite endearing trait. Pure boyishness, time and again, as though the years had never dimmed his ability to find wonder in the simplest things. It was, in part, the vestiges of his sheltered upbringing that made everything so new and fresh to him, but it was also the unquenchable attitude of curiosity and wonder that rose to the surface. Either way, it was a part of her fiancée that continually delighted her.

Kira had always thought of her extensive travels in the modeling business as a tremendous opportunity she had been afforded, but now being with Sean, she could almost wish to have never had those experiences so that she could delight in their novelty with him. This was certainly the next best thing.

Later in the afternoon, they stopped in a gift shop just to look around. Sean fell in love with a little carved, wooden model of the Bell X-1 jet, the first aircraft to break the sound barrier at the hands of Chuck Yeager. Laughing, Kira said she'd buy it for him while his eyes were already being riveted by something else. It was a display of mementos from World War II. Sean's eyes gravitated to a slender, old-style, lighter fluid powered lighter that said 'Remembering D-Day June 6th 1944', under a tiny picture of soldiers on the beach in Normandy; on the back was the simple inscription, 'let the light of freedom shine'. He held it reverently in his hand as he turned to Kira.

"It's incredible to think of how many people died in that war, isn't it?"

Abruptly catching his mood Kira answered, "Incredible isn't the right word. Appalling, would be much more appropriate."

~

Sean just nodded as he set the item back down, his thoughts floating back to the scene with his dad and the little lighter of his mom's that he had in his pocket. He hadn't yet mentioned it to Kira, or even that part of the story with his dad. He vaguely wondered why and decided he'd mention it to her later.

They left DC barely ahead of the afternoon traffic; both a bit distracted remembering the sights of the day. By the time they got back to Reston they were tired. Sean helped Kira carry in her supplies, and they slipped downstairs to dinner before making an early evening of it.

Once again dressed all in black, from her fireproof nomex mask to her black running shoes, Poena crept through the evening shadows of the neighborhood. She'd spotted the subdivision she needed when she was driving around earlier in the afternoon. It, too, bordered on the Potomac River and was a very ritzy neighborhood, and it, too, had very limited access.

The black canoe was tied securely to the shore a hundred yards away and slipping through the intervening woods in the night, she was about as visible as a shadow in a coal bin. Being careful not to let the tools she carried clink together, and at the same time attempting to minimize the sound of her footsteps through the dark arboreal maze, was taxing even her formidable powers of concentration. Moments later, she slid the tools under the tall wooden fence and bounded over the top of the six foot wooden fence in two easy movements.

When her grandpa made her take gymnastics as a young girl, she had never dreamed of how useful it might become to her later in life. The agility to traverse almost any fence quietly and easily was quite a useful ability for her current needs, not to mention those two early occasions before she was familiar with how fast the sun could spread when she'd been forced to make an unexpected exit out of a second story window.

Having checked earlier in the day, she was reasonably certain that there was no dog in this or the neighboring yards, but she recalled being fooled before, so her first few steps were all the more tentative. By the middle of the yard, she was certain of her safety and moved quickly to the right side of the house where she'd previously spotted the gas meter.

The oversized monkey wrench she'd brought was perfect for loosening the fittings. She had studied diagrams of these gas meters for hours and knew exactly what she needed to do. Quickly setting the wrench on the fitting she planted a foot on the side of the house and prepared to pull.

A noise from inside the house stopped her. Someone was home. It sounded like it was coming from the kitchen. Waiting patiently, she listened some more before deciding it didn't matter.

With the deep shadows outside she was virtually impossible to see, and she didn't plan on making enough noise to attract attention. Besides, she just needed a few more minutes and she'd be long gone. The air was cool, and there was a gentle breeze.

As she tightened her grip on the wrench again, she took mental note of the direction of the breeze. It might be useful here shortly. With both hands on the prodigious hand-tool and her foot pressing against the house for leverage she began to pull. For a brief second nothing happened and a twinge of fear raced through her, then with a small squeal of protest the fitting finally yielded to Poena's efforts. The sound almost scared her, until she realized how small a sound it actually was. The magnification she feared was only in her mind.

Steadily, she continued to pull and the fitting inexorably turned until she began to smell the mercaptan, the chemical that gas companies add to give natural gas its smell, and hear the slight hiss of the gas releasing into the night air. Perfect, she thought to herself. With another turn for good measure, Poena disengaged the monkey wrench and set it down. She was wearing gloves and still pondering the necessity of taking the huge wrench with her. Finally deciding that such blatant evidence of intent might hurry someone onto her trail, she decided to take the heavy thing with her at least back to the river.

Reaching into her little bag, she pulled out the odd homemade device she had fastened. It was a combination of a kitchen timer, a small battery pack, and an electric starter for a heater furnace. Next, she pulled out two plastic eggs filled with Silly Putty and affixed the timer to the siding directly above the gas meter.

Natural gas is lighter than air, unlike propane which actually sinks. Poena knew that the mixture of gas to air would have to be perfect for the gas to ignite in the open but even if it didn't, the leak itself would produce the desired result. It would just take longer.

One way or another, the fire department was going to be called to this location promptly. She set the timer for fifteen minutes, picked up the heavy monkey wrench again and, smiling broadly, turned towards the back fence and her waiting canoe. Sadly, she thought, if the gas actually did manage to ignite she would be in a poor position to enjoy the beauty of the flames.

Once back in the canoe, she picked up the black paddle she'd brought with her, paddled a few strokes, and then summarily dropped the wrench overboard. Stroking quietly through the black water, Poena relished the sensations surrounding her. Her muscles working the paddle in perfect unison produced the slightest sound of a gurgle in the water as the canoe sliced smoothly through the calm dark waters of the age old river.

Poena let her mind wander for a moment and listened to the crickets, the breeze, an owl, all the night sounds that she so loved. It made her think of Grandpa, he should be here too. He loved theses sounds as well and, before he became too ill, he had sat with her many nights on the front porch in their rockers as they listened to the night, and he told her the stories of his past agonies. The awful men in black. The horrible places. The screams in the dark that drove the sleep away, and the murmured prayers of his countrymen. The hours and hours he had lain awake and planned . . .

Something in the water ahead caught Poena's attention and pulled her from her reminiscences. At first she wasn't sure what it was, then realized that it was a floating log, nearly invisible in the moonless dark. Carefully she determined its direction and navigated the canoe around the back of it.

Feeling her muscles continue to warm with the work, Poena turned her thoughts back to the task at hand and the path ahead. She wondered if the husband would be at home. It didn't matter; if he was she'd deal with him. It was the woman she wanted, the granddaughter of one of those jackals.

Yielding to a sudden urge, Poena pulled her new mask from its little bag; black this time, with a twisted golden smile and black feathers dancing in the breeze. It was so beautiful. Another face to watch the demise of the next, just as Grandpa had told her he and his friends had been forced to do. Justice was sweet. Justice and revenge.

~

If anyone had gazed on Poena's face right then, lurking beneath that grotesque mask, they would have found it far more unnerving than any mask she might ever create, because, in that instant, that face clearly revealed blazing intellect coupled with twisted intent and malignant insanity. There was something especially grotesque and unnerving about malevolency engendered by such otherwise gorgeous features.

The time passed slowly as the canoe glided almost soundlessly through the water like the Indians of centuries past, on this very river, quiet and serene. The beauty of using the canoe was that the distance from her first point to her second was less than half a mile due to a sharp bend in the river, but by surface streets, the fire trucks would have to negotiate many miles to get to her next target, not to mention giving her an unconventional method of escape from the scene. In mere moments she could be back at her original starting point, probably just after it was vacated by the fire department, who would be rushing to the new blaze. It was a perfect plan.

Poena began to focus her gaze on the shore to her left. On the previous evening, she had familiarized herself with the pattern of lights on the shore that would mark her destination. Smiling, she recognized her goal about a hundred yards up ahead. Angling the canoe back towards the shore, she was just about there when a thunderous explosion rocked the evening stillness.

Glancing sharply back, Poena saw flames claw their way into the night. She grinned at her own surprised response. She was so focused, she'd almost forgotten the possibility of the detonation, but she only allowed herself a moment's glance at the glorious sight. The clock was ticking now; she had to concentrate.

The canoe bumped gently onto the shore. Poena laid the paddle down and grabbed the gunwales, gracefully duck-walking towards the front of the canoe. Quickly tying off the sleek little craft, she made her way up the embankment and onto level ground. There was a narrow expanse of trees between her and the wooden fence at the back of the yard.

She picked up speed as she padded through those woods, feathers waving in the night, eyes focused on the fence ahead, and her thoughts intent on her course. She was a stealthy, killing machine, sent from the past by her grandpa's words to bring the retribution that so many had escaped and so richly deserved.

When the sirens began to sound in the distance, Poena paused at the back of the fence to glance at her watch. It would take them ten minutes to get to the fire, but she was unsure of how long it would take them to extinguish the flames. She had to hurry. They had to remain occupied with that fire while she started the next.

~

Kira's eyes opened. The room was dark. She laid there wide awake wondering what had brought her up from the depths of sleep. Gossamer bits of images floated up to her in answer to her thought. She'd been dreaming. They weren't powerful dreams just vague bits and pieces of memories of other paintings she'd done since she'd decided to paint with the ashes of the deceased. Interesting, she thought, that she never had dreams of her modeling career. Save one she'd rather not remember.

Ever since she had conceived the idea for Canvas of Life, her world seemed to be moving at light speed. First there were odd images even with her very first painting of her mother. She'd dismissed those as coincidence until she'd done the second painting for her first commercial client, Louise.

She'd had nightmares at night and visions during her painting sessions that all seemed to coincide with what she was painting until Louise had confirmed that she had brought knowledge to her work that she couldn't have known. That had been a good experience, though and a very fulfilling one for Louise.

Then she met Sean and fell in love and begun Jason's painting, his supposed father. An uncaught serial killer, haunted by an evil he couldn't control, he died taking his secrets with him to the grave or at least he had until Kira began to paint his "Canvas of Life". The visions

117

and dreams she'd endured had nearly gotten her killed, and if it hadn't been for Sean's love and special intuition, she probably would have been.

It was an eerie chapter in her life, and one she didn't particularly care to repeat, yet here she was trying to help the FBI find another serial killer. *I must be absolutely crazy,* she thought to herself as she lay there watching the dim shadows dance on the ceiling of the hotel room. *Why am I doing this?* The sight of the dancing shadows only seemed to focus her forgotten fears and brought her senses back into the room.

She listened intently to Sean breathing, relishing in his warmth next to her, but the physical sensation from her skin as she lay there next to him paled beside what she felt inside. It was amazing to be in love with such a wonderful person.

The thought hardened her resolve. God had her here for a reason and had given her a great gift in her painting. It was her duty to use that gift for as much good as she was able. With that thought, she quietly slipped out of bed, taking care not to wake Sean.

The gentle rustle of the sheets seemed loud in the silence of the room but Sean didn't stir. She was awake, and she had work to do. She was going to take a few moments and sketch Poena's face. The quicker they could catch this crazy woman, the quicker she and Sean could get back to their lives and planning their wedding.

The room was large for a hotel room. It had two double beds and a wall running beside the one closest to the door, leaving an alcove that led into the bathroom with an open closet on the left. If Kira slid one of the chairs in there she'd be able to turn on the bathroom light without waking Sean.

Tiptoeing across the room, she picked up the chair that sat at the little desk and carried it back to the alcove. The chair was heavier than she expected, making it difficult to carry quietly. Her bag of supplies was already on the floor of the closet and taking what she needed from the bag with a minimum of noise was even more difficult. Kira agonized over the noise, continually fretting about disturbing Sean's slumber with her nocturnal enterprises.

CHAPTER

Sean sat up in bed and looked over at Kira there beside him. Even in the dim light he could see she was lying on her back with her eyes wide open, staring at the ceiling. "Kira!" He almost shouted at her. She didn't move. Leaning over towards her Sean realized she wasn't breathing. "Oh my God! Not again!" He whispered. Pulling back the covers as he turned to her, he shook her shoulders, thinking oddly that the covers on the bed weren't right. Shaking her again to no avail, he put his head down on her chest. No heartbeat. Frantic now, he shook her again. "No, please," he whimpered, a lump of panic rising in his throat as he continued to shake her shoulders. "What is wrong with you? Kira!"

~

Sean sat up in bed. He was confused. He looked quickly over for Kira. His breath was coming out in ragged gasps. She wasn't there.

He lifted his head and saw the light in the direction of the bath-room.

"Kira?" He rasped out, his sleepy voice not quite up to the task. No answer.

Clearing the fence with fluid grace and gliding through the shadows in the back yard like a malignant spirit of the dead, Poena
carefully observed the house she was approaching. It was after midnight and all the lights inside were off. It was a huge place; a two story
colonial, and like so many in this neighborhood, a relic from the past.
Soon it would be a smoldering skeleton of charred wood around the
ashes of the dead. Soon it would be a tribute to her grandpa's memory.

Stealing quietly up to the back door, Poena gently tried the lock.
Secure, as she'd anticipated. She reached into the little pouch around
her waist and pulled the lock pick kit from it, deftly unrolling the soft
leather and selecting two tools before replacing it in her pouch. Peering
through the window as her hands mindlessly felt their way into the
lock, she saw no keypad on the walls by the door. It always amazed her
how many homes didn't have security systems. She could defeat them,
but it took so much more time and planning that she typically would
move on to another target whenever she encountered one, which actually was the best reason for the system anyway.

With a soft click the simple lock yielded to her deft manipulations,
and with ears alert to any sound, Poena quickly replaced the tools in
her kit.

"They must pay!" Poena heard the words and briefly flinched. Then
an unseen smile spread across her face beneath the mask. Grandpa,
she thought to herself. He sometimes would talk to her while she was
delivering his justice.

It was unnerving, though, when she was trying to be so quiet to
have his voice return to her like that. It used to be much worse before
she became certain that no one else could hear him.

Now she delighted in hearing his beloved voice again, but it was difficult to concentrate when he was talking to her.

"Their families must pay! Remember the mask, always wear the mask," he droned on. Padding through the house, Poena tried not to focus on her grandpa's words. She needed to listen to the sounds of the house. If anyone awoke, she must know immediately. In the past she might have tried to hush Grandpa until later, but from experience she knew it wouldn't work. So she just focused her thoughts and continued her plan.

The dark, carpeted staircase had a gentle curve to it as it meandered up to the second floor. Poena's gloved hand slid quietly over the smooth lacquered banister as she flowed up the staircase alert for any sound. The house had a pleasant scent, she thought vacantly. All houses had their own smell, but this one was particularly pleasant. It reminded her of something back in her memory she couldn't quite place.

At the top of the stairs she turned unerringly to the right, towards the master bedroom. The thick plush carpet further muted the already silent footfalls from her well worn sneakers. As she approached the bedroom she slowly slid the knife from its sheath behind her back. It made a whisper of a hiss.

The bedroom door was partially open. Moving soundlessly, like the Grim Reaper himself, Poena gently pushed the door. There before her on the bed were the peacefully sleeping forms of the couple who lived here. So the husband was home. Damn! She thought quietly. It was trickier when there were two, and she really just wanted the female spawn of the jackal, not her misguided husband. Still, there was nothing else she could do. He was here, so he'd have to die too.

Knife poised before her, Poena eased up to the man's side of the bed. At that instant, roused by some primordial sense of danger, the husband's eyes popped open.

They locked on Poena as he tried to pull his hands from the covers. He was surprisingly fast, Poena thought, for someone who'd just been dead asleep. But not fast enough.

With deadly accuracy, she jumped across the husband, reached for the wife's throat with one hand and smoothly plunged her knife into his neck with the other.

121

The alarm, just beginning to issue from his mouth was drowned in the gurgling bubbles of his own blood. Poena felt the woman coming awake beneath her hand, and in one shockingly graceful movement withdrew the knife from the man's throat and angled its hilt accurately into the temple of the wife. She heard the distinct sound of skull cracking as the woman went limp beneath her hand. Poena's eyes never left the husband who was weakly struggling as he lay there and drowned.

Intrigued by his struggles, Poena indulged herself for a moment and continued to watch as the light left his eyes. Once he finally became still, she turned her attention back to the woman. She was dead. Poena had struck her temple far enough back so as not to interfere with what she had to do next; and she knew she had to hurry.

Grabbing the woman's face with her gloved hand, she rotated her limp head up then, shifting the grip on her knife, slowly began the cut starting at the hairline just above the forehead. She pressed until she felt the knife's tip touch bone then released pressure slightly and drew the blade deftly across the forehead, following the hairline, behind the ears and under the jaw line.

Though the skin itself is quite tough, most people don't realize how loosely it adheres to the muscle and fatty layers beneath. Once separated, a severed flap pulls away much like a layer of sliced American cheese from a stack.

Seconds later, amidst what should have been a sickeningly squishy sound, Poena pulled the woman's face from her skull. Setting her knife on the bed, she reached again into her pouch and pulled out a zip-lock bag, deftly placing the skin inside. Sealing the bag, Poena wiped the knife on the bed covers and sheathed it.

Taking her backpack off, she quickly opened it, put the zip-lock bag in there and pulled out another larger bag she had inside. The sun. Fortunately she had brought more of the precious powder than she needed because now she had two bodies to burn, and she'd need all she'd brought.

With one last indifferent glance at the intricate musculature on the woman's bloody skull, she slid back off the bed dragging her back pack with her. She liberally poured the powder over the two bodies leaving a little trail of it that extended off the bed onto the floor. It was time for her special match.

Poena slipped the backpack on again and reached into her belt pouch. She pulled out the permanent match as she spread the balance of the powder across the hapless couple covering nearly the entire bed. Pausing to listen briefly, she dropped the empty bag on the bed, slid over to the end of her little powder trail and brought the little hacksaw blade up. With the flint side of the bar towards her, she struck the spark. She turned her head anticipating the flash, and the white hot response lit the room like a camera flash. It was time to go.

Poena backed her way out of the room and took one more glance at the rapidly growing inferno on the bed, looking for any trace of her presence she might have inadvertently left. When she turned her head away the after image of the flames still occluded her vision. She blinked and there before her was the face of that woman. Kira. She squeezed her eyes shut and opened them again in an effort to dispel the unwelcome vision still lingering before her eyes. The high cheekbones and chestnut hair, it was definitely the same woman she'd seen before. And she was squinting as though she were trying to peer through something to see . . . to see me Poena realized in a sudden panic.

"NO!" She screamed out loud at the specter. Then she remembered she still had on her mask. Good, she thought. But she had to do something about this prying bitch. And even more than before Poena was convinced that this woman was one of *them*. She was going to have to find her. Poena mentally shook herself, her usual confidence failing her.

The sun was working even more swiftly than usual, she'd think about the woman later. Now she had to move or be trapped.

All stealth disregarded, Poena bolted out of the room and down the stairs, the growing flames crackling in her wake.

"**NO!**" Kira yelled. Sean bounded around the corner of the alcove, virtually skidding to a stop at the unexpected expletive.

Sean's mind was still sluggish both from sleep and his confusing and frightening nightmare. For a split second, he thought Kira was screaming at him, until he realized that she was sitting stone still on the chair with the sketch pad on her lap and her pen hanging frozen in the air. She looked like a statue. It brought back sensations from the dream and scared Sean vastly out of proportion to the event itself.

"Kira," he yelled, rushing to her and causing himself yet another déjà-vu as he began to shake her shoulders. This time, however, she responded, seeming to come awake at his first touch. She turned her head sharply,

"Sean," she began, "I . . . she was . . . Oh dear God, I think she just started another fire!"

"What?"

"The killer, she just started another fire." Kira was still talking as if she were in a trance. The timbre of alertness had not yet reentered her voice. She turned back to the sketch pad, and Sean followed her gaze. There before him he saw the hastily sketched bust of a woman with long black hair wearing a grotesque feathered mask with a twisted gargoyle like smile. The smile seemed to mock them. Smug. Self-satisfied. Instinctively, Kira tried something she'd never tried before. She raised her pencil to the pad and forced herself to concentrate.

"It was like she forced me to stop drawing by yelling at me," Kira's voice retained its dreamy quality, but now it seemed to convey concentration more than an absence of clarity. Changing her mind, she lowered her hand back to her lap without taking her eyes off the sketch pad. Blindly, she picked up an eraser and began erasing the masked features of the facial area.

As her hand moved gently and deftly, she began to speak again. This time, though, the tone of her voice sent chills of fear through Sean, and it suddenly occurred to him that he was completely unaware of what she was thinking or feeling. It was like a cold void where he was used to having a warm, friendly sense of knowledge. The sensation further raised his doubts and redoubled his chills. All he could do for the moment was watch as Kira worked, and listen in fearful awe as her voice changed. This was no longer the voice of the woman he loved.

". . . peels away much easier than you would expect . . . like cheese . . ." Her hand slowly and methodically continued to erase, erase, erase; in straight motions at first and then in careful circular motions.

". . . prying bitch!" Kira said with a vitriolic intensity.

Hearing those words and that tone come from the woman he loved nearly froze Sean's heart in his chest. He wanted to shake her or yell at her to break the spell she seemed to be under, but some intuition stayed his hand. Instead, he just remained standing close to her ready to . . . ready to . . . he had no idea what he was ready to do. He simply knew he had to stay close and keep his attention fixed on her face.

". . . trapped . . ." Kira said as she slowly lowered the eraser and, without a single glance away from the page before her, she delicately dropped the eraser in her lap and picked up the pencil.

Sean's eyes remained intent on Kira. Her features hardened into a visage of concentration. Her thoughts and feelings were returning to him. It made him think of a marshmallow slowly floating up from a cup of chocolate. He could almost feel the nexus of who she was rising back to the top, becoming more palpable to him as the seconds passed.

Kira's hand danced swiftly across the page, redrawing the area she had just erased. A split second before Sean's ears registered the sound, his mind registered the words emerging from Kira's mind.

"Stop dammit!" It was Kira's voice, and she nearly yelled the words, yet her hand never slowed on the sketch pad. The intensity of it caused Sean to flinch beside her. Kira's hand remained steady. Her hands continued to move fluidly across the pad. The eyes were beginning to reappear on the sketch without the distortion of the mask over them.

~

Poena stopped dead in her tracks on the stairs leading to the living room. What was that bitch doing *now*? She was still trying to see her. If she closed her eyes she could see the woman's face lingering before her eyes.

She furrowed her brows beneath the mask in an attempt to focus her thoughts. Concentrating as hard as she could on that beautiful, hated face, she screamed,

"NO! YOU CAN'T!"

~

Sean, standing beside her, saw Kira's head snap to the side slightly as if she was attempting to dodge a projectile. At the same instant her pencil snapped, and the blunted point drove into the paper. Sean moved so he could see her face. As he watched, more focus return to her gaze, but she didn't turn to him, instead a look of determination continued to crease her features, and her right hand reached to the floor and a second pencil.

The sensations he was getting were confusing. Kira was thinking about Poena, but Poena was doing the same thing. How could he be sensing anything from the other woman? Through Kira? It was as though some mental struggle were going on between the woman he loved and the killer that wasn't even there. Both were determined to foil the other, of that he was certain, and his gift allowed him to be an unwilling observer.

As he watched, Kira brought the second pencil back to the paper but before she could delineate five more strokes that point snapped too.

"DAMN!" Kira said, leaning back in the chair.

~

Poena was sweating, and it wasn't from the flames. She'd just done something she'd never done before even though she had no idea how she'd done it or even exactly what she'd done. Her surprise was over-ridden by her fatigue. Well, that wasn't exactly true. She did know that she'd stopped the bitch from seeing her, if only just in time. She felt as

126

though she'd just finished a four hour math test. Her mind was drained.

A thunderous crash rerouted her thoughts. The ceiling above her had partially caved in. The flames from the upstairs bedroom had made their way through the floor and she was about to be trapped. She'd only taken a few more steps down the staircase towards the living room during her battle with the woman, leaving her still in danger of the fire she'd just set. Thoughts shifted to actions as Poena turned to the large bay window on her left. Another explosion rocked the house and the ceiling gave way entirely, sending the chandelier crashing to the floor in another gout of flames.

Poena jumped sideways and juked around the new source of flames looking frantically for another exit. In front of her the big window again loomed like the answer to a prayer. Whatever awaited her from the maneuver she considered then was preferable to being trapped by the flames. The decision was nearly instantaneous, and, like a champion swimmer; she ducked her head and dove through the glass. She could almost feel the flames licking her toes as the in-rush of air caused them to chase her flying form through the opening. The sound of glass exploded around her ears while she squinted through the mask, trying to catch a glimpse of her landing spot.

Seeing the darkness rushing towards her, she instinctively ducked her head just in time, catching the ground initially on her hands, then shoulders and rolling easily down the slight slope leading away from the house. She rolled directly to her feet and turned smoothly back to the house in a single graceful motion. The maneuver would have qualified as a perfectly performed circus stunt.

All the upstairs windows were blazing and she heard sirens approaching, then saw the reflections of the firetruck lights dancing off the adjacent houses. Damn! Her mental entanglement had lasted longer than she realized.

She turned, running back towards the river, before remembering she had one more task to do. She stopped suddenly and pulled the mask from her face. It slid easily over the black nomex mask beneath it. Almost reverently she turned it towards the burning house, tilted it up slightly and paused to stare at the flames.

A fireman rounded the corner in his bright yellow slicker just as her fingers finally released the mask. She bent low as she began to run. The sound of the growing flames covered any noise her footsteps might have made. She took one last look over her shoulder to see if she had been spotted. No. The one fireman that had ventured to the rear of the house was too preoccupied with the burning building to worry about the woods.

The sweet cascade of her laughter as she entered the woods would have seemed an enchanting sound to any unaware of the horrible deeds from which it was born.

As she ran, Poena realized with certainty what her next task had to be, and with sudden clarity she thought she knew how to do it. She *had* to find that woman.

"Kira, are you alright?" Sean asked, putting his hands gently on her shoulders and staring intently into her eyes. She was all there now, aware, in the moment and, more important, she was alone. He could feel it. Just her.

Sean was still reeling a bit himself. His life had become a carnival of new sensations over the last few days, but even among those bewildering new experiences this one stood out. Sensing emotions and thoughts was horrible enough, but then, via the mask he had touched, it appeared he could pick up thoughts from the dead too, and now thoughts from people who weren't in his presence! This was all in just a few days! What would happen next? But maybe this new development had something to do with Poena's proximity to Kira and his connection to her. Somehow, that made it seem much less scary.

Interrupting his thoughts, Kira finally brought her head up slightly, her eyes shifting to Sean's.

"She's fighting me Sean. She's fighting me! Every time I try to draw her face she's fighting me somehow. I can feel her reaching out to fight me. And when she does, I feel connected to her in some way." Kira shivered, "She's so evil." Kira lowered her head as Sean felt the sensations of fear and sadness well up in her.

"It's okay," he said, kneeling down and putting his arms around her. "We'll get through this somehow." Sean could certainly relate to bewildering feelings, but he still didn't quite understand.

"You mean you can see her face but just can't draw it?"

Kira stared at him for a brief second her face still pale, "Well . . . yes . . . but no. It feels like . . . like . . . almost like I can see her face in bits and pieces, like I see her eyes by themselves then I see her hair and then the images are gone."

Now it was Sean's turn to ponder for a second. "What do you mean by 'fights you?'"

"That's just it," Kira said, "I don't know. I've never felt anything like it. It's like it's some sort of mental struggle, and the minute I try to draw her face, she becomes aware of it and resists me somehow."

Then it occurred to Sean that he wasn't finding this near as odd or frightening as he should. What the hell was going on here? It was beginning to feel like someone had dropped him and Kira into some movie called The Battle of the Psychic Adversaries.

'Psychic', he'd never gotten comfortable with that term applying to him. He was even less comfortable applying it to his fiancé, and now they were trying to catch this arsonist somebody who apparently had powers of her own. Madness. Oh Rod Serling, he thought, you'd be proud of me.

At some point, however, he was going to have to accept the fact that *psychic* was exactly what was going on with all three of them, and to some degree or another, this problem was going to have to be resolved on that level. Once you find yourself in a situation, denial doesn't improve anything. And in that brief instant, standing by Kira, he had detected the evil in Poena, just like Kira had described; and just like she said, this woman had to be stopped.

By the time Josh got to his office the next morning, he already had a message from Sean and Kira, and another one from Division relayed from a local fire department in a little burb called Shepherdstown, West Virginia, right up against the Potomac. There had been another fire, two actually, and another mask was left.

Josh already had a sneaking suspicion that the first fire was a decoy for the second. The first fire wasn't actually a fire so much as an explosion from a gas leak.

Once the fire department had the gas shut off they determined that the fittings on a gas meter had been loosened and some homemade timer device left there to ignite it.

It was hap-hazard and sloppy and there was no mask; definitely nothing like the typical forethought of his arsonist. On the other hand if it had just been to distract the fire department and slow their response to the real fire, well, it had certainly done that.

As he sat there and pondered, Josh looked more closely at the message from division. The time on the message said the fire had been started at about 3:15 am. He looked at the time stamp on the incoming message from Kira. 3:23 am. Impossible, he thought.

"Who am I kidding," he said out loud as he plopped down in his chair, "Typical would be a better word." Damn psychics, he thought next. The whole idea of dealing with these people continued to give him the jitters, and he was getting damn tired of feeling this way all the time.

The note also said that they'd be back in the office after breakfast. The thought brought an image of Kira into his mind, and he promptly felt himself getting aroused. That thought was immediately chased by his unreasonable belief that Sean knew when he was thinking of his fiancée.

"SHIT!" He said, and stomped out of his office to get some coffee.

~

Poena was standing stone still in the shower, letting the hot water run over her sore muscles. Her long black hair hung down between her breasts, and the steam billowed through the little enclosure, as she let the heat drain tension from her body.

Her right shoulder was badly bruised from the dive out of the window. She was pretty sure she'd rolled across a rock but hadn't noticed at the time. She'd had way too many other thoughts on her mind. Getting to the canoe had been a breeze, and the long paddle back down river in the dark had been relaxing in itself, but her mind was so full she barely remembered doing either.

She'd followed her regular procedure when she got back home, carefully putting her tools away, salting the new face she'd taken and storing it in the refrigerator.

Normally she would have stored the rest of the sun in its special hiding place in the false back of a drawer but this time she'd used all she'd brought with her, so that was one less task that needed doing. Yet, while her hands had tended to the mindless details that she was so familiar with, her mind had raced. That face. How could it keep reoccurring to her and why?

The thoughts had followed her into the shower, and now she began ruminating over them with the warmth and solitude of the shower helping give her thoughts focus. The woman was trying to identify her, of that she was sure, but why, and even more important how? Was she working with the police? More like the FBI by now, but *who* was she? She must be working with the authorities she decided, and that would be how she'd find her.

"Hurry, Poena!" Poena flinched upright in the shower and turned her head reflexively, then caught herself. That voice was in her head again . . . grandfather! A smile broke across her countenance as the warning repeated in her mind.

"You must hurry!" The smile faded slowly from her face as the

132

impact of his words sank in. He'd never spoken to her with such force since his death, and she knew what he meant. She had to hurry and find this woman. Well, at least now she knew how she was going to do that.

With a plan in mind she turned off the water, stepped out of the shower and reached for a towel. She had a rendezvous this afternoon and some work to do before she got there.

But as she dried, an uncharacteristic bout of shivers took her. The more she thought about it, the more she realized that Grandpa never talked to her so clearly. Hearing his voice like that brought back memories of the first time Grandpa's stories began to change. She'd been five years old. It was the day Grandpa had changed her name.

Watching her work around the house, being so industrious and helping to do the little things that were now so difficult for him, Isaac called little Sondra to him.

~

"Sondra come here and sit down in Grandpa's lap, and I'll tell you some more stories."

Sondra ran to comply with Grandpa's wishes. She loved his stories. Through his eyes she'd been able to see far off things and places she had never been, and it all seemed so magical. He'd described Paris to her from the many times he'd been there. From the Eiffel Tower, to L'Arc de Triomphe, to the myriad ornate bridges that crossed the Seine. It had all seemed so wonderful. Then there were the trips through the German wine country and down the Rhine to the great number of castles that overlooked it, tall majestic and all with their own history and stories. It was like walking through her own personal fantasy land to the tone of her grandpa's rich voice.

But he seemed to be having difficulty remembering things these days, and many nights she'd awaken to hear him moaning in his sleep. One night she'd even slipped into his room after being awakened by his sounds, only to find him tossing and turning in his sleep. He was talking in his sleep as well, and that had frightened her, but not as much as what he was saying.

"No. No. Not again. Please, I can't take it again. No!" And if the words weren't frightening enough, tears were squeezing from his closed eyes, and his sweet old face was twisted in pain. She had wanted to help him, but she'd been so frightened that she'd raced from the room and hid under her covers.

It had been awhile since he'd offered to tell stories, and she was eager to hear something more. Excitedly, she crawled up into his lap and snuggled into his shoulder. He continued to rock as he held her and finally, he began to speak. The first thing she noticed was that he wasn't telling this story as if he were in it. He told it as if someone else were telling it and he'd had no part. This was a sharp contrast from the way he had told stories before and little Sondra wondered briefly about the change. It didn't matter. It was still Grandpa telling a story, and she couldn't wait.

~

"It was the night of November the 9th 1938, which later became known as Kristallnacht or in English 'The Night of Broken Glass', but it could just as easily have been the night of broken hopes or the night of broken faith.

The Reich had orchestrated the systematic destruction of Jewish synagogues, businesses and homes all across the region that fateful night. Twenty six thousand Jewish men and women were taken and shipped to Dachau and other concentration camps amid the sounds of destruction, wailing, and death. The Nazi purge of the "Jewish problem", as Hitler referred to it, was well underway. It would be months yet before the edicts were passed requiring Jewish people to wear The Star of David on their clothing, denoting them as Jews, and still more time before the overt mass killings were to commence. But on this night Isaac and Rebecca Goldstein were dragged from their homes along with the other hapless victims and forcibly carted away.

They desperately clung to each other in fear until the SS troops beat them repeatedly for their efforts. It finally occurred to them to just lie in the rear of the truck back to back, touching each other but not outwardly acknowledging one another. In this fashion, they shared some comfort from their love without letting the Germans know of it, on a night that shamed nightmares in its unabated terror.

Eyes still wide with fear and red from tears, they could only watch as other Jews they knew and many they didn't, were beaten to death for speaking up or even casting a severe look at the wrong guard."

~

Sondra squirmed in her seat on Grandpa's lap. She didn't like this story already. It was scary and sad. She wanted to move but Grandpa's grip on her had hardened, and she had little room to even wriggle.

"I don't like this story Grandpa," she'd said, but he didn't seem to hear. She glanced back up at him and his eyes seemed unfocused and glazed. As she calmed slightly, his voice picked up as if nothing had happened, and his distant perspective seemed to make the story even more frightening.

Little Sondra's heart raced. This wasn't like Grandpa at all and now, not only was the story scary, but Grandpa was scaring her too. With mounting fear she was forced to sit and listen:

~

"The dead bodies were left among them, crammed into the overcrowded covered truck bed and the released excrement from the corpses on top of the horror of the beaten heads and bodies caused many to become ill. Ultimately, their emptying stomachs caused a chain reaction, and there was no getting away from either the smell or the vomit itself. The best that one could hope for was to turn your nose into the crook of your elbow and try to block out as much of the odor as possible, while avoiding any direct onslaught from others as they became sick.

Lying there like that in the dark, Isaac avoided being sick and from his shared contact with Rebecca he knew she did too. The moments seemed to stretch into hours before the truck finally bumped to a stop and the shouting began again. They were ordered from the truck and any that were unwilling or too sick to move quickly were viciously beaten with the heavy black sticks the guards, for that's what they were in truth, wielded so freely.

The sight that greeted their night vision added another dimension to their terror; Two, ten-foot chain link fences ran, one inside the other, twenty feet apart topped with another two feet of wicked looking razor wire. The fences seemed to race off into the dark leading to unimaginable places Isaac simply didn't want to know.

Rebecca had moved quickly enough and been silent enough to avoid the beatings so far, and she was quite adroit at remaining next to Isaac without seeming to be anymore than another figure crushed together in the crowd.

Now, looming ahead of her she saw the fortified gates roll back and the steel and the wire reminded her of nothing so much as the gaping maw of some ungodly creature from Hell preparing to consume them. And in a sense that's exactly what it was.

Rebecca had managed to grab a scarf as they were forced from their home, and she had used it to wrap her head and, as much as possible, conceal her face. The instinct that led her to this was a good one. One developed over a lifetime of living with a face so exquisite that often strangers would stop and blatantly stare at her in awe. Thankfully, her outward beauty had never managed to overshadow her inner beauty and her inability to be overly impressed with her own physical perfection had only made her that much more appealing in the eyes of all who knew her.

Isaac had already been a successful jewel merchant, following in the steps of his father, when his family had introduced him to Rebecca's family and Rebecca herself. The sight of her that first evening passed through Isaac like a sword straight to his heart. No one could have resisted her beauty, but to have that entrancing package hold, not only a heart of gold but a keen intellect too, was just beyond imagining and Isaac felt blessed to have met her. Isaac's tall, handsome features, in turn, had caught Rebecca's eye, and the union their two families had so hopefully planned was well on its way.

They had only been together a year and married less than that, amid the escalating turmoil that Germany had become, when the night of horror befell them.

Isaac had only heard of the "camps", as they were called, and scarcely dared to believe they existed. Now in the face of the reality, his fear centered more around Rebecca than himself. That scarf couldn't hide her forever, and in a place like this her face was bound to attract unwanted attention.

When selling jewelry, he knew, it was important to watch the faces of those that come into your store. Watch their eyes and it becomes apparent what they really want. It was even said that ancient street merchants could spot likely customers by noticing the dilation of their pupils when they beheld a thing they desired. That knowledge would allow the merchants to raise the prices to a customer that desperately wanted a thing they had. This whole process of observation had become second nature to Isaac. The side benefit was that observation was always a useful tool when dealing with people. The more you observed, the more you knew, above and beyond what the person intended to communicate.

Isaac was using those skills now as the group was herded through the ominous gates and into the bowels of oblivion. And what they were telling him was knowledge to freeze the heart. The cold remorseless eyes of the guards reeked of distaste and disdain.

These people cared less for their charges than an average person would care for a smelly dog digging through back street garbage. 'So much filth to be dealt with' was what he saw in their eyes. His hopes were on a slippery slide to despair even before the massive steel gates behind them ominously clanged shut.

The guards kept the group close together as they marched them across the compound. Stragglers were beaten first and talked to second, if at all. The lingering smell of death and sickness flowed with them, almost like a tangible blanket. But now Isaac noticed one more smell that mingled with the others. It was the smell of fear . . . terror. It grew with each step they took. A few people tried to speak to the guards or to each other in their nervousness, both actions brought the same consequence, a swift strike with the cruel cudgels they carried.

Sometimes no words would accompany the strike, just the blow itself serving to relay the message the guards disdained to speak. Occasionally, however, the blow would be accompanied by a quick sentence. "Seien Sie ruhig. Sie jüdischer Hund." Be quiet. You Jewish dog. Or something similar. The silence was better.

They finally entered a building on the far side of the compound. It was a low ceilinged affair devoid of furniture. A guard opened a door at the far end and stepped back to allow the procession to pass through. Unlike the other room, this one was more of a warehouse.

As Isaac looked around he saw huge piles of shoes on one side and even larger piles of clothes on the other. As the last person filed through the door the guards followed, closing it behind them.

"Remove your clothes and put them in the proper piles," the guard stated coldly in a tone that brooked no denial.

An unspoken murmur passed through the crowd and when no one immediately moved to obey, several of the guards stepped in and began to wield the sticks. Screaming and groans followed and others slowly began to comply.

As they undressed in the cold November night, Isaac noticed one guard fix his gaze on Rebecca and then another and a new fear slithered into his soul. Yet another guard distracted him briefly, pushing a wheel barrow full of burlap sacks. He unceremoniously dumped them on the ground near the center of the group of milling people.

"Setzen Sie diese an," the guard said roughly, 'put these on'. As he finished speaking the guard seemed to stiffen and instinctively Isaac followed his gaze. A tall man in a crisp, black uniform glided menacingly into the room, eyeing the new prisoners like a man selecting cattle."

~

Sondra squirmed again. Her face had lost all color. She didn't want to hear any more of this story, and she told Grandpa so. She was so frightened she was afraid she might wet herself, and she wanted to get away. But still her grandpa held her.

His face had become eerie, devoid of emotion; his cheeks hanging slack were making him look a bit younger than he was. He didn't respond to Sondra, he just stared into the distance with glazed eyes and continued holding her from escaping. When she quit squirming, he continued, again, as though nothing had happened. His voice became a low monotone, and he spoke as if describing someone else . . .

~

"Swiveling his eyes carefully to avoid attracting attention, Isaac stole a glance back at the man who'd just walked in. He must be the Commandant, Isaac thought and before the thought had even formed clearly, the man's gaze had fixed on Rebecca's lithe form. She was naked, still trying to get into the burlap sack.

There, in the man's eyes, Isaac saw what he had feared most. The tall man wanted her, and he wanted her badly.

~

The weeks turned into months and Isaac's emaciated form barely had the strength to do the work they required of him. Many had already died from starvation or the beatings or being shot during an attempt to escape. Too many nights he'd seen the barb wire fences lit up to reveal a poor emaciated being clinging to the fence or trying to cast their body over the deadly razor wire. The sound of the sirens was a backdrop to the staccato of the machine guns that invariably were used to annihilate the hapless victims, many of whom were simply left to rot on the fences as a reminder to the others.

Isaac and Rebecca were faring better than most, but the price being paid was high. The tall man whose gaze had locked so fixedly on Rebecca had proved to be both their salvation and their damnation. He was in fact the Commandant. Heir Eicke. He had gone to the women's quarters one night and ordered her to follow him back to the main building.

Fear had gripped her as he led her from the barracks and towards the building where the guards resided. He took her to the back and ordered her to remove her sack. Fear and loathing congealed within her, but an opportunity arose in her mind and in this human wasteland opportunities were few and far between.

Moments later she was standing naked before him trying to keep her voice calm.

"Heir Eicke," she said in the softest voice she could manage. "This can be so much more pleasant if you will just make things go easier for my husband and me."

"I can take what I want. Why should I do anything more?" he replied in clipped, curt German. But the disdain that the soldiers always offered their Jewish prisoners was not there in his voice and the difference was not lost on Rebecca.

"Because," she offered as she moved closer to him, "Taking me is one thing, but me giving myself to you is another thing altogether." The ploy would have failed miserably if Rebecca, even in her malnourished state, were not so gorgeous and the Commandant not so smitten.

The months dragged on and Rebecca was covertly allowed to talk to Isaac on certain occasions, and so he heard the story from her. He now knew why he'd been transferred to the main building and what the cost was. It broke his heart but saved his life. His work was getting lighter and his rations seemed to be increasing slightly while his fellow inmates (for, by now, that's what they knew themselves to be) continued to inch toward starvation. At first he simply wept bitterly, but then he realized what a great gift it was that Rebecca was sacrificing on his behalf, and he accepted it for what it was, a way to survive.

As the war raged, the prohibitions against the Jewish people escalated and though little of it had any effect on the occupants of Dachau, the new edict by the German high command prohibiting sexual relations between Germans and Jewish women put Heir Eicke at substantially more risk, and his liaisons with Rebecca dwindled.

For Isaac's part he learned to mask his feelings. He felt it to be one of his greatest accomplishments. Outwardly he never showed the fear or pain, disgust, joy or sorrow that tormented him. To those around him, he was an automaton, merely doing as he was asked. He found this to be the best way to avoid any attention from the guards, and no attention from them was good attention.

More prisoners were brought in day after day until the crowding began to be a problem and the gassings had begun. Isaac and Rebecca had been at Dachau now for almost a year when she managed a word with Isaac one evening.

"Isaac, I'm pregnant," she told him breathlessly, trying to ignore the feelings she knew those words generated.

Rather than reacting to the powerful feelings those few words invoked, Isaac instead responded with the simple facts. It was a fear they had both harbored for months and both were practically amazed that it hadn't happened sooner. Privately, Isaac felt certain that her borderline malnutrition had saved her from this fate until now.

"He'll have you killed if he finds out," Isaac said tersely.

"You mean *when* he finds out . . . I know," was all she said. But from that moment the notion of escape planted itself in Isaac's mind, and he waited and watched for a situation that would give his hope an opportunity. When it came he'd be as ready as possible.

The mask he wore over his emotions proved to have another benefit. Somehow he seemed slightly less disagreeable to the guards, and when they chose people to go to the gas chambers his lack of emotion seemed to cause him to disappear in the crowd. So far it seemed to be his salvation, that or Rebecca's unholy pact with the devil.

It was almost three months later when a fleet of trucks drove into the compound. By this time the only reason Rebecca hadn't been discovered was the bagginess of the sacks they wore for clothes and the fact that Heir Eicke had been gone out of the compound on many occasions.

The sight of the trucks was typical, except this time the trucks that entered were not full of new prisoners but were empty. By afternoon the whistles began to sound and through his little window Isaac saw the guards rustle the prisoners together out in the main courtyard where they were promptly ordered into the trucks.

The wretched humanity that barely had the strength to crawl into the conveyances had little concern for why they were being ordered to board, just that they were and had better comply quickly or be beaten. The fact that they were being moved to Auschwitz in an effort to consolidate the Germans efforts to resolve the "Jewish Problem" would have mattered little to them even if they'd known. The horror of their existence left little room for concern over what may come next. Merely getting through each day was all the courage any of them could muster. Many were already well beyond the point of caring about anything and, in truth, would welcome any end to the perpetual suffering that their lives had become. Isaac on the other hand, saw an opportunity.

Knowing he would be called soon, Isaac replaced the small brick he had so painstakingly removed. For many months he had worked to free the loose brick in the back of the little room where he slept, and using some precious paper he had managed to filch, a wood splinter from a chair for a quill and his blood for ink he related snippets of his and Rebecca's plight and her first conception within the walls of Dachau. He didn't know why he had bothered to risk writing the small note, and now he realized he wasn't even going to attempt taking it with him. When he heard the commotion outside, he'd merely slipped it back into its little hiding place.

The guards indeed arrived shortly and ordered Isaac out of his little room. He marched before them obediently, keeping his emotional mask firmly in place. It had saved him so much anguish. He scanned the prisoners as they were being loaded into the trucks and saw that Rebecca was being loaded into the vehicle right behind his. It would be the closest thing to an opportunity he may get, and if it arose he planned to take it."

~

Sondra had ceased her useless squirming. She was in shock by this time, but the tale that Grandpa was weaving had her enthralled. His detached perspective had allowed her to imagine that it wasn't really her grandpa telling her this horrible story. And certainly this wasn't a tale that *happened* to Grandpa. Grandpa wouldn't tell her such a terrible tale.

With her sweet little face ashen white, she now sat frozen in his lap and continued to listen as the distant voice, that couldn't be her grandpa, droned on. But her life would never be the same.

~

"Once the trucks were loaded, they began to roll. Isaac's senses had long since become accustomed to the stench of sick and dirty human flesh, but his special circumstances had not forced him to endure the cramped crowding that was so common in the compound.

Now he was so compressed into the sea of diseased and dirty humanity that claustrophobia was becoming an issue. He also suffered from a new intensity of odor accosting his sense of smell as well as being bruised by the bumpy ride on the hard truck benches and floors. Even the looks from his inmates chilled him.

They knew he was getting special treatment but didn't know why, and Isaac wasn't about to tell them, so they just assumed that whatever it was, it wasn't something in their best interest. Their stares were hard and incriminating. Again, his mask served him well. He did his best to simply close his eyes, block it all out and pray.

For some reason the trucks stopped forty-five minutes after they had left Dachau and several of the trucks were ordered emptied. This included both Isaac's and Rebecca's. The guards herded them over to a clearing in the primordial forest they had been traversing and threw them shovels. For over an hour they all dug and any who were too slow were beaten. One particularly emaciated man dropped his shovel, fell to his knees and pleaded with the nearest guard who summarily shot him in the head and kicked him into the hole.

Suddenly, Isaac knew why they were digging. This was to be their grave. Why they were going to kill this group here instead of elsewhere and why not all of them, he couldn't fathom, but it didn't matter. He thought to run, but there was no way he had the strength to move that fast, and he doubted that Rebecca was in any better shape. Could there be any way to hide, he asked himself as he continued to dig.

For the millionth time, as he bent to the labor, he prayed for God to deliver him and his wife, and this time God answered.

When the hole was about four and a half feet deep, the guards began bringing other prisoners from the trucks. As they approached the edge of the giant hole several guards opened fire with their machine guns. Screaming ensued and bloody bodies began to fall into the pit on top of the people that were already in there digging.

Isaac had managed to work his way over near Rebecca until he was actually digging beside her, and owing to their extra rations his section of the pit was a bit deeper. The bodies began to fall amid the screaming and chaos, and Isaac reached for Rebecca. As the bullets swept towards them and two mangled bullet ridden bodies beside them fell, Isaac pulled Rebecca down with him into the indentation. They had fallen into the hole before the bullets actually got to them. The other two bodies came to rest over them, followed shortly by many others.

As the bodies continued to fall, lying there quietly while other people's blood and entrails flowed down across his body proved to be the hardest thing Isaac had ever done.

The staccato of the machine guns seemed to go on and on until Isaac began to worry that the sheer weight of human flesh would crush them. Intermittently, they could feel the bodies above them jump and twitch as they were continually pumped with rounds from the horrible guns, which caused Rebecca to flinch slightly or occasionally whimper, letting Isaac know that she still lived.

Eventually it stopped, and through the ringing in his ears and the mountain of dead flesh Isaac managed to hear one of the guards say.

"The bulldozers will be here in a half hour. They were delayed." Moments later, to Isaac's surprise, he heard the trucks start back up and slowly move off until the sound of their passing faded completely.

It was the chance Isaac had hoped for, and he recognized it amidst his shock at the fact that they were both still alive.

Reaching for Rebecca's hand under the mountain of dead flesh he spoke the first words he'd dared speak in days.

"Rebecca we have to go." His words sounded croaky to his ears and distorted by the bodies around him. As he spoke he struggled to move and realized that escaping from that hell hole was going to be more difficult than he'd considered. The bodies were too pliable and the blood spread everywhere made them slippery. As he struggled he pulled on Rebecca's hand and finally brought a response from her. It was a whimpering sob. He could barely turn his head himself, and when he did he saw that Rebecca's head was turned away from him."

~

Suddenly Sondra's stomach heaved. She thought surely she was going to throw up, but somehow she managed to keep it down. "Grandpa," she squeaked looking back up at him, but whatever trance had taken him, it was complete. His eyes were distant and shrouded, and his grip on Sondra remained firm. He apparently had only paused at the convulsion of her stomach. Taking a few deep breaths, Sondra managed to calm her queasiness. She was beyond shock now. Beyond revulsion. She was trapped within her grandpa's memory and helpless to move until it was over. She felt like she was living this horrible story that had happened so long ago, and it was making her increasingly sick in more ways than just her nausea. Slowly she managed to calm herself, and when she did, Grandpa's voice suddenly picked up exactly where it had left off.

~

"Rebecca you have to help me," Isaac pleaded as he made his first real attempt to shift his position in the cauldron of bloody flesh. Rebecca finally turned to face him and at that instant, the look in her eyes and the coppery odor of blood that covered their bodies seemed to coalesce in his mind. He froze. Rebecca didn't look right. Her eyes had the wild, feral look of a cornered animal. Isaac's stomach heaved at the smell or the sight of her, he wasn't sure which. Time, marked by the beats of his heart, passed before clarity finally returned.

Tugging, sharply this time on Rebecca's hand he locked his focus on her eyes and spoke again, virtually yelling.

"Rebecca! We can escape but it has to be now!" Relief washed through him like a warm summer breeze as he saw sentience return to her eyes. Sentience first, awareness second, focus and then determination consecutively passed through those lovely eyes.

She began to move in earnest and replied. "Okay Isaac, let's get out of here!"

The next few minutes were frustrating at best as they attempted, in unison, to extricate themselves in the waning light from the slaughter house surrounding them. It was like swimming through mud. Wherever they pushed, the bodies gave or shifted or they slipped on the blood and entrails. It was all they could do to avoid looking into the horror stricken eyes of the victims piled around them. After trying several times, they finally figured out that they could make the best progress by using each other alternately as anchors to push or pull themselves towards the top. When they finally reached the soggy crest of tortured and dead human flesh, Rebecca belatedly vomited on the bodies around her.

They were both so drenched in blood and tissue that they looked like ghouls rising from some ghastly feeding and Isaac briefly found himself thinking of the baby within Rebecca, and the similarities between their current predicament to that of a newborn issuing forth from the womb amidst a flood of blood and tissue.

Isaac was the first to reach the edge of the pit, and he wasted no time in pulling Rebecca free. The woods looked inviting and a deep rumbling of machinery in the distance spurred them to race hand in hand away from the carnage.

~

Months later, virtually living in the wild, Isaac and Rebecca made it to France.

Isaac never did come to understand that what had happened to him in the year in that camp was not only damage to his body which slowly healed, but more importantly, it was the damage to his mind that never really did.

They'd been in France for only a few months when Rebecca gave birth to her first daughter. It took little deliberation for them to agree to give up their new child. Neither one could bear the thought of raising the offspring of that death camp Nazi. Rebecca had cried nevertheless when the attendants at the orphanage took the child away. It was only six months later when she became pregnant again and nine months after that she died bringing Sondra's mother into the world."

~

Grandpa stopped. His gaze slid down to Sondra and locked on her eyes. Sondra's eyes looked watery and glazed. The shock was continuing to settle in as the horrific images he had just described danced through her head.

"And now my little Sondra, you will be Sondra no more. In books when I was young I read of a wonderful deity that would exact justice from wrong doers and that is who you shall be. From today on you will be my little Poena, and someday you can deal out justice for me."

With those last words Grandpa's arms suddenly went limp and Sondra, now Poena, realized she was free. She looked back up at Grandpa. His eyes were closed and his breathing was even. Gently she slid off his lap. Now she knew how her grandmother had died, and she wondered if she'd died giving birth to her mother because of the things those horrible men had done to her. Slowly, she walked away from Grandpa. Her stomach still writhed. The shock and horror of what she had just heard had changed her more than she could possibly imagine. She was a child no longer. She was Sondra no longer. She'd been too young to bear the tale of the worst horrors man had ever done to man and the aftermath, at first, left her feeling like a burned out shell, but later that emptiness had been filled with hate. Hate for the people that had done those things to her grandpa and grandma, and it was a hate that would only grow with time.

The nightmares that followed in the weeks to come only served to harden her resolve. She would be Grandpa's Poena as soon as she was old enough.

~

Poena's eyes refocused. She was dry, and she was in her bedroom standing stock still and naked. She shivered. That memory had never, ever before come to the surface. Her mind had shunted it away in inaccessible dark corners for all these years, but now reliving it only served to intensify her resolve. There was a reason it had come back to her now. It was another message from Grandpa. Yes, there was definitely work to be done.

~

As for Isaac, possibly the death of his beloved Rebecca was the true beginning of the end for him. All the horror he had endured at Dachau seemed to culminate in the loss of his beautiful wife. Even after the war and his eventual return to the jewelry business, Isaac lived a breathing death. No profit brought joy, no relationship brought fulfillment; even sweet Kathleen, his daughter, brought precious little happiness to his life. Watching her grow seemed only to remind him of what he'd lost. Due to his listlessness, she became a cold and bitter child. She finally left Isaac's home at the age of sixteen, but not before Isaac had instilled in her the horrors of the holocaust and a deep and abiding hatred for all that was German.

Kathleen had a good measure of her mother's beauty, and it led her quickly into the arms and bed of a Jewish merchant who was willing to overlook her cold and bitter nature in return for ownership of a woman whose face would stop people in a crowd. Kathleen was pregnant before she was eighteen and gave birth to Sondra before the end of her nineteenth year.

Her woes were not to end there, however. Her husband was too insecure a man to bear the attention a woman of Kathleen's beauty inevitably accrued. He took to beating her and accusing her of intentionally garnering the attentions of the men around her. Kathleen bore this treatment for longer than she might have, and, to her credit, shielded Sondra from as much as she could, but one day sitting in the house with Sondra, nursing her bruises after having been beaten before he went to work, Kathleen snapped. She picked up Sondra, grabbed a few clothes and left. At three years old, Sondra barely remembered her mother dropping her off at her grandfather's house, but it was the last time she or Isaac ever saw Kathleen.

Even in his misery Isaac's intentions were good, but by the time Sondra was four and a half, his mind was truly starting to slip. He'd have lucid moments followed by periods when he'd slip into ramblings. Most of these were innocuous at first, and even when he mistakenly called Sondra, Rebecca, and expressed his love for her, it caused no harm. It merely made her feel sad for him, until that one fateful day at age five when he'd told her the whole story. That had been the beginning of the end for her, but also the beginning of her desire to avenge her grandparents. It wasn't until years later that she stumbled on the exact meaning of her grandpa's name change for her. 'Poena' wasn't a deity of justice. She was the Greek goddess of revenge.

Breakfast had been notably quiet as both Kira and Sean were enveloped in their own thoughts. They were both feeling a bit depressed and more than a little scared. Sean caught a mental glimpse of Kira thinking about doing Jason's painting and all the terror that had encompassed. The brief image sent Sean's mind casting back to the same events at his little farmhouse. A brief shudder coursed through him as he finished his last bite of sausage and leaned back, picking up his coffee cup.

"It's gonna be okay, Kira." His voice may not have carried the conviction he would have liked, but he meant it nonetheless.

Kira seemed to understand completely. "I know it will Sean, it's just that, even though this is frightening like what I've done in the past, it's different too. There is something unusual about trying to find Poena." Kira paused for a moment, struggling for words. "There's some kind of a connection that's different than any of the other ones I've ever felt. I just can't describe it."

But Sean sensed what she felt, and he agreed. He couldn't describe it either.

As he lifted his cup for another sip, Sean's cell phone rang.

"Hello," he said, hurriedly returning the cup to the table.

"Sean, this is Josh. I got your message this morning, and I'm planning to go to the crime scene this afternoon. Do you and Kira want to go?"

"Just a sec," he answered, lowering the phone from his mouth. Kira was already looking at him questioningly.

"Wanna go with Josh to the new fire scene?" She simply nodded, her expression and feelings devoid of surprise, as were his. He raised the phone back to his mouth.

"Yeah, what time and do you want us to meet you there or at your office?"

"Why don't you just meet me at my office at 1:00? It's about forty-five minutes from here in a small town up river."

"Sounds fine with me. We'll see you then."

Sean put the phone down and looked at Kira. "Well this ought to be interesting," he said.

"Yeah real," Kira answered, but as she lifted her own coffee cup, her eyes were reflecting what Sean was sensing both from her and in himself. Anxiety. Maybe even dread. Shit, he thought.

~

Josh hung up the phone, wishing he hadn't made that call. Whatever help these two might be able to offer, he considered, was offset by the intimidation of being around them. The same thoughts kept occurring to him over and over again. If it wasn't that damn girl having these eerie visions, it was her damn boyfriend acting like he could read his thoughts, especially when he couldn't seem to keep his thoughts off the girlfriend.

He picked up the reports in front of him and tried to focus, but his thoughts wandered back to whether *she* was the reason he had made the call in the first place. The thought nettled him, and it reminded him of the real reason he didn't date, or at least the rationalization he'd invented to explain it. Women were a nuisance, and once he found himself attracted to one, he couldn't focus on his work, which was *exactly* what was happening now! As a matter of fact it wasn't just women either. Ultimately, anyone seemed to distract him. It's why he didn't work with partners.

Even his superiors quickly recognized that pairing him seemed to slow him down or diminish his results. But these two with their weird abilities were something else altogether. The sooner he was done with this case the happier he'd be.

With renewed determination, Josh stared down at the report from the new fire. One item caught his eye from the local investigator's preliminary report; "temperatures at fire origin estimated to be in excess of 2000 degrees". Two thousand degrees! He'd realized the fire origins had been excessively hot but not *that* hot. It narrowed the possibilities down considerably.

After a moment's reflection, Josh shifted his attention to his computer and began to look up some reference information. There couldn't be that many substances one could get their hands on that would burn that hot. By the time Kira and Sean arrived, he decided, he would know them all.

Poena had slept for three hours, eaten quickly and dressed in non-descript jeans and a beige, button-down shirt. She wanted to get back to the burned house as quickly as possible. There was no way of knowing how long it would take until the woman arrived, but she *would* be coming and Poena had to be there first.

It was almost noon by the time she arrived. Parking two blocks away, she moved casually back toward the burned house. It was daylight now and too much stealth would, itself, attract attention, better if she assumed the mantle of a resident out for a walk in the upscale neighborhood. No one knew her and no one would notice. In upscale neighborhoods, people seldom knew their neighbors anyway. She smiled at the irony of that thought. In these times people seldom knew their neighbors in any neighborhood.

~

By 1:10, she had passed by the house three times. She was virtually certain the woman had not been there yet, but she was getting a little concerned about how to remain in the area, keep an eye on the house, and still not draw attention. There were other people milling about to be sure, and the police department had already taped off the perimeter, leaving only one bored officer pacing around. It gave her plenty of cover for a while, but the longer she stayed the more likely she was to garner some unwanted attention.

Finally, it occurred to her that the woods behind the house, which had earlier aided her escape, might again provide the cover and vantage point she needed. She initially moved away from the crowd, then ambled three houses away, where she angled down a driveway and between two houses, one of them, fortunately, unfenced. Not that a fence was any deterrent to her abilities, but bolting over a tall fence in a single bound was a poor method of maintaining one's anonymity.

She continued down the property line into the woods, and reaching the end, turned abruptly back toward her objective.

Her thoughts flashed back to that woman's face. Something about it was bothering her. It wasn't just the fact that the woman was hunting her, there was something else. A familiarity? It tugged at the back of her mind, but the more she concentrated on it the more it seemed to slip away, so she returned her attention to the task at hand.

The wind was blowing steadily, and the stirring of the leaves made a perfect acoustical cover for her footsteps. As she approached, she began to eye the trees for one large enough to conceal her yet still give her a view of the street in front of her handiwork. Finding the perfect place, she slowed then disappeared behind the tree and settled in to wait. She was good at waiting.

~

When they met Josh at his office, Kira picked up her supplies with Sean's help. She'd told Sean she wasn't going to do any more painting there. It was too uncomfortable.

They briefly exchanged stilted pleasantries with Josh. Neither Sean nor Kira really liked seeing him, and Sean sensed that Josh reciprocated the emotions most whole heartedly.

Using some lame excuse about later plans that no one was interested in questioning, they elected to follow Josh to the site rather than ride with him.

When they finally pulled up to the house, he tucked his car in behind Josh's against the curb and turned his attention to the devastation. Burned timbers protruded in disarray like the charred bones of a massive dinosaur. The lone chimney stood like a giant gravestone over the remains of the once resplendent dwelling. A wave of sadness swept through Sean as he stared at the carnage that was once someone's life and home. Abruptly, he sensed something similar from Kira and turned to look at her. She was staring at the house as intently as he'd been.

"Come on," he said, "Let's get this over with."

Kira merely nodded her head as they reached for the car-door handles in unison.

Sean waited for Kira to walk around the car and, almost reluctantly, they followed Josh who was already up at the site poking around in the rubble.

~

From her vantage point behind the tree, Poena saw the two cars approach. First the tall skinny guy got out and then, moments later, two people emerged from the other car. It was them. She was sure of it. Riveting her attention as they walked up to the house, the most important detail that caught her eye was that the woman wasn't carrying her purse. It was the break she'd been looking for, she thought. But then her attention was drawn to the woman herself. That face. Why was it so familiar? Unlike the visions she'd had recently, seeing the woman in person crystallized the feeling. Poena leaned back behind the tree, briefly, and closed her eyes. Where . . . where . . . she racked her brain for a moment but nothing would come.

Turning back, she realized they were all in the house now, occupied. Now was her chance. She turned and slipped back through the woods the way she'd come. Two houses away, she casually crossed the street and walked up a driveway to the row of houses on the other side where the two cars were parked.

~

Kira fought a sense of revulsion as she approached the violation that was once someone's home. For Sean's part, his sense of unease seemed to blossom into dread as he entered the ruins. It made him wonder if he was sensing a remnant of the terror the occupants had known before their death or something more personal to him and Kira. Either way, his senses were prompting him to get away.

Instinctively, he stepped closer to Kira and they crossed the threshold into what used to be the front door. The stench was almost overwhelming; the odor of charred woods, burned plastics, burned fabric and many other odors Sean didn't recognize. Unconsciously, he raised his arm to cover his nose with the crook of his elbow, noticing that Kira had already done the same thing. The sudden thought that there may be a burned body in here caused Sean to look down sharply. The idea of feeling the crunch of someone's dead bones beneath his feet added caution to his steps.

Kira began looking around, like she was trying to find something. He wondered if she was thinking the same thought he'd just had, and then he realized, to his surprise. that he wasn't getting a clear impression of Kira's thoughts at all. Whatever his new abilities, they certainly weren't consistent. With a rueful smile, he resorted to the commonplace and simply asked. "Kira, what *are* you looking for?"

"I don't know really," Kira answered rather distantly. "It's just ... it's just ... I feel like there must be something here that's going to give me a clue. Something ..."

Her voice trailed off and Sean's attention shifted to Josh who was kneeling down, picking something up from the debris. It looked like it might be something that had fallen through from the second floor, and Sean sensed his intense curiosity. It occurred to him to ask and then thought better of it. The less he talked to this guy the better, especially if it involved something that Sean had *sensed* from him.

Ten minutes of watching Josh and Kira peer fruitlessly around the wreckage was making Sean impatient, and he was considering going back to the car to wait when he sensed something new. Whirling back to face the car for reasons he didn't understand, Sean saw someone closing the passenger door with what looked like Kira's purse in her hands.

"No," Sean screamed, already dancing through the detritus to race back towards the car. Kira turned, seconds after Sean and fled right on his heels.

~

Poena heard the shout and looked up briefly to see the man racing towards her. SHIT, she thought, turning on her heels and sprinting away. She crossed the street angling back between two houses and glanced over her shoulder. The man was too fast. He was closing the distance. Fine, she thought, I have the remedy for that. She continued her track between the houses until she reached the fence in the back yard and dove over it, rolling smoothly to her feet in a dead run. She raced diagonally across the back yard and bounded over another.

~

Sean could see he was closing the gap but was shocked to watch the agility with which the woman went over the chain-link fence. She actually dove and rolled without slowing whatsoever. Sean had seen gymnasts do similar moves on TV before but never seen it done live. His hopes of catching her dwindled even as he pushed himself harder. The extra second or two it took him to clear the fence increased the gap, and by the time he was on the ground running again he saw her take the second fence with the same smooth motions. And then she cleared another even higher wooden fence, and as he belatedly recognized the sense of determination emanating from her, he realized it was useless.

Slowing, he put his hands on his hips and bent over. "DAMN!" he gasped. Then it occurred to him that she hadn't likely run all the way here from her home. He froze as the realization hit him, then with new found strength, turned and bounded over the fence he had just jumped and raced back to the car.

Kira was still trying to catch up to him when he raced by her going in the other direction. She twirled as he passed and yelled. "Sean, wait. Sean! Where are we going?" But she turned and raced after him even before she finished.

"Back to the car! Come on!"

~

Poena had crossed three more fences before she slowed, slipped up between two houses and peered around the corner of the brick house to gauge the pursuit. She looked just in time to see two figures racing back to their car.

"Damn!" She said turning and racing for her own car.

~

Josh watched curiously as the two jumped into their car then shouted, "What's the rush?"

"The killer", Sean yelled cryptically before slamming his door.

"The what . . . ?" But they were already turning the car around before the message sunk in, and by then it was too late to follow. Nevertheless, Josh quickened a few tentative steps towards his own vehicle, mouthing what Sean had yelled.

"The killer?" But they were gone. "You gotta be kiddin me," he said in utter disbelief.

Josh just stood there perplexed for a moment. It was too late to try to follow, and he damn sure wasn't going to call it in and have it turn out to be nothing. How could they have found the killer anyway? Or know it was her if they did? Oh yeah, he thought belatedly, psychic shit.

He walked back to his car in a funk of frustration and stark disbelief. He was frustrated at not finding anything more helpful at the site and in disbelief of the possibility of Sean and Kira having found the killer. I mean come on, this wasn't some Hawaii 5-0 episode, so why the hell had they torn out of there like Satan himself was on their tale? But a little seed of doubt was teasing his mind and he remembered he'd forgotten to check in the back yard for the inevitable mask.

Sure enough, there it was almost centered in the yard, black feathers swaying in the breeze mocking grin painted in yellow. He picked it up gingerly, thinking about what was plastered there under that heavy coat of black and yellow enamel. One more dead end but at least it would prove another murder had happened, and that the arsonist was the same one he'd been chasing for weeks.

He walked back around the house carrying the mask and opened the door to his car, taking one last look at the burned out residence. His nose twitched and as he rubbed it his thoughts shifted to the amount of soot probably residing there, one of the hazards of burn site inspection.

He slammed the door, rubbed his itchy nose yet again and turned his thoughts to Kira and Sean. Maybe he should call them. Maybe they *had* found something. He didn't believe it for a second, but without any other clues he didn't have much else to do. He needed to see where they were anyway.

Josh reached half heartedly for his phone, thinking that he really didn't want to talk to either Sean or Kira, when a car in one of the neighboring driveways caught his eye. It was a red '67 GTO with a white vinyl top and Mag wheels. It was almost identical to the one he'd had in high school except his had been a midnight blue. He'd loved that car, but he never had been able to afford those cool Mag wh...

"WAIT a minute!" he yelled. "Shit that's it! How could I have been such an idiot! Shit, shit, shit!"

With Sean and Kira abruptly forgotten, he started the car and turned back towards the station, suddenly in a hurry. He had a bit of research to do, but he was sure he was right and if he was, he'd just found the clue he'd been looking for.

~

Poena reached her car and looked in the rearview as she pulled away from the curb. No one yet. But the instant her car was into the lane, she saw their rented Dodge careen around the corner. With an effort of will she forced herself to keep her foot off the gas pedal. Her best choice was to look unhurried. They didn't know her car and would be looking for someone in a hurry. With forced casualness she turned on her left turn signal and gently took the corner. The other car was gaining rapidly as she eased gently onto the cross street.

~

Sean was puzzled. He'd expected to see someone racing away from the scene and there was no one, except one nondescript Subaru that looked like it was being handled by a little old lady.

As he closed on the little car, frantically trying to decide his next move, a sensation surprised him. Fear... anticipation... What? He looked at Kira. She was anxious even excited but not... wait... "SHIT!" he yelled abruptly, startling Kira. "It's her!" He swung the wheel and hit the gas.

"Sean how the hell..." but Kira didn't finish; her attention was riveted to the little Subaru ahead of them and Sean's sudden acceleration towards it.

~

Poena watched in the rearview as the other car pulled up to the intersection and hesitated, then to her dismay swung abruptly towards her and accelerated. "Dammit! How the...?" But there was no time to waste. She was sure they were after her now, and it was time to drive. Her face set in grim determination, and she shoved the gas pedal to the floor.

She knew this neighborhood well. She'd driven it extensively during her preparations for the fire. It was twisty and turny with a number of poorly marked dead ends. That information could serve her well if she could just get one corner out of site from that son-of-a-bitch behind her. Otherwise, it didn't mean shit. As she thought, she made a second abrupt turn.

~

Sean slid round the second corner just in time to see the Subaru in front of him career through another one. If he could even get close enough to read the license plate ... But his biggest concern was her getting two turns ahead of him. At this point, if she did, he'd lose her altogether. The thought sent his foot mashing down even harder on the gas pedal.

~

Kira'd never seen Sean drive like this before and realized she had no idea as to his ability to handle this type of maneuvering. She was afraid to speak though for fear of breaking his concentration, and merely clutched the hand hold on her door as her eyes darted back and forth from Sean to the car he was chasing.

~

Poena did manage to make a third turn, though, and then a fourth before her pursuers could make the third. "GOT YOU DAMMIT", she said as she raced to yet another turn that would quickly take her out of the subdivision and onto the main road.

~

Sean actually skidded around the next turn only to find his quarry already out of sight. "GOT YOU DAMMIT!" he suddenly heard in his mind. Sean physically flinched as he paused at the stop sign and Kira saw it.

"Sean, are you okay?" She asked, a twinge of fear in her voice.

"What the hell is going on?" He answered in an angry tone as he stomped the gas and swung the car to the left.

Perplexed and frightened, Kira tried again. "Sean what's going on? Why are we going this . . ." But Sean interrupted her.

"Kira, she's in my head!" Tires squealed as he straightened the car out of the turn. "Oh shit," he added suddenly as the car over corrected and he had to compensate for the slide.

"She what?" Kira was certain she'd heard him right but it didn't make any sense—then it did.

"Sean, you're hearing her thoughts?"

"Just a second—just a second," he answered as he finally negotiated the car back into a straight line and accelerated again. There she was but she was already turning again, this time out onto the highway.

~

Poena made the next turn, feeling satisfied with herself. She'd lost him, she thought, and then there he was. "What?" She exclaimed. "Who is this damn guy?" But even as she spoke she shoved the gas pedal to the floor. The light ahead was the highway; with a little luck she could maybe use the traffic.

~

Sean saw her barely hesitate at the red light before swinging right. Racing to the intersection, preparing to run the light, he took a quick glance to his left and stood on the brakes throwing Kira hard against her seat belt.

A long line of semi trucks was almost to the intersection. He couldn't turn, and even after he did he'd never get past that line of trucks on the two lane road, not in time anyway.

"DAMN IT!" he yelled, beating the heels of his hands on the wheel. "We could have had her!"

"And done what?" Kira asked quietly.

The calm timbre of her voice jerked Sean's attention more effectively than any expletive. His gaze riveted on Kira for a brief second, and his senses picked up the answer to his question from her even as he voiced it.

"What do you mean?" he still managed to get out. But then he answered before she could speak. "Yeah, we could have just held her till Josh arrived, or at least gotten your purse back."

"My purse!" she echoed. "I'd almost forgotten my purse. Sean, she's going to know who I am!"

Sitting there not moving when the light turned green, silence fell inside the car. Sean made no attempt to move and for a moment neither spoke.

Finally Sean answered, "I know Kira, I know."

~

Josh was excited. All thoughts of Sean and Kira's apparent chase were lost from his mind. He didn't believe them anyway. He thought he'd found the first real clue since the case started, and he couldn't wait to follow up on it. How could he have been so stupid, he asked himself again as he slipped through the traffic back to the office. The more he thought about it though, the more he was certain he was right, and if he was right he would finally have a positive lead on this damn arsonist. It would only take a few minutes with a reference book, and then he could start tracking the clue. FINALLY!

He'd never had a case elude him for so long, and he couldn't wait to get this perp in jail and out of his mind. His mind . . . that's what Sean and Kira were dealing with—the killer's mind,—hell *his* mind. If he could get this solved he'd have that crazy pair out of his life for good.

No more longing after Kira. No more of Sean's knowing glances. Eeesh, the memory gave him the willies all over again. That thought, in itself, was enough to push his accelerator pedal a little closer to the floor.

~

"Now what are we going to do, Kira?" Sean asked finally making the turn but in the opposite direction Poena had gone.

"I have a feeling all we're going to have to do is wait," she answered.

Sean sensed her next thought. "She'll be coming after us, huh?"

"Why else would she steal my purse? She wants us. She wants *me*."

The soft drone of the rental car moving down the highway was the only sound in the car for the next few minutes while both of them absorbed the import of her words.

"I guess let's go back to the hotel." Sean offered. "There's no reason to go back to Josh's office. We can tell him about your purse being stolen on the phone. Maybe he can get us some protection."

"Sean, the hotel is on my credit card. She'll be able to find us."

"Kira, she's an arsonist not the FBI. She can't easily track your credit card usage, but we can check out and check in under my name if you'd like, unless there was something in your wallet to lead her to me."

"I don't think there was, and yeah I'd feel better if we checked back in under your name."

"No problem, we'll do that, then give Josh a call."

"Thank you," she said then paused. "Sean, something bad is going to come of this, I can just feel it."

"I know what you mean, hon, but we'll figure it out. We've proven to be pretty good at that." Kira's smile was all the reward he needed as they drove for a while in silence.

"Sean," Kira asked, finally breaking the silence. "How did you manage to follow her? She was out of sight for most of that little chase?"

Sean hesitated for a second, reflecting. It seemed so bizarre, but he was certain Kira would understand. "I could hear her thoughts." He said simply.

"I figured you'd say that."

Sean sensed her discomfort and the half-formed thoughts in her mind. "Does it really scare you that bad?" He knew the answer but wanted to ask anyway. Somehow he had to help her be comfortable with his new found abilities.

"Well, a little bit," she said reluctantly, turning her head to him and smiling. "But it'll be okay. I love you."

Sean felt like the sun had just come out from behind the clouds. "I love you, too."

~

Poena was ecstatic and furious at the same time. She was thrilled to have escaped and angry at having been followed at all. How had that guy followed her, anyway? Could he be getting in her mind like the woman was? At least when the woman was trying to find her she was aware of it. If this guy was doing something similar, she hadn't noticed a thing. Something was definitely going to have to be done fast.

Poena made a bee-line back to her house. She wanted to get somewhere safe and alone so she could see what was to be discovered from the woman's wallet.

That's where the clues were she could follow to get close to them. She hardened her resolve; this woman definitely had to go.

"The flames can help you there, too." Poena flinched. Grandpa!

"Seek the source of the flames, Poena. Answers are there."

Just that and he was gone. Grandpa's voice was getting so much clearer these days. Now when she heard him, it was more like a real voice than a thought in her mind. Oh this must be really important, she thought, for Grandpa to speak to me this clearly. Unconsciously, she accelerated. She had to get home.

Josh was sitting at his desk going through a chemical reference book. His finger was tracing the lines down the page. There it was. "Magnesium. In a powder form it can burn extremely hot, around 4000 degrees, and isn't prone to explosion." Seeing the Mag wheels on the GTO had made the connection for him.

The bitch was using magnesium powder to start the fires. That would explain the lack of remains too. Magnesium burns hot enough to consume even bones and teeth in a short space of time. But where was she getting it?

Josh smiled; this was the clue he needed. Putting the reference book down, he reached for the phone book. There couldn't be too many places in town someone might be able to acquire magnesium powder. "Oh, I've got you now, you crazy bitch," His voice echoed in the empty office.

Having the arsonist turn out to be a woman was bringing Josh's latent misogynistic tendencies to the fore. His gangly frame and hawk-like features had never made him particularly popular with women, and as a result he had unwittingly cultivated a general dislike for them over the years. It wasn't a prominent trait, but having the 'bad guy' in this case be a 'bad girl' fueled his old feelings. It was as though he had found an appropriate target for his dislike of the gender that had so often spurned him.

Fifteen minutes later, he'd made a list of five places that might possibly have magnesium powder. It had occurred to him to research the chemical supply houses, but not only would that be expensive, the quantities she was using would arouse suspicion. So he'd turned his search to metal salvage shops. Magnesium was a valuable metal and most of those shops carried good quantities. Now he had some calls to make.

Initially, he began calling the different shops to question them about their customers and see who was buying scrap magnesium. As it turned out, all of those were corporations or viable businesses of some sort. Hmmm, he thought, maybe she was buying through ... she ... why did it have to be a she? Just because Kira said so? That was stupid. Anyway, maybe it was a corporation, but that just didn't seem right. He puzzled some more until it occurred to him that he was looking for magnesium in a particular form. Magnesium in a shredded or pelletized form didn't burn so readily. To be easily flammable, it had to be in powder form. What the metal shops called 'the fines'. Armed with that bit of deduction, he began calling back the different shops and asking for the form of magnesium the customers were purchasing. It didn't take long for him to get frustrated, though. No one was purchasing fines. Finally, on the fourth place in the second round of calls, an affable fellow named Fred took an interest in what Josh was looking for.

"Well if you're looking for people buying fines, I think your outta luck, but if you need some there sure are plenty of 'em on our floors."

"Really," Josh said, letting Fred continue.

"Oh sure, we get big piles of them from our cutting processes that we have to have cleaned up every day so we don't have a fire hazard ourselves."

"And who does that?" Josh prompted.

"We have maintenance people that handle all the floor clean up. I can get you their names if you like."

When Josh was finished calling all the places back a third time and getting a list of their maintenance people he had a list of seventeen names. Only two of them were women though: Sondra Maslin and Elizabeth Sanchez.

"I'll be damned," Josh said to himself as he sat at his desk staring at the list. "Sondra and Elizabeth" Not the names Kira gave him but female anyway.

Only two women. It was too much of a coincidence to be ignored. At the very least he could start there. With a wry look on his face he called back the shop where Sondra and Elizabeth worked and got their addresses.

CHAPTER

The voice in Poena's head was getting louder.

"It's time to leave now, Poena. Time to go." The voice had been loud on her drive back to her house.

For the first time in her life, Poena found herself a bit disquieted by the sound of her grandpa's voice in her head. It was loud and insistent making it difficult for her to think.

She was in her house, sitting on her dingy brown couch, dumping the contents of Kira's purse onto the coffee table when the voice spoke again.

"Hurry Poena! You must find out the source of the flames."

Poena shook her head. What did that mean? The 'hurry' part was clear enough but the source of the flames? Before she could sort that out, the voice continued.

"This is it Poena. The first shall be the last. Hurry!"

Poena shook her head again, sat back in the couch and waited for more, but the voice had stopped. "Is that it Grandpa? What do you mean? What first? What source?" She waited moments longer but there was no more. Grandpa was done.

Frustration gave way to curiosity, so she leaned forward to rummage through the belongings on the coffee table before her. Her first target was Kira's wallet and as she opened it to look at the driver's license, she saw the picture then stopped cold, her eyes slid down to the name, Kira McGovern.

Seeing the close up photo had a different impact on her than previously seeing Kira's face in her mind. Her mental image brought no real recognition but this photo . . . those high cheekbones, those eyes, even the thick wavy hair . . . she *knew* this face, but where had she seen it before? Where?

Absently, she flipped through the rest of the wallet as she tried to recall. There was another photo in there of a woman, an older woman. Poena guessed it was Kira's mother. She looked familiar too but not nearly so much so as Kira. Where had she seen that face?!

She continued to fumble through the wallet as her mind worked on the puzzle. A receipt fell out that she ignored while she pulled out an expired library card from New Orleans. New Orleans? She glanced at the driver's license reading the address. Hmmm . . . Reaching back down, she picked up the receipt. It was from a tollway. "The Kansas Turnpike," she mumbled to herself. And another receipt from Victoria Secret. The address was someplace called the Plaza in Kansas City. She wondered if maybe the boy lived around Kansas City. Kira must have visited him. Poena considered this as she played some more with the wallet. It had a little leather flap on one side with a tiny writing tablet under it. Lifting the flap, she saw a hastily scribbled note. The name Sean Easton, the boyfriend maybe, was written first, followed by a phone number. Maybe she was just staying with the boy friend. Maybe he was new. At least now she had his name.

Glancing again at the address on the driver's license she made a note. That's where she should pay her next visit. She could come back for the boy, but she'd just as soon stay away from him as long as possible. Even if Kira wasn't there at the moment, it would be satisfying to destroy everything she owned. Who knows maybe she'd get lucky and catch Kira there too. The sudden decision and her grandpa's warning jarred her off the couch. It *was* time to go, and now she knew where. There was so much to pack. She had a feeling she wouldn't be coming back.

Moving with a swift and determined grace, Poena turned to her bedroom and retrieved her suitcase from the closet. Opening it, she checked the zip pocket that ran down the side, hundreds and twenties lined the slender space. Money she'd saved. Grandpa had always said it was good to have cash. She hastily threw some clothes into the case and turned towards the kitchen.

The small ice chest under the sink was the perfect size. She opened it, dumped in some ice from the freezer then carefully took the plastic bag from the refrigerator, gently laying the face on the ice. She had another mask to make, she thought, and maybe one more face to take.

The rhyme made her smile. Could this Kira be one of the *spawn*? And if so, was this going to be her last one? Is that what Grandpa meant? But he said 'the first shall be the last' what did that mean? It didn't matter, the woman had to die anyway, and Grandpa would tell her when it was time to know. But how would she even get the woman if she was still in Kansas? A smile spread across her face. She wouldn't have to. The woman would do it herself. Next time that woman popped into Poena's mind, she'd be ready.

Her thoughts turned back to her packing. Certainly there'd be time to carve on her way to Kira's house, which reminded her to bring her carving tools and the wood. Next, she turned to her special nook and pulled out the box with the sun in it. She'd need the sun, and she didn't know when she'd be able to get any more, but this was more than enough for her current mission. She could worry about replacing it later.

Twenty minutes later, her car was packed. She slipped in behind the wheel and with one last look at the little place she'd lived for the last few years, she started the car. Yes, this was an ending.

Sean's adrenaline had finally dissipated to the point that he could think clearly. He was pondering his connection to Poena and paying little attention to the road when Kira spoke.

"Do you even know where you're going?"

The question yanked Sean from his thoughts. "What? Oh—yeah. I was driving back to Josh's office, I guess."

"What for? I don't really want to see him. And anyway, if we need to talk we can call him from the hotel." Kira was feeling nervous and tense and the strength of her emotions was dragging Sean into her mood. He had no better plan in mind, so he agreed.

"What do you want to do when we get back there?"

"I want to try to draw Poena one more time."

The simple resolution in her voice surprised Sean. When he glanced over at her she was staring straight ahead, already lost in her own thoughts. Her determination was in the forefront of her emotions. Fine, he thought. At least I'll be there.

With that, he turned his attention back to the road and the puzzle of his connection with Poena. It occurred to him then that the only person he had that powerful of a connection with was Kira. But why? Why was his connection to her so powerful? Was it because she was threatening them? He didn't know. Maybe he'd figure it out later.

~

Josh had the address of both Elizabeth and Sondra. It hadn't taken him long to locate both places, but it had taken a few hours for the damn HR person to call him back with the info he'd requested. Looking at his watch, he decided he'd make a call to the Judge. May as well try to get a search warrant, though with what he had to go on at the moment he was doubtful.

Kira and Sean flickered across his mind. Where the hell were they? They hadn't called or come back to the office since the chase. Hmmmm . . . That didn't sound good come to think of it, especially the way they'd bolted off, not that he believed they'd really found the arsonist or something. Hmpf! He'd been so preoccupied with his discovery that their absence had barely registered. He picked up the phone and dialed Sean's cell.

"Hi Josh," Sean answered, apparently recognizing the number on the caller ID.

"Hi Sean, are you guys okay? I haven't heard from you since you tore away from the burn site."

"Yeah, we had a little aborted car chase. I thought we had her, but she got away."

"You really think you were chasing the perp?"

"Yep. Almost had her, too. She stole Kira's purse, Josh. I saw her leave the car with it."

"Stole her purse!" That put another wrinkle in Josh's thinking. There's no reason that arsonist would want to risk going for Kira's purse unless she was trying to get to Kira. Suddenly those two addresses became a lot more urgent. He only hoped that one of them proved to actually be the perp. But it was going to hurry him up. Now, if he could just catch a break with the damn Judge.

Another thought occurred to him, but he almost didn't want to ask. "Sean how did you know it was the arsonist?"

"Uh, well we just knew okay?" Sean answered, dodging the question.

Josh figured that's what he'd hear, and he wasn't in the mood to push it, so he changed the subject. "Well, I have some news myself. I figured out what she was using to start the fires, and now I have it narrowed down to two possibilities. I have addresses on both of them."

~

"You found her?!" Now Sean's attention was riveted.

This little tidbit was the first news Sean had heard from Josh that surprised him since he'd arrived here, well except Josh's attraction to Kira. It was also the first lead he'd heard Josh mention on the case. "So what's the accelerant?" he asked, using the term he'd heard from Josh

"Magnesium. It burns at 4000 degrees and accounts for the lack of remains at the sites. And once I figured that out it wasn't too hard to find her."

"Well, I found two likely candidates anyway. I'm just waiting for the Judge to get me a warrant then I'm going to go check them out."

"Do you want us to come?"

Shit, Josh thought. I didn't think they'd volunteer. He definitely didn't want them along on this trip.

It occurred to him that Kira would be able to identify the girl for him, but he dismissed the idea. He couldn't bring himself to believe it, anyway. "I think I better do this one alone, Sean. Who knows what we might find there."

~

Sean could sense his thoughts. He thought they'd be in the way and another worry he'd have to deal with when he went to her door. It was fine with him, though, so he didn't even pretend to argue.

"So, will you call us when you get there?"

"Sure. Are you guys at the hotel?" Josh was a little surprised not to get resistance about going, but he was certainly willing to let it drop.

"Yep. I think we're going to be here awhile. Kira wants to try to paint some more." And Sean wasn't *about* to explain that to him.

"I appreciate that," Josh answered, "but I don't think it's going to be necessary. I'm almost certain it's going to be one of the two we have now, and we'll have her in a few hours."

"By the way. What are their names?"

Josh was almost excited to confirm that Kira had been wrong but that was just silly, so after a brief hesitation he answered. "Sondra Maslin and Elizabeth Martins." It was all he could do to keep the smug tone out of his voice, and he wondered if Sean would sense it anyway. Shit. Now he was beginning to believe all this psychic crap.

"Maslin, huh? Sounds like that one might be Jewish." Still sensing Josh's thoughts, Sean decided he was ready to be done with this call.

"Well, just call us when you know something, okay?"

"Sure. I'll talk to you later then. I have a few more calls to make."

"Okay bye." So he wanted off the call as bad as I did, Sean thought, wondering at the feelings of satisfaction floating in Josh's mind.

Kira, who'd been listening quietly to the whole thing walked over to Sean as he set the phone down. "Sondra Maslin, huh?"

"Yep that's her name, and Elizabeth Martins."

"That has to be wrong. I'm certain it's Poena. What's he going to do?"

"He's found where they live, and he's trying to get a warrant."

"I have a feeling it's not going to do any good. I think she'll be gone."

"Why do you think that?"

Kira hesitated as she searched her feelings. I don't know, but I'm still going to try to draw her again in the morning.

Poena had been driving now for seven hours. She was halfway through Indiana and barely remembered any of the road. Her grandpa was talking to her a lot, but mostly he was repeating what he'd already said.

"The first shall be the last."

"Seek the source of the flames."

"Hurry Poena, hurry!"

It was giving her a headache. Everything had become so difficult since this Kira and her boyfriend had come on the scene.

Her delightful sense of purpose and her methodical search and destroy missions to eradicate all of *them* had all been so easy and gone so smoothly, but now it was —hurry this—hurry that— get chased by the boyfriend . . . Just thinking about it made her blood boil, and why the hell did Kira's face seem so familiar. Try as she might she could *not* place where or why that face was so familiar. It didn't matter. It didn't *matter*. She'd see her face soon when the woman tried to see her again and . . . Poena's thoughts flickered to an image of her boning knife slowly slicing through Kira's skin, pulling the face away from her skull but even as she imagined details she knew so well, something was different.

In her mind, as the razor sharp blade slid through the skin of that woman's face light erupted from around the edges of her incision. As though the woman's skull contained some sort of iridescent flood light or something, shining through as she took her face . . .

Shaking her head to clear the image, she focused on the road. She didn't know what the hell was going on, but she knew she had a rendezvous with destiny of some sort and it was going to be something . . .

something big. She had to make Grandpa proud again. Maybe then he'd stay out of her mind.

The thought shocked her; she'd never resented Grandpa's voice before. Ever! Not since his dying words had set her on her path. His voice had always been the calming sound of focus and encouragement. But now it was so loud and so insistent that she found she really did want it to be gone. Gone for good . . . Soon, she told herself. It would be soon.

With renewed purpose she centered her attention back on the road. She still had a long drive before she could sleep.

~

Josh walked warily up the cement walk to the small dwelling. The still calm of the evening did little to ease his nerves, if anything it seemed to magnify the sound of his approaching steps. He had picked Sondra Maslin's house first. He wasn't sure why, maybe just because it was first on the list.

His gun felt awkward on his hip. He never carried one. Though he was proficient with the weapon, it gave him no comfort. Even Malcolm, the officer beside him, was doing little to settle his jittery nerves. He was typically an analyst, going to actually apprehend a criminal was not part of his usual repertoire. But if this was *the* woman then she was different. This woman might be a ruthless killer and her behaviors had proven too odd to anticipate, as if you could anticipate anyone's reaction when cornered.

She'd eluded him too long, and he couldn't bear to let someone else capture her. He wanted to be there to see the look in her eyes when she realized she was caught.

Josh's eyes carefully examined the exterior of the premises as he approached. Any observation might be the difference between life and death. All the lights were off and the blinds all closed. It was fairly late in the evening. Maybe she was asleep, that might even be the easiest.

Before knocking on the door, Josh sent Malcolm around back to check for possible exits. There was no car in the driveway but there was a garage. The car could be in there.

Malcolm radioed he was in place, and Josh took a deep breath, steeled himself, and leaned forward. This was it.

Rapping loudly on the door he said, "Sondra Maslin, open the door. This is the Police." Josh felt a fleeting hint of pride at the timber of his voice. He didn't sound scared at all. Seconds stretched. The breeze picked up. He could hear it approaching through the trees in the distance. No lights clicked on.

"Anything back there, Malcolm?" he radioed.

"Not even a light here." Josh almost resented how calm Malcolm sounded, but then why shouldn't he, he reasoned. He did this all the time.

Virtually pounding on the door now, Josh repeated in his best booming voice, "Sondra Maslin, this is the police. Open the door or we'll break it down." Nothing. He waited just a few more seconds before calling Malcolm again.

"Okay, let's go in." As he spoke the words he noticed a light pop on in the neighbor's house. Shit, he thought, we woke someone else.

"Roger that," Malcolm answered calmly.

Josh reached down and picked up the metal battering ram they had brought and as he swung it, he heard the crash of the back door caving in. It preceded his only by seconds. Swiftly dropping the ram and drawing his gun Josh entered the dark living room, yelling again.

"This is the police. Give yourself up." He wasn't sure if he needed to keep yelling at this point, but it seemed a good idea if for no other reason than to let Malcolm know where he was. It wouldn't do to get shot by your own partner.

Seemingly in answer to his thoughts, Malcolm turned on a light on the other side of the house and yelled, "All clear here."

Belatedly it occurred to Josh that he should turn on a light too. This definitely wasn't his bailiwick.

"All clear here too," he was saying as Malcolm entered the room. "Let's check the back," he told Malcolm as his eyes fell on the items on the kitchen table. There was a purse, a knife of some sort and a wadded up rag. The purse snagged his attention. Surely it wasn't Sondra's. She wouldn't have left that. In that case maybe it was Kira's. He picked it up as he moved. Time enough to deal with that in a moment, he thought, then followed Malcolm down the hallway to the bedrooms.

"What's that smell?" Malcolm asked, keeping his eyes roving as he waved his gun around. "And why are you carrying that purse?"

"It was on the table," Josh answered, with a hint of annoyance. Now he focused on the odor and wondered why he hadn't smelled it sooner. It was a vague chemical smell that Josh recognized but couldn't place.

~

Flicking on light after light, Malcolm moved through the house, accurately training his weapon wherever his gaze fell.

He got to the back bedroom, flicked on the light, and moved to the dark little bathroom. Nothing. The bed was unmade and clothes were on the floor.

Josh moved to the closet and opened it quickly, imitating the motion with his gun he'd seen Malcolm do. "Looks like someone left here in a hurry," Josh offered, lowering his weapon.

"Yep, that's what it looks like to me."

"Look around and see what you can find. I'm going to go back and look in the den."

"Gotcha, boss." Malcolm answered.

~

Josh's thoughts turned back to the items on the kitchen table. If it really was Kira's purse he wanted to know, and he wanted to know if anything was missing. Josh's eyes continued to wander as he entered the den again. This *was* what he did regularly, look for clues. The furniture in the place was ragged and mismatched. Purchased at garage sales with only thoughts of utility in mind, Josh surmised. He sat down on the faded flower-print couch and laid the purse down, moving the other clutter to the side to clear a space. Opening the purse, he found a lipstick, spare key, and tiny folding knife in there beside the wallet. The wallet? Why was the wallet still there? He glanced at the credit cards still in their slots. It was Kira's purse, and everything seemed to still be intact except cash which Kira may or may not have been carrying. But why leave everything after going to the trouble of stealing the purse to begin with, he thought as he put other items back in the purse. He paused. Wait a minute, he thought, and pulled the wallet back out.

Where's the driver's license? It was missing. Why would Sondra take only the driver's license? Was she planning to use Kira's ID for something? Was there a facial resemblance possibly?

His thoughts were interrupted by Malcolm's voice from the kitchen.

"I still don't know what that smell is, but I know where it's coming from."

Josh looked up in time to see Malcolm closing the refrigerator door. Then it hit him. The masks. She must have been keeping the facial skin in the refrigerator until she made her masks.

The thought sent a tiny wave of nausea through him. Sometimes chasing sickos got old. And this was definitely one of those times.

At least finding Kira's purse was going to save them having to go to the other woman's house.

Malcolm had verified there was nothing in the garage and they were heading back to the car when Josh turned at the sound of a voice.

"Excuse me." It was the neighbor. He was short and slender and was wearing a dark robe.

Josh moved to him. "Yes. Can I help you?"

The neighbor looked only a bit nervous and Josh fleetingly thought that that was actually a strange reaction to the sight of two policemen leaving a neighbor's house they'd just broken into.

"Well, I heard you yell a name just before you busted down the door. It didn't surprise me though, you being here I mean. I always knew that girl was a whack job."

"You knew her?"

"Well, I had talked to her a couple of times. She wasn't home often and kept strictly to herself but still, being next door, it was hard to miss her completely."

Josh's interest was piqued. "What's your name?" he asked, moving in the man's direction and pulling out a pad.

It was as if the guy suddenly realized that he was getting himself involved in something he didn't want to be a part of. He involuntarily backed up a step and stuttered. "Uh, Michael. Michael Barnes."

"Michael, can you tell me anything about Sondra?"

Josh noticed Michael get a funny look on his face and whatever he was thinking replaced his nervousness. "Yeah, I heard you yell that name before you broke down the door, but her name wasn't Sondra, it was Poena."

At that word Josh froze. No, he thought. It can't be! Kira was right after all. His eyes refocused on Michael, who was now looking at him strangely. "Can you tell me anything else about her? Like what car she drives?"

"Well, she drives a little brown Subaru wagon, and she must work several jobs cause she's never here, and I've never seen anyone else come to visit. I always thought that was strange too, cause she's so damn beautiful."

"Beautiful, huh? What does she look like, Michael?"

Michael didn't hesitate at all. It was obvious he had given this a lot of thought and had a very clear picture of Poena in his mind. "Long black hair, olive complexion, built like an athlete. I guess she must be around 5'5" or so. You didn't know what she looked like?"

"Thank you Michael. You've been very helpful. Can I get your phone number in case we need to ask you anything else?"

Michael got that nervous look back on his face before giving Josh the information he'd requested. Josh thanked him again and turned to leave with his thoughts in a major whirl.

Making one stop to drop Malcolm off at the station, Josh was back on the road alone fifteen minutes later.

Damn, he thought. He had her, except that she was apparently gone. He still had to figure out what Poena wanted with Kira's ID. The adrenaline rush was definitely fading, leaving in its wake a bone deep fatigue and cloudy thoughts. He'd worry about it tomorrow, tonight all he wanted was to get to sleep.

Then he stopped as a thought occurred to him, the address. That ID had her address on it. Didn't Sean mention to him that Kira had recently moved in with him? Yeah. So was it her new address with Sean or her old one? Either way, he had a phone call to make.

"Rebecca!" Poena gasped, exploding up from her little motel room bed. She had been dreaming of her grandpa sitting in his rocker telling her his stories; so many of them had had to do with Rebecca, his wife, and then, all of sudden, her sleeping mind put the clues together. That was where she'd seen that face before. Kira looked like Rebecca. Very much like Rebecca. But how could that be?

Poena visualized the old tattered photo that Grandpa had kept hidden away in his little memory box. The photo was of a young woman, an exceedingly beautiful woman. The woman he finally married and the woman that had been taken away with him that one horrible night in Germany. Her grandmother.

She'd seen the photo many times while Grandpa was alive. Coming into his room to bring him some tea she'd see him holding that photo and sometimes crying. So many times he'd tell her that she'd have to pay them back for what they'd done to her, and maybe it was even grandma he was referring to with his dying words. The words that had given Poena her life's purpose.

How odd, she thought, that the last face she would take would resemble her grandmother. How fitting, she decided. Maybe this mask she wouldn't paint. Maybe this mask could just have makeup and be kept with her, a reminder of her successful mission for Grandpa. The thought made her smile. She hadn't kept any memorabilia of her work, and that lovely face that reminded her of the grandma she'd never known would be the perfect memento.

Her eyes returned to her surroundings. Her thoughts drifted into focus on what she had left to do. She had many more hours of driving and then she had a house to burn.

~

"Rebecca!" Kira and Sean voiced together as they bolted up in bed. Sean had picked the word up from Kira's mind, and it had been so charged with emotion that it had drug him up from the depths of sleep right along with her.

Turning to her he asked, "Kira are you, okay? Was it a nightmare?"

Kira was shaking her head almost dazedly. "I was dreaming about my mom and trying to paint Poena when all of a sudden that name popped into my mind. It scared me enough to wake me up."

"Who's Rebecca?" Sean asked.

"I have no idea, but I have a feeling that Poena does." It didn't even cross Kira's mind to question why Sean had awoken. She was getting comfortable with how close they were.

"You think that word came to you from Poena?" For Sean's part, he was passed being surprised at these connections, either for himself or for Kira, especially when she was painting.

"Yep, and I'm going to try to find out right now." Kira threw back the covers and marched to the bathroom with Sean calling behind her.

"What're you going to do?"

"I'm going to take a shower and then draw Poena's face." The determination in her voice was a pale reflection of what Sean could sense coming from her. Wordlessly he got out of bed and followed her into the shower.

The next morning Josh was in a hurry to get to work. He'd woken up late and was frothing at the bit to get going. He'd already put out an APB on Poena's car and was hoping to have some word waiting for him when he got to the office. He was also in a rush because he'd forgotten his cell phone when he left the office last night, and he felt absolutely naked without it. It was the center of his business, not to mention people could have been calling back about leads and he wasn't getting the information. How did people ever function without them anymore? He didn't even *own* a home phone.

To make it worse, he'd woken up certain about the answer to his little puzzle from last night, and he was feeling stupid that he hadn't been sure of it immediately. Kira's ID. Poena definitely wanted Kira's ID for the address. It was a good bet she was headed to the address on that ID. That was another reason he needed his damn phone!

His frustration mounted as he stepped on the brakes. Damn morning traffic!

~

Kira had acquiesced to Sean's push for them to eat breakfast before she started to paint, but in return she'd forced him to hurry, and he was feeling a little testy as he followed her back to the room with his coffee still in his hand. He couldn't hold the emotion though. It ebbed away before they even got back to the room. He was more into admiring the view from behind her than worrying about being rushed to eat his breakfast.

Kira grabbed her sketch book and plopped down on the bed. She reached for her pencil and looked up at Sean.

"This shouldn't take too long," she offered briefly. Then, turned her attention to the book.

Again, Sean could feel the rigid determination waft from her, so he turned his own attention to the newspaper he'd brought back from the restaurant.

A moment later she got up and moved over to her stool. Sean looked at her quizzically, and she answered his unasked question.

"Gotta get in the right frame of mind and this helps." Sean just nodded and went back to the paper.

~

Seconds later she was staring at the sketch pad, listening to the soft drone of the hotel air conditioner. Okay, she thought, let's start with the curve of her cheeks. Gently she touched the pencil to the pad and struggled to visualize the details of the face she'd seen in her dreams . . .

~

THERE she was, Poena thought, leaving her gaze fixed on the road. It was like a dim flickering of a bad movie reel in her mind. That face would flicker then go—flicker then go. But it was her. She'd been waiting patiently, knowing that sooner or later Kira would try to *see* her again. Poena really had no idea what Kira was actually doing, she just perceived it as Kira attempting to see her. Well, she would see her this time and get a little direction too.

~

Kira experienced what felt like a jolt go through her. She could see the face. Poena. She was driving in a car.

Suddenly Kira was sitting in the car beside her, staring at the road. This was new. Kira was certain that this new perspective was not something she had done. After a moment she realized she knew this road. With an effort of will she pulled her gaze from the road and turned to look at Poena again. The profile was striking; long dark hair, almost black, high cheek bones. This woman was beautiful. The thought had barely formed in her mind when Poena turned to face her and grinned. But the grin went from lovely to odd as her mouth spread too wide, too gruesome as the smile seemed to split the skin on her cheeks and

183

stretch almost to her ears.

Then her face at the hair line began to fall away from her head in a precise line, as though sliced by a surgical laser, right along the sides of her head behind the ears. The flap of skin from her forehead was drooping down over her lovely brown eyes exposing a bare and bloody skull and still the horrible caricature grinned. Kira began to scream, but as her scream slipped past her lips the horrid visage turned back to face the road. Involuntarily, Kira followed the gaze but the road was gone. There, outside the window, was a home in flames. Kira saw it as Sean's farmhouse, her new home, burning in great gouts of flame. Flame shooting from the upstairs windows. Flames everywhere. Now the scream blossomed in full from her panic stricken throat . . .

~

"Kira! KIRA! Come out of it!"

She became aware of her head shaking like a rag doll. She blinked. Poena's face before her. But no, she was looking at her sketch pad and there it was, Poena's face in detail in a partial profile. She gasped and turned to Sean who was now kneeling beside her looking into her eyes.

"Oh my God, Sean. I know where she's going. She's going to our home!"

Sean was trying to wade through the avalanche of emotions that were streaming from her. He'd become comfortable weeks ago dealing with any emotions he felt from Kira but these were too raw, too profuse, and too powerful. Recognition, revulsion, horror, fear, guilt, shock.

It was like she'd opened up Pandora's Box of emotions, and they were all flying out at once. All he could do for a moment was hug her, close his own eyes, take deep breaths and let it wash through him like water through a river rapid, flow past and go, flow past and go. There, it was passing. Gently, he pushed back from Kira and looked into her eyes.

"To our home you said?"

"Yes, that's what I saw and she's driving there now."

"I guess I don't need to ask if you're sure." Sean took another deep breath. "Okay. I'll call the airlines. You pack our bags."

Quickly accepting the extraordinary events as if they were normal, Kira stood up and set about doing what Sean asked.

As Sean reached for the phone, it rang.

"Hello," he answered, having already looked at the caller ID.

"Sean, this is Josh. I had a break through, and I have some disturbing news."

"Well, what a coincidence. We had a breakthrough too and also have some disturbing news."

This statement caught Josh off guard. He hesitated a moment taking it in. "Er ... eh what's your news then?"

"You first," Sean countered, feeling again the mild aversion to even talking to this guy. Besides, Sean could tell he was excited, so he may as well let him get it out.

"Uh, okay. Well, after I figured out the accelerant. I hunted for sources of magnesium powder, and I figured out where she lives. And uh, Kira was right about her name after all, it is Poena, Poena Maslin."

Now Sean was interested enough to interrupt. "So did you find her?"

"Well, we went to her house, but she was gone. It did look like she'd left in a hurry. We also found Kira's purse and everything was there except ..."

"Josh she's heading to Kansas," Sean interrupted again.

And again Josh found himself caught off guard, and he was beginning to have the distinct sensation that he didn't like it.

"I know. She took Kira's license, but how do *you* know that?" He asked, afraid he already knew the answer.

"Kira had an episode while drawing her face. Which, by the way, we'll send a copy of to your office. I imagine it's a good likeness." An episode, he thought as he finished, sounded like an incident in a mental ward. He was still regretting the choice of words when he realized that Josh was speaking again.

"That should help a lot. I already put out an APB on her vehicle, but it might take a while before it becomes really effective across state lines. You're sure she's going to Kansas? I didn't know which address was on the license, so I figured it was either Kansas or New Orleans."

"Kira changed her license over last week, but yes, she seems sure she's going to Kansas. We're already packing but our flight out doesn't leave for a few hours yet."

"Sean, you should wait for me before going back. I'll check on flights when we hang up."

"Josh, this is my home you're talking about. We'll meet you when you get there."

"But . . ." Josh lowered the phone, the bastard had already hung up. That's just what he needed, a couple of amateur psychics chasing a killer on their own. Damn!

Just then the fax started ringing. It was Kira's drawing.

~

Poena took a deep breath and let her mind clear. That was the strangest sensation. The face just appeared in her mind, and she found that by concentrating she could affect what was going on. She'd visualized the flames she planned to start at the house, and she even tried to visualize the cutting off of Kira's face, all the time trying to direct evil thoughts at her. She felt sure it worked, but she really had no idea of what Kira actually saw. It was satisfying though, to turn that bitch's magic around on her. What was she doing anyway when she was trying to see her, some kind of incantation or something? Well, it didn't matter for long.

They'd be trying to race back home now, and she had to get there first. She wasn't going to burn the place till they got there, though, oh no . . . they'd be in it when she lit the fire, but she had to make some preparations before they got there for sure.

"NO POENA!"

Poena almost veered into the other lane. Her grandpa had virtually yelled at her. He'd never ever done that before.

"No what, Grandpa?" She said to the empty car. Moments passed with no answer and Poena was beginning to question what she'd heard. Maybe it had something to do with the episode with Kira.

"NOT THERE, POENA. The source of the flames. You must go to the source of the flames! Bring her and find me!"

"Find you? Grandpa you're gone. How can I find you? And what *is* the source of the flames?" Poena pulled over. The car and the voice in her head were both quiet. What could he possibly mean? Furrowing her brows, she tried to concentrate. She had a headache. What did he want her to do? Well, she knew what he didn't want, but it was too late for that now. That house was going to burn, and after she took Kira's face she could worry about where it was she was supposed to bring it.

Poena saw the street sign. 93 miles. She'd be there in another hour and a half, she thought as she glanced again at the driver's license on the seat and the map where she'd circled the address. She'd be there just after dark. Plenty of time to make her preparations and leave.

~

Josh was just livid, sitting there in his office. The more he thought about those two racing back to meet that killer, the angrier he got. Who the hell did they think they were, anyway? Mr. and Mrs. Smith? They had no training and were barreling home to meet a determined psychopathic killer. It was ridiculous.

The flight schedules weren't cooperating so he'd tried to get a hold of the local law enforcement people; even that John guy that had worked with them on their previous case, but it was getting late in the afternoon and all he'd gotten was voice mail. As an afterthought, he'd called the emergency number and some old lady had answered, got his info and said she'd get a hold of John, but he still hadn't called back.

Josh glanced again at his watch. The first flight out he could get was 6:00AM and he had a feeling that would be too late. Damn!

CHAPTER

The plane didn't touch down till 8:30 and Sean was fidgety. They had checked bags, too, so by the time they got back to the house it was going to be closer to 10. Damn! He just hoped it wasn't too late. Kira was feeling the same way and their combined nervousness made for a kind of enforced silence. Neither one could imagine what might happen next, only that they had to get back to the ranch to save it.

~

Poena had already switched cars. With some difficulty, she found a Rent-A-Heap-Cheap place that would rent her a car with Kira's ID and cash.

She'd left her car in a nearby covered Mall parking lot and taken off the tags. She was afraid that if the local authorities weren't looking for her car, yet, they would be soon. The tag thing would at least slow them down.

She drove slowly through the narrow streets entering the French Quarter. It was a Friday afternoon in late August and the air was thick and humid. The address on Kira's license was clear enough, but actually finding the place in this labyrinth was going to be another matter altogether. The whole place had a swampy feel and smell to it that Poena hated.

That, combined with the heat, was making her irritable. The further she penetrated into the area, the thicker the crowds seemed to get, too, making her even more annoyed. Crowds were never good for what she did.

Grandpa's voice had been quiet since his last foray with her and Poena couldn't help but wonder why. Was he upset with her? She had a vague sensation that she'd dreamed about him last night and awakened feeling a little scared. She was never scared. What was going on? She couldn't worry about that now. She had work to do, and if she didn't concentrate she might make a mistake. Mistakes were something she couldn't afford to make.

She got lucky and saw someone pulling out of a parking space on Decatur Street just down from a place called Café du Monde, so she slipped neatly into the spot and got out. The traffic had already been bad, and it appeared that walking anywhere in the immediate area was going to be easier than trying to negotiate these bumpy, narrow little streets in a car. The thought of the crowds almost made her shudder. She calmed herself with the thought that, if this really was the area that Kira lived, the fire she set was going to be glorious and might even take out a little of this awful crowd. None of that mattered right now.

According to the map, the open space across the street was Jackson Square. Standing there looking at the map, she almost jumped as a horn blast from a Sternwheeler on the river behind her echoed through the square. The jolt served to break her hesitation and started her walking. She crossed the street, angling towards Main. Her destination should be just a few blocks away.

As the five o'clock hour approached, the crowds seemed to thicken and change moods. Work hours were ending and people were already gathering in the open bars on several corners.

Raucous voices and happy faces appeared in every direction. As she passed them she caught snippets of conversations from the many patrons and eventually discerned an undertone of tension among the weekend revelers. They all seemed a bit excited about some weather. More than once she caught the word hurricane, but she didn't give it any thought.

She only listened at all because a heavy rainfall would alter her plans somewhat.

Focusing her thoughts, she continued to stroll toward the address on Dumaine, right before Bourbon St. When Poena finally arrived at the address on the ID, she stood there looking around. From the dark brick street beneath her feet, to the slightly slanted buildings lining it, the placed screamed history. To Poena it simply looked old and smelled nasty. She was standing in front of an intricate wrought-iron gate that had had some sort of painted metal attached to the back of it. To prevent people from easily looking in, she assumed. She leaned over to the small space above the lock and peered in to a gorgeous courtyard. She barely registered the rainbow of flowers and greenery populating the area between her and the front door. What she did notice was that all the lights in the structure were off. Nobody home.

The gate itself was obviously old but judging by the lock and the screws mounting it to the adjoining brick fence, it had been recently repaired, and she could see the deadbolt was in place. Glancing to the left and right at the rows of buildings, whose walls and railings seem to be immune to the general construction tendency for straight lines, Poena had the oddest sensation. Everything about this city was so foreign to her. She had the brief impression that she might have left Earth altogether. The flora, fauna, structures, and smells of this strange part of the world felt like a throw back in time. Poena was suddenly reminded of the stories Grandpa would tell. A land far away and long ago. That's what this place felt like; a land far away and long ago. She gazed again through the gate into the courtyard and turned the knob. The heavy lock was engaged and she leaned back slightly, considering the effort it might require to scale the brick fence which not only stood unusually high but slanted like every other structure in this part of town. Even the gate was tall with some more blunt wrought iron spikes above it.

As she continued to ponder the possibility of going over the brick fence she was surprised to notice chunks of broken glass had been cemented into the top of it.

This barrier had actually been constructed to keep people out. Not just to discourage the casual passerby. It didn't matter, though, she decided, she was certain she could pick the lock when it came to that, she just needed a few seconds of being unobserved.

People were passing her in uneven clumps, and she began to be concerned of arousing suspicion. She hadn't taken a step after that thought when a woman leaned in beside her and peered through the gate. She hid her surprise as she stared at the woman. With a camera hanging around her neck, the woman's demeanor suggested a tourist that had already spent a bit of time at one of the local drinking establishments.

"Beautiful, isn't it?" The woman stated as she continued to stare through the wrought iron.

"Uh, yes it is," Poena answered stiffly. Her social skills ranged from rusty to non-existent, especially when her first reaction was resentment at being interrupted. She immediately began to calculate her best exit from this overtly friendly woman.

"I've always been amazed at the beauty of the little places hidden along these old dirty streets."

"Uh, yeah. Me too." Poena spotted a bar down at the corner that seemed to have a crowd with tables set up outside. Turning, she hurried away from the woman. "Have a nice evening," she muttered, for no other reason than to keep from arousing the woman's curiosity. If the woman decided to follow her she might end up having to kill her, and Poena was certain that she just didn't have the time, much less need another detail to attend to. As those thoughts slid through her mind, it occurred to her that a woman wandering alone in this area might seem a little suspicious in itself. She let the thought go. She didn't care about that woman and as to her own situation, there was nothing to be done about it anyway.

Crossing the uneven street she again registered the builder's apparent aversion to straight lines in their construction preferences. But it wasn't the builders. It was the land.

She had read somewhere once that the street below her was originally built by forcing cotton bales into the shifting, swampy muck to stabilize it before covering it with brick and then later the blacktop she now trod.

The sounds from the bar were increasing as she approached, and glancing back she was happy to see that not only had the woman moved off in the other direction, but she was going to have a line of sight to the gate she'd just left.

Piano and harmonica music began regaling the customers of the lively little bar, dragging Poena's attention back to all the antique, wrought iron trim work which only added to the other-worldly feel of the place. The bar was situated on a corner, and slatted wooden doors were folded back on both sides, leaving the place primarily open. The little tables and chairs set up on the sidewalk were wrought iron as well, and exuded a charm that Poena could never appreciate. As an afterthought, she donned a smile. It was simply a necessary part of her disguise for awhile. It felt foreign on her face.

"Whatcha' havin' ma'am?" the bartender asked as she seated herself at one of the outdoor tables. He was old, black, and looked more worn out than the place that employed him. But his smile seemed genuine, as though serving her was actually something he enjoyed.

The man's eyes were, despite his age, taking their fill of her and suddenly Poena became aware of other eyes on her, too. For the thousandth time she resented the beauty that caused her so much attention. It was a thing most women would kill for, but it seldom suited her purposes.

"What do you have on tap?" she asked absently. She had seated herself at one of the heavy metal chairs that allowed her to easily divide her attention between the bar itself and the gate down the street.

"Jax beer, if you want something local. Bud or Bud Light if not."

"Jax is fine thank you." Poena had no idea what Jax beer was, but she didn't care either. She wanted to minimize her contact with the man. The waiter had barely walked away, however, when another man appeared at her table. He was tall, slender and well dressed. His dark hair and bright eyes would have been considered attractive by anyone's reckoning.

"Whateveh is such a lovely lady doing imbibing by herself, ma'am. Surely you are awaiting someone?"

His southern drawl caught her by surprise but his presence in general annoyed her. She didn't need this. Her anger began to flair. On the other hand, she considered, quickly checking her initial reaction, if she rebuffed this man someone else was likely to take his place and in the long run annoy her more and waste more of her time. Besides, he *was* cute.

"I'm afraid I'm not waiting on anyone," she answered, now donning her most engaging smile. "I was here in town on business and decided to stay an extra night. I'd never seen the French Quarter before."

"Really?" The man drawled, making the single word come out as three syllables. "Alone in the French Quarter. Surely that must qualify as some form of sin?"

Poena smiled but said nothing. There was no feeling behind it either. She felt certain the man didn't notice the deception as he seemed to have his interest focused elsewhere.

"Would yah mind if Ah joined yah for a bit, then?"

"No, that would be fine."

"Mah name is Benson," he began. "James Benson." He seated himself smoothly, his gaze riveted on Poena's face.

"Kira," Poena said without hesitating. She wasn't sure why she'd picked that name, other than it was on her mind, and she had no inclination to offer a surname. As an afterthought, it occurred to her that maybe the use of that name in this vicinity might not be such a good idea.

She glanced around nervously to see if she'd gleaned any new attention, but the only other people gazing in her direction were a couple of men at the bar and, judging by their expressions, it wasn't her name they were interested in. She shifted her eyes back to James.

"Nice to meet yah, Kira."

Poena saw that he was about to ask another question and decided to head him off. Men love to talk about themselves, and he couldn't question her if he was busy answering her question. "Thank you. What brings you to the French Quarter this evening? Are you from here?"

His expression flickered as he absorbed the change from the question he was about to ask to his response to hers. Not a real fast thinker, Poena observed. Making the shift seemed to require a bit of effort.

"Well Ah'm from the Atlanta area actually and like you, Ah'm heah on business but unlike you Ah have decided to leave early. Ah was supposed to stay through the weekend, but Ah changed my flight to one late this evening due to the approaching storm."

"Storm?" She prompted. This was the second or third time she'd heard something about this storm, but it was the first chance she'd had to actually question anyone about it.

"Yah haven't heard about the approaching hurricane? Kathleen's her name. They felt that it would miss Naw'leans once it struck Florida, but it seems now to be bearing down upon us and picking up strength as it does. Ah can't imagine how you missed hearing about it."

"I don't listen to the news much, and my business here was a research project so I haven't been talking to the locals." The excuse sounded plausible but Poena felt certain he was going to question her further, and her mind was working furiously to fabricate something acceptable while she deflected him with a damsel-in-distress act. "My though, that sounds dangerous, maybe I *should* shorten my stay."

"Well, that certainly was mah thought ma'am. As it is I'm afraid mah flight might be diverted north due to the storm, anyway. Ah certainly hope ah don't end up spending the evening in DC or worse."

The mindless chit-chat seemed to stretch on forever. Poena was only on her second beer, but James was on his third or fourth whiskey drink. Her gaze kept shifting from James to the gate at Kira's place. The sun had slid behind some of the building tops. Shadows were intermittently beginning to dance across the street and the crowd was thickening. She was sure James noticed her distraction, but he was apparently too polite to ask anything about it. She was preparing another rapid reply to keep him occupied when she noticed someone stop at the gate. It was a man. He paused briefly, produced a key and apparently turned the lock. A man? Could that be the one she'd seen with Kira? The one that was driving the car that had chased her?

She had no way of knowing from this distance but her prolonged gaze drew James' attention. He turned his head to follow her gaze, and Poena figured she had better make up an excuse quickly.

The man at the gate had already disappeared into the building, anyway.

"That's strange," she began drawing his gaze back to her. "I saw someone down the street who I thought looked familiar. It must have been a trick of the light. I certainly don't know anyone around here."

"Well yah do now," James said obviously pleased by the return of her attention.

"Well, yes, now I do," Poena responded putting on her best dumb smile. This guy is such an idiot, she thought. Visions of stabbing him flickered through her mind. They seemed more pleasant than continuing this conversation. No time. There was just no time. She had to get to that house again and see who that man was, where Kira was, and now, apparently, she was going to have to hurry to get out of town.

Also, if the storm started too soon it would mitigate the effect of her fire. She hated to have anything interfere with the sun, but it would still consume the interior quickly and spread fast. She could barely imagine fire engines negotiating these narrow streets, especially on a weekend with all the crowds. Her thoughts floated back. James was speaking again. She just wished this jackass would go away.

"...so Ah'm afraid that Ah'm going to be forced to relinquish yo company rather soon if Ah'm going to make mah flight. Though, I do regret the necessity to hurry off." He signaled the waiter as he finished his sentence.

It looks like I get my wish, Poena thought, as the first sincere smile of the evening bloomed on her face. "I do understand James and thank you for the company you did offer. It made the afternoon go so much faster." Poena thought she would choke on the blathering platitudes she was spouting, but the waiter brought the check, James paid for her drinks, and he was gone moments later. Five minutes after his departure, even before the waiter began to ask if she'd still like to stay, she left.

Though the crowd was not yet thick, having to negotiate it at all roused Poena's temper. Once she got to the gate, however, she was beyond that and again focused on her goal. She tried turning the knob on the gate, and it was still locked. She imagined it was set to stay that way in this neighborhood.

She thought of the soft leather lock-pick kit in her purse but was hesitant to use it with so many people on the street. Even if she could open the lock quickly it would still be a minute or so of her standing plainly out in front of the gate with some strange tools in her hand. Not an ideal situation. Then a thought struck her as she noticed the small black button mounted on the wrought iron that she'd somehow missed earlier. Without any further hesitation she slung her purse up and over the brick fence, ripped the sleeve of her shirt, then knelt quickly and rubbed her hands in the soil and gravel by the gate. Standing back up she flipped her hair forward and back letting it just hang, then pushed the button. A chime answered her action that sounded like a soft Big Ben coming from within the house.

"Who's there?" A male voice came from a speaker that must have been mounted inside the brick fence to her left. Poena almost jumped.

"Hi, I'm Sarah. I was just mugged, and my purse is inside your courtyard. Could you help me?"

"Uh . . . well yeah . . . just a sec."

There was a crackling electric sound, presumably as he released the button and then silence for a few seconds that seemed to Poena like years. Finally, the front door opened and a non-descript man appeared on the porch walking determinedly toward the gate. His head was swiveling both directions as if he expected some ambush from within his own courtyard.

His movements suggested to Poena a lack of coordination and athleticism. This man would be easy to overpower. He was only about 5'8" and just a bit too heavy to be called thin. His hair was black and he was wearing jeans and a plain yellow T-shirt. As he approached, she could see his face was as non-descript as the rest of him, definitely not the face she had seen with Kira. She assembled her best damaged-maiden expression as he came to the gate.

"Thank you so much," she began. "I was just walking and this guy grabbed me, and when I fought back he took my purse. Do you see it over there? Oh, I'm certain I saw him throw it." It all rolled out of her mouth with such gusto that she found herself being mightily impressed with her own fabricated histrionics.

The man glanced around first. "Ah," he said then moved off to his right. He came back a second later with Poena's purse in his hand. "Is this it?"

"Yes," she answered smiling, and for one brief second she thought he was going to pass her the purse through the bars but his gaze shifted taking in all of her, and she saw the change in his expression before he spoke.

"Uh, would you like to come in a second? Collect yourself maybe, see if anything is missing from your purse? I could make you a drink to calm you, too if you'd like."

"Oh, that would be wonderful."

"Are you by yourself? That's not such a good idea in the French Quarter." But he was opening the gate as he spoke, and at that point Poena didn't give a damn what he was talking about. He'd most likely be dead in a little while anyway.

"Well, I was here on business. I didn't plan on coming here, but I had a little extra time and I'd never seen the French Quarter before." It was always helpful to be able to add a touch of truth. It made the lie so much more believable. As they reached the front porch, the man focused on her more attentively, taking in her face and figure. Poena acted like she didn't notice.

"Um, my name is Mark, by the way. Mark Heinz." He opened the door offering her the chance to enter ahead of him.

"Thank you, Mark. I'm just so shaken. I've never been attacked like that before." She let her head swing left and right taking in the place. "Oh, this place is so beautiful. You'd never guess it from the outside." She turned to him; he was closer behind her than she'd expected. She almost flinched back a step to get him outside her personal space but then thought better of it.

"Thank you again. I don't know what I would have done without my purse. You're a life saver." She flashed her very best smile and locked eyes with him as she spoke. The ploy worked, he seemed to lose his concentration altogether. Contrary to her previous thought, this was one of the few occasions where her feminine appeal worked to her advantage.

"Um, uh, have a seat, Sarah, I'll make us both a drink. What would you like?"

"Do you have a beer?"

"Sure."

"That would be great." She sat down on the couch as he moved off into the kitchen. She let her eyes wander around quickly. Kira obviously wasn't living here.

So what the hell was the deal with the address? She must have moved recently, probably in with that man she'd seen. Damn! Now where the hell were they? Somewhere near Kansas City?"

Mark came back in with two beers and walked up to the couch. He sat next to her, but not too close, as he handed her one. Another Jax beer. She smiled as she took it.

"Thank you again, Mark."

"You're more than wel . . ."

That was as far as he got before Poena's beer bottle connected with the side of his head. Blood spurted as the bottle shattered and his eyes rolled up. She snagged his beer as he fell off the couch. She didn't think she could take anymore bullshit conversation tonight, anyway. Hmmm, she thought as she got up off the couch, ignoring Mark lying on the floor. She took a swig of his beer and moved into the kitchen.

She spotted the kitchen knives in a block on the counter and considered killing him right away, but after thinking a moment longer, she decided that she might need to ask him some things first. Besides, she might want to stay here tonight. It was as good a place as any and wouldn't be a problem to check into like the hotels. That was another good reason to keep him alive. She didn't want to have to drag his rotting carcass around, and she certainly didn't have any good place to store a body.

So with a plan in mind, she began rifling through the drawers and cabinets until she found what she was looking for. Duck tape. Ten minutes later she had him securely taped to a chair with his mouth taped shut. She'd taken his pants off but left on his shirt and stuck his big French knife firmly into the coffee table in front of him. It'd be the first thing he saw when he awoke. If that didn't scare him enough to talk, then it would be much easier to convince him with his pants already removed.

Next, she began looking through the little home for any hints to Kira. Everything in the place had been updated fairly recently, but despite the modern décor, all the actual living spaces were tiny. Everywhere she looked, care had been taken to save as much space as possible. She was almost through the whole place and not having any luck when she heard a muffled moan from the den. Good, she thought, now I can get some answers.

As she moved back into the den, she flipped the TV on. If he yelled she wanted it as muffled as possible.

She knelt down in front of him and jerked the knife from the table. His eyes were as big as saucers. "Mark, I'm going to remove the tape to ask you some questions, okay? Now, if you yell or don't answer my questions I'm going to cut you. Do you understand?" As she said it, she shifted her glance down to his crotch then back up to his eyes. He definitely understood. Without concern for his pain she yanked the tape from his mouth. He barely managed to stifle a yelp as he remembered her warning.

"What do you want?" His voice was trembling and she could see sweat popping out by his temples and upper lip.

"I'm just going to ask you a few questions. But I wouldn't ask me anymore if I were you." She shifted the blade to let the light from the ceiling flicker off it. He nodded.

"Do you know a girl named Kira that used to live here?"

"Yeah. I sublet from her until her lease runs out in November." His voice was shaking. Good, Poena thought.

"How long have you been here?"

"Just a couple of weeks. Listen, why . . ."

Poena jammed the knife back into the table hard and released it. It stood there quivering in the solid wood. "I told you not to ask me any more questions didn't I?" Her voice was icy calm. Mark just nodded. For a moment Poena got concerned that he might pass out from the fear, so she decided to hurry.

"So do you have a forwarding address for her?"

"Uh, yes. It's somewhere near Kansas City. Uh . . . it's in the drawer by the kitchen table."

My, he was being helpful. She rose slowly, and Mark seemed like he was trying to back the chair he was taped to away from her with his toes, but it only tilted slightly. Poena glanced back over her shoulder as she walked to the kitchen. "I wouldn't do that if I were you, Mark. If you tip that chair over it might crush your hands and I'd probably just leave you like that."

There was a little thump as the front chair legs clicked down on the floor. She imagined he didn't even know he'd done it. His eyes were rolling around wildly. Maybe he would pass out. If the address was there she didn't care what he did. It was there. She read the little note that looked as though it had been written by a woman's hand; Kira no doubt. Louisburg, KS, it said, with some farm road address.

Where the hell was Louisburg, Kansas? It had to be near Kansas City, she thought, remembering the receipts in Kira's wallet.

Sticking the paper into her pocket she thought for just a second about what to do with him. It was then that the TV caught her attention.

"...its winds are back up to category three after clearing the northern peninsula of Florida and seems to be on a direct path to New Orleans. Residents are advised to stay tuned for updated reports..."

"Really is a hurricane," she said. She had unconsciously moved back into the den by Mark as she'd listened to the broadcast. She turned now to look at him. He was pathetic. Sweat was rolling down both sides of his face and his breathing was coming in heavy gasps. His fear sickened her. She had a sudden urge to slice his cowardly neck and actually turned towards him. He gasped but then she remembered that she intended to stay here tonight.

She slammed the knife back down in the table making him flinch and marched back into the kitchen. She hoped he had some food.

After raiding Mark's refrigerator, she'd gotten tired of him staring at her, so she'd finally taped his mouth shut again and found a ski cap to pull down over his eyes. Then she watched the news story in peace. This *was* one serious hurricane coming, which was fine with her because she was leaving this damn swamp hole, anyway. She then spent quite a while on Mark's computer. She looked up Louisburg, Kansas, finding that it was near Kansas City, just as she had guessed.

She then began researching the Kansas City area to familiarizing herself with the surroundings of Kira's new home. It was many hours later, after Mark had apparently fallen asleep, that she'd finally gone to bed herself, amid the increasing booms of thunderstorms.

CHAPTER

Standing at the luggage carousel, Sean glanced at his watch again; 9:10. Shit, just like he thought, they were going to be about 10 o'clock getting home. And it was starting to rain too. That would slow them down even more.

Worry chaffed at him even as he caught sight of Kira's bag coming up onto the carousel. Oddly though, he sensed calm coming from her. How the hell could she be so calm? Because it wasn't her house? He dismissed the thought, disgusted with himself. It was calloused and unlike Kira, and he was very much certain that she felt like it was her home now, too. But then how could she be so calm?

~

Kira's thoughts were far away. For the last hour or so she'd become caught up reflecting on the turn her life had taken in such a short space of time. It had only been five months or so since she'd conceived Canvas of Life and embarked on these new special paintings. Every one had been a revelation or a shock of some sort leading up to meeting and falling in love with Sean, and doing that catastrophic painting for him . . . and now this.

The countless shocks to her system, either in the form of visions while she was painting or nightmares when she wasn't, were beginning to take their toll. If she kept this business going, was each and every painting going to be such a trial?

Even her first painting after her mother's, her first commissioned painting for Louise, whose situation was totally innocuous, had resulted in emotional shocks as she relived emotions from the subject's life. Where was it all going to end? Did she even want to deal with this anymore? For certain she'd have abandoned it already if it weren't for Sean. He'd been her lifeline and confidante through almost all of it, and she couldn't imagine anyone who could have suited her better, especially under such unusual circumstances. But that was another question all together. Sean's special gift was part of what made him so perfect, except that it had now evolved from being aware of feelings to reading hers and others thoughts. She was still intermittently unsure of how she felt about that. HELL, he could be reading my thoughts right now! Somehow it wasn't working that way though.

Either he couldn't read her thoughts all the time, or he had found some way to avoid doing it. She took a deep breath and asked herself as she turned to watch Sean reach for her bags on the carousel; did it really bother her? Could she really spend her life with a man who could be inside her mind at any moment? But the moment of fear dissipated and the answer came quickly enough; no it didn't. The *idea* of it bothered her much more than the reality, and giving up the love she felt for him was not something she could even consider.

But what if his abilities continued to expand? No. There was no sense borrowing problems, and if that was the case then she'd just forget about it and not question herself or him again. Besides, she had plenty of other things to think of right now. You know, little things like a killer waiting for them at their house, wanting to burn it down with them inside. The absurdity made her chuckle slightly and Sean turned to her abruptly.

"There you are," he said.

"What?" Kira answered, eyes widening.

"You went somewhere for a while there, and I couldn't figure out why you were so calm, but you're back now."

Kira tilted her head slightly. This was exactly what she'd just been pondering. It made her smile and prompted one of the questions she'd just been asking herself. "Why didn't you just read my thoughts?"

Sean got a twisted little grin on his face that promptly faded as he led her out of the terminal carrying the bags.

"It's not quite like that," he spoke over his shoulder. "Sometimes your thoughts just come to me and sometimes I can pick them up if I really focus, but I don't like to do that; it feels . . . wrong somehow . . .

like a peeping Tom. They're your thoughts, and I'm quickly learning that I don't want to know every thought that everyone around me is thinking. It's too confusing and really . . . just too much information."

Kira smiled again. She wouldn't have believed she could have loved this man anymore than she already did, but that little confession just ratcheted her affection up another notch. "Come on sweetie, we've got a whacko to catch."

Sean's answering smile radiated love as he stepped onto the shuttle bus, but doubts haunted him as another concussion of thunder rocked the night.

"Yeah, before she catches us."

~

The thunder was still escalating as they crunched down the driveway and the famous Kansas wind had begun to howl like a werewolf in the woods. Debris was blowing in intermittent bursts, but so far the impending rain was holding back. Sean scanned the area closely as he approached but any motion that might otherwise signal an alert was obscured by the fierceness of the wind and the increasing lightning flashes. It felt like a scene from a horror movie, Sean thought, and unfortunately that might not be too far off. Why did it always have to storm on scary nights anyway? What was it, some kind of law of the universe?

He pulled the truck around back, still wordlessly searching for any hints of danger. The house was dark and quiet.

"You think she's here already, Sean?"

Sean could feel her fear much more strongly than what her voice conveyed.

"I don't know, but I bet if she's not here now, she has been. Surely she's had time to get here before us."

All of their senses were in overdrive as Sean led the way to the back door. The wind was still picking up, deafening them both to any covert sound that might alert them. A bolus of thunder exploded as Sean opened the squeaky back door, and Kira, right behind him, jumped and grabbed his shirt.

Sean had jumped, too, at the great peal of thunder, and for a second he had the powerful urge to giggle. Only it wasn't funny, and their fear was founded in recent experience. Still, being back at his home it was hard to imagine the reality of a crazed arsonist driving half way across the country just to come here and burn down their home. But then again it was difficult to imagine the extraordinary experiences they had already lived through in this house. Why should one more amazing incident be any different?

Kira's tugging on his shirt distracted him. He turned back as he stepped into the kitchen. "What Hon?" The look of fear in her eyes was accenting her feelings, and his too, for that matter.

"She's not here Sean. I can feel it."

"Feel it? Isn't that my department? But you're right, I don't sense anything, yet."

"I'm telling you, she hasn't been here yet. Somehow I think I'd know."

His own words had made a thought occur to him. He stood stock still and concentrated. Even though he didn't really understand the 'how' of what he was doing, he somehow sent his senses out. It was the strangest sensation, part of him thought as he 'listened' for thoughts, to be standing here reaching out with his mind. Even without an understanding of the process, however, he was still filled with the certainty of the result. If anyone else was near he'd know it. All he sensed was a fleeting image of his father's face. Smiling. It puzzled him, but he let it pass.

Kira stood still, also apparently understanding and content to wait.

"Well, there's definitely no one here now," he finally said resuming his steps through the house.

"Good." Kira answered unconsciously accepting Sean's amazing statement as simple fact. She flicked on a second kitchen light as Sean moved into the den, head swiveling, trying to see every direction at once.

A second later he caught himself and realized he was acting as if he didn't believe his own statement, which he did. He visibly relaxed and picked up his pace towards the staircase. She may not be here now, but he could still be alert to anything missing or changed.

The air in the house seemed to be charged with energy and Sean couldn't decide if it had something to do with his own nerves or some odd aspect of the impending storm. He was moving quicker now, though still observing everything as he walked up the stairs.

Ten minutes later, they finished walking through the house anyway even though they were both certain that their efforts were needless. Sean plopped down on the bed.

"Well, what do we do now?" Kira began, looking as jittery as she felt.

"I don't know what else we can do, Kira. Lock the house up tight and try to get some sleep I guess."

"Sean, how could you possibly sleep?"

Sean thought for a moment staring at Kira and a grin slowly appeared on his face. "Well, we have to get some sleep sometime . . . but I guess we could have a glass of wine or two and try to relax each other."

At first Kira got an expression of disbelief on her face, but it quickly morphed into the same lascivious grin Sean was affecting. "Hmmm . . . that might not be such a bad idea. I'll get the wine. What did you have in mind to relax each other?"

Sean found the mock innocent expression she was wearing so irresistibly cute that he leaned over and grabbed her, kissing her with an ardor far beyond what he'd intended. Kira was taken a bit by surprise, but when Sean finally pulled back, she stared at him a moment, reeling from the feelings, then spoke.

"Oh. That kind of relaxation. I'll be right back."

While she went to get the wine, Sean went back down to the car to get the bags they had intentionally left there until they had finished their search of the house. The wind was really howling now, and as he grabbed the two bags he sent his senses out again. All he picked up were Kira's thoughts in the kitchen and that brief intrusion surprised him enough to quicken his steps. She had some plans of her own it seemed.

When he walked back in, and after he locked both locks on the door, she followed him upstairs with the open bottle and glasses in hand. While he set the suitcases down on the floor, Kira set the wine and glasses down on the dresser, and as he was unzipping the first one she came up behind him and gave him a hug. He almost turned around too quickly and Kira had to pull back slightly to avoid an elbow, but she promptly leaned back in and put her hands around his neck.

"Now you want to show me that relaxation technique again?" The heat was building within her, fueled not only by his first kiss but by her own imagination while she'd opened and poured the wine. Sean delighted in the sensation of it, and his own arousal was immediate.

Moments later Kira pulled back and looked up into Sean's eyes. "Sean, there's something I need to tell you."

That phrase and tone sent a little needle of fear racing through Sean's stomach until he sensed the warmth coming from her, so he simply smiled and said, "Okay, you have my attention."

She held his gaze for a moment almost losing herself in the simple feel of his touch but finally she spoke, "Sean I know that you know that I've been concerned about your new ability to read thoughts; mine in particular."

At those words Sean actually did read her thoughts, easing the moment but he prudently kept the knowledge to himself.

A tiny flicker of a smile, however, still crept onto Sean's face and a miniscule lessening of the tension in his eyes. He'd read her thoughts already, Kira thought. She smiled. He wasn't the only one who could be perceptive. She continued anyway,

"And I've decided that they don't bother me. I've decided I'm comfortable with it being another part of who you are, and I can't tell you how much I love you, but before we do anything else I have to go to the lady's room."

The biological interruption somehow tickled Sean, and he just smiled as Kira got up and left. Seconds later though he burst up off the bed at Kira's yell from the bathroom.

"Oh my God!"

Bounding into the room on the heels of her exclamation, Sean looked around for the source of her shock but saw nothing except one of her purses on the counter.

"What?" He exclaimed. "What's wrong?"

The pause seemed to stretch forever as Kira lifted something from her spare wallet and turned to him. "She's going to the wrong place."

"What? How could . . . ?"

"Sean, I forgot to switch my IDs before I left for Virginia. I'd been using my spare purse for days and in the rush I didn't think to switch my license before I left for Virginia. She's going to New Orleans."

Sean let the words sink in. Poena wasn't on the way here, at least not yet.

Tension seemed to drain out of the room like cold bathwater; not only his, but Kira's too. He could feel it. They were safe for now. They had time to plan.

All of a sudden Sean's thoughts returned to the previous topic and now with the danger gone for the moment, his ardor returned with a vengeance. Kira's next comment encapsulated his feelings.

"We're safe for now," she said and smiled as if she'd just read his mind.

Sean thought his heart would burst for the joy it was containing. For a reply he pulled her back to him, and let the smell and feel of her envelop him as he kissed her again.

The passion of their union drained what little energy the travel had not, and spooning each other tightly, they quickly fell sleep.

Poena opened her eyes. Muted daylight came in through the window and thunder still rumbled in the skies. She stretched where she lay in Mark's bed and wondered what time it was. The very next thing she noticed was the smell. Something smelled like a toile... Mark. She'd forgotten Mark. Damn!

Dreading the problem she'd made for herself, she marched into the den where the TV was still droning softly about the approach of Kathleen. The smell increased dramatically as she rounded the corner. Mark's eyes looked drowsy but were opened and turned sharply to her as she entered the room. Fear, shame and anger were mingled in that gaze. She didn't give a damn. He sat there still tied to the chair, with no pants on, covered in his own excrement. She went back to the kitchen, grabbed the butcher knife and walked back over to him. His eyes widened, and he flinched as she approached.

"I'm going to cut you loose. You can take a shower, then clean up your mess, but let me warn you I can throw a knife even better than I can swing one and if you force me to I'll cut you into pieces small enough for the crawfish around here. So just do what I tell you, and I think I'll let you go in a little while. I don't care that you've seen me and there apparently really is a hurricane coming, so I'm going to bolt this damn swamp anyway. You got it?"

He nodded his head and a touch of the fear seemed to leave his eyes.

It almost nauseated her to have to get close enough to cut the tape. He still flinched and she almost cut him anyway. When she finished he stood up shakily. Fear radiated from him as he moved his limbs, probably trying to stir up a little circulation.

"Now hurry up before I lose my patience."

Without a word he turned and angled toward the bathroom. She'd have to keep an eye on him, but he was too scared and weak to be much of a threat. The TV caught her attention again. They had called for a voluntary evacuation of New Orleans. The city was going to start emptying out. I wonder how well that will work, she thought. Maybe it would be better if I wait until much of that traffic leaves.

It seems like these things always turn at the last minute anyway and maybe the whole evacuation will be for nothing. The house in Kansas isn't going anywhere, anyway. There's plenty of time.

Josh arrived in KC on Saturday and the first thing he did was call Kira and Sean. He hadn't talked to them since they left Virginia, and he was almost certain that he would have heard from them if anything had happened; like coming home to a burned out house.

The phone rang twice before Sean answered.

"This is Sean."

"Hi, Sean. This is Josh. I assume you two got back okay and everything is fine?"

"Yeah, so far. Josh, Kira realized last night that she had her old ID with her. Poena has probably gone to New Orleans." There was a pause on the other end of the line.

"Well, I wish I'd had that info last night. It might have saved me a trip."

"Sorry. We were real keyed up when we got home, and it wasn't until later in the evening that Kira realized her new ID was in her other purse. By that time it didn't even occur to us to call you."

"That's all right," he said, but Sean knew he didn't mean it.

He hung up the phone just a touch too fast.

Since he'd already made the trip, Josh decided to go on out and at least talk to Sean and Kira. He didn't expect it to be particularly fruitful, and as it turned out it wasn't. The only consensus they had come to was that Poena probably did go to New Orleans and one look at the TV was sufficient to convince Josh that he wasn't going to be able to track her down there. At least not now. What Kathleen wasn't destroying, the hysteria in the city was. The voluntary evacuation had already begun. There wasn't a way into the city now unless you were stupid enough to attempt something by air.

Josh hung around for another hour or so talking about details with Sean and Kira but nothing new came of it. To make it worse, he quickly became anxious all over again about being around the couple. His attraction for Kira was still there and his discomfort around Sean, right there with it. Psychics, he thought disgustedly. It was crazy.

So with a stilted attempt at seeming causal and calm, Josh said good bye and drove gladly back to the airport. If he was lucky he could still catch a flight back to Austin this afternoon.

For his part, Sean was glad to see him go. The hawk-nosed man just about pissed Sean off every time he was around. The situation made Sean truly wish that he couldn't read thoughts, especially not from this sleaze ball.

The minute the door closed on Josh, Kira turned to Sean.

"Well now what are we going to do?"

"I guess we do what Josh said. Stay alert and let him know if we learn anything else."

Kira just stared at him. The initial lessening of tension they had both felt when they'd learned that Poena had gone to New Orleans was now reversing itself. The undefined waiting for some anticipated danger *somewhere* in the future, brought with it brand new tensions. Kira was absolutely certain that Poena would still come for them once she figured out where they were now. Sean wasn't so certain. He felt that it was just as likely that she'd get sidetracked and never make it back to them.

"In the meantime," he continued, "I guess we just get on with our lives."

"Oh, great," she countered. "Just get on with our lives, and try to forget the maniac that's coming to kill us and burn our house down."

"No. Don't forget. Pay attention, but still Kira, what else can we do?"

"I don't know."

The exasperation in her voice was once again a pale echo of what she was feeling. Sean was beginning to understand that often times peoples' words didn't rise to the intensity of the feelings behind them. It was an interesting perception, he thought.

"Kira, something else will turn up. This can't last too long before we learn something, you'll see."

"I hope you're right."

No matter how much Kira tried to get her mind on something else, thoughts of Poena augured their way back to the forefront. At last she decided to try to do something constructive about it. Without consulting Sean, who was busy in the barn with his recently neglected horses, Kira set up her easel and stool and prepared to paint. She was immediately struck by the fact that doing something so common felt so unusual. It had been many, many months since she had begun a painting that didn't involve ashes. Her paints were thinner than usual and she spent some time thinking about the different techniques for painting with mediums of different consistencies. As she did, Poena's face floated into her mind with an uncommon clarity and sent a chill down her back. The fear strengthened her resolve, however, and with a grim, determined set to her mouth she brought paintbrush to canvas.

The image of Poena's face began to take shape on the canvas. She made several uncharacteristic pauses, expecting some sort of resistance from Poena, but none was forthcoming. She had no idea why, so she continued. She still had no clue what setting she was going to use for it, so she had started with just the face in the center of the canvas.

She couldn't have even said how she decided on the size of the image, but as she sunk deeper and deeper into her work, an image began to appear.

Kira took a deep breath and leaned back. Surprise dominated her expression. She had apparently sunk into the same type of trance she always did when painting with ashes, only this time there were none involved. In the past she had been struck by how much deeper her trance seemed when painting with ashes, and this session, without ashes, felt just like that. Hmm, she thought. Unusual.

Nevertheless, there before her was a picture of Poena viewed from the side through the window of what Kira could now see was an old pickup truck. The tops of her hands were just visible above the door, firmly clenching the steering wheel. A look of determination dominated Poena's face.

She's coming, Kira thought, fear lacing through her like a hungry snake. At that moment Sean burst in the back door.

"What's wrong?" He asked, his eyes riveted on the portrait.

"She's coming, Kira said.
"But there were no ashes," he began.
"I know."

CHAPTER

Saturday flowed into Sunday, and though Poena now had proof that the hurricane was going to hit New Orleans she still wasn't in a hurry to leave. Time was on her side now.

She'd decided that since she'd lost the initial element of surprise or the possibility of actually beating Sean and Kira back to their home, for surely they'd have guessed her intentions with Kira's purse, her best bet was to delay and let them get lulled into believing she wasn't coming. At this point, the longer she waited, the more surprise she could regain. People can't maintain a vigil against a possible threat forever. Eventually they lose their belief, or at the very least their degree of alertness. Besides, this hurricane was only a category three. It wasn't going to be near as bad as the news media was making it out to be, but that's what the news media did. Make news.

Mark sat on the couch watching the TV. She wasn't bothering to tie him to the chair anymore during the day. He had become quite docile; she figured he believed she was going to let him live if he behaved. Hell, she might actually do that; she still hadn't decided. It wasn't that killing him bothered her that much, but the only ones she'd killed so far were *them* and their relations, and part of her felt that killing anyone else besides them would make their deaths less special, somehow. It would also be cheapening Grandpa's revenge, and she really didn't want that. Still, if she felt it was absolutely necessary, she'd gladly end this worm's life. After all, Mark wouldn't be able to give any information that the hawk-looking investigator didn't already have, and by the time they caught up to her she would have finished Grandpa's work, and it wouldn't matter what happened to her.

The TV was showing more and more people evacuating as the

sporadic thunderstorms that had lashed the city preceding the hurricane now became straight winds and torrential rain. Kathleen was finally focusing her strength on the heart of New Orleans. The tone in the news reporter's voice was taking on an almost frantic quality as he reported the growing panic of the residents. Poena snorted with disgust. Idiots.

They'll trample themselves and each other to get out of town because the media was frightening them. A category three! Weren't they listening? The storm was not going to be that dangerous. Coastal towns had been hit with much worse and survived just fine.

The day passed slowly for both Poena and Mark as the storm's intensity continued to increase, but when Sunday slid into Monday an event occurred that galvanized Poena's actions and made her decision about Mark, too.

She was listening to the TV, munching on a sandwich from Mark's kitchen when a news flash interrupted the ongoing drone of the reporter's broadcast.

"I have just been informed that the Canal Street levee has given way. I repeat the levee has given way. The city is flooding!"

She turned to Mark, her decision already made. Now was the time to act.

"Mark! Go get some clothes and get out of here. The city is going to flood."

He only hesitated a second before jumping up off the couch and hurrying out of the room. The instant he left, the power went out and Poena made straight for the door. Perfect timing. She no longer cared what Mark did or thought. It was time to leave.

Though it was daytime, it was still nearly pitch black in the apartment. Even so, she had no trouble making it to the door. She just hoped she could still get to her car. There was no way of knowing how much time she had or what the roads would be like now, but the quicker she left the better her chances.

The roar of the storm when she opened the door surprised her. Even though she'd been hearing it from inside, she was shocked at the increase in volume. She'd had no idea how much the little residence's walls had been muting it. The fierce winds were blowing the rain horizontal and debris was flying down the streets. Two steps out into the fray she was not only soaking wet, but those little droplets felt like pellets of ice being driven as they were by the tremendous winds. The thought flickered across her mind of the suitcase she'd never even taken out of her car. She'd never intended to be in New Orleans this long, but she was glad she wasn't carrying it now. Squinting as much as she could against the fierce rain droplets she began to run through the empty streets. Even in this storm, the deserted streets of the French Quarter should have seemed eerie to her, but her thoughts were else-where occupied.

The sheer velocity of the winds coupled with the increasing flow of the water across the sidewalks and streets caused Poena to fall twice in her flight back to her car. She finally thought to stay close to the building walls to shield herself from the worst of the onslaught. It was almost ten minutes later when she turned the corner onto Decatur. Her car was there, standing out because it was almost the only one to be seen. Crossing the ankle-deep water in the street, she made it to her car, jumped in and tried the ignition. It started right up. The sound of the raindrops hitting the car sounded more like hail than rain. If it was possible, the intensity of the storm was still building.

Now the real challenge begins, she thought as she glanced at the map on her seat and pulled away from the curb.

Trying to get on with their lives proved to be a daunting task for Sean and Kira, but for different reasons.

By Saturday afternoon Sean found himself sitting on his tractor feeling like he was being baked alive in the middle of a field; in spite of this, his thoughts were far away.

His recent experiences with Kira had seen more changes inside him than just his gift. They had expanded his thinking about life and the world in general, and to his surprise, he found he wasn't quite getting the fulfillment that working the farm used to bring him.

And another thing; these images of his dad flashing into his mind were becoming a more and more frequent occurrence. At first they had truly just been flashes, a quick picture of his dad's face in his mind. But as it was progressing, those flashes were getting to be longer, and with each one he came away with some particular feeling or sensation that he would swear was coming from his dad. Was Aubrey trying to send him these, or was he just becoming continually more connected to him now that they'd met? Is this what happened when two people with his kind of psychic gift meet? Not once did it occur to him that it might not be real.

There was no answer to either that puzzle or the other one about the farm, but Sean was smart enough to recognize that what he'd found fulfilling for so many years here in his little corner of Kansas was no longer going to be able to make him feel happy. The same old farm and the same old house and the same old life had suddenly lost their luster. Just being with Kira made him enormously happy, but now he found he wanted more. He had now been introduced to adventure and was finding that his soul had a real taste for it.

A drop of sweat slipped from his eyebrow into his eye, pulling his thoughts back to the task at hand. He flinched, suddenly shaking his head before wiping his shoulder across the eye. The sun had heated up the baseball cap he was wearing and he was now sweating seriously. The little burning sensation in his eye continued to short circuit his mental meanderings. He just wanted to finish with this field and get back to Kira.

Kira on the other hand was happily working away in the house having almost the opposite train of thought from Sean. She'd spent years as a model traveling around the world and the adventure and glamour of it all had finally morphed into a lonely monotony of changing scenery. It ceased to mean anything. Being here on the farm with Sean and painting, however, was making her feel as complete as she'd ever imagined.

Certainly it had supplanted the lost empty feelings she'd struggled with right after her mom died. Even ideas of children were beginning to trickle across her mind, which in her life, was a first. She'd spent so many years chasing her dreams that the concept of being tied to kids had never occurred to her, at least not as anything more than something to be seriously avoided.

Both of them had money, and being in love and having her painting, plus the work around the farm, gave her a sense of belonging she didn't recall ever experiencing before. That thought led her to thinking about marrying Sean. They really hadn't had a chance to consider the wedding. As a matter of fact they'd had precious little time to think about each other at all since he'd asked her. Had it really only been a little over a week? She couldn't believe it, people just didn't move this fast into a serious relationship, but contemplating it got her excited all over again.

So, with pleasant thoughts of wedding plans dancing through her head, she got back to cleaning.

It was a measure of how happy the idea made her that for a little while Kira forgot about the wacko arsonist who still had her and Sean in her gun sights.

Poena was furious. She had made it out of the French Quarter with very little trouble but between the panicky drivers, the ferocity of the storm, trying to look at a map, and the changed highway entrances, she'd taken the wrong road. She'd ended up on Canal Street and then somehow on Veteran's Highway which caused her to keep wondering why the canal was actually on Veteran's. Was it some kind of joke? The water was flowing over both roads, but it had been worse on Canal though the canal on Veteran's was overflowing, too.

She kept trying to glance at the map to see which direction she needed to turn to get on I-10 but was afraid to look away from the road for too long.

The water was up to the middle of her tires and debris as large as chairs and trashcans was being hurled intermittently through the blinding rain by the still rising winds. The size and mass of that debris increased noticeably as she drove. The rain itself was alternating between coming down in slanted sheets or horizontal buckets.

During one of her quick glances at the map she thought she saw a major road—Causeway Blvd.—that would cross her path. If she found that one she could go left and get to Interstate 10 and just pray it was still open. She was finding plenty of time to regret her decision to stay in New Orleans while this monster of nature approached.

Thirty minutes later Poena made it to I-10 to find that all the inbound lanes were closed and traffic was being diverted into the opposing lanes. She didn't want to do this, however, because she was low on gas, and if she took that option her choices for getting off to fuel up would be limited.

She hugged the right hand lane as she maneuvered the heavy traffic.

It appeared that there were still many folks who hadn't opted for the voluntary evacuation two days ago.

Poena was finally experiencing shock at the ferocity of the storm. Hearing about a hurricane and actually being in the midst of one were certainly two different experiences. The trees were standing at horrendous angles trying to resist the pull of Kathleen's mighty winds. The traffic was now moving so slow that she had ample opportunities to watch the drama unfolding all around her.

Though the water wasn't pooling on the highway yet, she could certainly see it rising on the side streets. On some, it was already up to mid-door on the cars still parked in the streets.

She was still focused on the drama of a woman trying vainly to start her car which already had water in it over the floorboards, when a jarring crash swung her head to the left and her car to the right.

She was already in the right lane so she had some room to maneuver but not enough. It was a pickup that had struck her and seconds later it had forced her off the shoulder and into a guard railing.

Poena's shock shifted abruptly into anger, and her eyes blazed at the cab of the pickup, looking for a target for her fury, but to her surprise there was none. Her eyes narrowed as she searched for signs of the driver since her car and the truck had now come to a stop on the side of the road. The pickup was still pressed up against Poena's door, so exiting from that side wasn't going to be an option. The nose of her Subaru was crushed into the guardrail and the engine had quit. She felt pretty sure that the vehicle was done for. Remaining calm was something she was good at, however. She slid across the seat to try the passenger's door which opened readily once she applied enough force to overcome the howling wind.

She was still drenched from her walk to her car so another dousing at this point made little difference. She crawled out, noticing some bruises on her chest and legs as she did so, while having to shield her eyes from the velocity of the rain drops. Even with glare not being an issue, sunglasses would have been welcome. Keeping her hands on the car to steady herself against the wind, Poena walked around the car to the pickup, which was still running. The passersby on the freeway barely gave the wreck a second glance. They were occupied with their own escape.

She decided to approach the pickup from the passenger's side giving her a bit of protection from the wind and rain. As she reached for the door handle, she glanced into the cab. A woman was face down on the seat and wasn't moving. Poena opened the door and reached for the woman's neck to check for a pulse. The woman was dead. Poena's glance moved over the woman's body. There were no apparent marks on her. Had she had a heart attack? An aneurism? She didn't care. What she did care about, all of a sudden, was the fact that this pick-up was a four wheel drive, and its gas gauge was reading nearly full. All at once what had been a problem was turning into a fortuitous event.

Undoing the seatbelt, she started to pull the woman out of the cab then thought better of it. She got her close to the passenger side door then closed it, and went around to driver's side. She hopped in and put the vehicle in reverse which produced some tortured screeching of metal before it pulled free from the doomed Subaru. She quickly retrieved what little luggage she had in the Subaru and raced back to the pickup. Hopping in, she adjusted the seat and mirrors and looked at the oncoming traffic. She found a break moments later and reentered the exodus from New Orleans.

Now she didn't have to stop for gas. There'd be plenty of chances to dump the woman's body later. As she sat there in the truck, stuck in the line of cars, listening to the radio scream about the levees giving way and reports from the Ninth ward of explosions preceding their levee flooding, Poena began to smile. Grandpa was watching over her.

Monday flowed into Tuesday and the changes on the farm were only those that couldn't be seen. Sean had been testy this morning when he'd left to go tend to farm chores, and Kira had been bothered by it for awhile. Finally though, she dismissed the thought and settled into her newest painting; a commission she had received from a lady in Atlanta. Her sixty year old husband had passed suddenly, and she wanted to commemorate him in some special fashion.

After receiving the ashes via UPS, Kira had picked up the urn and knew what the painting would be even before she talked to his surviving wife, Beth. The instant Kira put her hands on that urn she received a powerful image of a bright yellow bi-plane partially inverted in a bright blue sky. It had an open cockpit and a tiny confederate flag was whipping from the top wing above it. The grasses and trees below were myriads of variegated greens. It was an incredible image, and she was already excited to paint it.

When Beth had finally called, Kira had shocked her by suggesting that she make the painting of a yellow bi-plane. The silence on the line told Kira she'd hit the mark:

"How did you know . . . ? That's exactly what . . . Oh Kira, that would be wonderful!"

"This is what I do Beth," Kira had said. "I assume he owned one of these planes?"

"Well yes. We . . . I mean I, still do. It's called a Starduster, and it was the love of his life. When his heart condition prevented him from flying it anymore I think he died right then. It just took another few years for his heart to figure it out."

Now Kira got silent hearing the pain in the woman's voice.

Unfortunately, this was a part of the business she had chosen, but she was continuing to struggle with getting used to it. Still, she was getting better.

"Beth, I'll do the best I can. I'll be in touch."

"Thank you Kira. I'm ... I'm glad I decided to do this. It would make him so happy. Call me if you need anything."

"I will. Bye, Beth."

~

The memory of the conversation faded and Kira turned to the fresh canvas in front of her. Another Tabula Rasa ready for her creation. She seated herself on her stool, left hip on the stool, right foot on the ground, her thumb through the palette balanced on her left wrist. With a wistful smile, she touched brush to canvas, and her thoughts soared off into the bright blue sky.

~

Sean was out in the wooded section of the farm on his little John Deere Mule. The wind had whipped through the trees the night before, and he was taking the opportunity to gather up kindling for the upcoming winter, while at the same time clearing the woods of a lot the debris.

He wondered if Poena was still coming. He wondered if they were actually through with that adventure. And he wondered what it was he wanted to do with his life now.

He was afraid that these changes in his feelings might affect his relationship with Kira, too. What if he couldn't find something else he wanted to do? Would this vague dissatisfaction grow into frustration, then apathy, and then maybe even anger?

As his hands worked, his mind trod off into the philosophical. One could never miss the taste of chocolate if one had never tasted it. Now he had tasted something more, and he wanted it. But how or what? Where could this desire possibly take him? Adventure wasn't a vocation, was it? What do you do with such a desire, especially when you have found a love you'd die for, and she seemed more than thrilled with the complacency the farm could supply? The thoughts gnawed at him with no answers forth coming and before he knew it the little Mule was filled with twigs and branches. He'd pray about it and wait. Answers always seemed to come to him that way, though that didn't stop the anxiety in the interim.

The week drug on. Wednesday became Friday and then the weekend was upon them. For days now both had avoided the topic of Poena and the specter of her vengeance looming over them, but neither forgot it. It was just that there was nothing they could do. The idea of taking security measures barely even crossed Sean's mind. He was still wrestling with his restlessness and trying to divine what course to take. In truth, as the days slipped by, he was slowly becoming less and less concerned with Poena. He was actually starting to let himself believe that it was over. Even Kira was apparently letting her thoughts move on to other subjects. She seemed so thrilled with her new commission.

~

By Saturday, Kira decided that she had something to discuss with Sean and, even though his mood had continued to gravitate to the surly side, he went out of his way to try to hide it from her. She appreciated the gesture, even if the feelings behind it were troubling her.

They had made love the night before and spent the rest of the evening in each other's embrace; tightly holding on to the love they were feeling. By morning though, Kira knew it was time to talk, and Sean felt it coming.

They were sitting at the breakfast table drinking coffee when Kira finally unloaded.

"Okay Sean, what's going on with you? And also, have you given any more thought to our wedding? And what do you think happened to Poena?"

The triple whammy of emotionally charged topics took Sean by surprise, which didn't happen very often, and he was silent for a moment.

As if understanding his need to take all that in, Kira continued unabashed, "Would you like some more coffee?"

Wordlessly, Sean held out his cup and smiled while Kira poured. He finally spoke.

"Okay, I think I'll answer those questions in reverse order because that'll be the easiest. First, I'm beginning to think something else happened to her. For all we know she died in the evacuation from New Orleans or found some other target to occupy her or . . . who knows? Second, I'm ashamed to say I've been so preoccupied I haven't thought much about it, but I love you and we can do the wedding any time, any place and any way you want. And third, well, I'm not so sure, Kira. After what we've gone through together I guess I'm finding that I'd like a little more excitement in my life, but I don't know what to do about it. I have spent my entire life on this farm and in many ways I love it, but I just know that a part of me has come to feel a little empty and somehow having you in my world makes this new emptiness seem even more pronounced. I just don't know what to do. I know it's been affecting me though, and I'm sorry for that."

They both sat there at the kitchen table, silent for a moment, thinking about the different topics. Kira was the next to speak.

"Why don't you get your pilot's license?"

It crossed her mind that her recent painting had been the source of this left-field idea, but it seemed to fit somehow.

Sean was too stunned to respond for a moment. From his perspective, the comment was so far out there that he wasn't even sure what he thought about it. Kira, however, continued.

"I mean really, Sean, who said that your excitement has to come from work? Take up a hobby that offers you the excitement you're needing."

The idea itself was growing in his mind but even more, the idea that Kira understood and respected what he was feeling was making his heart soar. He wouldn't have believed he could have felt any closer to her, but here it was one more facet to adore. Still, the more he considered it the more he liked the idea. Flying. That *would* be exciting! The thought had never crossed his mind before.

"How did you come up with that? And yeah, I like the idea! Thank you!" Then an image of her new painting popped into his mind. Whether it was from her thoughts or his own he couldn't tell. But she was already finished with most of the bi-plane itself and was working on the background. "Oh, I know where you got the idea."

Kira just smiled.

They sat there for a bit at the kitchen table, each mulling on their own thoughts, sipping their coffee and generally enjoying each other's company. Kira's thoughts finally slipped off in another direction and Sean saw the smile on her face slowly give way to a look of concern. He was preparing to eavesdrop on her thoughts, something he'd been pointedly avoiding whenever he could, when she spoke, saving him the guilt.

"Sean, are you really thinking that the danger from Poena has passed?"

"Well, that thought has been crossing my mind more and more often I must admit. Maybe something did happen to her in New Orleans. I don't know."

"Yeah, I've let that thought roll around in my mind, too, but my gut tells me she's not gone, just waiting."

"Yuck, Kira. That is not a fun thought to consider."

"But wouldn't we be stupid *not* to consider it?"

"Well, I can't argue with that. I wonder if it would occur to Josh to call us promptly if he apprehended her."

"Lord, I'd think so. I don't know if I want to wait for that though."

"What are you thinking?" He already had an idea he knew where this was going and the idea was already making him nervous.

"I think I'm going to try to do another painting of her . . . "

"I was afraid you'd say that, but on the other hand if we can learn anything maybe it's a good idea after all. At least it is, if I'm not too far away when you do it."

Even as he finished his sentence he found his thoughts wandering back to her suggestion about him. Flying. Would that really suffice for his restlessness? If it would, it would certainly solve this new conundrum. He let the idea roll around a second more but was jarred back to the present by Kira's next statement.

"Well, since you're not going anywhere today, I think I'll start on the painting tonight. I have made good progress on the commission for Beth, so I don't think a small detour would even be noticed. I didn't bother to mention how fast some of these paintings go together so she wouldn't be expecting it this soon anyway."

"Tonight, huh?"

"Yeah, at least to start it."

"Okay. I think I'll go into town and get a couple of bottles of wine.

We might need them later."

Again, Kira just smiled.

~

On his way into town Sean experienced another image of his father. This one however seemed much more personal than any before. A distinct impression of his father's face congealed in his mind and the expression was unmistakable. He was worried. Worried? Why would he be worried? The experience so struck Sean that this time, he resolved to do something about it. When he got back home he'd give him a call or maybe even on the way back to the farm from town.

~

Kira spent the day flying through the skies of her painting with the Starduster. Fortunately, her ability to paint didn't require her conscious attention, because her thoughts were flying off in several other directions, too. Had her flying suggestion really helped? She couldn't help but notice the subtle changes in Sean since they'd come back from Virginia, and even the idea of something coming between the two of them rocked her to the core. Part of being in love was to actively help the one you love become the person they wanted to be. She'd read that somewhere years ago, and it struck her now. Love wasn't just a passive feeling, it was an act, or rather an ongoing series of acts. Besides, the idea of doing anything to help Sean grow and be happy filled her with more joy than she could have imagined. Maybe joy really was in the giving.

She leaned back from the canvas and shook her head. What's up with all this philosophical monologue, she thought. Now that she'd paused, she refocused her gaze on the canvas in front of her. She was doing mostly sky now, and it was coming along nicely. As she shifted her stance and touched her brush again to the canvas, her thoughts jumped directly to Poena. But why? It was her connection to her subconscious through her painting that was giving her this glimpse, she realized, and suddenly she knew the reason as well. She *was* coming. Kira could feel it. She was pretty certain she'd know for sure tonight, if she didn't already.

~

There were a couple of other errands Sean had in mind when he had left the house, besides the wine, but through it all he couldn't get his thoughts off his dad. Two hours later as he was driving back to the farm, he decided to make the call. It only rang once.

"Hi son."

Hmmm, Sean thought. Caller ID or . . . it didn't matter, nor did it surprise him.

"Hi Dad." There it was again. That strange awkwardness about calling Aubrey dad. Well, he *was* his dad but he . . . Shit.

That didn't matter either, and Sean was beginning to get annoyed at himself for having to have this same internal conversation every time they spoke. He was about to have plenty of other thoughts to occupy his mind, though.

"I've been thinking about you," Aubrey continued.

"Yeah, well, you've been on my mind too." Then he decided to just spit it out. "As a matter of fact, I've been having these flashes of you in my mind, and they're more than just images. I keep sensing emotions, I'm guessing from you, every time I get one.

"I understand. Truly. Why don't you tell me about Poena?"

Sean stopped cold. Poena. How could he know . . . He searched his memory, but it had been too recent, and Sean knew he hadn't talked to his dad since learning her name.

"Well, I guess you haven't just been 'thinking' about me either, have you?" Sean wasn't sure how he felt about his dad having that knowledge. It certainly gave him a taste of what it must be like for Kira when he read her thoughts. It was a bit unnerving at the very least.

Sean decided he was going to do his very best not to tap into her thoughts anymore. Somehow it felt a little too . . . personal . . . In the meantime, Aubrey hadn't answered Sean's question. He just let the silence hang there across the phone connection.

"Can you do this with other people too, Dad?" It was a given that both knew what the other was talking about.

"Well, yes but not like with you. I usually have to be around them, and I usually have to *try* to catch their thoughts. But since I met you I can hardly help it. I imagine I'm sensing you every time you're sensing me."

Sean let this sink in a moment not saying anything, so Aubrey continued.

"So why don't you tell me what you know about this Poena woman?"

Fifteen minutes later, Sean finished relating his and Kira's story of their adventures since they'd talked last.

"Wow," Aubrey said. "This one sounds dangerous. Not only that, but it sounds like she has tapped into you and Kira too. What're you going to do?"

Tapped into us? Why did it seem that everything in his life these days revolved around something psychic? This was nuts! He had to think for a moment. What to do? It was the same question he'd been asking himself for days, and he wasn't at all sure he had an answer yet.

"Well, at the moment we're doing nothing. I was beginning to hope that maybe Poena had found some other target, and we were done with all this, or maybe she got herself killed in the hurricane."

"Don't count on that one, son. From what you're telling me, she doesn't sound like the 'give up or get distracted' type. I'd expect she's still coming. Maybe she's delaying for just that reason, to get your guard down."

"Yeah, that's what Kira thinks too. She's decided to try to do another painting of her and see what happens."

"Probably not a bad idea, as long as you're there when she does."

Sean smiled. "Yes sir, that's exactly what I told her."

"Well, the only other advice I'd give you is not to forget your own gift, Sean. For as much as we try to deal with the problems of having it, there are moments when it can be quite useful. Life saving in yours and Kira's case, I think."

"Thanks dad, I will." Life saving? Sean's heart skipped a beat as he considered the possibility of losing Kira.

They chatted for a few more minutes about what was going on in Aubrey's life, which centered around the problems with and prognosis for the stock market. When they hung up, Sean was left with a warm sensation again and reflected on the thought that he'd never had the opportunity to feel this way with his adopted dad, and what a nice feeling it was.

By this time, Sean was sitting in the driveway in the truck, and as he opened the door he wondered if Kira had seen him sitting there wondering what the heck he was doing. Sure enough when he walked in, he found he was half right.

"Talking to your dad, were you?" She began.

"Yep, and he agrees with you. He doesn't think she's given up or become distracted. As a matter of fact, he suggested she was taking her time now to throw us off her scent."

Kira was nodding and smiling. "You really enjoy talking to him don't you?"

"Yeah, it gives me a sort of sense of belonging that I've never felt before. Well, not until I met you anyway." That comment earned him a protracted hug.

~

It was about 5:30 that afternoon when Kira decided to go ahead and start the painting. The day had waxed hot, and Sean had come back in from the fields about forty-five minutes before, dripping with sweat. He'd smiled at her in the kitchen as he'd come in and swiveled with a determined step toward the upstairs bathroom.

"No kisses till after I shower," he mentioned as he passed her, smiling.

"You think I'm afraid of a little sweat?"

"Oh, alright then," He turned back toward her reaching out his arms. Kira squealed and ran with Sean chasing her for about four steps.

"Not scared, huh?"

"Okay, I lied. Go take a shower."

Kira was tickled by her own chagrin as she watched Sean chuckle and bound up the steps.

Kira had heard the shower water stop a few minutes back and knew Sean would be down shortly. She'd removed Beth's painting from the easel, and set it under the window on the floor.

It was nearly complete, and she felt good about it. Beth would be pleased.

Rather than a canvas, she placed her large sketch pad on the easel.

She'd thought about this, and had the feeling that she wasn't going to get very far anyway, so she didn't want to actually bother with paint. Pencil and charcoal would do fine for this attempt.

Standing in front of the easel, she hesitated. She found that she really didn't want to start without Sean being close. While she waited, her memory drug up images of her worst experience with Jason's painting. Surely nothing could be worse than those . . . but still, she worried that something different might happen, something she couldn't imagine, and the fear blossomed. He'd be down in a minute.

When she heard him on the stairs, she raised her pencil to the sketchbook and began to draw. She let her mind drift to the details she remembered of Poena's face. The oval face, the long dark hair, high cheek bones . . . The slender nose was giving her a bit of a problem when she noticed her hand was sweating. Pausing briefly, she put her pencil into her left hand and wiped her right one on her jeans leg. As she took the pencil back and touched it again to the paper, she realized her hand was getting even hotter. It wasn't like she touched something hot though, it was more like the blood inside her fingers was heating up. She'd barely managed two more lines drawn before the heat had ratcheted up to the point of pain. Still she drew. Sean, who had quietly seated himself on the couch beside her, stirred.

As the pain in her hand began to feel like her own personal bonfire, an image appeared in her mind. It was Poena. She was in a vehicle driving. It was a truck. No sooner had the image formed in her mind than Kira saw the expression on Poena's face change. The face had been passive a moment ago, but now she saw the brows furrow and the jaw muscles tense. Anger swept across that beautiful countenance and quickly escalated to rage.

Sean was off the couch a split second before Kira screamed and dropped the pencil.

The pain had gone from bonfire to nuclear, and she backed off the stool so fast she tripped and would have slammed her head into the coffee table if Sean hadn't already been there.

"My hand!" She yelled as Sean dove across the coffee table catching her in his arms, altering her trajectory, and carrying them both gently to the floor. "It's burning!"

Sean didn't hesitate to discern what she could be talking about. He simply got up, carried her into the kitchen, turned on the water in the sink and shoved her hand into it as he set her down. Without even the slightest hesitation he turned to the refrigerator and came back with two handfuls of ice and dropped them into the other side of the sink. He stoppered the drain, shifting the faucet and Kira's hand at the same time letting the water begin to fill it.

~

Poena nearly gasped before her rage replaced her surprise. That damn woman was trying to see her again! How could she do that? Then the rage displaced clear thought, and all Poena could think of was that she was heading there now, and she'd burn that bitch and her boyfriend and their house and be done with them.

~

Sean still stood silently by the sink gently holding Kira's hand in the cold water. He'd fetched another couple of handfuls of ice, then simply stood with her holding her hand at the wrist.

"Is it any better?"

"Yeah. It's finally starting to cool . . . She's coming Sean. I saw her driving a truck. I'm afraid that trying to draw her might have hurried her up a bit."

"Good. I'm getting tired of thinking about this hag. The sooner she gets here the sooner we'll be done with her."

As Sean gently pulled Kira's hand back out of the ice water, Kira began to sob. The sensation of sadness and fear had struck him a split second before her sobs, and he was already reaching his arm around her and walking her towards the nearest chair.

"It's alright Kira. It's alright. It's over for now."

At least now they knew, and Sean's mind was working furiously on how else he could prepare for it.

After she left New Orleans, she drove straight through Mississippi up to Memphis, where she found a small back road on the Arkansas side of the river to dump the woman's body. She was tired of sitting beside the stiffening corpse.

She was careful to remove all of her ID before simply slipping the woman into the dark swirling waters of the mighty Mississippi. When somebody did find her, she'd probably be miles downstream and even then they'd play hell ever identifying her, and that's assuming some monster catfish didn't save everyone the trouble. Poena figured she wouldn't have to worry about anyone reporting the truck missing, either. It was perfect.

She went back across the great old suspension bridge into Memphis and ended up staying at some flea bitten dive off of Beal Street for twenty-five dollars a night. The sounds of the partiers in the downtown area filtered easily through the paper thin walls, but Poena found the noise of other's activity comforting somehow, though late in the evening the sounds seemed to transform into the screams of the tortured and dying from one of Grandpa's stories. She awoke sweating; clutching the filet knife she kept under her pillow.

For the next few days, she spent her time wandering around the back roads of Arkansas taking in the scenery, pondering her grandpa's most recent words and wondering even more why they had stopped. There seemed to be no answer, so she let her thoughts meander back to the scenery and found herself thoroughly surprised to discover that the state of Arkansas was so beautiful. No one ever seemed to associate scenic beauty with this state, she thought.

At any rate, there were plenty of cheap, out-of-the way, little drive-in motels that didn't seem to care if she had a credit card or not, as long as she had some cash. The only drawback to these little back-waterholes-in-the-wall was her beauty. She could tell by the looks she got, especially at the little diners, that many of these hill people weren't likely to forget her face. It didn't matter, she decided, she'd never pass this way again, anyway.

~

The days trickled by peacefully. She wandered up highway 65 out of Arkansas, almost to Branson, Missouri until that bitch intruded on her thoughts.

Now Poena realized that the time for delay was over. She was certain they knew she was coming, and the best thing she could do was get there as quickly as possible.

If she pushed it, she could be there in three hours.

Kira was exhausted. The pain in her hand had subsided with a little time and a couple of glasses of the wine Sean had bought. Sean had had a couple with her. She was more than a little surprised the incident didn't leave a mark on her hand, just in her mind. Sean displayed no surprise at all.

"Sean, what is going on with this woman? I mean I'm not even painting with ashes or anything, but every time I try to draw her we connect. It's weird. I guess I should be glad that she can't seem to connect to me on her own. It's only when I try to draw or paint her."

Sean sat there for a minute just holding Kira on the couch. He didn't like the thought that had crossed his mind at her words.

More of a question really, and the question was 'could she'? Could Poena connect to Kira by herself and Kira not know it? He fervently hoped not.

Kira, snuggling into him, redirected his thoughts. He turned to face her and found her lips already heading in his direction. After a sweet, soft, lingering kiss, she gazed up into his eyes.

"I love you, Sean Easton. In such a short time I find myself wondering how I ever managed to live without you all these years."

As was becoming the norm when dealing with Kira, Sean found the emotions coming from her much more overwhelming than the words themselves. To his surprise and embarrassment he realized he was tearing up. In an attempt to hide the unmanly moisture, he kissed her again.

This one, however, was several steps further up the ladder on the passion scale, and he realized that it was more than just her he was heating up.

~

Kira purposely ignored the glistening in Sean's eyes and let her self sink into the passion of his kiss. She had never met a man remotely as sensitive as this one, who could still evoke her femininity with the depth of his masculine aura. He was smart, brave, industrious and quick thinking. How oh how could she have been so lucky? It was not as if she hadn't been exposed to a lot of men, either. In her years as a model they virtually flocked to her. But none had captured her imagination and heart like this amazing Kansas farm boy. All these thoughts melted into the back ground as Sean lifted her from the couch in his arms and slowly ascended the staircase still kissing her.

Kira's mind and body were responding so strongly that clear thought dissipated into the heat and moistness between her thighs. As he laid her on their bed and began to undress her, the world narrowed to tactile sensation only, and she responded with excited abandon.

Sean thought he was going to explode. He wanted to tear her clothes off, he was so excited.

Making love to Kira had proved to be a new experience for him, not that he hadn't been with other women, but with Kira there was a new dimension. There was a powerful desire for closeness beyond just the physical gratification. It was as though being inside her was just one more way to be as close to this woman as possible. Yet even that seemed to fall short. In Sean's mind he couldn't possibly ever be as close to Kira mentally or physically as he wanted, but as he pulled her jeans off her shapely legs he was reminded it was OH so fun to try.

An hour or so and another glass or two of wine later, they lay tangled up in each other, completely spent and asleep. For the moment Poena was forgotten.

Poena was hyper alert as she slowly steered the pickup down the long gravel driveway leading up to the house. She'd already circled the area several times and had found this road leading to the back of the property. It was the property diagonally connected to the back of Kira's new address. The boy's house, she figured. The crunching of the tires over the gravel sounded like artillery in her ears, and she was glad that the dilapidated old house at the end of this long road was abandoned.

She parked the car at the end of the road after turning it to face back out. She then turned the lights and the engine off, grabbed her backpack, got out, and just listened. Thunder rolled in the distance and the outlines of the clouds intermittently assumed eerie shapes as the accompanying lightening lit them from behind. The wind howling through the trees would cover the noise of her passage.

She took one look back at the big old house. Lightning silhouetted it briefly. It must have been a hundred years old and looked to have not been lived in for half that long. She liked old things. Something she maybe picked up from Grandpa. Smiling, she turned again and with the wind blowing her long hair back, she began to walk.

~

In her dreams Kira was walking in the woods behind the house. The wind was whipping her hair and making shadows dance across the entire canopy of trees like a procession of ghosts. Her steps were slow and metered with her shoulders back and her arms trailing behind her. She pictured photos she'd seen of woodland fairies tip-toeing through the forest in green gossamer grace with sparkles and lights all around.

But somewhere in this forest was a shadow stalking the fairy, stealthily approaching with dark, dangerous steps. Lightning flashed and for an instant all the shadows froze in place, seeming to suspend the entire forest in a moment of time. Tip-toeing she walked, not knowing where she was bound and less concerned with that than with the approaching shadow.

Closer it came and she could sense its malintent growing in her mind; growing as it drew closer. Black evil expanding in her awareness with every step she took. Another lightning flash and again the shadows froze. This time, though, the wind seemed to battle the momentary stillness with a renewed fury. Thunder exploded and the vibrations of it sent ripples through her very bones. Almost there. She could feel it was almost upon her. Another lightning flash, and there before her, framed by the twisted shadows of the night, was a figure in black with long black her whipping wildly in the wind. One arm thrown out to her side, fingers splayed, and the other, raised above her head holding a knife. So strong was the light reflecting from the smooth metal surface, it seemed she held a bolt of lightning. Her gaze shifted to the face, contorted in a snarl of malevolent glee. The knife began to move. She wanted to dodge, run, anything, but her feet felt frozen in time as the lightning bolt accelerated towards her.

~

Poena waited a hundred yards away in the woods. She'd been waiting for hours. The impending storm had released its rain for a few moments then subsided, and the cover of the trees had kept her even drier than she'd hoped for. Her black runner's suit helped to shed the water and her black hair was already dry from being blown by the gusting wind. Glancing up at the sky, she watched the low dark cloud shapes race away. The wind was even stronger up there than on the ground.

She glanced at her watch; 3:55am. It was time. She'd chosen her location not only for the cover of the trees but also due to its position downwind from the horses. She'd heard them on her approach and hoped the wind wouldn't change directions. So far it hadn't. She didn't need any nickering horses alerting them of her approach as they'd alerted her of their presence. She eased out from the canopy of trees, merely another moving shadow in the tempestuous evening.

"No, Poena. The Source; you must go to the source!"

Her footsteps froze. Damn! Grandpa again. What was going on? Why was he now so insistent and what *is* the source? Waiting momentarily for more from Grandpa, she resumed her silent steps when she decided he was finished. She'd be through here shortly and could take the time to figure out what Grandpa was trying to tell her.

She scanned the terrain ahead of her for any sign of life. No lights were on at the farm house, but there were two vehicles in the driveway. Perfect she thought. They were both home.

Moving up to the side of the house, she paused. Farm smells, she thought. How can anyone live around that? She smiled. It would all smell different soon enough. Another bolt of lightning framed her in the night. She froze. All in black, standing still, she presented just another shadow in the night.

Finally, she approached the back door. The horses hadn't nickered and the storm was still approaching. The thunder and lightning were getting closer together. She set her small backpack down.

Whatever it was she was going to have to do to get in, she was certain that doing it to the back door was a much better idea.

Opening her pack, she searched and searched, then realized her first mistake; she'd forgotten her pick set. Damn! She tried the door, and it seemed both the latch and the deadbolt were engaged. Picking her backpack up once more, she moved around the back of the house checking the windows as she went. She finally stopped at a large den window. She could see the latch above her. It was unlocked, but at this section of the house the ground sloped away and the window sill was near the top of her reach.

Poena smiled as she slipped her pack from her shoulder. This was proof that her delay had accomplished what she intended. Surely if they still expected her they wouldn't have left a window unlocked.

She reached up and pushed on the window which gave way smoothly. Next she released one strap from its bottom buckle which allowed her to put the pack through, and slowly lower it to the floor. She then grabbed the window sill with both hands and smoothly pulled herself through the opening. Lifting her weight gave her no pause whatsoever, and her incredible agility added whole new dimensions to her ability at stealth.

As she stood up and silently slid her pack back onto her shoulder, thunder cracked again. The wind and the thunder were doing a tremendous job of covering her approach, but she needed to close the window quickly before the wind disturbed something inside the house. Her only concern was for the occupants of the house. In a rural area such as this, even the closest neighbors could be as much as a mile away.

Still, she waited almost thirty long seconds, straining her ears for the slightest sound before stepping any further into the house. An unlocked window, she thought again as she waited.

"Country hicks," she murmured into the night, then again began to move.

She stepped through into the kitchen and slowly pulled a small Maglite from her pouch.

Switching it on, she was careful to keep the beam pointed down so as not to have any strange lights showing through the windows. That could attract attention from even further away than a noise. Well, probably not in this area, but caution was her habit, and she intended to stick with it.

As she moved slowly through the house she played the flashlight around, more out of curiosity than anything else. She wanted some clue as to how these people had tracked her and why. The flashlight beam slid across the coffee table where she noticed a loose piece of paper. It looked like a proof for an Ad. Picking it up with a gloved hand she read: A dignified approach to the preservation of cremains. Canvas of Life.

What the heck was the Canvas of Life? Hmmm . . . cremains? Must be the ashes from cremation, but what did that have to do with a painting? She walked further through the house noticing the painting on the wall. It was of a man sitting in a rocking chair on the front porch of . . . this house. Then the man must be a relative of Kira's boyfriend; his father maybe. It didn't look like an ordinary painting, though. It had much more texture to it. Like the paint used was extra thick. Wait a minute, was this Kira woman mixing those ashes with her paints?

Canvas of Life. That made sense. What an interesting idea, Poena thought, mixing the ashes of the dead with paint and doing paintings from it.

Thinking back on all the brass urns she'd seen at the funeral home, she decided that she really liked this idea. She almost wished she could have done that for Grandpa, but he was adamant about not being cremated and given his stories she guessed she understood that.

The more Poena thought about it the more she felt a kind of kinship with this Kira woman. She worked with the ashes of the deceased, too. But that's where it stopped, Poena thought. Kira didn't work with the flames, and *they* were the life force, not what was left after the flames departed.

Her flashlight continued to dance around, and it settled on an open sketchbook standing on an easel. She froze. Poena hadn't spent much time looking at herself in the mirror. As a matter of fact, she went out of her way to ignore how attractive she was, but she knew her face well enough to recognize the partial likeness of her standing there on that easel. Was that how Kira was doing it? Did the attempt to draw her, connect them? Suddenly, she was certain of the truth and even more certain of why this woman had to die.

"No Poena. Not here."

The voice in her head made her jump. Or was it in her head? She couldn't tell anymore. Before arriving at the farm, she hadn't heard his voice in days and the abrupt change had startled her. First he leaves her and now he gets insistent? Why? And what did he mean? But the jolt made her abruptly realize she was wasting too much time, possibly time she didn't have. So she resumed moving through the house. She needed to make a few preparations, find the master bedroom, then finish this.

Mute lightning suddenly lit every window in the house causing her to flinch, then freeze. Her jump suit and mask seemed to absorb the light making her nearly invisible when she didn't move. For seem reason she didn't even understand, Poena removed her mask and tucked it in her shirt. It was something she had never done before. Five full seconds later a great peal of thunder rocked the old farmhouse on its foundations. Poena felt the vibrations through the soles of her feet as she listened for movement from upstairs. While she froze she thought about her carved mask. It was plain now, awaiting the face that she would soon use to adorn it. She listened again. Nothing but the wind. Like a wraith in a basement she crept toward the staircase.

~

He was in a place of darkness, and it was calm. A gentle fog rose up to his knees and little wisps of it wafted up like ghostly tendrils reaching ever higher to tickle his torso. The quiet was eerie, and as he turned his head in an attempt to make sense of his surroundings he saw impossibly tall fences in the distance. Chain link, topped with razor wire.

Cruel, forbidding barriers that whispered of rent flesh and agony. As he looked, the fog seemed to follow his gaze and flow up the base of the forsaken fence.

Continuing to walk, he was struck again by the silence of his own footsteps. It was as though the fog itself was swallowing the sound. Fear lanced through him. Where was he? Something was approaching, he thought suddenly, but still there was no sound. He made several more footsteps, continuing mindlessly to approach the fence. He was looking for a gate, but the fence stretched first into the fog and then into the gloom in the distance. No break to be found. Fear again. And then from nowhere a sudden burst of thunder exploded causing his heart to jump wildly. He wasn't sure if it was in his dream or not, but as the lightning followed on its heels he abruptly knew Kira was in danger. Sensing a presence he whirled to find the threat but only the swirling fog met his gaze.

No. Not the dream.

Something else . . .

A KNIFE! He had to . . . !

~

Sean reached up before his eyes opened, and even before they could focus, his fingers were clutching a descending wrist holding the knife. The outside light shown through the window, reflecting off the gleaming blade he'd miraculously arrested. His eyes focused on the attacker above him leaning over the bed. The figure standing there in black with a flap of black fabric stuffed in the collar of her blouse startled him with her beauty, then made his heart quail. Evil flowed from her in great ebony waves. If ever Sean wished for his gift to be gone this was it. The hateful intent streaming from her made his stomach clench even as he realized she was trying to pull her hand back from his grasp.

Kira's scream punctuated the instant as Sean reached up with his other hand to try to take the knife. She was strong, but Sean was stronger. He sat up further letting the covers fall from his naked body and prepared to lunge at the woman.

~

Damn, Poena thought, how did he do that? He had awakened at the very instant she was about to end the girl's life, and his hand had reached for her even before his eyes had opened.

If she hadn't seen it with her own eyes, she wouldn't have believed it. And now he had a grip on her and a damn strong one too. She smiled to herself. She wasn't through, yet. There were a few surprises still awaiting this country hick.

~

Sean made the lunge forward grabbing Poena's wrist. The blade nicked his arm as she pulled back, but the maneuver caused it to slip from her hand. She continued to pull and to Sean's surprise, grabbed his wrist with her other hand. Sean was still lunging forward while she twisted his wrist and continued pulling. In a split second, he realized he was losing his balance and the second after that his wrist was being painfully contorted while she turned her back to him and continued to use his momentum to yank.

With both her hands still engaged with his, she dove off the bed and ducked her head to roll. Sean's hands were so totally entangled that rolling wasn't an option for him even if he'd thought of it, so he found himself suddenly flying through the air over her head. He also had no time to react when she abruptly released her grip causing his head to smash into the dresser against the wall. Lights exploded behind his eyes, then nearly went out.

Dimly he heard Kira scream again as he picked up Poena's thought.

"Now burn!" Came through to him like a pistol shot.

"NO!" He yelled, looking up in time to see her strike an entire book of matches and flick them towards the bed. In the bright flash he saw the line of powder just under the edges of the bed and was already diving towards Kira before the matches ever landed.

Taking a cue from the painful lesson he'd just learned he used his momentum to knock Kira from the bed and continued to roll with her towards the corner of the room, feeling the breath leave her and dimly hoping his spontaneous maneuver hadn't seriously hurt her.

Swinging his head back towards the bed, he heard the sizzle of flames; his eyes caught the black figure darting for the door just before the blinding white flash blocked out all other sights. It was like a hundred camera flashes all exploding at the same instant. The effect was as disorienting as a military flash-bang grenade.

They still had to get themselves out, and if they hurried they could just make it to the door before flames blocked them. And maybe not lose the chance to catch that witch.

Lifting Kira up, he realized they were still both naked. No time to worry about that at the moment, he thought. He almost drug her with him, angling sharply toward the door, and it occurred to Sean that she was acting particularly bewildered. As they stepped through the portal Sean turned to her.

"Try to do something about the fire. I'm going after Poena." When she didn't respond Sean shook her gently lowering his head to catch her eyes.

"Kira? Kira. Come on! We have to move!"

Either the raised voice or the shaking did it, and he saw focus come back into her eyes. Sean actually felt her thoughts coalesce. It was an odd sensation, but he wasted no more time. Releasing her abruptly, he turned and ran.

~

Kira couldn't believe how bright the initial flash had been. What the hell was that? And she could barely get her mind around the last couple of minutes. Her mind had been jolted from that nightmare in time to see Sean already holding Poena's knife above them and fighting. It made it difficult to tell where the nightmare stopped and the living nightmare began.

The flames were already reaching from the bed to the walls and ceiling. In a bare few seconds the bedroom was going up before her eyes.

The thought of getting the hose crossed her mind, but it was too little too late. She raced to the phone downstairs. Her cell phone, on the bedside table, was already engulfed.

"911 operator." The voice on other line said.

"Fire," Kira yelled, "at the Easton ranch." She gave the drowsy sounding woman the address and hung up, only then remembering she was naked. All her clothes were in that bedroom. But there was a coat in the coat closet. Grabbing it, she raced outside to get the hose, not at all sure if it would be of any use, but she didn't know what else to do. Outside, Sean was nowhere to be seen, and she could hear the horses bumping and neighing in the barn. The smell of smoke was already scaring them.

~

Sean never saw Poena leave the house but, naked, he charged unerringly into the woods. Once again he was following the trail of her thoughts.

Frustration, fury, determination all led him as surely as a leash. He'd been on this trail before though, he thought, chasing this woman, and she'd out run him then. But no, she hadn't out run him, she had out climbed him. He'd been closing on her in that subdivision in Virginia until she'd gone over those fences. "Well, there are no fences now, and it's dark and these are *my* woods."

~

The only thing abating Poena's fury as she raced through these God forsaken woods was the sound of her grandpa's voice.

"To the source, Poena." He said, and he'd been right about trying to finish it here. That man-devil must be reading her mind. How could he possibly catch a knife *before* he woke up? It was crazy. But her thoughts were interrupted again.

245

"It ends where it began, Poena. Come find me."

What the hell did that mean?

"The first is the last but you must find me."

Poena was listening to Grandpa so intently she barely managed to duck a low hanging branch. But her frustration was at such a crescendo she found herself yelling out loud.

"Where, Grandpa, where?" She was shocked to hear her own voice and even more disconcerted by how far it seemed to carry. She had to hurry; she had a feeling that boy would be trying to chase her.

The pickup was parked just beyond the fence on the back of the property. Once she was there she'd be free. Panting hard, she tried to listen for pursuit, but surely if they weren't burned, and somehow she didn't believe they were, then they'd be fighting the flames. No. The boy would follow. As the thought crossed her mind, she heard the faint sound of a siren in the distance. They were already coming. She strained her ears again and caught the sound of another passage through the woods.

That damn boy. She'd been right. The barbwire fence was just ahead, and she could see the truck, but she wanted to slow this asshole down first, maybe even kill him this time. She'd lost her knife somewhere in the woods, but it wasn't necessary for what she had in mind.

In one smooth motion, she reversed her direction and ran back toward where she'd heard that last sound. A huge oak dead ahead was exactly what she needed. She ran straight to it, stopped and spun so her back was to the tree and again listened. He was coming.

~

Racing through the woods on bare feet wasn't the best of ideas, and Sean knew he was losing ground. He looked up to see if he could make out his quarry when her voice rang out in the night.

"Where, Grandpa, where?"

Sean was so shocked to hear her voice he slowed down briefly. It was a rich, melodious voice and somehow seemed wrong coming from something so wicked. And why was she yelling at her grandpa? He redoubled his speed, ignoring the damage it was doing to his feet.

~

She'd picked the right spot she was almost certain. It was a bare few seconds before Poena heard him racing toward the tree she was behind.

As he flashed by, she swung her arm back intending to catch him in the throat with the knife edge of her hand. But years of running through the woods had taught Sean the danger of running straight up, especially in the night, so he'd been in a partial crouch when her arm lashed out.

A split second before the impact, he caught the thought of her intentions coming from her, but it was too late to adjust. The thought had barely registered before her hand impacted with his nose, and another blinding flash struck him, this one from inside his head as his nose made a crunching sound. His feet flew out from under him, and he landed hard on his back, the air leaving him. His own blood nearly choked him when he tried to draw a breath until he thought to open his mouth to let in a great gulp of air.

~

"DAMN!" Poena yelled as she realized she'd missed his throat. But she watched as his body sped past her, feet swinging up and out in front, then landing flat on his back. It was the perfect time to run, but something stopped her. Was it his naked muscled form lying there on the ground or something else?

Poena froze. He lay there groaning and an impulse took her. She jumped over his body and came down straddling him, intending to choke him. He barely moved, but she was surprised that he was conscious at all. Between the obvious damage done to his nose and the impact of his landing on the hard ground, he should have been unconscious.

As she reached for his throat another urge seized her, and she bent down and kissed him solidly on the mouth.

Shocked beyond words at her own action, she jumped back up and turned to the barbwire fence. Racing toward it, rather than slowing, she accelerated and dove over the top of the fence, rolling in the grass and coming to her feet fluidly, reaching for her keys. She took one more glance back at the boy, well he wasn't a boy was he, still lying there naked on the ground. A smile played across her face for a second, but as she opened the door to the vehicle, Grandpa finally answered her earlier question.

"Dachau, Poena. Find me at Dachau."

Stunned, she paused a second. Dachau? The prison camp he'd told her about from the war. The one where he and Rebecca were imprisoned. Alright then, now she knew. She started the truck and roared off through the field.

~

Struggling with the pain and shock, Sean still managed to look up just in time to see her break free of the woods and launch herself over the barb wire fence in the distance. He'd been closer than he thought. But when his eyes locked on the vehicle, he knew it was useless. He could barely move, and even if he wasn't hurt it was too late. He slowly began mopping the blood and tears from his face and eyes. He took several slow, deep breaths trying to calm down and think.

Then something began to tug at the back of his mind. Something about the way she turned her head... Did it remind him of... but the thought was interrupted as another powerful thought came from Poena, a thought just as clear as her words had been a moment before.

Dachau. Find me at Dachau.

Where was Dachau? What was Dauchau? The engine roared to life, tires spewed gravel, and she was gone.

The sirens howling in the distance were getting closer.

The house.

He needed to get back.

~

Kira's pathetic attempts with the garden hose had been more than futile. The flames had simply spread too fast. By the time the fire department got there, the upper stories were thoroughly ablaze, and Kira was beginning to worry about Sean.

In a burst of forethought she'd grabbed a long raincoat looking thing, called a duster, from the closet when she'd grabbed the other long coat for herself. It was pretty certain that he'd bolted out of the house naked, as well. And both their clothes were gone. She kept glancing back over her shoulder at the woods hoping to catch a glimpse of Sean returning.

Flashes of that knife above her being arrested by Sean's two handed grip kept coming back to her mind. It was amazing. He must have picked up Poena's thoughts from his sleep. He certainly wouldn't have laid there awake waiting for her to get that close.

Sirens blared and lights played across the house. There were three fire trucks arriving now, and they were getting the blaze under control. She'd only talked to one fireman, and he'd merely asked if anyone else was in the house, before returning to his truck. Other questions could wait for later, she figured. He barely glanced at her odd attire. She imagined he'd probably seen worse.

Thinking of Sean again generated another glance back towards the woods. There he was behind a tree apparently trying to decide whether to walk up to the group naked or not. She smiled at him and moved towards the edge of the woods.

Holding out the garment for him as she approached, Sean finally stepped out from behind the tree and took it.

Kira gasped, "My God, Sean, what happened to your nose?"

"She waylaid me from behind a tree. I'm lucky. I think she was aiming for my throat." Now he found that he was feeling a bit sheepish about letting Poena out maneuver him again, so he changed the subject.

"Boy, that crazy woman can sure clear a fence fast."

"Got away again, huh?" Kira asked rhetorically. She was caught between admiring him as he donned the slicker and worrying about his nose. She put an arm around his waist as they began walking back towards the house and a wave of sadness took her as she looked on.

"She had a car waiting on the other side of the fence," he began, as his eyes focused on the flames lighting the night. "Oh my God."

Now Kira forgot her own feelings of sadness and instead felt sad for him. Even though it was her home too, it didn't hold a lifetime of memories for her like it did for Sean. Wordlessly, she squeezed him tighter as he walked slowly towards the fire trucks.

~

The reflection of the flames flickered across Sean's face as he watched the only home he'd ever known, burn down. Emotions flickered inside of him as well seeming in tempo with the light. Bitterness, regret and nostalgia all sought to gain ground in his heart, but with Kira standing by his side they all faded into the background. It was just a new beginning.

~

"I did the best I could, Sean. I got the garden hose out after I called 911 but it didn't do much good. That stuff she uses sure burns fast."

"And hot too. That was the magnesium Josh told me about."

"Magnesium?" Sean hadn't gotten around to mentioning that little fact to her.

"Yeah, he figured out that the accelerant she was using was magnesium powder."

"And that's what she planned to use to burn us alive in our beds?"

"Yep."

"It would've worked too," she continued, "if you hadn't of swept me out of the bed so fast. You must have been reading her thoughts. Were you?"

Sean turned to face her. "Yeah, even before I woke up. Before she raised that knife, before she threw those matches and then *after* she dove over that fence."

"After? What other thought did you get from her?"

"Well, it wasn't just a thought. While I was chasing her through the woods I heard her yell, 'Where, Grandpa, where?' and then when she was about to get in the car I got a thought from her." Sean paused thinking back, "At least I think it was from her . . . it must have been . . ."

Sean lingered a moment thinking.

"Well? What did she say . . . er . . . think?" Kira's impatience urged.

Sean's eyes seemed to come back into focus, and he locked gazes with Kira, then spoke.

"Dachau, she said. I think she's going to someplace called Dachau."

"Good Lord," Kira said.

"Do you know where Dachau is?" he asked.

Kira was shocked. "You mean you don't?"

"No clue."

"Didn't you study any history in college? Dachau was one of the more notorious German prison camps in World War II. The only one that was more infamous was Auschwitz."

"I do remember reading about Auschwitz. Don't know how I missed Dachau. And I wonder why the hell she was yelling out loud to her grandpa."

"Yeah. What's up with that?"

"I don't know, but I'm almost certain that's where she's going."

"What do you wanna do?" Her eyes followed his gaze. They were both staring at the house. The flames were almost out and one of the fire trucks had already left.

"Well, for starters, why don't we go see what's left of our home. And somewhere in there we might want to think about some clothes."

Kira smiled at him and in unspoken agreement they began moving back to the house. "I bet we're going to have to answer a few questions, too."

Sean just nodded.

They were still about seventy five feet away when one of the firemen caught sight of them and started walking their direction. It was the same one that had asked Kira earlier if anyone else was in the house.

"Hello there," he said approaching.

"Hi," Sean answered.

"I guess you're the other one that lived here? . . . Oh wow, what happened to your nose?"

"Uh, I ran into a branch in the woods and yeah, I lived here." Sean said, noticing his use of the past tense and hoping this guy wouldn't ask any more questions about his nose.

"Well, hopefully it's not broken. Uh, I'm Billy Creighton, fire chief. I'm really sorry about your home. We did our best, but that fire was burning fast. Aren't you Jason Easton's boy?"

Sean paused for a second considering the question about his adopted dad, before answering simply, "Yeah, that's me."

"Well, I sure am sorry. Do you have any idea what caused it?"

"Yes, I do. It was intentional; an arsonist that was trying to kill us. She used magnesium powder to set our bed on fire."

Billy's jaw dropped, and it was several seconds before he responded, his words falling all over themselves. "Holy SHIT! Magnesium powder? Where would she . . . she? An arsonist? How did . . . Wait a minute, maybe we should wait till we can sit down to go over this." The guy's general level of shock at Sean's prompt answer was such that the part about attempted murder seemed to have slipped by completely.

Sean barely noticed the shock and surprise coming from the guy. He was too worn out. Instead, he just kept drifting towards the house holding Kira as he spoke. "Yeah sure, we can do that."

The first floor was still standing but most of the second floor and the roof were gone. Wisps of smoke wafted up from the corners and the smell of wet char filled the cool night air.

"Our home is gone, Kira." It was a simple statement, but Sean gathered a weight-of-the-world sensation from Kira, nevertheless. She understood.

"Our home is with each other, Sean, and that's still intact . . . thank God"

It wasn't her words so much that turned Sean's head, but the feelings and images he got from her as she said them.

Tears were already running down his dirty cheeks as he turned to her and smiled. "Thank God is right, sweetheart. Thank God for you."

Kira's tears were already answering Sean's even before his reply, but as a new thought from her struck him, they came down full force, and she hugged him fiercely.

"This is my fault," she finally said.

In a voice tinged with anger Sean answered. "You're not an arsonist, Kira. Poena is. The only thing you've done is agree to try and stop a monster. Don't you dare feel guilty around me."

Kira lifted her head from Sean's shoulders, surprise at the fierceness of his tone evident in her expression, and squeezed a smile out from behind her tears. "Thank you."

With the steel still clinging to his voice Sean continued. "And we're going to stop this monster too, dammit. Kira, have you ever been to Germany?"

Sean felt fear laced with determination coming from her before she finally answered. He heard the words in his ears and mind in sort of an out of sync stereo effect. Sean just smiled because there was nothing left to explain.

"It's beautiful this time of year," she answered. A smile bloomed at the corners of her mouth, but her eyes reflected the hint of steel in Sean's voice.

"Good, I guess we're going to Germany then."

"Shouldn't we call Josh?" Kira asked tentatively.

"And have him tell us we are crazy while Poena gets away? And even if he did believe us, do you think he would be able to convince the

German authorities based on yours and my gifts? No. If Poena is going to be caught it is going to have to be you and I doing the catching."

Kira simply nodded in agreement.

They had continued to drift closer to the house when another fireman called out to them.

"Folks, I wouldn't be walking into that rubble with bare feet. If you don't get cut you'll darn sure get burned."

Sean and Kira stopped abruptly, looked down and then turned to each other sheepishly, and laughed. "Maybe we should find some clothes first," Kira offered.

Another fireman yelled from inside the house. "Hey Billy, come look at this!"

Sean and Kira circled to where one of the walls was burned through, allowing them to see into the den where the other fireman awaited. As Billy crossed over to him, Kira and Sean could clearly see what had so attracted his attention. There on the wall was the picture of Sean's adopted dad, Jason, the one Kira had painted with the man's ashes. It was completely unscathed. While the firemen chatted excitedly about the phenomenon Sean turned to Kira grinning.

"Kind of nice to have a fireproof painting, huh?"

"Yeah, but it's not like this was news or anything," she answered smiling back, remembering their first experience with it.

"Ain't that the truth." They both chuckled, causing odd looks from the firemen in earshot.

At that moment the edge of the sun peeked up over the horizon between some low lying clouds. Red-gold beams lanced through the woods and cast a beautiful but eerie light on the remains of the house and the barn. It seemed to catch everyone's attention for just a moment and a general silence ensued. Then the rooster crowed.

"Okay boys, let's go," the fire chief yelled to the others, then turned back to Sean and Kira. "And could ya'll come in to town and give me the details on this a little later?"

"Sure," Sean said. "As soon as we pick up some clothes."

~

Fortunately, the Wal-Mart was already open. Sean sensed Kira's distaste at the styles available, and Sean had to repress a snicker. Some vestiges of the fashion world never dissipate.

The funny looks they had received when they marched into Wal-Mart, barefoot wearing a long coat and a rain slicker, with Sean's eyes beginning to blacken, were augmented when Sean paid for their articles with a crisp hundred dollar bill he kept in the glove box of his truck for emergencies. They changed in the car and used the last of the hundred at McDonald's getting coffee and Egg McMuffins while they waited for the bank to open. Fortunately, it was a small town and Sean had been banking there for years. With his wallet lost in the fire, he was forced to use the drive through and actually talk to someone. The teller knew him, however, and with a brief explanation that brought groans of sympathy, she cashed a temporary check for him.

They were both pensive as they drove away, the shock continuing to settle in.

"Kira, I wonder what this deal with her Grandpa is."

"Grandpa?"

"Yeah, I told you, remember? Just before she dove over that fence like some kind of circus performer or something, She stopped and yelled, 'Where, Grandpa, where'?

"Oh yeah," Kira answered, "I do remember you telling me that."

"Well, is she hearing voices in her head or what? And I guess maybe the next thought I got was ... what ... Grandpa answering? Dachau? I think this woman is a certifiable nut case."

Kira was quiet for a moment. "Do you think these voices in her head might be her motivation for the fires?"

"I guess they could be, but anything could be with a whacko like that."

"Hmmm," Kira mumbled, thinking, "do you think her grandpa might have worked in Dachau?"

"Well, Josh said her last name was Maslin. That sounds Jewish to me, not German."

"My God!" Kira said suddenly, swallowing another bite. "What if he *was* a prisoner there? What if this is all some sort of retribution for her grandpa?"

"That would mean all the victims would have to be German wouldn't it?"

Kira turned to Sean, eyes wide. "We should call Josh and ask him to check on it."

"If she's going to Germany, what difference does it make? Which reminds me, if we're going to Germany, we're going to have to get passports. Hell, we're going to have to get IDs and credit cards for that matter."

"Well let's just hope that she's got to get one, too. Otherwise we'll never catch her there. As far as what difference it makes, I don't know about you, but if we're going to run off chasing this lunatic, I want every bit of info I can get on her, don't you?"

Sean's head nodded in agreement as he finished his last bite of sandwich.

~

They checked into a little motel to take showers. By this time they were used to the odd glances from people which included the hotel's proprietor, who for some strange reason, decided not to ask any questions. They were still covered with dirt and soot which now stood in sharp contrast to their new clothing. The whole situation would have been just too surreal if it wasn't for the recent events in their lives. After what they'd lived through in the past few weeks, the term 'surreal' had lost some of its luster.

What Sean and Kira might now term surreal would probably qualify as unimaginable in the minds of most of the world.

Once they had taken showers, both of them began thinking about the next step.

"Sean, we should pick up some more cell phones, too."

"Good idea," he said, "I'm glad you thought of it. I was having a hard time focusing."

"All the people?" she asked.

"Yeah. They were all so curious and judgmental. One guy was thinking we look like terrorists."

Kira grinned. "I understand. Okay let's hurry and get out of here. We can drop by the fire station and then go take another look at what's left of our house."

"Sounds good," Sean replied.

Thirty minutes later they walked into the fire station, finally looking and feeling like normal humans. A man they didn't recognize greeted them just inside the front door.

"Can I help ya?" He asked affably.

"Uh, yeah," Sean began, "We're here to see Billy Creighton."

"You're the ones whose house burned last night, huh? I'm really sorry about that. I wish we could've done more."

"That's very nice of you, thanks," Kira ventured.

"Sure," he answered. When silence lingered for a few seconds the man finally spoke up again. "Uh, just a sec, I'll go get Billy. Make yourselves comfortable," he added pointing to a couple of raggedy looking chairs over by the wall.

"Okay, thanks," Sean answered making no move to sit.

Nervously, the man left, and Sean followed Kira who had decided to avail herself of the chairs.

At about the same moment that Billy walked into the room, the front door opened again and in walked John Thornton.

John Thornton was the detective that had helped them when they were trying to solve the mystery surrounding Jason, Sean's adopted dad, and finally finish Jason's painting. It was John who had given them the background information on the murders, and John who had been there near the end. He'd had the opportunity to see and experience some of the unique talents of both Kira and Sean, and it was John's account of events that had ultimately ended up in Joshua's hands and interested him in Kira to begin this whole ordeal.

"Hi, John," Sean said warmly, standing up as he reached to shake the big man's hand.

"Hi, Sean, what happened to your nose?" he answered in his booming deep voice before turning to Kira, "and hello to you, too, Kira." John leaned over and shook her hand as well, forestalling her need to rise from the chair. "I'm so sorry to hear about your home. I kind of feel responsible since Josh found you due to my report."

"It's not your fault, John," Kira chimed in, smiling inside at his attempt to assume guilt just like she'd done. "We were supposed to do this. This woman has to be stopped, and Sean and I are the ones to do it. Besides, who could have possibly predicted the set of circumstances that would have led to this?"

John smiled. "Well thank you for that. Do you mind if I sit in and listen to you tell Billy what happened?"

"Feel free," Sean answered. He was happy with the feelings he was getting from John, the warmth, and compassion mixed with John's ever-present curiosity. "Oh, and my nose? The arsonist blindsided me in the woods."

John's curiosity came on point, but he was distracted as Billy sidled over and sat down. John remained quiet while Billy sat and made some notes on a tablet in front of him. Finally, he looked up, apparently ready to get on with business. Billy only had a few questions, and Sean related the tale, reiterating his knowledge of the magnesium and how it was Josh who had discovered it. Fifteen minutes later, it was all over and Billy was excusing himself.

"Thanks, folks," he said. "If I need anything else I reckon I can get it from this Josh guy. You've been most helpful, and again I'm sorry about your home."

They got up to leave, and John turned to go with them. He'd been quiet throughout the whole story but seemed to have something else in mind now. "Sean, would you two mind if I go with you? I'm guessing you're going back out to your home, and if you don't mind I'd like to just tag along."

Sean and Kira looked at each other briefly, and Sean immediately sensed her agreement with the proposal. Then he smiled because he sensed that it had just occurred to Kira, maybe for the first time, how convenient his ability could be.

She'd wanted to encourage him to let John come but hadn't wanted to say anything. So she just thought it as she looked at him and knew he understood. Sean was reassured that his gift could also bring them closer, rather than become the wedge he feared.

"Sure," he finally said, "Why don't you follow us?"

Moments later, they pulled into the long driveway. Sean glanced into the rearview mirror and could barely make out John's truck in the dust cloud behind him. The wind picked up again as he returned his gaze to the ruined house before him. The blackened shards of the simple old farmhouse stood out starkly against the blue morning sky. The black fingers of burned timbers reaching up like a burned hand from the grave. A wave of sadness washed over him, and he realized at least part of it was coming from Kira. Sean turned to look at her, catching her gaze still fixed on the house. Following her eyes back to the home of his youth, his sadness abruptly turned to anger, then subsided with Kira's next words.

"I'm sorry about your home, Sean."

"Our home," he said reflexively. "We'll build a new one, Kira, and it will be all ours. Maybe it's a blessing to put the last of the ghosts to rest once and for all."

She turned to him and smiled, overwhelmed with the flood of emotions assailing her as she watched him put the truck in park. "I love you, Sean. I never thought I could be so happy."

The miraculous sensation, of feeling her emotions at the same time he was hearing her words, especially when they were words of love, was Sean's favorite expression of his ability. It made everything else bearable. "I love you, too, Kira. You can't know how much you've completed my life."

Sean was starting to get teary as was Kira, so he hurried out of the truck, wiping his eyes before turning to face John.

"So I know you have some more questions for us, John. You want to just spit em out?"

John grinned the tight little smile that was as close as he typically came to humor. "You do get to the point don't you, Sean? Well yeah, I guess I'm pretty certain that you didn't give Billy back there all the details.

For instance, you mentioned that she came into your room to start the fire, and that you woke up and scared her off, but that doesn't quite explain why you have that new slice on your wrist or how you knew she was coming here to begin with, and why you both left in such a hurry that you couldn't grab a stitch of clothing.

I know you two are both capable of some unusual things, and I suspect that the brevity of your story was intended to leave those details out."

"Okay, John," Sean started, "To begin with, is this of *personal* interest or are you supposed to be investigating this?" The burned wet char smell still lingered in the air, momentarily distracting him.

"Well both, actually. I've rather come to like you guys and someone, anyone burning down a home on my turf gets my attention." John spoke as he followed Sean and Kira up to the remains of the house.

The warmth Sean was sensing from John surprised him. The detective truly did like them both, and there, down deep beneath the softer feelings sat a well controlled spike of anger, neither of which he'd ever let show. It reminded Sean how much he, in fact, had come to like this man himself.

"Alright, let me give you the Reader's Digest version. You knew Josh called us indirectly as a result of the report you did on our little adventure here and Kira agreed to do a painting for him to try to help catch some crazy arsonist he'd been chasing. Well, as you might expect when she did, she got something, only this time it wasn't a victim she was getting images from, it was the killer herself. And somehow this nutcase has become aware of me and Kira and has decided to come after us. I picked up a thought from her when I was chasing her from a crime scene in Virginia, and we tried to get here before she did. Apparently we did, but only because she'd taken an old ID when she stole Kira's purse. So she apparently went to New Orleans first and, we assume, got caught up in the evacuation from Kathleen. After that, she apparently took her time getting here, and Kira tried to do another sketch of her early last night. She saw her in a pickup driving and knew she was heading for us. Too bad we didn't know how close or maybe we could have been more prepared last night.

At any rate, she managed to get into the house without waking us and had already placed that accelerant around the bed before she attacked me.

I was still asleep and dreaming when I sensed some danger to Kira, which woke me up just in time to catch her knife before she stabbed Kira, but I got a little nick when I relieved her of it." Sean stopped there suddenly. It occurred to him that he didn't want to share with John what they were about to do. Dachau, he thought again. What's that going to be like?

~

John absorbed the information. Certainly he knew of Kira's abilities, but Sean had let something new slip. A thought? John knew Sean was extra sensitive to feelings, but he'd just casually mentioned that he'd picked up a thought . . . Could he read thoughts too? And Sean had stopped rather suddenly, as well. It sparked a question.

"Well, do you think she's coming back here?"

"No. She's not." Sean looked up as he answered and realized he might have just hinted at what else he knew.

The front door to the house still stood, and as he answered, Sean led them both through that way. The porch creaked badly, and Sean was glad he'd bought some sturdy boots for him and Kira this morning.

"So, you know where she's going?" John asked casually.

Sean's attention had been riveted by the devastation around him so he answered before he thought. "Yeah, we know she's going to . . ." He stopped, suddenly realizing what he was saying, but decided it didn't matter after all. "Dachau."

"The prison camp, Dachau?" The surprise in his voice was a ghostly image of what Sean sensed from him at the unexpected statement.

"Yep, the prison camp," Kira chimed in. "And that's going to be our next stop."

"You and Sean are going to chase a crazy arsonist-murderer to Dachau Germany? Sean, how do you know that's where she's going?"

There really wasn't much of a way around it now. John was going to figure it out one way or another anyway.

"Yep, we are. I chased her out of the house and before she cracked my nose and dove over a barbwire fence I caught a thought from her. It was almost like some other voice was talking to her. It said, 'Find me in Dachau.'" Sean didn't look at John as he finished. He just leaned over to move a shattered picture frame out of the way before changing the subject. For his part, John was completely silenced by Sean's candid answer.

"Kira, it looks like everything is lost. If the fire didn't get it, the smoke and water did."

"I know. It's horrible." But as she spoke she moved slowly into the den area where the painting she had done of Sean's adopted dad had been on the display easel. The easel itself had been partially burned and the painting had fallen to the floor. It was still lying on its side against the wall as Kira gently bent to pick it up.

"It's amazing that picture didn't burn," John observed, as Kira lifted it.

Kira's innocent expression belied her thoughts which centered on the previous mutual experience with Sean and that painting.

"What a surprise," he said with a straight face, and they both cracked up. But the laughter abruptly ended, amid John's questioning gaze, as Sean picked up Kira's sudden change of thought to her mother's painting. Instinctively, he moved to put his arm around her and answered her thoughts. "I'm so sorry, Kira. I know it's gone."

The sadness suddenly so present on her face seemed to soften at Sean's comforting touch, and the only response she managed was a little nod of recognition and a bitter sweet smile.

Sean was quickly distracted by thoughts from John. He felt John's complete bafflement at their vague interactions. John had realized there was much more going on here than was being said, and felt oddly out of place being in the midst of all this display with no context to understand it. The term, unreadable mime, floated into Sean's mind from John and Sean smiled. Then he spoke.

"Does Josh know you're planning on going to Germany?"

"Nope." It was Kira that answered, and when she didn't volunteer anything else, John asked another question.

"Well, why haven't you told him? Don't you think he needs to know where his perpetrator is headed?"

Suddenly everything seemed to coalesce into anger for Sean. Stepping back towards the kitchen where John was standing, he moved in close and answered, "John, Josh thinks we're weirdoes, maybe even crackpots, and even though we've been right every time, he treats us like disobedient children. AND he's got the hots for my fiancée, which I'm unfortunately aware of whenever I'm near him. Our home has just been burned down and someone tried to kill us and we're *still* the only ones that know where she's going. So basically my feeling is SCREW Josh! We'll find this lunatic and deal with her ourselves."

The heated words flowed from Sean like a dragon's breath and seemed to leave him slightly deflated. Kira was stunned. It was the first time she'd seen a real flash of anger from him, and it seemed so out of character that for a moment she just stared.

John had no such reaction, however. He merely absorbed Sean's words, thought for a second, then calmly launched a tirade of his own.

"So what do you think you're going to do when you find her, Sean? Are you going to kill her? In a foreign country? Do you even have a gun? Not that you could travel with it if you did. And what if she tries to kill you again? Are you prepared to kill her without any hesitation because from what you're telling me she's not going to hesitate to kill you? And any hesitation on your part may not only get you killed but maybe Kira, too. Is that what you want? You better think this through very carefully my friend."

Sean hadn't thought it through, and now John's cool dose of reality deflated him even further. The anger that had swelled within him drained away completely and sadness and confusion rushed in to replace it.

"So what do you think I should do, then? It's not like Josh is going to send someone to Europe on a clue I picked up from a fleeing killer's mind."

"I think you should do what you're planning to do except that I should go with you."

Two heads turned sharply at the declaration, and two smiles slowly grew from the initial shock, first Sean's then Kira's, but it was Sean who spoke.

"We accept." He said simply and reached out to shake John's hand.

~

Numbly, John took Sean's hand. The idea had come to him abruptly, and he'd blurted it out in an atypical rush. He'd just done what he'd warned Sean not to do. Not think it through. Normally he thought things through very thoroughly, but somehow his sense of being family with these two kids was provoking his fatherly instincts and overriding his typical cool logic. He'd never been able to save his Laura, but maybe he could keep these kids safe. Hell, he'd never even been out of the country, it would be an adventure.

So as he reached for Sean's hand he also reached the conclusion that he liked his idea after all.

~

They spent part of the rest of the day picking through the charred ruins of their lives, looking for odds and ends that were still intact. Fortunately, Sean's adopted dad had owned a fireproof safe that was kept in the garage and Kira had put her important papers in there, too, when she moved in. They were going to need them now to see how fast they could get Sean a passport. Kira already had hers, and John's credentials should expedite his, if he didn't already have one.

CHAPTER

DACHAU! DACHAU!
Poena's head was pounding mercilessly as she drove mindlessly down the road. She'd been driving, probably in circles for a couple of hours and Grandpa's voice had been getting louder and more insistent by the moment. She'd never felt anything like this before, and trying to answer him wasn't helping, either. It was goading her on like a cattle prod.

Beyond that, she was furious with herself. How could she have failed to kill them? She wasn't used to failure. And how did that boy manage to follow her, *again*? And why the HELL had she kissed him?! As she tried to wade through the anger and confusion, she decided that she should just keep on driving. An idea formed in her mind and as the sun finally peeked over the horizon in front of her, she made a decision.

Her thoughts were too jumbled at the moment to make any serious plans, but at least now she knew where she was going. Grandpa was always right, so she needed to leave the country and now was going to be much better than later. She'd brought her passport with her when she'd deserted her house in Virginia, not that she'd planned on leaving the country, she'd simply made a point of taking *all* of her ID with her, and now she knew why. She just needed to hurry to stay ahead of any pursuit by the law. But they couldn't act that fast, anyway, she decided, not since she was going straight to the airport; just not the Kansas City airport.

Having made the decision, she smiled to herself. The trip would give her a chance to clear her mind and maybe give Grandpa a chance to tell her what to do next. Besides, if she didn't get to Dachau soon, she was convinced that her head would explode from Grandpa's growing voice.

~

By mid morning she was almost back to St Louis and in a much calmer state of mind. She'd made as good a time as she dared. She couldn't afford to be stopped for speeding right now. Killing an officer would certainly make things too complicated at the moment.

As she pulled into the parking lot at Lambert Field, Poena realized that Grandpa's voice had settled into a sort of pattern. First, he'd nearly yell the word 'Dachau' at her a few times, then he'd tell her to hurry, then he'd repeat that 'the first would be the last' comment, and to find him at Dachau. Then it would start all over again. His voice had quieted for a while, but now it was back, and it was becoming increasingly difficult to concentrate.

As anticipated, the woman at the ticket counter gave her a strange look when she pulled out cash to pay for her ticket. You'd think the woman had never seen money before. With a glare that Poena decided wouldn't be any more memorable than the cash itself or her appearance in general, which was still mostly in black and tight fitting, she checked her bag and looked for a nook to grab a bite to eat. A quick glance told her that she'd have to go through the security line first. She'd already lost her knife and with Grandpa's voice in her head it was difficult to concentrate, so she forgot all about the permanent match in her purse. She'd not even used it at Kira's house because she had had to light that fire so quickly, but she'd had it out of her suitcase anyway.

Her stomach twisted nervously as the guard at the security check asked to look in her purse after it went through the X-ray machine. It had already jumped twice in this line when she presented ID. Would the search for her have made it this far yet? Had she forgotten anything else? When he pulled out the permanent match, he gave it a funny look, then turned to Poena with a questioning glance.

"What's this?" He asked.

Putting on her best smile, Poena decided to play dumb, "I have no idea. I picked it up at a souvenir shop in Mississippi, and I thought it was cute. I meant to stick it in my suitcase, but I forgot. Do you know what it could be?"

The officer was shaking his head as he put it back into the purse. The little hacksaw blade was being contrary and he had to scoop it up on its leather lanyard and slip it back in separately.

"No ma'am, I haven't got a clue, but whatever it is it looks harmless enough."

Poena continued her vapid smile, finally noticing the guard notice and smile back.

"Thank you," she said as he handed her back her purse.

"Have a nice trip ma'am."

Poena could feel his gaze on her as she walked away. She was just glad that she'd lost her knife. She probably would have forgotten about that, too. Her thoughts were too jumbled, and it'd been a very long time since she'd flown anywhere.

By the time she got her food at the little sandwich shop, her head was aching so bad that her eyes had begun to throb, and she was feeling sick to her stomach. The voice was back in her head, and it was pounding. She barely managed to restrain her volume as she caught herself grumbling out loud over her sandwich, "I'M GOING GRANDPA, I'M GOING ALREADY!!!!"

Fortunately, no one was sitting too close and her histrionics went largely unnoticed.

She finished her food in concerted silence as the voice finally subsided.

Her flight left in two hours.

When John got back to his office the next morning he made some calls trying to find out if his status as a detective could expedite getting him a passport. As it turned out, it could. Next, he started checking for flights.

Maybe he could save Sean and Kira some time if he had that info in hand when he talked to them a bit later. That thought made him wonder if they had *their* passports. Surely Sean didn't.

The feelings of closeness that had prompted him to volunteer to help, somehow continued to grow. It felt good, though he found it more than a little surprising. Maybe it was because he didn't have any other family, and they had helped him finally bring closure to the disappearance of his Laura. Maybe he just needed a change.

Whatever the reason, he felt very strongly that what he was doing was the right thing, and to that end, he wanted to be as much help as possible.

Sitting there at his desk he pondered what he did know. What kind of a crazy who starts fires on the eastern seaboard decides to drive all the way out to Kansas to burn down the house of a couple of strangers?

He hadn't been involved on this case at all and only knew what Sean and Kira had told him, but there was also a part of him that still felt a bit responsible and the more he knew the more effective he could be.

With that thought in mind, he picked up the phone and hunted around for the phone number. It just took him a moment to find and the call was answered on the first ring.

"This is Josh."

John noted the practiced briskness momentarily before responding. "Josh, this is John Thornton in Kansas."

~

Josh's thoughts were so far away it took a moment for the words to sink in. He'd heard nothing on the APB, so even after his breakthrough on her identity Josh was again feeling stymied. But he had received word of the fire already and had cancelled his flight to Kansas until he could talk to Sean and Kira, which he as of yet had not been able to do.

He focused his thoughts. Ah, he finally remembered. This was the guy who wrote the report that had motivated him to get involved with those two psychics. Great.

~

"Good morning, John. What can I do for you?"

"So where are you?" John asked. "Are you in the Kansas City area now?"

"No, actually I heard about Sean and Kira's house, and I cancelled my flight until I could talk to them, which I haven't been able to do."

"Well, I spent the afternoon with them while they dug through what was left of their house, and it occurred to me to see how things were coming on your end with this lady firestarter." John was pretty sure that his note of recrimination wasn't being missed, but Josh apparently chose to ignore it. He probably just took John for another country bumpkin.

"Well, we know where she lives, and we have her house staked out, and there's an APB out on her car."

"Was there an APB out on her car here in Kansas? I don't recall hearing about one."

"No, the multi-jurisdiction thing was slowing things down, and I suspect she has already left the area by now."

"And what makes you so sure of that?" John didn't like this guy's attitude. He had only talked to Josh once before and had paid little attention at that time, but now he was beginning to sense what Sean was referring to or maybe his own opinion was being colored by Sean's words. Either way he was developing an unusual opinion him. It was sort of an 'I've-only-known-you-for-five-minutes-but-already-I-don't-like-you-for-years' sort of feeling. Probably much the same as Sean felt.

"This fire doesn't fit her MO, and I'm pretty certain it was done just for vengeance. If that's the case, she should be heading back to her home base."

"Well, Sean and Kira feel pretty comfortable that they know where she's going."

"They what? How would they know that? No, on second thought, don't tell me. I don't want to know. So where do they think she's going?"

"Germany. Dachau, to be precise."

"Why the hell would she go to Dachau?" Josh was obviously stunned, but to his credit, he adjusted quickly. "Well, if she's really going to do that, she's going to have to have a passport. Maybe we can head her off there."

"Actually, Josh, I think we should just let it be. I believe Sean and Kira are right, and this way we know where's she's going. If she gets deterred getting her passport, she may go to ground, and we wouldn't have any idea where to look until the next fire."

"What's this 'we' reference, John? You're not part of this investigation, and for that matter, don't you think it's a little dangerous letting them do that by themselves. This woman is a killer after all and a cold blooded one at that."

"I agree," John answered. "That's why I'm going to go with them."

"John, let me say this again. This isn't your case and I don't think . . ."

"It became my case," John interrupted, "when your nutcase set a fire in *my* town and tried to kill two of *my* residents. Now, whether you like it or not, I'm going. For that matter, Josh, you're going to have to do something about your own jurisdictional issues if this woman leaves the country."

"You have the same problems there that I do, John."

"I know that, but I'm not going as a Sherriff. I'm going with them as a friend. Now do you have any more information that can help me or not?"

"John, I'm still going to try to head her off before she gets out of the country, and if I get any information that might help you, I'll let you know. But frankly I still know precious little."

"I appreciate that. I'll let you know how it goes."

"Fine, John. Be careful though. This broad really *is* a nut case."

"Thanks, I will." John was a little surprised at both the warning and the sudden acquiescence to his suggestion based on Josh's general demeanor, but he brushed it off and said goodbye. He had a lot to do.

Sean and Kira found out that they could accelerate the passport pro-cess, too, if they had a ticket in hand. It took them just forty-eight hours to get Sean's passport after much running around and scads of phone calls, but they did it. The whole time Kira kept getting tickled over Sean's grumpiness about his still noticeable black eyes.

"It makes me look like a raccoon," he'd said to another bout of Kira giggling.

Very shortly after that, they found themselves at the airport where John was waiting for them at the gate for the flight to Munich.

"Hi, John, I see you made it," Sean said extending his hand.

"Was there any doubt?" He answered shaking Sean's hand but smil-ing at Kira.

"No, I guess not."

~

As they seated themselves to await their flight, John looked back over at Sean and Kira. These paternal feelings were completely new to him. He was not only surprised by them, but it also kept him feeling a little awkward. It made him thankful for that tacit acceptance.

~

Sean, for his part, was sensing the new feelings from John and even aware of John's curiosity about them. It almost made Sean laugh. Curiosity had always been John's hallmark, and it was humorous that he was turning that proclivity onto himself. On the other hand, Sean found the sensations very endearing and all in all he decided it was best to keep his entire awareness of the subject to himself.

John's big voice interrupted his thoughts.

"Did either of you by chance call Josh to let him know what was going on?"

Sean and Kira looked at each other, sharing a slight guilty expression. It was Kira who spoke.

"Well, we talked to him the day of the fire and told him what happened, but not since."

John just nodded his head. "Well I did. I told him you were going to Dachau and why and that I was going with you."

"And how did he take that?" Sean asked, feeling pretty certain he already knew.

"He didn't like it. But I didn't give him much choice. He said he was still going to try to catch her when she tried to get a passport, but I guess he hasn't or he would have called me."

Sean could just picture Josh, seething with anger over someone taking over his investigation. Hell, it wasn't even an investigation anymore, it was a chase. His fleeting feelings of satisfaction were quickly chased away by guilt at having such petty thoughts.

He turned to look at Kira who was staring at him as if she'd just read his every thought, but rather than say anything she grabbed his arm. He turned back to John.

"Well, I imagine it'll be us calling him soon enough. Have you ever been to Germany, John?"

"Never been out of the country. Haven't ever been much for travelling."

At that point the overhead speaker came on announcing their flight.

~

Josh slammed down the phone. "DAMN that BITCH!"

He'd just received word that Poena had made it onto a flight. How had she made it to an airport with a passport so quickly? She hadn't been back to her house. Had she known she was going to Germany even before she left for Kansas? He didn't believe that.

It seemed everything he'd done this whole case added up to chasing his tail or, more to the point, her tail. He'd been two steps behind all the way. The brief thought crossed his mind that he was glad John had gone with those two. He had a sneaking suspicion that events were going to turn very nasty in Germany, which reminded him, he did have one more phone call he could make to an old friend that now lived in Germany. Maybe he could do something right before this case was over.

~

Sean's eyes opened, and he glanced out of the window. It was dark and the ocean below had few lights to offer other than occasional dots from a ship. He turned his head to Kira to find her staring at him and smiling. Suddenly her thoughts came flooding into him as she began to speak.

"I think I was right about the connection here," she said randomly.

"Poena Maslin, huh?" He'd picked up the name from her mind, and she'd smiled.

"Yep. It reminded me of what you said about her last name sounding Jewish."

It was hard for Sean not to race ahead, and he'd found that when he focused on her thoughts while she was speaking them it was like an out of phase stereo and to that end, confusing. So he made the conscious effort to tone down his perceptions so he could just feel her feelings without getting the words. "Go on," he urged.

The funny look on her face suggested that she knew what he was doing, but she continued anyway. "Well, the whole idea of the flames and her being Jewish got me thinking of the Holocaust."

"You're still thinking she might be doing some kind of vengeance thing? Isn't she a little young to be seeking retribution for events from the Holocaust?" Kira smiled again and for a second all Sean could think of was how gorgeous she was.

"You're the one who told me she said something about talking to Grandpa. He'd be about the right age."

"You think he's still alive?" This was much better Sean thought. Tuning out her thoughts was working. It was comforting to practice exerting some control over the whole thing. He'd barely been able to before.

"I don't know. Maybe we can call and ask Josh when we land, or get

John to."

"Well it might be interesting to actually know if the victims were German, even though I'm not sure what good it'll do us."

Kira furrowed her eyebrows. "Don't you think any information we can get might be helpful. I mean who knows what this crazy woman is really planning, but the more we can find out before we confront her, the better off we'll be."

"Well, that certainly makes sense." Sean could feel another question in Kira's mind, but he waited patiently knowing it was coming.

"Sean did you remember that I'm of German decent from my mother's side?"

Sean thought for a moment. "Yeah, Schultz right?"

"Yep."

Silence hung in the air for a moment. The low lights of the cabin seemed to complement the gentle roar of the plane's progress, not only chasing across the expanse of the Atlantic but also racing through time. Seven hours forward to Munich local time.

Without mentally peeking, Sean couldn't stand the suspense. "Well, what of it?"

Kira focused her gaze upon him with a somber look on her face this time. "Nothing I guess. It's just curious. I never knew my granddad, and I guess there is some chance he was a Nazi."

"Didn't your mother ever talk about him?"

"Actually no. I don't think she knew anything about him, either. She was in an orphanage when she was young."

"Really?" There was a wistfulness about her that Sean found a bit unsettling. He'd never sensed this from her before. Another question occurred to him. "Where, Kira?"

"Where what?" Apparently her thoughts had moved on, and Sean's question caught her off guard.

"Where was she in an orphanage?"

"I don't know. Germany somewhere."

Hearing those words come out of her mouth left Sean with an eerie foreboding, but when he glanced at her, her thoughts had moved on again so he let it drop.

CHAPTER

P oena was feeling energized. She'd managed to sleep most of the way over on the plane and had awakened when the plane touched down, realizing that for a brief space of hours Grandpa had not been haunting her thoughts.

As she followed people off the plane, it occurred to her for the first time in her life that maybe she *did* want this to be all over.

She'd been following Grandpa's words for years now, carrying out the mission he'd left for her, but she was getting weary. Maybe that was why she'd rushed to come to Germany when he'd told her to. "The first will be the last," he'd said and maybe that meant that her mission would soon be over. She had money. Grandpa had left it to her. It was hidden in banks around the world. Grandpa's stories had not inspired confidence in government, and as a result she'd not trusted a single institution or even a single country to hold all of her assets. But these thoughts led her to an even more disturbing thought. What would she do next? If she completed Grandpa's mission in Dachau then what would she do with her life? The thought had never crossed her mind.

Now, as she made her way down the unfamiliar hallways of the glass encased terminal in Munich, more than just the airport seemed other-worldly. All at once her entire life seemed like a gaping black maw before her, beckoning her to dare that next step. What would she do?

The baggage conveyor drew her attention back to her surroundings. Her bags were coming off. She'd have plenty of time to forage through that dark forest of possibilities later. Right now she had to finish her mission.

Retrieving her bags, Poena thought briefly about what her next step was going to be. She could go straight to the little town surrounding the prison camp, but part of her wanted to relax a little and have a chance to think about what might occur in Dachau and what had happened with Sean and Kira. She couldn't quite set aside the disturbing sensations she was getting both from the woman trying to draw her face, and the boy who seemed able to read her thoughts. And the reason she had stopped to kiss him.

On another, profoundly deep level, she found it disturbing to be here in this country full of the people Grandpa had directed her to kill. She knew it wasn't all of them. It wasn't really Germans in general, just those particular ones. Still, the sensation of being a stranger in enemy territory plagued her.

The taxi driver had asked her for a destination in passable English and without any better ideas, she simply told him to take her to an open place with lots of people.

An interminable amount of time passing red roofed buildings and eclectic architecture later, he delivered her to what he called the Marienplatz. It was an open courtyard which, in years gone by, had been an outdoor market. The market was gone but the people remained.

It seemed as good a spot as any to decide her next move and Poena thought it might be pleasant to sit here awhile and think.

Marienplatz translated to 'St. Mary's Square' according to the writing at the base of the tall column in the center, which was itself, dedicated to St. Mary. Christianity had never had much impact on Poena, and the closest she ever got to caring one way or another was when she was presented with artifacts such as these which merely left her with a mild discomfort, as though she was missing something she didn't understand.

Watching the people go by in the warm afternoon sun for a couple of hours finally had the desired effect. She decided to stay in Munich tonight and maybe even check out a bit of the nightlife. Time enough for Dachau tomorrow.

After amiably asking a few of the passersby in the great courtyard, Poena decided she'd stay at the Platzl hotel. It was only a half mile away and was close enough to town to be walking distance from much of the night life.

By late afternoon, she was checked in and jetlagged. The hotel had exceeded her expectations. When she walked in the door with her suitcase rolling behind, her eyes were greeted with rectangular martini glass columns flowing up to the ceiling and a parquet wood counter framed by a hexagon tile floor. Even the multi-bulb lighting sprinkled throughout the lobby added to the Bavarian feel of the place. Poena was pleasantly surprised with having to settle for the Bavarian Suite as the last room they had available. Money wasn't an issue with her anyway. She was feeling drowsy, and not knowing about how to deal with jetlag, she headed up to the suite for a nap before braving the night time in Munich.

The room itself was, again, more of a pleasant surprise. The entire interior of the Platzl Hotel's very best accommodation was a wonderland of light colored, inlaid wood. It covered the walls, dormer window with built in desk, part of the ceilings and even a carved half-canopy overhanging the bed. Poena took it all in in one breathless glance, then promptly plopped herself down on the bed.

The last thing she remembered was staring at the carved wood above her before she slipped into sleep.

~

That same wood looming above her caused her to flinch when she opened her eyes and saw it. She smiled at herself as she glanced at the clock. It was 8:30. She'd slept for three and half hours. As she got up and showered, trying to shake the cobwebs from her mind, she tried to decide if she still really wanted to go out. In the end, she did for several reasons.

One, she thought that maybe staying up later would help her body adjust to the new time zone, and two while she'd slept she'd found herself dreaming of kissing that boy, and now she was aroused for the first time in a long time. So she planned to do something about it.

After the shower she felt invigorated and awake. Without really thinking any more about it, Poena walked over to her suitcase, reached in and pulled out a pair of tight jeans and a dark blue nylon pullover. It was long sleeve and low cut and whether she thought about it consciously or not, it was guaranteed to glean attention to her shapely form. She donned the clothes and moved back to the bathroom to brush her hair and apply the small amount of makeup she was willing to wear.

Her thoughts were once again far away. She was thinking about the woman's face and, more importantly, the face of the man that had chased her. He really was attractive. Poena wasn't used to thinking of men in those terms. Her relationships over the years had been quite limited and inevitably devolved into sexual gratification. That's all it could ever be. Her mission allowed no room in her life for anyone else to get closer to her than that. For one thing they wouldn't understand. And once the relationship got to the point where those intimacies interfered with the goals her grandfather had left her, they had to be terminated. Nothing could hinder her mission. Nothing. Sex was just a way to get what she wanted, like her grandma had done to save Grandpa.

She ran the brush through her long black hair as these thoughts tumbled through her mind. They weren't new. But what was new was the sensation she had gotten from that man when she'd kissed him. Why had she done that, she asked herself again?

The only answer that came to mind was the feel of his lips in that brief second and the smell of him, and the sight of his naked body. She loved smells, and this man smelled so much like a man!

She put down the brush and absently noticed the lovely sheen to her hair. It made her think of an Indian princess.

She was fond of stories of the American Indians. They had been so strong and brave and their women had been capable. They could fight, as well as handle their domestic responsibilities, and woe be to the man who thought he could easily take an Indian woman. He was likely to find his throat cut in the middle of the night. Poena smiled at that as the thought of a nightclub drifted into her mind. She actually liked to dance on those few occasions when she would allow herself any social activities at all, and she'd asked at the front desk when she'd come in where to find a club close by. The concierge had told her of a spot but that it was dark and loud and the music was generated by a DJ who never grew out of the 70's and 80's American music.

She was still struggling with that other-worldly sensation from a combination of the new surroundings and the jet lag when she got in the cab and told the driver her destination. The distance didn't really warrant a cab ride, but she didn't have any desire to walk even half a mile in the heels she was wearing. She was unsure why she had packed the heels to begin with and, given her lifestyle, it was a minor miracle she had ever even purchased a pair. She had, however, and now they felt strange on her feet.

The club was called the White Raven and was patterned after the era whose music it played. As Poena strolled in she felt eyes turn to her. The interior of the club featured a number of circular dance floors on different levels that were lit from the bottom. Imitation chrome and mirrors gleamed from the walls and railings, making the roving colored spotlights from the ceiling cast rainbow reflections in all directions. The effect was dizzying, and no doubt intended to enhance the experience of whatever drug was bending the senses of its patrons on that particular evening. Poena had never tried any drugs, and had no intention of it. Her mind was busy enough, and she could never do anything that might dull her abilities and threaten the success of Grandpa's mission.

With an exaggerated saunter she continued across the place and over toward the bar, letting the dancing lights play over her as she approached.

She made a point to casually notice the men's eyes that followed her, looking for one she found attractive, maybe not as attractive as *that* man, but enough to get her mind off him anyway.

This particular club allowed smoking, but the air circulation was such that the smoke didn't linger. To Poena's mind it was a distinct perk to the ambience. She hated cigarette smoke. It had none of the wonderful qualities of the smoke she created with her fires. She had attracted the attention of several men by the time she reached the bar, but none of the ones she'd noticed caught her eye. She'd have to keep looking.

"Ginger Ale," she said to the bartender.

He hesitated just briefly, and Poena wondered if he spoke English or was just surprised at her choice of drinks. A second or two passed as he took in her face and form then promptly smiled.

"Certainly," he said with a heavy German accent while he turned for a glass. It hadn't really occurred to her that there might be a problem with not speaking the language, but apparently English was common enough at this place.

Poena turned to face the dance floor and leaned back against the bar. The heels she had on made her appear even leggier than she already was, and the total effect of her appearance and pose was captivating; a fact of which she was well aware.

She heard the bartender slide her drink onto the bar beside her. Without turning her head she thanked him. There was a dark haired man on the dance floor moving athletically to the music of "Beat It" by Michael Jackson. He was tall and lithe and obviously had wonderful rhythm. The girl he was dancing with was a slender blonde in a short skirt who was definitely more interested in how she looked on the dance floor than with the dancing itself. Poena smiled. This was going to be fun, she decided.

She continued to stare at the man until his gaze eventually crossed hers. Two surreptitious glances later, and she knew the man knew she was staring at him, which was exactly what she intended. To the chagrin of the blonde, the dark haired man thanked her after the dance and moved straight for Poena.

"Guten Abend," he said simply as he approached her.

Poena didn't understand the language, but assumed the greeting and donned her most engaging smile then said, "Hi there yourself."

He paused for a moment as the language change sunk in, then promptly switched to English.

"I couldn't help but notice you looking at me." His accent was thick, but his English was perfect.

"You'd have to have been blind to have missed it," she responded catching him off guard with her candor. His smile grew as he hesitated for just a second before continuing.

"Can I buy you a drink?"

"No, but you can buy yourself one and drink it with me." Again her candor stopped him for a second.

"My, you are direct aren't you? American, eh?" Now he was engaging *his* best smile. Her beauty along with her unusual demeanor had had the intended effect.

When he'd introduced himself as Wilhelm Kohl the smile he got from Poena should have frozen his blood, but instead he missed the nuance, being much too engrossed in the other signals she was sending.

"Please, call me Will," he said.

Poena's feelings were mixed. She was definitely getting aroused by this man, but the sexual tension was mingled with something else. Another type of lust. It never occurred to her that her ability to kill was in the least bit perverse or strange. She was simply better than other people, especially *them* and as such she wasn't subject to the rules others must live by.

And suddenly she was certain that this man *was* one of *them*. She wasn't sure how she knew . . . but she always knew . . . and this attractive dark haired man was definitely one of *them*. The descendents.

"Certainly, Will,"

The lust in her smile now was a deadly one, but his eyes were busy flickering between her wan smile and her alluring figure. Tonight she was going to take her pleasure from this man and give him the last and greatest pleasure he would ever know.

At the thought she felt her arousal heighten. She squirmed slightly on the bar stool and mis-reading her body language, Will asked her to dance.

It had been his last chance to escape, and he'd missed it.

Two hours later, she was in his car heading back to his place. Sitting on the contoured seat of his two-seater Porsche, she smiled at him seductively as she noticed him eyeing her again.

Soon, she thought.

His place was a two-story townhome in a swanky little suburb. When they arrived, Will went out of his way to open both her car door and then the one to his home.

Poena ignored his courtesy, instead taking in the pleasant sensation of the warm calm night. She could very easily be walking away from this house before sunrise, and it was nice to know that the weather for it would be pleasant.

"May I get you a drink? Some brandy perhaps?" Will was absolutely exuding charm, and being that he was indeed a handsome man, Poena should have found this somewhat endearing. All she could think of were the stories of her grandma's abuse at the hands of a man like this. On the other hand, some brandy did sound nice.

"Yes, thank you," she replied as she let her eyes roam about his domicile. He seemed to be a lover of the outdoors and of skiing. Photos of him in ski attire with different companions littered the room, especially on the antique, upright piano. The piano itself seemed somewhat out of place, in that most of his other furnishings were modern while the piano was obviously from another era. A music score was open on the tray. Wagner. It figured. Poena turned from her scan and faced Will who was approaching with two undoubtedly expensive snifters in his hands.

"Please," he began, gesturing with his free hand after handing Poena's glass to her, "make yourself comfortable."

He pointed to the overstuffed couch and Poena complied.

They only chatted briefly before he made his move and even that short interval had tried Poena's patience.

She wasn't interested in getting to *know* this man. Her intention was merely to quench a physical desire.

He *was* a good kisser. Her thoughts flashed back to the boy in the woods. Why did she keep referring to him in her mind as a boy? Some kind of self defense maybe, or a subconscious intent to demean?

A few moments later, with both of their clothes substantially loosened, Will led her upstairs. Poena had to make a special trip to the bathroom before she undressed, however, because she wasn't ready to let Will discover the six inch skinning knife she had in the slender sheath strapped to the inside of her waistband. She came back from the restroom naked with her hair swaying across her breasts and a two pronged lust in her eyes.

She could feel Will's heart pounding in his chest as he took her into his arms. Their lovemaking was wild and passionate and his extreme tenderness elicited a tiny stab to her much eroded sense of right and wrong. She quickly subdued the sensation, however, amid the urgencies of the moment, along with any lingering thoughts of Kira's boyfriend.

Three hours later they were both spent, satiated and asleep.

Two more hours, and Poena woke up and slipped into the bathroom.

When he awakened to her slicing his throat with her hand over his mouth, his struggles were surprisingly violent, throwing her off of him and onto the floor. They were also exceedingly brief. His life bled out too quickly for him to do much else. Poena was back up on the bed in time to watch the extreme shock and surprise fade from his eyes along with his life.

One more gone.

But even as she wielded the knife again to remove his face she heard her grandpa's voice again.

"No, Poena. Not here. You must find me at Dachau." And he was gone. Poena jumped at his words, shocked to hear them at that moment. The surprise faded quickly, though.

Not long after that she was gone as well, in Will's car, with his face in a baggie on the seat beside her.

Kira's eyes wandered the empty expanse before her, looking for clues as to where she might be, but the fog was thick, and all she could discern were the outlines of the roofs of a few buildings in the distance. The fog swirled around her. When she looked down, she couldn't even make out her feet. Where was she? She took a tentative step and her pulse shifted into a higher gear as she heard the laugh off to her right. There was no humor in it. It was the gleeful cackle of a broken mind, and to Kira it could only denote some horrible act that either had been done or was about to be. She hoped it wasn't the latter.

In her heart she felt there was something here to find; something important, but at this point she didn't have a clue. She took a few more steps and the laugh broke the silence again, jerking Kira's gaze further to her right. Had she seen something? The fog swirled in the direction she now looked as though something had just passed through it leaving unsettled eddies in its wake. She took another step as her pulse found yet a new gear and raced ahead of her. With the fog moistening her cheeks, she thought briefly that this must be what clouds would feel like on your face.

Suddenly, a figure came flying out of the fog, screaming. Appearing like an apparition from Hell with a gleaming knife raised and a face twisted in hate. It was Poena.

"Your face is mine, you Nazi bitch. How dare you imitate *her*!"

Kira didn't really have time to think. It was react or die, and she reacted by diving off to her right and, to her surprise, rolling smoothly away into the fog. The surface must have been black top, though, because a pebble dug itself into the muscles near her spine as she rolled, causing her to groan involuntarily.

She feared the sound would direct Poena towards her and as she regained her feet, she turned to see the screaming figure coming at her again from the fog . . .

~

Gasping, she opened her eyes with a jerk to see Sean staring at her intently. She was still on the plane.

"You alright?" he asked.

Before she could answer, Kira glanced down in her lap. The little sketchbook was there and a face was on it. It was Poena. Kira hadn't even known she was drawing that face or intended to, but there it was. Feeling the weight of Sean's stare, she finally answered him.

"Yeah, now. Bad dream I guess, or vision or something."

Sean's eyes glanced down at the picture on the sketchbook. "My money says vision. Did you learn anything?"

"You mean other than that the woman hates me? No."

Sean put his hand on her thigh and rubbed.

"Put that pad away and try to get some sleep. There'll be time enough to deal with it later."

Nodding her agreement, Kira put her head on Sean's shoulder.

~

The plane touched down gently and the jolt awoke Kira from a restless sleep. She looked up at Sean who was staring intently out of the window at the surrounding countryside. Kira followed his gaze briefly, but now there was only runway and airport to see and she'd seen so many airports before that it didn't hold any interest for her.

"Munich," Sean said almost to himself. "I've never been to another country before."

The yesteryear look to the red rooftops and the great expanses of green in the distance riveted Sean's gaze.

"There's such a sense of history here," Sean said wistfully. "It's like going back in time. There just aren't any buildings in the States as old as some of these."

Kira's gaze had slid over to Sean as he began to talk. There it was again, the little boy fascination. She absolutely loved that about him.

It was one of the many things she had fallen in love with about this man who'd barged into her life and become one of the many dramatic changes she'd experienced since beginning her new business, The Canvas of Life. It was a good name for what she did and now thinking about it, it seemed to encapsulate her own life, too. Sean wasn't merely part of the paint in that life, he was more like the frame that supported the canvas, and given the experiences they'd both endured since meeting each other, just a few short weeks ago, she was certain she'd never have made it without that support. Focusing her thoughts outward again, she realized Sean had turned to stare at her. He was smiling.

"I love you, too, Kira."

Even that, she liked. The 'always knowing' sensation was slowly becoming a comfortable backstop and cushion to her feelings for him. Moments like this left her amazed that she had been so concerned about his abilities. It was just another part of who he was, and she loved it all.

~

John was still drowsing in the seat across the aisle as he had been for most of the fifteen hour flight. He'd awoken long enough to eat the numerous meals they offered, read a bit and then settled back into a comfortable repose. But as the wheels thumped to the runway his eyes fluttered and opened.

It took a second for his mind to focus, then a quick glance out the window before he turned to Sean and Kira.

"Welcome to Germany, I guess." His big deep voice caused a few heads to turn, as Sean answered him.

"Yeah, welcome to Germany. It's beautiful, huh?"

Looking at John, Kira was struck by the sense of age there. When she'd worked with him before, she was only aware of his probing questions and whatever his purpose had been at the moment.

Now, seeing him awaken from sleep, the years seemed to weigh heavy on him, and she was left with the warm feeling she'd have for a grandpa. She smiled at him and, after a few seconds, he actually smiled back.

She'd found a Hostel about half a mile from the prison camp, thrown her things on the bed and walked straight over to the camp, but not before she started the preparations for the face. She was in a hurry, so she utilized the little kitchenette in her room, the main reason she'd rented it besides its location, and treated the skin, then placed it in the oven on low. She wanted it ready soon. She'd thought to bring one of her carved wooden masks with her, so if she didn't paint this face like the others, it could be ready in a few hours.

It had been a clear day when she first arrived, but clouds had gathered since then, and the light was waning fast as she approached the front gate.

"*Arbeit macht frei*" The sign said on the front gate in big, roughly fashioned, wrought iron letters. She didn't speak German but Grandpa had recited this phrase to her often enough. "Work shall set you free" he'd translated, and he had proceeded to give her the work to set her free, or was it to set him free? The work was vengeance. Vengeance is mine sayeth the Lord. God had judged, according to her grandpa, and she was God's executioner, appointed by God himself via the ramblings of her Grandpa.

Well, now apparently her work was almost done. She'd methodically hunted down the progeny of the officers and guards of the Dachau Concentration Camp and killed them. Burned them in the flames of justice and forced each one after the first to literally 'Face' the demise of their successor.

And here, according to Grandpa, was the source of the flames and the site of the last task she had to perform.

Poena had the sensation that she could hear echoes as she passed through the front gate. But there were no echoes to be heard in this open courtyard unless it was the echo of the travesty of the past, the echo of suffering unimaginable and despair incomparable. No, there were no echoes in this blatant reminder of man's capability for cruelty, only the echoes of Grandpa's words in Poena's mind.

The place was a vast emptiness. There were no longer guards here, not even the type that accept a ticket for admittance to such a place, and Poena thought the solitude felt perfect. She could imagine the pervasive smell of burning flesh that must have constantly hung in the air once the cremations had begun; a grim reminder to those who still drew breath under the oppression of the Nazis.

She couldn't help but imagine what it must have been like for Grandpa, how he'd managed to survive here for so long, and what survival had cost him. For sure, his words had described it to her in vivid, gruesome detail from the time she had been old enough to understand what he was saying. At first he'd only spoken of his incarceration at Dachau in the evenings when he'd had a bit too much Scotch. Those musings were brightened by his descriptions of the beautiful French and German countryside, but as the years went by and his faculties diminished, his meanderings increased in frequency, darkness, and detail. Until she turned five. Until he changed her name and completely relived for her, his experience in Dachau.

At such a young age the details had been horrifying. Her dreams had been plagued with visions of human skeletons protruding from tightly stretched skin, the product of severe starvation. Broken, twisted bodies hanging from razor wire fences, caught there attempting to escape and becoming entangled. According to Grandpa, the guards would often let the bodies remain there, dripping blood and then rotting in the sun to be eaten by birds, as a reminder and a deterrent to the other prisoners.

Open graves piled with emaciated, rotting corpses that lay there awaiting the bulldozers to cover them up after being shot by a dozen guards with machine guns. Screams at all times of the day or night as other prisoners were being burned alive; and of course the smells of burning flesh.

These were the childhood stories Poena had been raised with, and the images she had in her mind as she attended kindergarten and then first grade. Her grandpa had always taken good care of her, physically anyway, and as his dotage increased, she in turn took care of him. But her mind had been forced to experience in repetition and detail the vilest acts that humans had ever performed on other humans and in such vast numbers as to make the stoutest heart quail.

Grandpa's hearing had been failing since Poena was young and therefore he didn't hear her screams, as night after night she awoke with images of people burning, blood dripping, and dying people begging her to help them . . . There was no comfort from that terror in the house Poena lived in, and the arduous attention to her physical needs was a stark counterpoint to the unintentional torment of her innocent young mind.

Her only escape had been to turn cold inside; to make hardness a part of her very being. To blot out any care or concern for any other human beings outside of her beloved Grandpa, and most importantly to learn to mask her lack of feelings. Just like Grandpa had told her:

"Poena you must wear a mask over your feelings. Never let them see how you feel, for if they see fear, they choose you sooner, if they see determination they quash it, if they see hope they increase pain . . . no . . . you must always wear your mask."

Poor Poena had no way of knowing at her tender age that Grandpa's words were disjointed ramblings meant only to describe his method of surviving the horrors of Dachau and not words to live your life by. But she had learned, and those words had helped her survive the horrors of her night times and the solitude of her childhood, until as she grew, one day the nightmares were gone. And now, two years after Grandpa's death, he was still with her helping her accomplish the task he and God had given her. And here, in this place, the source of the flames, it was all going to end. All she had to do was wait a little longer and locate whatever it was Grandpa wanted her to find.

She was already pretty sure what it was supposed to be. It would have to be about the one she had missed, about General Theodor Eicke, the commandant of Dachau when he and Rebecca had arrived. Grandpa had spoken of him often and of the sacrifice he and Rebecca had been forced to make to him to survive the hell into which they'd been thrust, though he had never been quite clear as to what that sacrifice was. It was *his* progeny she'd been unable to locate on her quest from God, and therefore it was bound to be something about him that Grandpa wanted her to learn.

Her steps took her slowly across the main courtyard. It was an eerie feeling being here. Grandpa had described it to her so many times and in such detail, that she felt like she'd lived here herself. But some things had changed from Grandpa's descriptions. The lines of wooden barracks that filled the courtyard were gone. In their place stood four new buildings, replicas of the ones used during the war that had been too dilapidated to save. These were the quarters for the endless parade of hapless Jews that were being rounded up all over the country and sent into hell. They were stacked 1,600 to each barrack that was designed to hold 250. But it wasn't where Grandpa had lived, or Rebecca either, for that matter. No, they lived in a small corner of the main building, actually two small rooms. Grandpa had told her that being in that building was part of the compensation he and Rebecca had earned for their sacrifice. She hadn't understood as a little girl what that could be, but now she had a pretty good idea.

Finally crossing the courtyard, Poena walked up to the metal artwork that was part of the memorial to the prisoners of Dachau.

It was a powerful piece; an almost abstract graphic of vaguely human forms intertwined in a black metal fence, as if caught forever in their final attempt to escape, or perhaps the bodies in the representation were supposed to comprise the wire of the fence itself. To anyone else the artist had clearly captured the sense of torment, which was the essence of the camp, within the image of a fence that was symbolic to it. To Poena, it was a centerpiece depicting the reason for her life's work. She felt no sense of despair or depression at the reminiscences of horror all around her, only a sense of approaching the final completion of her work. There, in the building before her, was whatever her grandpa wanted her to find, and soon, she somehow knew, the couple would come after her. Those two things were all that was left to do.

With a growing sense of peace, the antithesis of this place, she crossed the threshold into the building. The cool breeze on her back went unnoticed.

"That way, Poena. Follow the hall."

Poena flinched. It was the first words Grandpa had spoken to her since she'd taken Will's face, and this time they weren't loud in her mind. As a matter of fact, they almost sounded ... scared? ... no, not scared but calm somehow, and she found that she knew exactly which way he wanted her to go. Slowly, in the echoing quiet of the abandoned old building Poena moved towards the far corner where Grandpa was directing her. Casually, she glanced up at the photo murals that covered much of the large expanse of wall: huge black and whites depicting scenes from the heyday of the Concentration Camp. The whole wall could have been entitled 'A study in human suffering'; emaciated bodies, pleading eyes, and steely eyed guards looming everywhere. The entire scene barely registered for Poena. She'd had it described to her so often as a kid, that it had long since lost any emotional impact for her, and besides, she had already donned her mask. Her facial expression was as blank as the cement floor beneath her.

"All the way to the end, Poena."

Soothing, that was how his voice was sounding. Soothing. She'd never heard Grandpa's voice sound so soothing before, or at least not since she was a kid. Unconsciously, she matched her movements to the timber of that voice, gliding across the floor with unhurried, catlike grace. Even so, her footsteps made soft echoes as she moved into the hallway. Her eyes barely shifted from the path Grandpa set for her; not taking in the other rooms and no curiosity about anything else around her. She was here because Grandpa wanted her here and nothing else mattered, except the certainty that those two were following her. That was her other task. Find what Grandpa wanted her to find, and then finish off the bitch and the boy.

"On the left, Poena, in here."

Poena turned into the small room almost expecting to see Grandpa standing there. Why was his voice so calm? Her eyes slowly panned around the room. Two of the walls were painted brick and two were made of wood. The dingy color remaining might have once been manila, but now it had a patina of green that was reminiscent of mold, or maybe it actually was mold.

"Find me, Poena. I'm here."

Here? What did he mean, here? Poena's eyes continued their sweep. The room was empty. No furniture, no pictures on the walls, nothing. The room was absolutely bare.

What could Grandpa possibly be talking about? Was he going to appear to her? He'd never done that before. Then another thought occurred to her, and she began to look more closely. Maybe something was hidden somewhere like she always did in her own home.

Moving closer to the walls, she bent down and began to inspect the seams between them and the floor and then stood up to search the seams between the walls and the ceiling. Nothing. There were no cracks on the wooden walls, so she moved slowly along them tapping, listening for a telltale hollow sound. Nothing. Methodically, patiently, she moved to the two brick walls and began to give them the same scrutiny she'd directed at the wooden ones.

Tapping, searching, looking for the slightest ... Then she found it. In the corner, where the two brick walls met. The second brick up from the floor wasn't aligned perfectly. It sat at a slight angle to the ones surrounding it. Casting her glance quickly across the wall, she could find no other brick that was canted in that fashion. There were no cracks around the brick but that didn't mean anything. She had no idea when this room had been painted last but she suspected it had been painted at least once since the liberation of the prisoners in 1945.

Squatting down, she slipped a knife from her pocket and opened the blade, keeping her gaze on the brick. Taking the blade point, she gently pushed on the mortar surrounding it. It crumbled easily, and then as she moved the point, it suddenly slipped in all the way to the hilt. Almost nothing there but paint, she thought. Working quickly now, she moved the blade around the entire perimeter of the brick. It was surprisingly easy going, and it made Poena wonder how it had even stayed intact so long. With the mortar removed she slipped the brick from its resting place and peered in the hole. She could see something in there and reached in boldly to grab it. She'd never been afraid of rats before, but sticking her hand in there made her think of the ramifications of a rat bite. It didn't matter, though, there wasn't any choice. Her fingers closed on something that felt like wood and was fairly flat. Flat enough to be pulled back through the opening she'd just made if she grabbed the edges.

She sat back on her haunches and stared with stunned surprise at the little flat box with the carved Star of David on the surface. How could Grandpa have managed this? A Star of David in this camp was as good as a death sentence, but then again, this whole place was a death sentence wasn't it? So what difference was one more thing? Still, there was death, and then there was death. Abruptly, she realized she was just sitting there contemplating. She turned the box in her hands to look for hinges. There were none. The dark wood was rough and unadorned except for the Star. Where could he have gotten it?

Awe was not a feeling that Poena was familiar with, but here, now, sitting in this place she'd heard so much about and holding a box she was sure belonged to her grandpa, elicited that emotion clearly. A violent shiver wracked her whole body.

Setting the box down, she gently moved to lift the lid. It fit snugly but otherwise didn't resist her efforts. The lid came off, and inside was three items; folded paper, a picture and a long slender piece of wood. Poena picked the piece of wood up first, curious as to its purpose. It was strangely smooth with a darkened tip on one end. The wood itself was a lighter color almost as light as pine except for that tip. The tip was darker than mahogany. With almost reverent motions she set it aside and lifted up the picture. It was an old black and white of a young couple. The edges were brown and the image was the worse for wear but as she stared at it, she realized it must be Grandpa and if that's Grandpa, she thought, then the other person must be ... Rebecca. They must have both been in there late twenties or so in this photo and the picture of Rebecca struck her. There was something ...

"Oh my God!" The sharp intake of breath she took as she dropped the photo seemed to sear her lungs. It couldn't be! But then maybe that would explain ...

She suddenly turned back to the box and reached for the paper, but now she had a good idea what she was going to see.

"Find me, Poena." Now she knew what Grandpa had meant. She *had* found him. Carefully, she unfolded the darkened paper and began to read, noting absently that the ink was the same mahogany color as the tip of the piece of wood:

November 15th 1938

I guess I should be thankful but the emotion eludes me. It has been less than a week since the Nazi's Kristallnacht, and already I have watched hundreds, maybe thousands die. Hell could hardly be much worse than what I've already witnessed being done to my brothers, and I know it's just beginning.

January 5th 1939

I already feel like a traitor. The night we arrived, the Commandant, a General Theodor Eicke, happened to catch sight of Rebecca and God help us, but he became smitten with her. He called her to him later, and in return for her willing affections, she negotiated for me to act as a servant in the main building and to see her occasionally. I'm not forced to live with the others in the barracks, but who knows how long this tenuous bargain with the devil will last, and the price my lovely Rebecca is being forced to pay makes me weep every night.

March 1939

I'm so weak. Some days I am shocked that my body hasn't given out. This deal with the devil is all that has kept us alive, but I fear that it is indeed costing us our souls. When he comes for her, he takes her in the next room or if she's with me he'll often force me to watch. He's never gentle. I've wanted to kill him so many times . . . but even if I wasn't weakened from starvation, the Commandant is a large, strong man and were I lucky enough to succeed, it would be the end of me and probably worse for Rebecca. I cannot allow that. I cannot allow her sacrifice to be in vain. No. There is no bravery here in the Death camp except the bravery to remain alive and the bravery to dare to hope. And I do dare to hope. I pray that some day Rebecca and I may be free of this place and even that she and I may someday have a family . . .

June 1939

The heat only makes this living hell worse. Dying could not possibly be worse than living under these conditions. So many others have already been killed or succumbed. It is such a strange reality to live in a place where violence, cruelty and inhuman death are a daily occurrence.

The spark of hope is a bare flicker for any of us. To maintain it has truly become the only badge of bravery available.

October 25ᵗʰ 1939

I happened to overhear the date when the Commandant was speaking on the phone. The months have ground past. I can barely stand to see the hollow look in my lovely Rebecca's eyes. I feel like such a coward. I'm wracked with guilt; guilt for not fighting back, guilt for not suffering as much as the others in the camp, guilt for not trying to escape. Some days the guilt is even worse than the despair and the lack of blame in her eyes haunts me. Rebecca is my hope. She is the star that drives me on. It has seemed such a cruel joke that God would bless me with a woman as wonderful as she, and then deny us the opportunity to spend our lives together.

December 1939

Rebecca is pregnant. I can't imagine how she could conceive in the state her body is in. She's so thin. Still though, she fares better than most. But our time is running out. General Eicke can't afford to have anyone know he's been taking Rebecca. The new laws were passed months back. It's against the law for a German to have sex with a Jew. Even in his position of power the General couldn't survive that. The SS would see to it. No, we have to leave soon if we're ever going to leave, and this upcoming transfer may be our only chance, even if it's a small one.

January 1940

I'm not going to be able to write much more. My fingers are constantly swollen and sore from the continuous pricks for 'ink' and they're all getting infected, but somehow it felt important to at least get some of my feelings down, even if writing them is only a salve for my guilt.

We got word the Nazis picked a location for another Death Camp; Auschwitz, I heard them say. Maybe if they move us that will be our chance. With his help, I have managed to hide the surprising bit of treasure. It is, in itself horrible, and I do not think I'll be able to take it with us anyway, but if we need it someday, maybe I'll come back. It resides at the foot of the first fire, two paces to the left of death.

February 1940

They're supposed to be taking us away tomorrow, to Auschwitz I think. I've already heard bad things about that place but how it could be worse than this? I can't imagine. It doesn't matter, though, Rebecca and I will never see Auschwitz. We're going to escape ... somehow ... or die. I've already told Rebecca and she says she's ready. There's no choice anyway, another few weeks and her pregnancy will be apparent ... That is a death sentence we won't survive ... Dear God please spare us ...

Poena put down the paper and looked again at the long thin piece of wood. The dark stain now had meaning for her. It was Grandpa's blood. Fifteen months in a German death camp, and he and Rebecca had survived. It was incredible. They apparently had not only survived, but they had escaped with Rebecca three months pregnant. So Rebecca had had a child before her own mother was born, a half-sister who was the seed of that Nazi commandant. This was a piece of the story Grandpa had never shared. Slowly, Poena lifted up the photograph. Staring at the picture of Rebecca, the truth finally sunk in. Kira looked identical to her. "The first shall be the last ..." Kira was also the granddaughter of Rebecca ... Her cousin and the daughter of Rebecca's first born child.

It was Kira that Poena had been sent here to kill; the granddaughter of the First Commandant of Dachau. Treasure? Grandpa had saved a treasure? Poena couldn't care less about that. She had enough money.

She dropped the photo and stood up, leaving everything on the floor. Mementos had no hold on her mind. They were coming soon, she reminded herself, and she had to get back to her room before she returned here. There were preparations to make.

Rather than checking into a hotel, Kira directed them to a little hostel, Europe's version of a bed and breakfast but much more prevalent. Sean was delighted with the arrangement. The quaint house with the three stories of narrow stairs and smaller rooms screaming of history, were an absolute treat for him. John, however, was somewhat less than thrilled, that is until he tasted the proprietor's cooking the next morning.

The room had been rather chilly and Sean and Kira had slept close to each other, like two spoons in a drawer. When she awoke her first thought was of the feel of Sean's arms around her, her second thought was that she'd made it through the night without any nightmares. She was thankful for that. So far this whole adventure had been less bur-densome in that fashion than doing Sean's adopted dad's painting, but this felt much more personal somehow.

The little hostel was only a mile from Dachau, as was the outdoor beer bar Sean had spied on the way in. Sean and Kira decided to walk to the old camp this morning, again much to John's chagrin. He also tried to encourage them to wait until later in the day, but neither of them would hear of it. They were here now, and they wanted to get this over with.

"What makes you think she's even there yet," John asked, "If she's going there at all?"

"Oh she's going there alright," Sean answered. There was no deny-ing the certainty in his voice. "And it occurs to me that getting there before her, if we can, is not such a bad idea either."

Kira merely nodded her head in agreement, and John decided it wasn't worth the argument, so with a bit of a disgruntled look on his face, he followed them out the front door and down the street towards Dachau Death Camp.

It was a brisk gray morning with wisps of ground fog seeming to linger in the crevasses between the buildings, but as they walked on, the fog continued to gather, and Sean seemed to be getting depressed. His shoulders sagged uncharacteristically, and the spring fell out of his step.

By the time they had walked half the distance, the fog was swirling around their feet and sometimes up to their chests. It was reminding Kira way too much of her last nightmare, recalling the mental image of strolling through a gigantic witch's cauldron. The whole feel of the day seemed to deteriorate the closer they got. To make it worse, Sean's condition was worsening. Kira wasn't sure why. It finally got to the point where she felt compelled to ask.

"Sean, are you alright?"

He hurriedly lowered his hand from his head where he'd been rubbing his temples and answered. "Yeah, I'm fine. I just keep feeling more and more depressed, and I'm not sure why."

Kira stared at him as they continued walking and had just glanced back to John, who was following along doggedly, when Sean spoke again.

"My God! This is more than depression. This is despair! And pain. What is going on? Does anyone still live in Dachau?"

Kira's eyes reflected her concern. "No, nobody has lived here since the Allied forces liberated the camp at the end of the war."

They'd only gone a few more steps when Sean paused and grabbed his temples with one hand, covering his eyes. "I would expect to feel this way if I was forced to walk down death row in a prison Kira. The lingering emotions are *so* powerful."

Even though John was well aware of Sean's abilities, it was still strange watching him utilize them, and he voiced what both of them seemed to be ignoring.

"Well we are approaching the site of one of the most horrible atrocities that man has ever committed on man."

Sean turned to him, seemingly surprised. "But all those people are dead or gone."

"Does that matter?"

Sean froze for a moment, caught off guard by the question. "Well, I guess I've always thought it did but . . . no surely I can't . . . well . . ." At that moment Sean reached for his temples again, with both hands this time.

It was hurting Kira to watch Sean like this, and instinctively she took him by the arm. "Come on, let's get this over with." She pulled Sean along as she spoke, and they all proceeded through the rising gloom toward the front gate.

~

"*Arbeit macht frei*", they all read as they paused at the gate.

"Work makes you free," John translated, causing Sean and Kira to both turn and stare at him. He just shrugged his shoulders and answered their unasked question. "I used to study stuff about World War II and the concentration camps held my attention for quite some time."

They continued through the gate. The fog was thick now but still clinging close to the ground, and with the overcast above them, it left Kira with the odd visual sensation of floating in the sky between two layers of clouds. The moisture had become so heavy that she felt her skin grow damp, and her fingers were moist enough that she couldn't even register the dampness on her clothes.

Twenty steps inside the tall gate, Sean suddenly released his temples and looked up, acutely alert. John looked at him expectantly, and a second later Kira followed suit.

"What is it, Sean?" she asked.

"She's here." He said simply.

Kira shivered. Sean's words sent a reed-thin icicle slithering up her spine.

No one had to ask who Sean was referring to, and seconds later Sean himself led them on again into the heart of the former death camp, while the fog continued swirling up around their thighs.

Tentatively, almost afraid of the answer she would get, Kira asked, "Sean do you know what she's thinking?"

"You mean other than that she intends to kill us?"

"Uh yeah, other than that." Kira didn't really want to be reminded of what they all already knew, but she was hoping to coax Sean into connecting more with Poena. It just might save their lives, but Sean's struggles were increasing, and it was distracting him from concentrating on the immediate danger.

"Aaaah", Sean groaned and grabbed his head again. "It's like I can still hear all the people that were here, Kira, sobbing, crying out in pain, whimpering or just struggling to draw the next breath. Despair. Horror. Terror. I've never felt anything like this before in my life. It's horrible."

Her concern for him shoved her previous thought from her mind. "Can you just turn it off?"

"Well, I'm trying, but I'm afraid that if I manage to shut it out it's going to stop me being able to pick up Poena's thoughts, too, and I don't think we can afford to have me do that."

The pleading look in his eyes broke Kira's heart, but she was at a loss for words. John, however, was not.

"You're right, Sean," he added, his big voice taking on a strange quality in the sound deadening fog. "We can't afford to have you lose track of her in here. If we don't know where she is we surely need to know what she's thinking."

"Grandpa," he answered obtusely. "She keeps thinking of Grandpa or about Grandpa, NO she's talking *to* her grandpa. Isn't he dead?"

"I thought so," Kira replied. "but I guess I don't know for sure."

Sean stopped again and bowed his head rubbing his face. "My Lord, the suffering . . . How could people do these things to each other?"

"Let's move on toward the main building," John said. "It seems as good a place to start as any." He began to move and Sean and Kira followed him woodenly. Sean was still holding his head and Kira was holding Sean's arm as the fog continued to swirl with their passing.

While they walked Sean suffered in silence, but he continued to let Kira lead him. He finally looked up again in time to behold the huge metal artwork in front of the building. It was a heavy-gauge twisted metal scene about thirty feet long and twelve high; an abstract representation of people being strung into or tangled in razor wire. The caricatures of the people looked as thin and twisted as the wire itself.

The artist had done a magnificent job of capturing the hopelessness and horror of the place with an economy of material. It was supposed to be a memorial, but the effect on Sean was to augment the sensations he was struggling with.

After a brief fixed stare, he quickly averted his eyes, and Kira led him past it into the main building.

~

Poena moved carefully out from the side of the main building as she watched them enter. She'd been watching the trio approach from several positions. Evading them had been easy, and the fog was a wonderful surprise. She could almost imagine that Grandpa had ordered it special. It was going to make her job so much easier. Her next thought was that she had no idea who the old fat man was, or what he was doing here with them, but it didn't matter. She'd laid her plans, and he would barely register as a nuisance to the little surprises she had prepared for cousin Kira and her beau. Roughly, she adjusted the mask on her face. It had been an effort to get the skin ready in such a short time, but since she'd decided not to paint this one, she'd managed.

Without paint on it, however, the skin stretched over the carved wooden mask was a wicked caricature of its original owner. It seemed to retain the frozen expression of the shock of his demise, locked forever on that wooden facade. It was a hideous sight to behold, Poena's live eyes staring out from that dead face. Yet it almost seemed normal in this crucible of atrocities.

~

Once in the building, Sean lifted his eyes to the huge mural covering virtually the entire back wall of the main room. It was a black and white collage of photos from Dachau during its heyday, if you could call it a heyday.

Sean's stomach clinched as he looked up. The feelings of pain and suffering intensified to the point they forced all other considerations from his mind. It was like this tremendous avalanche of despair and torment had just grabbed his soul in a spirit crushing grip. He retched and had to kneel down with Kira right beside him trying to be of whatever help she could and acutely aware of her inability to fathom the depths of his distress.

"Sean, are you okay?

"It's this place, Kira. I can barely stand it. Too much suffering happened here. I would never have imagined anywhere in the world could make me feel like this." Suddenly an image of his dad, Aubrey, flashed into his mind. Hadn't he said something about being able to filter things selectively? Hmmm . . . Maybe if he concentrated on Poena . . .

Kira stole a quick glance at John, and the look of utter disgust on his face caused her to follow his gaze. Her eyes focused on the giant mural, and her stomach almost caught up to Sean's. The photos of the camp were of twisted emaciated bodies piled in a pit or standing alone, in some cases, with these haunted, hunted looks of hopelessness on their faces. Or in the case of the ones in the pit, the glassy eyed look of death.

There were photos of the guards with their steely, unfeeling eyes holding machine guns, their expressions virtually screaming their desire to use them. The sky depicted in black and white was gray, the same as it was today. Was it always dismal weather over Dachau? Even the caste of the black and white photos lent itself to the sensation of despair that permeated the gigantic mural.

Kira turned her head sharply away from that depiction of abominations and back to Sean. He was breathing deeply through his nose and seemingly gleaning some control over his recalcitrant stomach.

"Are you going to be okay?" She asked.

Sean continued to take slow deep breaths as he focused his thoughts and rotated his head up to look in Kira's eyes. A moment later he finally spoke, but the look of nausea she'd seen on his face was now replaced with cold flinty anger and determination.

"Yeah, I'll be okay. I can do this. I can push these feelings away. I've just never had to overcome so much emotion at once. Kira, this place is hell on earth, or was at least. No being should ever have to endure what went on inside this place."

"Do you think Poena's Grandpa was here? Is that why she came here?" Kira could see the light go on behind Sean's eyes at the suggestion.

"I bet it is . . . matter of fact, I'm certain that's it. I wonder if the people she's been killing are somehow connected to her Grandfather's experiences in this place, just like you thought on the plane. I wonder if her Grandfather is even still alive? She sure talks, or rather thinks, like he is ..."

Sean watched Kira nod her head in unconscious agreement, and then shudder. Then he picked up her thought. 'What if some relative of mine actually had to endure this place?' A grimace swept across her features as a chill slid across her spine. Sean heard the thought and even felt her feel the chill as clearly as if it were happening to him.

"We better keep moving," John finally chimed in. His big voice echoed in the building, and his expression mirrored Sean's. Determined disgust. Sean could sense it easily.

At his words, Sean took one more deep breath and stood up from the crouch he'd assumed a moment before.

"Yep. Let's get moving. We have a crazy to catch and the sooner we do it, the sooner we can leave this damned hell hole. And I'm telling you if I NEVER see this place again it'll be too soon."

"Okay, stay behind me," John said as he turned towards the hallway on the right, the other two following silently behind.

~

Poena waited patiently. She knew they'd come back out after awhile. Then a thought struck her. Why wait here? And she abruptly turned and started toward the crematorium. Moving through the fog in her tight black jump suit, she looked like a spirit of death, wearing a face of death. She'd still be able to see the front of the building from there, she thought, and it would be easy enough to lure them in her direction when she was ready. She smiled again at the fog surrounding her, thinking that it left the whole compound looking like a miniature city in the clouds. She felt comforted here somehow. Maybe it was because Grandpa had spent so much time here, or maybe it was just because she was about to complete Grandpa's work and bring some justice to the victims of this place. But she didn't really care about the others; this was just for her grandpa.

"Soon, Grandpa, soon," she muttered as she padded off, crouching low into the fog.

~

Sean noticed the echo of his footsteps as he moved through the huge, empty hall. He was managing to get the sensations under control like he'd told Kira, but it still felt like a constant mental tug of war and the queasiness in his stomach had yet to subside. It surprised him when he stole a glance at John and noticed he'd drawn his gun, and was moving carefully from room to room in the classic ready position like a scene from a spy movie.

Kira was following quietly. Sean sensed only her tension as she gently squeezed his hand. Following behind John, Sean tried tentatively to reach out and find Poena with his mind. The other emotions flooded in causing him to recoil and slam his newfound mental barriers back into place.

"Sean?" Kira must have been looking into his face when the mental backlash hit, concern was evident in both her gaze and her mind.

"I'm okay. I'm just trying to feel for Poena and keep the other feelings down at the same time. It's not working very well, yet."

Kira just nodded understanding, and they both hurried to catch up to John.

Reaching the last room and peering in, John raised his gun to point safely up to the ceiling and took a deep calming breath. Then, a moment later, he called to them.

"Over here."

He was already bending over a loose brick and some debris on the floor when Sean and Kira knelt down beside him. From the dust John had picked up an old yellowed photo. He was still bringing it to his face when Kira, who was peering over his shoulder, gasped.

"My God! That looks like me!" The exclamation drew Sean's attention immediately.

"Wow. It really does," Sean agreed.

They were both leaning closer to the photo while John, who was still holding it, had turned his attention to the notebook still lying on the floor.

"But how could . . ." Sean never got to finish that sentence.

A scream tore through their nervous systems. It was loud and penetrating but distant. Sean's head popped up immediately.

"It's her."

Nobody needed to ask what he meant. They all jumped up and were following Sean before anyone had a chance to consider what they were doing.

Back through the building and out into the compound and the fog, Sean moved with a swift and certain grace. The other two remained several steps behind, much to John's chagrin, and Kira kept glancing nervously at the fog.

Turning her gaze upward, briefly, at the overcast sky, she felt like they were walking between cloud layers. It would have shocked and dismayed her to know how close her thoughts followed Poena's from a moment before.

Sean was all the way to the middle of the compound when he pulled up short. All of a sudden he wasn't sure anymore. Think, he told himself you can do this.

"Focus" he heard his dad's voice say. And then he could.

He turned his head toward the smaller crematorium and at that moment another shriek filled the air. Much closer this time. Sean had it right. With a fixed gaze and a determined step, Sean marched through the fog toward the smaller brick building. Kira followed, watching the fog churn around his feet and feeling more helpless and scared by the moment.

Sean stepped cautiously through the door to the crematorium and peered around intently. Rough wood beams framed the ceiling and dark red brick walls; otherwise nothing. But he knew she was here somewhere. He decided to wait for John to come in with the gun before going any farther. He took the moment to read the framed words on the wall by his head.

"This was the smaller crematorium and many prisoners were hung from the rafters above. These three ovens were used more for disposing of bodies than for the mass murders of the larger crematoriums."

Sean's gaze returned involuntarily to the brick ovens, and his queasiness wound even tighter in his stomach. He wanted to get out of this building, but he was certain that Poena was here somewhere. He could feel her. As that thought occurred to him, he realized he hadn't bothered to question 'what' she was feeling or even thinking for that matter. Now he turned his attention toward the task with a grim determination. He peeled her emotions from the knot of other sensations and managed to catch what he was looking for.

Hate, glee, anticipation, all overlaid with a patina of evil. What an odd combination of emotions he thought as John shouldered his way past him towards the first oven. The ovens had two foot square, heavy metal doors and John went to the first one and peered around both sides then reached for the door.

"You're going to look *in* the oven?

"Did you notice that this is the only one that's not completely closed? John answered in his deep metered voice.

"Well yeah, now that you mention it, but surely . . . "

"Sean, the sound came from here somewhere. Where else do you think someone could hide?"

Sean glanced around cursorily and shrugged his shoulders. "It just seems wrong somehow . . ." But he knew it had to be done, and except for all the lingering emotions of this place, that he was now successfully suppressing, this was reminding him way too much of when the three of them were standing around his mother's grave getting ready to dig. Frankly he didn't relish that ghoulish sensation or the memory.

Just as John reached to pull the door open with one hand, gun in the other, he spoke to both of them without averting his eyes. "Do you smell something?"

There was a distinct scraping sound that Kira recognized as the sound of a cigarette lighter's wheel turning across the flint.

At the same instant Sean caught an emotion coming from Poena. Anticipation, excitement? Right off the chart. Oh my God he thought. "John, NO!" he yelled as he dove for John's midsection again reminding himself of that other graveside scene.

A gout of flame exploded from the door of the crematorium and Sean heard the beginnings of Kira's scream as his shoulder slammed into John's side. They fell to the ground where Sean's senses dimly registered the fact that Kira's scream had cut off abruptly, but he couldn't attend to that detail yet.

John's clothes were on fire on the right side and it looked like the side of his face was badly burned. Sean yanked off his own shirt and used it to quench the remaining flames. John was apparently out cold. That was probably a blessing. Quickly, Sean yanked his attention back to Kira in the doorway.

She was gone.

"Kira!" he yelled. "Kira!" He ran back to the door and through it as he yelled. All he could see was layers of fog swirling in all directions like tendrils of smoke creeping beneath a fire-backed door.

~

Poena had not been in the crematorium for many minutes. The idea had struck her that the perfect hiding place was all around her and she had been barely behind the crematorium lying on her belly beneath the fog when they had all entered. The idea of using the unexpected cover to such an advantage tickled her. Grandpa was definitely watching out for her.

From her hiding place on the ground it had been easy to slither closer to the door. She wanted to be close enough to see if anyone fell for her trap, but she couldn't risk being seen and the fog wasn't penetrating into the crematorium. So she waited.

She didn't have long to wait, either. She heard Sean yell NO, and then heard Kira scream. The scream had startled her because it was so close. Kira must be near the door and in that case it must have been the fat man who had sprung the trap. Perfect!

Trying to breathe beneath the mask she was wearing was making her feel a bit claustrophobic, but she didn't have time to dwell on that. The moment to take the girl was now. Silently, but quickly, she rose up out of fog like a denizen from the depths and rapped Kira on the back of the head with the butt of her knife. Kira's scream cut off with a satisfying suddenness. Poena caught her body as it slumped to the ground.

Poena was dragging her away in the fog almost immediately. She had to get as far as she could before the boy started to look for her. And then she could cut the bitch's face off and be done with her mission. But not yet, she needed Kira alive a bit longer. She needed bait. That boy had to die, too. An unwelcome memory of his lips on hers slithered through her mind, and she shoved it roughly away. No time for that, she told herself. Concentrate.

"Kira!" She heard the boy yell. It was time to be still and Poena just lay there next to her cousin. Her face was so close to Kira's that she could make out her features easily in the fog. Exactly like her grandma, Rebecca.

It was amazing how much Kira looked like her, but that didn't change the fact that Kira was still the bastard granddaughter of that devil spawn Commandant of Dauchau, General Theodore Eicke. For that she would die and soon, then Grandpa could finally rest in peace. This was the goal Grandpa had sent her here to accomplish: the final act of her long mission. The first would be the last. It all made sense to her now.

It was only then that it occurred to her that Grandpa hadn't talked to her for a while now, probably because he didn't want to slow her down, now that she was finally on the right course. She smiled to herself lying there beneath the fog.

~

John felt several sensations so close together as to be indistinguishable and none of them were pleasant. He felt searing flames on the side of his face and then a tremendous concussion on the side of his body. Even as he was falling his mind was trying to take in what had happened. The word 'trap' made it into his awareness before another concussion on the side of his head sent a shower of sparks shooting into his vision, and then blackness swallowed him.

~

Sean was beside himself. He was torn between wandering around trying to find Kira and going back in the crematorium to check on John. Where could Kira have gotten to?

Then it occurred to him to that he could do both if he quit using his eyes and started using his mind. Think Sean, he told himself as he walked back into the crematorium. He called Kira's name a few more times, as he tried to think and then the leaden weight of past emotions from the former occupants of Dachau trickled into his mind. They felt like they were closing in on him, begging for attention. Forcibly, he pushed them down again. He would *not* deal with that now. It was only one mind he was looking for, and he *was* going to find her.

Continuing to concentrate on Kira, he went back in to check on John. He was still out cold and breathing steadily. Sean moved back from the crematorium and out into the yard of the compound. There was no more he could do for John at the moment. He stood stock still. He had to focus. If he did, he was sure he could pick up another thought from Kira or maybe even Poena.

The cloud cover was still descending and between that and the fog, the day was transposing itself into one of utter gloom, totally befitting not only his mood but the mood of the place itself.

He narrowed his thoughts to his feelings for Kira. All she had come to mean to him in such a short time and all they had already shared. He tapped into the memory of having to save her when one of her nightmares about his dad had stopped her heart. He had delved deeper into her psyche—her soul—that night than he ever had with anyone in his entire life and come away with a new bond with her unlike anything he'd ever felt before or since. In his mind he reached for that bond.

Nothing.

He couldn't sense anything from her, but how could that be unless . . . no he wouldn't even let himself consider that she might already be dead.

Unconscious maybe, but not dead. With renewed resolve, he moved his focus to Poena. He seemed to be gaining ground at suppressing the other voices and emotions.

Fog. That was the word that came to him.

Hidden. And a picture of the fog swirling.

Sean's gaze slid down toward the ground, and his eyes stopped on the vapor dancing up around his knees, thicker than smoke, billowing across the expanse of the camp. Of course! She was using the fog for cover! Lying down. But that meant she could be anywhere, near or far, and he had no idea if she had a gun or a knife or maybe even another trap set somewhere. If she caught him, he was certain that Kira was doomed. How had she even known they were following? The thought almost made him laugh. How had *they* known to follow? Why was it so hard to accept that Poena had some skills of her own? She'd already shown them, and now it seemed she'd planned this whole thing out much better than they had, but she hadn't planned the fog. She did seem to know how to take advantage of the situation, though.

Sean backed up a step, then froze. The fog really did look like smoke but without the smell. How appropriate for this resort from Hell. Visions of his smoking ruined home welled up in his mind. More like, how appropriate for an arsonist, he thought. Still, if Poena could use the fog, then so could he and with that thought he slowly knelt then laid down in the fog himself and he, too, disappeared.

Now if he could just figure out what to do next. Then another word congealed in his mind almost as if had floated to him from within the fog itself.

Lure. She wanted to lure him somewhere, probably John, too. That meant that nothing was going to happen until John regained consciousness. But no, Poena wouldn't know that John even *was* unconscious. Still, it did mean that Kira was relatively safe until they sprung whatever trap she was trying to set. Kira was the lure. What he needed was another clue from Poena, and he might as well be with John until then. Poena wanted him to come to her, so there would be another clue. Sean stood back up, deciding that hiding wasn't going to accomplish anything for him right now. Once he reached his feet, he turned back toward the crematorium.

~

With her hand resting gently on Kira's throat, Poena was aware the moment Kira began to arouse. After taking one quick peek up out of the fog and assuring herself that Sean wasn't any closer, she turned to Kira.

"You make even the slightest sound and I'll rip your throat out here and now. Do you understand me?"

Kira's first glimpse at Poena had clenched her stomach and caused her to flinch back, instantly tightening Poena's grip on her throat. On the woman's face was a mask of unspeakable horror. A man's face obviously stretched over some sort of wooden carving glared back at her. Real skin, she was certain of it and real terror frozen in its expression. Thoughts of the process necessary to produce the atrocity she was seeing further clenched her stomach, and Kira began to wonder if explosively vomiting on this woman might allow her to escape. The idea melted away though as Kira realized she wouldn't even be able to run right now as she was still dizzy from the blow to her head. Even if she tried, she had no idea where to run to.

~

To Poena, Kira's only response was the slight flinching away and the terror evidenced by the widening of her eyes. She assumed it was fear of her, the mask on her face completely forgotten. Her deceptively gentle touch on Kira's throat tightened instinctively and seemed to render the woman mute.

But that didn't satisfy Poena, so very softly and even more intently, she repeated herself. Kira nodded her head. She understood.

~

Kira could feel her pulse racing. The sensations she was experiencing were so surreal and foreign to her that she was having a difficult time believing she wasn't in the throes of one of her painting-spawned nightmares.

Here she was, lying on hard ground in a Nazi death camp in another country, surrounded by an eerie fog, pinned down by some crazy woman dressed in a skin tight black jump suit and a hideously grotesque mask composed of the removed skin from some poor soul's face.

The woman's hand was at her throat in what felt like a loving caress except Kira knew for certain this maniac was just itching to murder her. She had no idea where she was or where Sean was or what happened to John, and her head was pounding so horribly she thought it might be cracked.

She knew she had to do something, but without a little more information, anything she might try was tantamount to suicide. She was *not* going to let this woman win. She had to be patient and wait for whatever she might learn. As her thoughts slowed slightly, she felt her pulse pounding against the grip of Poena's hand on her throat. That unwilling evidence of her fear only served to further spark her anger. Still, she thought, patience was the only action for her at the moment.

~

Finally, Sean received a sensation from Kira: fear, revulsion . . . a dead man's face? What did that mean? Nothing that served as a clue, though, and a groan from John redirected his attention. At least now he knew Kira was still alive.

John's eyes were beginning to flutter as Sean knelt down and looked more closely at the burns on the side of his face. They were bad. Sections of his cheek were bubbled up and a few spots by his ear and down the right side of his neck were black. After the initial shock, Sean thought it could have been so much worse. His right eye was apparently unaffected which was a miracle in itself. At that point in his inspection John groaned again and opened his eyes.

"Ow." He said in his deep baritone causing Sean to nearly chuckle, but he caught himself and then felt guilty.

"I would ask how bad it hurts, but I'm thinking that's a stupid question right now."

"I'm afraid I'd have to agree with that," John answered as he struggled to lever himself up into a sitting position. "Where is Kira?"

"Poena took her."

Sean could sense John's pain and also his compassion. He concentrated, and it suddenly felt like his own face was burning. Mentally he flinched back from John's feelings.

Oh my God, Sean thought, the pain. As he watched, John slowly lifted his hand as if to touch his face, then thought better of it.

"Shit. Well, I guess we know what's next for us to do, then."

"I'm not so sure what to do just yet, John. Poena's using the fog for cover. I think that's how she snuck up on us. She could be anywhere. I'm certain she's fairly close, though. I'm also sure she plans to keep Kira alive long enough to lure us somewhere."

"Okay, so where is she?" John asked simply.

Sean could barely stand to look at John's face, and pointedly avoided letting any of John's feelings creep into his mind again. He couldn't imagine how the man could be functioning with the pain he was enduring, but he needed to be careful not to let those feelings distract him anymore. Therefore, the import of his question took a second to register. John expected him to know. But he didn't know, at least not yet.

Nothing he could do seemed to be helping him locate Kira. He'd finally managed to stem the pervasive sorrow and despair that lay over this travesty of humanity, so accurately referred to as a death camp. Now he should be able to utilize his ability, but still he wasn't getting any useful clues from Kira, and it was frustrating him.

Poena, damn it! He needed to focus on Poena. Why did he keep forgetting that *she* was the one he needed to concentrate on? Maybe it was because all of the little forays he'd had with her were unnerving. He didn't want to be in touch with the lunacy she harbored; or maybe it was just because he was used to touching Kira's mind, and that was where his heart wanted to go. It could simply be the overwhelming sensations from the dead in this place. None of which was going to help him find her, so he'd better shift gears and fast.

Do it, he told himself, so rather than answering John verbally, Sean stood stock still and concentrated. The first sensation that hit him was Kira.

She was in pain and she was scared but she was conscious, now. She was also confident that he'd find her, but she had no idea where she was ... Shove it away ... shift your focus ... to ... to ... there.

Poena. She was there lurking in the fog. Further away than she had been and trying to get herself and Kira over to ... large crematorium? Sean whirled his gaze back to John who was standing in front of the crematorium they had just left. The small brick building filled his vision. She couldn't have gone in there.

~

John watched as Sean first froze momentarily then turned to look past him to the crematorium, a look of confusion on his face. The searing pain filled his mind, but he refused to give in to it. He could attend to that later, if they made it out of here alive. He waited just a moment longer before being compelled to ask.

"What's wrong, Sean?"

"Crematorium. That's the word I'm getting, but she can't be in the crematorium. We're standing right here at the entrance."

"Maybe it's the other crematorium. The big one."

'Large.' That was the word he'd received. Sean shifted his gaze to John's wrecked face and schooled his own expression to neutral. "What other crematorium?"

"The big one on the other side of the compound. Over there." John pointed sharply to Sean's right as he finished his sentence, and Sean's eyes followed his direction.

"How did you know there was another one over there?"

"I saw it with some of the information on a map in the great room at the main building before we left."

Sean turned and looked back in the direction John had pointed. "That big building over there?"

"That's what it said. Apparently that was the one where they did the mass cremations. This one was just for disposing of bodies that had been executed some other way."

"You mean that one was for . . ."

"Burning people alive," John finished. As he spoke his hand drifted back to his face. The place his touch contacted must have felt foreign to his fingers judging by his expression.

"Does it hurt?"

"Actually, it doesn't *feel* at all. I guess that's a bad thing. Some nerves must be destroyed, too."

The reminder of his expression turned flinty.

"Maybe it's just shock." Sean answered.

"Whatever. Let's just go over there and get her and be rid of this God forsaken place."

Sean's head was nodding agreement but he said, "Not just yet. Let me get a better idea of what she's planning. We can't afford to spring the trap too soon or we might be caught by it. It would mean a quick end for Kira and *that's* not going to happen. Still, I think we can move in that direction at least, while I'm trying to get something clearer from Poena."

His feet began moving as he finished the last sentence, making the persistent fog swirl around their legs. It was rising. The image of a shark rising from the depths of the ocean popped into his mind. Not so far off, he thought ruefully. The cloud cover continued to lower. If it kept this up, the fog and the clouds would meet before too long, and their visibility would disappear completely.

The crematorium seemed to be drawing him. It occurred to him that moving around to the back of the thing might not be such a bad idea. At least they wouldn't be where Poena expected them, and it was as good a place to stand as any while he continued to try to pick up Poena's thoughts. He glanced back at John who was trudging along behind him. John needed a hospital, and he needed it sooner than later.

As they approached the larger crematorium, Sean was mesmerized by its construction. It was triangular shaped with two vertical cinder-block walls and a concrete floor. The third side was a giant lattice work of wrought iron with the image of a Jewish Star of David in the center of the door. What a horrible gesture to put that icon of the Jewish faith on the entrance to a structure built for their destruction. It reminded him of the artwork in front of the main building that had so engrossed him. That and the sensations he was receiving seemed to clutch at his soul.

The bars in the tangle of metal were not tubes of iron but square bars, giving the whole structure a sharp and even more forbidding feel. A shiver ran through him and a sudden surge of terror mixed with despair and hate flooded into his mind. His steps faltered. Being this close to the nexus of these atrocities filled with such hate was absolutely overwhelming. He'd thought it'd been bad before, but this was worse. It taxed his new found abilities to block it out, and his concentration flagged.

The passage of decades seemed to have had no bearing on the intensity of those residual emotions. Yet, he had to fight it. Push it down. Kira's life depended on it. Hell, *all* their lives depended on it.

Carefully he maneuvered around the back looking again to be sure John was still following. Sean could sense him, but the fog continued to deaden the sound of any footsteps, and John certainly wasn't in a chatty mood, so he felt the need to keep checking.

Sean continued to move towards the rear-facing apex of the triangular shaped structure; the fog catching his attention again. What had been a knee-deep, almost solid layer, seemed to be rising and thinning as if some suction was occurring from above, causing it to rise.

Slowly it crept up, waist high, then chest. It was the oddest sensation. It appeared like water rising in a container threatening to drown him, but the only sensation of touch was the increasing moisture on his exposed skin. The fog continued to thin out as it rose but was still thick enough to obscure vision at a distance of only a few paces. The cloudy undulating mass seemed to be swallowing up the entire compound. Sean looked at John to see if he was registering the change, but his eyes were drooping and downcast. The pain was finally getting through his shock and resolve. Sean let a tiny sliver of John's sensations trickle into his awareness.

His pain was intense.

A little shudder passed through him. He couldn't do that again, not if he wanted to be able to concentrate.

"Come on, John, just a little further, and we can sit and wait. The fog will keep us hidden. Hopefully our ears or my senses will give us the edge we need."

John just nodded wearily and followed as Sean moved on a few more steps, staying near the wall for direction. Sean was at a bit of a loss as to where to stop. His senses weren't giving him any more clues at the moment. The further back they went on the triangle the worse their view was of the opening to the crematorium. Sean did have one powerful sensation; that opening was where this was all going to end one way or another.

~

Poena was watching closely as the fog rose. It was both good and bad from her perspective. It would make it easier to move to the crematorium with Kira in tow, but it was also going to make it harder to see the boy and the fat man.

She was somewhat disappointed that the fat man was still alive. She'd hoped her trap would have finished one of them, but she'd caught a glimpse of him following the boy as they moved away from the small brick crematorium. Now she needed to get to the far side of the next structure where she had a few supplies stashed in preparation for this moment. It wouldn't be too long now.

Her thoughts turned to Kira. The woman was behaving at the

moment, but she was still debating the pros and cons of leaving her conscious. If she was unconscious she wasn't going to be trying to escape, but then Poena would have to carry her, and that was a burden she didn't need, especially after she reached the supplies. She'd have to knock her out again in a little while, though; right after she got the woman into position and made her scream, then the trap would be set.

Poena stood stock-still for a moment just to listen. It was too quiet, she thought; no movement to be heard anywhere not even any birds. It didn't matter anyway, she decided. It was time.

"Come on, let's go, Rebecca," she said.

~

Kira's eyes narrowed at the unexpected moniker, but she was too afraid to ask anything and figured it didn't much matter what this lunatic might call her, or for that matter what answer Poena would give if she asked. Before she could ponder it much further Poena touched her again, and all she could do was flinch.

~

Grabbing Kira by the neck again produced a little chirp from her, and it was all Poena could do not to smash the butt of her knife into that pretty face.

Rebecca's face.

Grandma's face.

She shook her head. It wouldn't do to let that thought keep floating around in her mind. It might slow her down.

~

The woman's hands were so cold on her neck that she squeaked involuntarily. Poena probably thought it was from fear. Good. Let her think that. It would improve her chances when it was time to move.

Kira didn't have any illusions about being sensitive like Sean, but she could still feel the hate coming from this woman in palpable waves.

What had generated such a malevolent spirit in her? She'd probably never know.

She wondered where Sean was now. It had occurred to her that if she even knew where *she* was then she might be able to get the information to Sean by thinking it. Surely Sean could find her thoughts, but right now she didn't know anything that would help. The pounding in her head was only getting worse, and she was beginning to worry about having a concussion. She could only hope Sean would hurry. Hurry Sean . . . please.

~

Sean bridged his temples with his hand. Kira's head was hurting, and she was thinking 'hurry Sean'. Well, he intended to hurry, but he had to know exactly where to hurry to. Even so, it felt nice to be connected to her again, comforting to know she was no worse off than she had been . . . at least for the moment. Hurry was right.

The fog had now risen to well above their heads, and everything was enveloped in the cloud. Even the back of the crematorium ceiling disappeared from view after a few paces.

The diminished visibility gave the impression of the death camp closing in on him as if it was trying to swallow these puny mortals who'd dared to linger within its walls. The emotions of the dead rose up briefly in his mind, and he had to double his efforts to quell them. It was all too eerie, and the waiting was excruciating. Poena was moving now. She was headed to . . . to . . . her supplies? What were her supplies, Sean wondered? Nothing good for him and John he was pretty sure. It was time to move closer.

Sean turned to John and caught his attention through the fog. Locking gazes with him, he held an index finger first up to his lips then curled it in a beckoning gesture and turned to move slowly along the tall crematorium wall.

John followed doggedly, his own pain continuing to intensify. Sean could sense it from him and wasn't sure how much longer he had before he passed out.

They had only gone about twenty feet when the sound of a rusty wrought iron gate screeching softly on its hinges shattered the silence. Sean froze while he listened to the sound and envisioned Poena opening the gate to the crematorium.

He could visualize the Star of David in the center of the gate and then had to wonder if it was his own imagination, or if he was picking up on what Kira or Poena were actually seeing. Either way he knew exactly where they were for at least a moment or two, and it accelerated his steps.

Inside the massive wrought iron wall that represented the entire front of the huge triangular crematorium, the concrete floor sloped gently upward towards its apex at the back. Poena shoved Kira roughly inside the iron door and hoisted the duffel bag carrying the supplies she'd procured. She wasn't worried about the sound the old rusty door made or at this point about any sounds Kira might make. She wanted the other two coming towards her anyhow.

~

Kira was seeing the Star of David at the instant Sean saw it in his mind, and she felt certain that he was getting the image. He would be coming, if Poena didn't just kill her first.

It was the strangest thing, watching this crazy woman execute all these plans while wearing that wretched mask. What did that mask have to do with them? And who was the poor soul whose face she'd taken? A shiver coursed through her again at the mental image of that act.

Was the mask some kind of symbol or something? And for that matter, why did she wear that skin tight black suit? Oh it was flattering, okay, and she certainly had the body for it but who was she trying to impress? It would certainly be useful at night, but in the daytime it seemed absurd. On further inspection Kira noticed that the fabric was especially slick looking. Maybe it was some special fabric to protect her from fire like what the race car drivers wear. Nomex, she remembered. That was the name of that stuff. Maybe that's what it was. Which wasn't a very reassuring thought. If she was wearing Nomex she was expecting flames, and if she was expecting flames then Kira was soon going to be wishing for Nomex herself. Again, she consoled herself. Sean was on his way, and there would come a moment when she'd have the opportunity to act, to do *something* to help extricate herself from this hellish situation.

Her thoughts continued to wander, sliding back to the items that John had found in the main building. That woman pictured in the photo, an old photo. Rebecca. Poena had called her, Rebecca. So who was Rebecca?

Poena's mother? Grandmother? John had also retrieved a little notebook, but no one had taken the opportunity to read it yet. Maybe that contained the answers to the puzzle. And poor John; she hoped he was okay. She'd only been able to see the gout of flame extend from the oven and Sean dive, before Poena had struck her from behind. Surely he was alive. She hoped he was.

That was as far as her chain of thought progressed, though, because they'd reached the back of the triangular chamber and Poena had stopped and was turning towards her.

Glancing around once as she reached the back of the crematorium, Poena reached for her knife bringing the butt up suddenly. Kira saw it coming an instant before it smashed into the side of her head.

She flinched sharply, turning her head and dissipating much of the force of the blow but went down in a heap anyway. If Poena wanted her unconscious, she was going to be unconscious at least as far as Poena was concerned anyway.

It was one of the toughest things she'd ever done. Lying there pretending to be unconscious, knowing that Poena was standing over her with a knife she was more than willing to use. But she managed it, even when Poena knelt down, her face close and spoke to her.

"Sleep well, Rebecca," she said and then stood back up.

~

Sean's head was starting to ache massively. The strain of filtering out all the emotions of this place, plus the pain coming from John, and the fear from Kira, all the while remaining open to what Poena might convey, was wearing on him badly. He had no experience in utilizing his gift this way, and the strain was increasing steadily. It would be easier if he could at least filter out John and Kira, too, but he needed to know their thoughts. See what they saw, know what they knew. He already knew Kira had gone through the gate with Poena, even without Kira's thoughts he'd heard the squeal of the old gate's hinges. But that was too easy. Obviously that was where Poena wanted them to go. So for Kira's sake they *had* to go there or at least seem to.

His thoughts continued to race. John was thinking that he'd about reached the limit of his ability to cope with his pain. Sean let himself feel John's pain again for a second, and the effort made him recoil. My Lord, how was he doing it? Sean pulled his thoughts back abruptly. It was time to move.

Seem to ... seem to ... Sean kept thinking as they moved through the fog and then through the squeaky gate. Was that coming from Kira?

John was two steps ahead of him when he spoke slightly louder than was necessary.

"John, keep it quiet. I think she might be back here."

But as he said the words, he touched John's shoulder, pointed ahead, then pointed to himself and jerked a thumb over his shoulder. John nodded briefly and turned into the fog. Sean back peEricd towards the gate and was soon invisible in the seemingly supernatural mist.

He had moved all the way to the entrance of the gate and now moved along the wrought iron barrier to where it met one of the tall masonry walls. The limit of his vision in the mist was a bare few feet, so he squatted down and began to concentrate. He needed to catch Poena's thoughts, and he needed to do it now. Drawing a deep breath he closed his eyes and focused his thoughts. First filter out all the old emotions, then separate out John and Kira and then what was left was . . .

Poena! He had her.

Poena was actually in a squatting position similar to Sean's on the opposite end of the wrought iron wall. She was unpacking the last items from her duffel bag including the box she had brought along that contained her supply of the sun. It was almost time.

The sun? Sean opened his eyes. Poena was thinking about the sun. It caused him to glance up and out through the wrought iron bars. Judging by the dim light above him, the overcast was still hanging there either above or continuous with the rising fog. There was no sun to be seen. So why was Poena thinking about the sun???? Closing his eyes again he caught 'box with the sun in it' and then something about an odor. Worrying about an odor? What was she talking about? His concentration slipped slightly, and the old emotions crept back in. Sean suddenly felt depressed. No! He thought to himself forcefully. I don't have time for this.

~

John inched his way back through the fog, holding his hands out in front of him like a blind man. The fog seemed to congeal in this narrow space and with each step he took, his visibility diminished further. He must be near the back, he thought, through the haze of anguish filling his brain.

He was getting a bit dizzy and expected that he was on the verge of passing out. A person could only tolerate so much pain before the body decided to shut down.

Suddenly, a figure rose out of the fog and lunged for him. He and Kira recognized each other a split second before they collided and the scream beginning in Kira's throat died unborn. John staggered back, his heart racing, trying to maintain his and Kira's balance, as they both heard Sean's voice at the same instant that Kira recognized a smell. Gasoline.

"Kira this way," Sean screamed as he raced across the wrought iron barrier towards Poena.

~

Once he had seen her through her own thoughts, squatting on the opposite end of the wrought iron entrance, Sean suspected that his time was running out. But when he caught the thought of a lighter and a flame he knew that whatever the 'sun' was, it pertained to fire, and it was time to act. He charged across the barrier, racing blindly through the earth born cloud and before he saw Poena herself, he saw a tiny flame appear in the fog.

"NO!" He screamed as he barreled towards the tiny light.

Four things happened in the next couple of seconds that in years to come Sean would struggle to separate in his mind. A breeze picked up and began to sweep through the crematorium, swirling and clearing the fog around him. A line of flame seemed to shoot through that fog straight towards the apex of this man made death box. A second point of flame appeared in front of him and suddenly Poena's form in some grotesque human-faced mask appeared out of the mist. His hand reached unconsciously into his own pocket as he saw her holding a lighter in her right hand and with her left she was casting a cloud of dust towards him.

His hand, on its own, had found the lighter his dad had so recently given him. The one his dad had bought for the mother he had never met. The one he had carried with him ever since and for some unknown reason had brought to Germany. The thought of that inscription flashed through his mind as he flicked it open with one hand and drew its wheel across the flint.

"*To Laura with Love, a reminder of the little light you brought into our lives. Aubrey.*"

Without really knowing why he was taking such unusual actions he tossed the lighter toward Poena as he heard her voice.

"Let the Sun take you," she screamed as she tossed her own old style lighter after the cloud she'd just thrown.

Sean was trying to fathom what she meant and why he'd just done what he'd done, when she screamed again, throwing her hideously masked face back in glee and her arms into the air in exultation.

"It is done, Grandpa! The first is now the last! I've done it!"

At that moment, the gust of wind that had swept into the crematorium, apparently having hit the back of the building and swept back out, blew the cloud back towards her face. Sean's lighter was now in perfect position to ignite that cloud of dust and the sudden blast of light that struck Sean felt like staring dead-on into a lightning bolt. A fraction of a second after that, a blood curdling scream rang out from the spot where Poena was standing.

~

Poena felt the heat of the flames as the sun ignited her face. In her hurry she had only donned the recently crafted flesh mask and had left the Nomex undermask she usually wore, back in her hotel. The immense pain raged through her and for the brief instant before she screamed, she felt the flesh of her face melt and run. As she gasped for breath, she thought of the bodies she had burned in fires just like the one that was now consuming her. Suddenly, there in her mind, came one last thought from Grandpa.

"It is over my child. I am sorry."

With that her consciousness fled, and she knew no more.

It took a moment for the color spots to recede from Sean's stunned eyes and what he saw soured his spirit. The wave of pain he suddenly felt coming from Poena matched the scream he'd just heard and the combination clinched his stomach, then just as suddenly, subsided. There she was, lying on the ground, hands clutching that hideous mask which had burned and melted utterly.

Poena was apparently unconscious or worse because she wasn't moving at all. Tearing his eyes away from her, Sean turned to look back down into the crematorium suddenly afraid. But before he could even focus his feelings, John and Kira appeared out of the rapidly dissipating fog. John was beginning to limp and leaning slightly on Kira. Kira was the first to speak.

"Sean, are you okay?"

Sean took one appraising look at Kira before answering. He was filling himself with both the vision of her and the thoughts coming from her in an effort to assure himself that she was alright. A second later he knew she was, and he answered her, first with a hug, then with a reply.

"Yeah, Sweetie, I'm fine. I'm not sure about Poena, though." He turned his gaze back towards the still heap in the tight black suit. The mask itself was indeed melted, with all the skin scorched and drooping in a wicked parody of what everyone assumed had also happened to the face beneath it. That stolen face seemed to have reformed itself into the lopsided caricature of a one-sided smile, as if to express satisfaction at the outcome. The whole picture was too grotesque and surreal to bear continued viewing, and all three turned their faces away from it after their brief rapt stares.

"She tried to throw something at me and light it, but the wind blew it back in her face and it ignited from my lighter."

"Magnesium," John said. "It was magnesium powder. That was the accelerant she was using to start the fires."

"Your lighter?" Kira turned a questioning glance at Sean.

"Yeah, I threw the lighter my dad gave me at her for some reason." And with that thought he turned back to Poena; after a brief scan he saw the slightly marred metal lying on the ground behind her. He walked over and picked it up, then returned to Kira's side, absently putting an arm around her.

For another moment or two everyone just stood quietly as the breeze continued to pick up, thinning out the fog. Finally, John broke the silence.

"I think I better make a phone call."

With slow, weary motions, John reached into his pocket and pulled out his phone, wincing in the process.

"The burns are bad, huh, John?" Sean asked, but even as he spoke he let himself feel what John was feeling and realized his mistake.

"I'm not sure what hurts worse; the burns or … well I think you might have cracked some ribs with that flying tackle you saved me with," he answered, turning his attention to the phone again to dial.

"Can you hold off on that phone call for a moment, John? I think we have one more thing to do before we call in the cavalry."

"What's that?" John asked, turning slowly to look back at Sean.

"We have a couple of things to retrieve from the main building, and I don't want anyone telling us we can't take them. So let's get them first."

John nodded. "The book and the photo."

"Yep. I think there'll be some answers in there for Kira. Don't you?"

"Oh, I bet there are."

Kira didn't say a word. She just slowly turned and looked down at Poena.

The fog was continuing to dissolve as the breeze freshened. Oddly, no one had moved to check on Poena, lying there beside them. They didn't know if she was just unconscious or dead.

Sean found himself strangely hoping she was merely unconscious as he opened his feelings to her. At once his mind reeled with the wails of those who had perished here in the past, mixed with the echoes of her scream. Otherwise there was a blank. After so many years, this compound had claimed one more victim with fire, and though one voice was now silent, Sean still struggled with the mortal wails of the past victims of this building. Mentally he flinched, closing off the connection again, wondering how that small amount of fire could've killed her.

"She's dead." Sean pronounced, "though I don't know how."

"I imagined she suffocated when that mask melted onto her face,"

John added as he turned away. "Come on folks, I need to get to a doctor."

With that, all three turned and trudged away from the looming edifice of death and walked back across the compound towards the main building. The breeze now qualified as a wind and the last vestiges of fog evaporated along with some of the cloud cover. Small beams of sunshine slipped through the gaps and the trio saw the first glimpse of sun they had seen all day. In its way the sunlight was as mysterious as the fog before it had been. It slipped through the waning cloud cover like little columns of light in the path before them and brightened their moods even more than it brightened the day. When they reached the main building Sean pointedly avoided looking at the wrought iron art structure in the front and told John to go ahead and make the call and he'd retrieve the items from the building.

Alone, walking through the building, listening to the echoes of his footsteps, Sean heard a voice. He flinched and then realized it was in his mind. Suddenly he knew he was catching one last thought from Poena . . .

"Tell my cousin I'm sorry . . . "

And it was gone.

Sean pondered the concept that Kira was related to Poena, then thought again of the photo he was going to retrieve. But he was temporarily distracted by another revelation. Now he was receiving direct thoughts from the dead as well as emotions and thoughts from the living. Was there no end to where this ability of his was going to go? He shuddered at the possibilities as he reached the back room and picked up the little book and the photo.

He glanced again at the photo, thinking again of Poena's last message. The resemblance was astounding. Family, he thought, bits of family history. Now Kira would have some unexpected information about her family just like he'd experienced about his.

It made him feel even closer to her for the connection. First the inadvertent quest with Kira that resulted in answered questions of his life, then being thrust into a path that resulted in the same thing happening to Kira. What could possibly be next for them?

That line of thought made him want to contact his dad again and, come to think of it, he wanted to quiz his dad more about his own abilities. Maybe he knows more than he told me. And then, he was certain he did.

A great weariness settled into Sean as he marched slowly back out of the old structure. A siren was wailing in the distance, and by the time he reached the outside, the ambulance and Kira were waiting for him. John was already inside. As the ambulance pulled away, the hearse from the coroner's office and two police cars were pulling in. Sean was glad to be going, though he knew there'd be endless questions later.

Leaving the former death camp in the back of the ambulance was the perfect compliment to the surreal quality of the day. They'd barely left the compound when the weight of emotions from the dead abruptly lifted from Sean's mind. He sighed a great sigh of relief as he realized he could no longer sense them, and his mood lightened perceptibly. Kira noticed the change.

"Glad to be out of there?" She ventured.

"More than I can tell you." The bone weariness made his voice sound flat even to his own ears.

Kira leaned over onto his shoulder. "I know what you mean. Did I mention I love you lately?"

"Not in the last few minutes," he replied smiling.

"Sean?"

"Yeah."

"What are we going to do with ourselves? I'm beginning to realize we're a couple of weird ducks."

"You noticed that did you? Well for starters, I'm thinking we have a wedding to attend to and who knows, maybe we could try for a few ducklings. Come to think of it, I guess we have a house to rebuild too."

Though Kira's smile was all the answer Sean needed, they were both silent for a moment. John was unconscious from the painkiller the emergency techs had given him and the sirens from their passing just seemed to meld into the thrum from the engine and the swaying of the ambulance.

As it turned out, Joshua's contact in Europe was not only an old friend but had quite a bit of clout as well, and at John's request he'd sent the report to the man, explaining most of the goings on at the Dachau Memorial. There was one less murderer on the streets. This simple act saved Sean and Kira hours of questioning by the German authorities.

They were still sitting at the hospital waiting for word on John's condition when Sean pulled out the photo and the notebook and handed them to Kira.

"I think you'll find some answers in there. I'm thinking maybe even some answers to questions you've never known to ask."

At the questioning look from Kira, Sean continued, "I also better tell you I picked up a thought that I'm sure came from Poena when I went in to get these."

"After she was dead?"

"Yeah. Great, right?"

"My God, Sean, is there anything you can't do?"

"Yeah. Make these abilities go away."

"What was the thought?" Kira asked.

"Tell my cousin I'm sorry."

A little gasp escaped Kira, and she promptly looked again at the photo in her hand.

"Cousin?"

"That's what she said ... er eh thought ... oh whatever the hell ... It's what I heard in my mind."

Right then a doctor rounded the corner and walked over to them.

"Uh, Mr. Easton?"

"Yes," Sean replied, catching the man's thoughts before he spoke them. Without thinking, Sean continued before the doctor had a chance to speak. "So John's okay, other than some facial scarring."

The doctor's mouth sagged and the look of shock along with his feelings caused Sean to realize what he'd just done. Lamely he tried to undo some of it.

"Did I guess right?" He added.

The doctor, for his part, was glad to have an easier explanation to what he'd just experienced, and his shock faded abruptly.

"Yeah, good guess. He also has two cracked ribs which might hurt him as much as the burns, but all in all it sounds like he came out rather lucky."

"When can he travel," Kira asked.

"Well, if we give him pain pills for those ribs, he could probably travel in a week or so."

"A week?" Sean was thinking that he was ready to get home, but he didn't feel comfortable leaving John here to travel by himself.

"Sounds like we might get a chance to do some real sight seeing," Kira chimed in.

Sean turned to her and the look on her face belayed his rising comment. Maybe seeing a bit more of Europe other than Dachau might be a good idea after all, he thought. Especially with Kira.

~

That evening over some Jaeger Schnitzel and a mug of Spaten pilsner on tap, Sean and Kira sat together, trying to make sense of what they had just experienced.

The Inn was a large place with dark heavy wood throughout and a muffled roar from the other patrons that served to give, if not true privacy, at least anonymity to their conversation. Kira and Sean both had taken some time to read the little notebook of Isaac's that accompanied the old photo. Kira was still holding the photo.

"So if Poena referred to me as her cousin, and we assume from the resemblance that Rebecca is our grandmother, then Isaac was her Grandfather and I was . . . ," her voice faltered, "Sean, that would mean I'm the granddaughter of the Commandant of Dachau prison camp!"

The horror in her voice short circuited the quip that came to mind and resonated with the sensations he was getting from her. It made him want to hug her so bad, but this didn't feel like the right place for physical emotions, so he tried something with words. "Yeah, but you aren't the crazed killer here," he offered reasonably. "Poena was. It doesn't matter who your grandfather was, what matters is how you've lived your life. And Kira, you're a wonderful person. Don't let this eat at you."

Tears were welling in her eyes as she looked into Sean's, but he already sensed that his words had had the desired effect. Now the primary sensation he was receiving from Kira was love.

She leaned across the table and kissed him. "Loving you this short time has been the greatest pleasure in my life."

Even though Sean had sensed the emotions, the words brought reciprocal tears to his eyes, and he fought to hold them back. Crying in public was definitely not on his list of manly acts, but sipping his beer to hide them was . . .

As if to help Sean, Kira abruptly changed the subject.

"Sean, what about this reference to treasure in the note?"

"I've been thinking about that, and from the hints he gave, I have an idea that we could find it, too."

Kira looked pensive for a moment. "Do we really even want to?"

"Well, on the one hand I guess it technically belongs to you since you're his only living relative, but I guess that's up to you. Whaddya think?"

"I don't know. Part of me is curious more as to what or how Isaac managed to squirrel away what he called treasure. I mean what could it be? He said it was 'horrible *in itself*'. What could that possibly mean? But we don't really need the money, and I'm not so sure I want to go back to Dachau *ever*."

"Amen to that. But listen, you think about it, and we'll do whatever you want."

Kira just nodded her head and, for the moment, let the subject drop.

They spent the week enjoying the sights around Germany, everything and anything other than prison camps. They took in Neuschwanstein, the gorgeous castle that King Ludwig never finished due to his bankrupting his country with its construction and the very same castle Walt Disney used as the model for the Disney castle and the icon on its logo. Sean found that he couldn't get enough of those ancient fortresses, and he and Kira spent most of the week touring up and down the Rhine, visiting the myriad of them on its banks.

Every one of them spoke to Sean, in more ways than one. Whispers from the past at every single location left Sean with a unique perspective of the mood of the castle from centuries past. It greatly added to the general awe for the years gone by and the bit of masonry left as testimony. Sean shared it in detail with Kira who not only enjoyed the added color, but continued to wonder at the depth of Sean's new abilities. The initial fear she had experienced at the waxing of her fiancée's capabilities had blown away like the fog in Dachau. In its place was a new depth of love that Kira felt like she could have only imagined in dreams.

Still, the week finally passed, and they got a call from the hospital saying John was cleared for travel. Reluctantly, Sean and Kira gave up their sojourn along the Rhine and aimed their rental car back towards Munich. As they drove, Kira returned to a previous topic.

"Sean, I think I want to stop back by Dachau."

"Want to see if we can find it, huh?"

"Yeah. For one, it'll bring more closure to this thing. I don't want any details or questions of this whole ordeal lingering after we leave; and secondly, if we do find anything of value, I have an idea for how to use it."

It was all Sean could do not to snatch the thought out of Kira's mind, but he liked the mystery of it and so, forced himself to wait for her to reveal her thoughts in her own time.

"In that case," he finally answered, "I guess we may as well go there now. It's kind of on the way."

"Do you really think we can find it?"

"Well, I've been thinking about Isaac's note ever since we read it, and while we were trying to find Poena I read something on one of the signs that tweaked an idea. It'll be easy enough to find out, though."

They both fell silent for a while, and when Sean pulled into the parking lot for the Death Camp museum he breathed a heavy sigh. He wasn't looking forward to experiencing the mental weight of this place again, but at least this time the weather was cooperating. The sun shone brilliantly out across the expanse of the camp, giving it a much improved aspect from the dreary gloom of the fog on their previous visit. Sean realized now that the fog and the cloud cover that day had gone a long way to enhancing the general feeling of despair that clung to the place.

Still, as they again walked through the gate under the '***Arbeit macht frei'*** sign, those horrid thoughts and emotions tried to clamp down on him again. His previous experience, however, had given him new tools to deal with it, and he blocked them out with relative ease.

"Okay, where to now?"

Sean took Kira by the hand and walked directly across the campground. "This way," he said. "We're heading to that small crematorium."

Kira grimaced at his words but followed him without any of her own.

Sean walked straight back into the small crematorium they'd entered first and stood there looking around. Kira pulled up beside him.

The sudden transition from the bright sunlight to the shade in the building gave her a chill, or at least that's what she attributed it to, and her eyes took a moment to adjust. When they did, she followed Sean's gaze. He was glancing at another placard on the wall by the far cremation chamber, which stated that it was the first of the three to be used in that wretched facility.

Releasing Kira's hand, Sean walked tentatively toward the far wall. *It resides at the foot of the first fire two paces to the left of death.* The words echoed through his mind as he walked along the far side of the first chamber. Each individual chamber was made of brick and stone and was the size and shape of an oversized coffin. Sean could only assume that the victims were slid in feet first, therefore the foot of death would be the far end of this first chamber. Once he reached the back end, Sean knelt down and began to look at the earth at his feet. He'd expected cement for some reason, but it was hard packed earth. *Two paces.* He raised his head and looked at the brick wall in front of him. He took two normal steps which brought his nose right up to that wall.

Remembering Isaac's hiding place in the other building Sean began to inspect the wall. At first he couldn't see anything, but when he used his fingers to test the mortar between the bricks, it began to crumble out like so much sand. Sitting down cross legged, Sean reached into his pocket, pulled out a coin and began to go to work on the mortar in earnest.

Kira sat quietly beside him and, without a word, handed him a pen from her purse. With the much improved tool Sean's work accelerated. The mortar came out leaving a single two brick, stair-step piece. Even the mortar between the two bricks remained intact as though the two brick piece was the original intention.

Sean paused briefly as he set the piece down, wondering when Isaac could have possibly had the time or opportunity to put this cache here. Glancing at Kira first, he turned back to the hole. The wall at this point was double thick, and they had no light to peer in, so Sean simply reached in with his bare hands and no small amount of trepidation. His fingers met not one but three cloth lumps. The material felt like heavy canvas as he drew the first one out. Once in the light it proved to be just that, a heavy dark canvas material with an equally heavy canvas tie strip around the neck.

Sean could almost hear Kira's heart pounding as she barely managed to contain herself while he unwrapped the package. His fingers fumbled slightly as he noticed the heavy clink coming from within the pouch. Once open, Sean simply upended the bag and to both their surprises a pile of gold jewelry fell out. Watches, rings, pendants, necklaces, and earrings all in gold and some with jewels lay in the dirt before them.

"Oh my, God," Kira gasped as the contents were revealed, "This must have all come from the prisoners."

Sean merely nodded his head. A small group of tortured voices added themselves to the ones he was already muting in his mind. These new ones he was certain were connected to this jewelry. It made his stomach queasy even as he muted these, too.

Without saying anything, he reached back into the little hole and pulled out the second pouch. It was heavier and had a higher pitched jingle. When he upended its contents this pouch proved to contain coins, all gold and all from around World War II Germany. It was a treasure to match the jewelry if not in intrinsic value certainly in historic value.

They were both dumfounded, and Kira could scarcely imagine the worth of what she'd already seen, even as Sean reached in for the last pouch. When he emptied the last pouch, however, the one with the dullest clinking sound, Sean and Kira both stared in wonder at the large pile of odd shaped bits and pieces of gold. Neither could make out what it was they were seeing at first until, with a gasp, Kira's stomach clenched, and she broke the silence.

"Oh God! Those are . . . they're from teeth!"

Even as Kira finished her sentence, Sean finally understood and his stomach hastened to catch up with hers.

"They are gold fillings and teeth from the prisoners!" She continued needlessly. Neither of them could speak for a while as Kira recalled reading about this procedure in Death Camps. Gold was in short supply during the war, and Germany was in desperate need of more money to drive its war machine. So they simply relieved all of the prisoners of any gold they might have had on their person when they were captured, then later had their own dentists extract the gold fillings and gold caps from the teeth of the prisoners . . . without anesthesia if she remembered correctly.

"I don't want any of this," Sean finally said, breaking the silence. "And we don't need the money, anyway."

Sean and Kira stared at each other for a moment before Sean's expression changed to one of curiosity. Wordlessly, he reached into his pocket and again pulled out the lighter his dad had given him. He paused again to read the now slightly charred inscription before flicking the wheel and producing a flame. In one smooth motion he turned back to the opening in the brick wall and extended his arm into the hole.

In the little light from the lighter he saw one last package he had missed. It was in the same dirty dark canvas as the other pouches, but this one lay flat in the dirt and was easily missed without the aid of a light. Still holding the lighter with his left hand, Sean reached in with his right and withdrew the little packet. It was dirtier than the others as it had been on the bottom and since it lay flat, had been nearly covered in dirt.

Sean pulled back both hands, extinguished the lighter, then turned to Kira and sat heavily on the ground. He crossed his legs, then looked up at her and handed her the pouch.

"Here. Why don't *you* look."

Kira slid in closer to Sean and almost reverently took the flat parcel from his hands.

"What do you think it is, Sean?"

"Open it and see."

Gently, she began to unwrap the layers of canvas and found an envelope inside. The exterior was blank. When she opened it, however, she found not one but two letters in it. Enthralled by the wonder of the whole experience, Kira slowly unfolded the first letter. They were in surprisingly good shape.

The penmanship was somewhat mechanical, but Kira's amazement echoed in her voice as she began to read out loud.

"To my dearest Rebecca,

The simple act of writing this to you will be more than my life is worth should anyone but you read it, but I cannot let these feelings pass unacknowledged. I found myself drawn into this war early on, and at first I felt as though the goals of Der Fuhrer and the Third Reich were righteous ones. But the lofty goals that Hitler used to persuade so many of us quickly revealed themselves to me for what they truly were: the ravings of a power-mad lunatic. Yet, once I became caught up in the war machine, I have striven to be the best I can.

To my greatest shame, I have found that cruelty is a part of my character, and it seems as if that trait alone could have propelled me high in the ranks. Still, what my innate cruelty could not gain me, my intellect did and with no family and no love in my life I allowed the war to consume me.

Rebecca, I took you for your beauty and for lust. You were simply a desire I wanted to fulfill. At first, I cared nothing for you or your feelings, but as time wore on I found a grudging respect for the sacrifice you were making for your husband. Even so, I couldn't bring myself to give you up. My selfishness is another trait in which I am not proud. It was months later when I realized that somewhere during our physical couplings you had managed to make me your prisoner or at least my heart. I have come to love you with an ardor I have never known, and it has caused me to see my entire life in a different and not very pleasant light. I am not fool enough to expect you to reciprocate my feelings under these circumstances, or that we could do anything about them even if you did.

My life is too much of a moral ruin for that, as is Germany itself. However, I now feel compelled to at least let you know that before it was over you had won my love. I am truly surprised to find myself even capable of such emotions but here they are.

Rebecca, I love you with all my heart, and I truly expect you to be the only love I ever get to know. As I write this, however, I sense the change in the fortunes of war, and I doubt that my life or the Nazi cause will last much longer.

To that end, I'm offering to you and even Isaac these packages. I cannot help you escape this place, but I can offer Isaac the chance to hide this and should you ever have the opportunity, however slim a chance that may be, I hope this small gift will help the two of you with a new life. It is meager indeed compared to the precious gift you gave me. There is no more to say.

All My Love,

Theodore Eicke"

Kira lowered her hands to her lap. She and Sean were dumfounded.

"This explains a number of things . . ." Kira's voice had a far away quality about it as they sat there in the dirt. "Isaac didn't mention any of this in his journal. Surely he must have known!"

"Why don't you read the other letter. Maybe it explains." Sean said.

"Oh, yeah, I guess that would be a good idea."

It was from Isaac:

"Dearest Rebecca,

I wanted to leave this little note here with the other letter from Eicke. He gave it to me when he distracted the guards to allow me to hide the treasure. Apparently, he knows we are among those to be transferred. To my shame, I opened it and read it and found myself both unable to destroy it or to give it to you.

So I left it here with the treasure and this apology; in the event we ever come to retrieve it, you will finally get to read it. I guess it shouldn't surprise me that your love could animate even the heart of one so wicked, but I am doubly ashamed at the doubts it has arisen in me.

You are and always will be the heart of my heart.

Isaac

This has got to be one of the most tragic stories I have ever read," Kira said as she slowly lowered the note.

"And far reaching, too," Sean added. "This tragedy has stretched across generations."

"It's so hard to believe that I'm reading histories about my grandparents. It's just so incredible. Isaac was my step granddad and Rebecca my grandmother."

Moments passed. Two lovers sitting alone in the dust in a crematorium at the site of one of the most horrible atrocities in human history, and they were both contemplating their respective lives. Surreal, didn't even come close.

"I don't want this stuff, either," Kira finally said. "But I would like to see all this suffering finally do someone some good. Let's take it Sean. I think I have an idea."

Sean gave Kira a quizzical look but gathered up the stuff into the pouches, all the while forcing himself not to 'peek' into her mind and glean her thoughts.

"How are we even going to get it back?" Sean asked.

Kira looked at him and smiled. "I have an idea for that too. If my friend is still here, and I bet she is . . ."

This time Sean barely managed to stop himself, but not before he plucked the words 'Air Force' from her. So, still curious, he trailed Kira out of Dachau Death Camp, and as he crossed the wrought iron threshold, he felt the weight of those tortured souls drop from his mind for the last time.

Sean was curious, but Kira wanted to keep her secret, and he let her. The trip back to Munich was uneventful and, after checking with the hospital, they confirmed that John could leave in the morning.

Back again at a hotel near the hospital, Sean got on the phone to call the airlines while Kira left saying she was going to go to the front desk. She returned a while later and Sean watched in curiosity as she took the dirty pouches and placed them into a box she had acquired, then sealed it up.

"What're you going to do with that?" Sean asked.

"I'm leaving it in the hotel safe for my friend to pick up."

"What?" Sean exclaimed, but a look from Kira stopped him. As much as he wanted to ask her, he not only refrained, but he also forced himself to steer clear of her thoughts again. Still, he couldn't avoid catching the sensation of her excitement and self satisfaction. With an effort he let it go at that.

~

The next morning they picked John up at the hospital, still with major bandages on his face and made their way to the airport. The effort of getting checked in and through security was all John's weakened body could handle, and he slept the entire way back to the States.

Arriving back in Kansas City had been a bit of a letdown, and Sean felt a mixture of relief at being home combined with a renewed twinge of sadness at being faced with rebuilding his and Kira's house.

~

It was a week later when Kira got the call from Josh. She was both surprised and apprehensive about hearing his voice.

His company had never been something to be relished, and his attitudes didn't seem to be improving with time. Still, curiosity reigned supreme because she couldn't imagine why he'd be calling at all.

"Hi, Kira, it's Josh."

"Hi, Josh." She said certain that the tentativeness was apparent in her voice.

He hesitated just a moment confirming Kira's suspicions.

"Uh, I have been trying to clear up some loose ends on this case, and I've been talking to John and well, we found something in Poena's house that concerns you."

Now Kira's attention was riveted. She'd spent the last week with Sean trying to forget about Poena and making plans to rebuild their home. Hearing that another connection had been found sent an icy shard of anticipation through her.

"What is it, Josh?"

"We discovered Isaac's journal in a safe deposit box that we found from a Will he'd left. We're pretty certain Poena never read it. It confirms what John said ya'll read in Isaac's note from Dachau. Poena was your cousin, and as near as we can tell you're her only living relative."

This part, at least, wasn't truly news. John didn't know about the thought Sean had picked up from Poena when he went back to retrieve the letter and photo, or the other notes they'd found with the treasure, much less the treasure itself.

Josh's next statement, however, was . . .

"So it looks like you're the one to inherit all of her belongings. For starters I sent you the journal in the mail. It explains a lot and should be there in a few days."

Kira was stunned. The shard of anticipation had shattered into splinters of revulsion that rippled under her skin.

"But Josh what if I don't want . . ."

Her sentence was interrupted by Sean entering the room and putting his hands tenderly on her shoulders.

341

"It'll be okay," he whispered.

Kira felt a welcome sensation of warmth at his presence and his words, then she was ready to be off the phone.

"Never mind, Josh. Thanks for the call. I'll call you when we get the journal."

"Uh, okay, Kira, and uh ... thanks for all your help. You and Sean were great."

Taken by surprise by the uncharacteristic compliment all Kira could do was acknowledge it simply.

"You're welcome, Josh. Glad we could help."

"Okay, bye then."

Kira turned to Sean as she put down the phone.

~

The journal arrived a couple of days later. Sean and Kira were living in a motor home Sean had purchased and parked on the farm while they rebuilt the house. The familiar rooster had awakened them to a beautiful, clear Kansas morning. The birds were singing and there was a slight chill in the air, rather strange for that time of year.

The mailman arrived at 11AM and Kira was the first one to the mailbox. The package was there. She walked back into the kitchen holding the small parcel like it was some kind of religious object. Sean was already there having just returned from working at the house. He was making himself a sandwich.

"Would you like something to eat?" he asked amiably until his senses caught something else. "So it came, huh," he offered, picking up Kira's thoughts accurately.

"Yep," Kira began. "Do you want to read it?"

"Maybe we can read it together."

"Sure," Kira answered sounding tentative ...

"Why don't you make me a sandwich, and I'll read it out loud."

"Sounds great," Sean answered. "But Kira whatever it says, it's going to be fine."

Kira offered a weak smile as she opened the package. She knew he sensed her feelings and it was comforting.

The old little notebook had a simple worn leather cover that was curled on the ends. She opened it, and was surprised to see her own hands shake. What was her problem, she thought. The worst that can be here is some unhappy family history. She began to read:

~

"It was fourteen days since Kristallnacht and my beloved Rebecca and I had settled into a routine and an uneasy accommodation within that God forsaken place. I guess I should be happy we both still lived but . . ."

~

The reading was poignant, startling, horrifying, and gruesome. It related the tale of Isaac and Rebecca's capture and eventual acceptance of servitude to Commandant Eicke in return for her and Isaac's improved circumstances. It continued through their horrifying trial, the horrors they witnessed and felt guilty for escaping, right up until their bloody and amazing reprieve from certain death during their supposed transfer to Auschwitz.

From there, however, the journal took quite a different turn. After recounting the birth of Rebecca's first child, it mentioned getting a note from an adoption agency years later informing him that the child had been adopted by a family named Schultz who had moved to the United States. The girl's name was Dawn. Isaac didn't mention why the adoption agency had sent the note, only that he had the information.

Kira paused with a little gasp as she read this part and Sean sensed her shock.

"Dawn Shultz," she said. "My mom." If the resemblance to Rebecca and the parting thought from Poena had left any doubt, now there could be none. Kira truly was the illegitimate granddaughter of the Commandant of Dachau, Theodor Eicke. And the crazed murderer that had tried to kill them and burned down their house was her first cousin.

It was merely confirmation of what they had already surmised, but it still sent cold shivers through her, and before she was aware he'd moved at all, Sean was behind her laying warm, gentle hands on her shoulders.

"It's the past, Kira. And it's not even *your* past. It's merely the past of someone biologically related to you."

Kira turned to him, tears streaming from her eyes. "But, Sean, to be related to a person who's committed *those* kinds of atrocities to other people ... It makes you wonder what's inside of you that you don't know about. Am I capable of the things they did? Am I capable of what Poena did?"

Sean gently turned her chair around and knelt before her.

"Kira I know *exactly* how you feel. Remember? I went through these same thoughts and feelings and the truth, I believe, is that all of us have the capability to commit horrors to one another, and all of us have it in us to do acts of selfless wonder. In the end we are what we *choose* to be. We make the decision. And I have seen the result of your decisions. Kira, you're a wonderful person. That's why I love you. If it helps, think of it this way, maybe in some way God is allowing you to be the balance for the evil of your forefathers."

Sean's words hit home, and a slow smile chased the tears that were still gently leaking from Kira's eyes.

As it continued, the journal accurately depicted the slow downward spiral of Isaac's mental condition. At one point Kira read:

"Images of the past still haunt me. What used to be simply nightmares of my experiences are now beginning to trickle over into the daytime. I can't escape it."

And then later:

"There must be some retribution for what was done to me, and my beloved Rebecca. But I'm too old to do it. Maybe our granddaughter can visit on them and their children the retribution they so richly deserve. Maybe she can find them. Maybe she can even find that demon spawn that my Rebecca was forced to bear, the one that weakened her so that she could not survive the birth of our own lovely child, Kathleen. Maybe then the nightmares would stop ... "

"I'm afraid I'm hurting Poena. I can't tell these days which things I've told her and which I've merely remembered to myself. She has been a good granddaughter, but she is so quiet ... I can only pray that it is not because of me that she draws inside. Still, she must help me find some peace. If she cannot find Eicke's daughter then she must find the children

of the other officers and make them pay . . . "

"As long as she wears the mask over her emotions she'll be safe like I was . . . as long as she wears the mask . . . "

Kira stopped reading and turned to look at Sean, tears glistening in her eyes. The journal had moved her on a number of levels.

"Oh my Lord, Sean, can you imagine being raised by a delusional survivor from the holocaust and one of the German death camps? It sounds like Isaac didn't know what he was saying half of the time. If he'd been filling Poena's mind full of the images of the horrors he'd experienced even when she was a little girl . . . Those are images even an adult shouldn't have to bear, and now it looks like we know where she came up with the idea for the masks. It was a little girl's interpretation of a survival tool her grandpa had discovered at a death camp."

~

Sean shivered. He could only imagine what it must have been like for that poor little girl, but what he didn't have to imagine was the twisted, hate filled thoughts that seethed from her on the number of occasions he'd received them as their paths intersected. It was an experience he hoped never to repeat.

Kira laid the book down, and they both sat there quietly at the table for a moment lost in their own thoughts. Finally, Kira looked up at Sean.

"Sean, I don't know if I want to do this business anymore."

"Canvas of Life?" He responded, knowing full well what she meant.

"Yeah, it seems like it's caused nothing but heartache and these visions and nightmares that have gone along with it . . . they've been too horrifying . . . "

Sean hesitated for a minute thinking, then looked up into Kira's eyes and spoke.

"First, Kira, I want to tell you that I love you more than anything in my life, and I'll support whatever decision you make. But before you make your final decision, let me tell you this; you've done a lot of good with your work already, from the painting you did of your mother to the one for Louise and Wes. You've brought peace and closure to the people you've encountered.

And I can't even imagine what would have happened to me at that farm after my Dad . . . eh . . . Jason died if you hadn't been there. Even here, Kira, you didn't just help catch Poena you saved lives."

He paused to let his words sink in then continued, "And another thing occurred to me when we were leaving Dachau. Maybe there's another use for my new abilities."

Kira looked up sharply, her curiosity aroused. "What?"

"Let me think about it a little more and I'll tell you, but I think it'll help with your decision."

~

Days passed and the construction of their new home moved along. One afternoon while Sean was out taking instruction in his new found passion, flying, the package finally came.

Sean sensed her excitement as he walked in the door late that afternoon, and it was so strong that it even over shadowed his own excitement about his first solo flight.

"What are you so excited about?" He asked as he threw his arms around her.

"The box has finally arrived."

Sean knew what she meant immediately. "So how did you get that shipped back over here, anyway?"

"I have a girlfriend in the Air Force in Germany, and she shipped it back for me. They rarely check packages coming back into the country from military personnel."

"So you got the Air Force to circumvent Customs. Nice."

Kira just smiled. "Now we have a few museums to call."

"Museums?"

"Yeah, I've contacted some holocaust museums, and they'll pay much more than any antique dealers would, and the antique dealers would pay more than the gold was worth."

Now it was Sean's turn to smile. "Well haven't *we* been doing our homework? I thought you didn't want any of this."

"Not for us I don't. I've decided to give this all to John."

So that was the secret she'd been keeping. As he thought about it, the thought warmed him, and Sean immediately decided it was the perfect idea.

"I bet he won't take it," he added.

"I've already contacted his secretary. It's just going to appear in his account."

"Huh. Well, that ought to do it."

"Sean, he's going to be scarred for the rest of his life. I just thought maybe this would help some."

"No. I agree with you. I think it's wonderful."

Kira got a playful look on her face and said, "How was your flying lesson?"

Sean's face lighting up like a kid at Christmas was all the answer she really needed. Still she listened attentively while he related the whole experience. After a few moments he stopped suddenly and stared at her.

"Okay. Nice change of subject, but now it's my turn."

"What do you mean?"

"Have you still been thinking about whether or not to continue with Canvas of Life?"

"Yes."

"Well, what I was going to tell you before was that the next time you do a painting or have a vision . . . I'm going with you."

The import of the statement slowly hit home with Kira. And what he was actually saying. "Do you think you can really . . . "

"Yep. Next time you have a vision or even a nightmare, I think I can put myself there with you. You won't have to deal with those alone anymore."

~

A brand new warmth stirred inside Kira. How could a man like this exist? Everything she could hope for in a kind strong man plus some things way beyond hope. She couldn't imagine having had fear about the escalation of his abilities. It was just a part of him that made her love him all the more. She looked up into his eyes, and he was smiling.

He already knew.

THE END

Follow Kira's and Sean's mysterious brushes with supernatural evil in the next book in the series, A Brush with Evil

An Unspeakable Power

A madman who moves particles with his mind laughs when he twists the small bones of a victim's foot for kicks. Soon, he is closing throats and pinching blood vessels to extort money.

Kira and Sean hunt the killer and are forced into a deadly negotiation with him. Will the madman double-cross them and kill them silently with his incredible ability? Or will they be able to manipulate him to help with a medical crisis of their own?

About the Author

Born in New Orleans, Jody Summers' life has been filled with unconventionality. The adopted son of a prominent Texas restaurateur, Jody grew up in New Orleans, Memphis and then Houston, learning the restaurant business while he built a career as a competitive gymnast that propelled him to a scholarship at the University of Kansas.

After college, Jody followed in his father's footsteps owning, at one point, three 24 hour restaurant franchises along with four tanning salons in Tulsa. Finally leaving that business, he turned his entrepreneurial skills to everything from a patent in the Pet Industry to a Single's website.

A restaurateur, a gymnast, a stunt man, an entrepreneur, a pilot, skydiver, scuba diver, and an accomplished martial artist for twenty-five years, Jody Summers has tried it all. Now he brings all those experiences to paper in his first novel, the romantic thriller, *A BRUSH with DEATH*

www.ingramcontent.com/pod-product-compliance
Lightning Source LLC
Chambersburg PA
CBHW031428240626
47154CB00001B/244